The Street Hawker's Apprentice

Kabir Kareem-Bello

JACARANDA

This edition first published in Great Britain 2020
Jacaranda Books Art Music Ltd
27 Old Gloucester Street,
London WC1N 3AX
www.jacarandabooksartmusic.co.uk

A CIP catalogue record for this book is available from the British
Library

ISBN: 9781913090234
eISBN: 9781913090432

Cover Design: Rodney Dive
Typeset by: Kamillah Brandes

Printed at Thomson Press

This book is dedicated to my wife Milensu and my Angels—
Funmilayo and Ntanda—Daddy loves you.

Also to

To ALL children living in poverty across the World and the street
hawkers of Lagos.

PART ONE

PART ONE

CHAPTER 1

"Oya, oya, get up, get up my friend, you are blocking my shop!"

The boy opens his eyes, awoken abruptly by three rapid slaps on his back, to see an unfamiliar woman staring back at him, shouting angrily. He lifts his head so that he can properly see the woman staring at him, squinting as he adjusts to the bright, shining sun. His eyes scour her light, pudgy, stocky face and he struggles to compose his thoughts. As she comes into focus he sees, spread sporadically across her skin, dark pigmented spots, still visible despite her heavy makeup.

"What…" He puts his palm on his forehead as he sits upright. Grunting he asks, "Where am I?"

She kisses her teeth. "My friend, you are wasting my time." She grabs him by his right arm, yanking him up. "Does my shop look like your father's parlour? Oya, cummutt!" He is too startled and disorientated to resist as she propels him out of the doorway and into the street, where he lands on his buttocks.

"If I see you here again, I will call police for you, stupid boy," she scowls at him. As she waddles back into the building through a red steel door, his eyes land on her humongous buttocks, undulating with each step, and he wonders what he had done to warrant such anger. The unpainted, single storey building has a fading sign above the doorway that reads 'Comfort Travel Agents'. Even in his confused state, he can not help but acknowledge the irony of the situation; the proprietor had certainly not made him feel comfortable. The two pillars leading to the doorway are completely covered with multi-coloured posters, umbrella and broom logos and words such as 'PDP', 'APC', 'Senate', 'Vote', 'Trust', 'Governor' that clutter the flyers, and are accompanied by images of smiling or stern looking men.

He stands up slowly, wipes the dirt from his hands and takes a long deep breath. "Oh my goodness," he says, heaving and coughing at the pungent smell—a combination of raw sewage, diesel engine and exhaust fumes. He covers his nose and mouth with his right hand and looks around. He squints and tilts his head to the left, then widens his eyes and tilts his head to the right. He turns around full circle as his brain attempts to identify a familiar entity and his eyes dart from one thing to another in desperation.

"What… the… bloody…" his mouth moves but no words come out. He closes his eyes and shakes his head hard. He wipes the sweat that has begun to accumulate on his forehead, bites his bottom lip and spins around four times with his arms flailing. His chest muscles tense up when he realises he is in a foreign and possibly hostile environment. His mouth dries up, his breathing becomes shallow and his legs begin to wobble. The people and objects become a blur and it's only through sheer willpower that he is able to stay upright. It's as if time stands still and he becomes frozen in the moment as he attempts to compose his thoughts. This is impossible due to the ear splitting noise bellowing from the horns of cars, minibuses, motorcycles and trailers. He closes his eyes for a few moments, in the desperate hope that when he opens them, he will awaken from what is surely a nightmare. The only thing he is certain of at this moment is the blue sky. He takes another deep breath.

"Uhhgg, God help me, whooo…" He screws up his face and sticks out his tongue as he gasps for air. He takes a pair of tepid steps to the right, stops, turns around, takes four steps in the other direction and stops again. Desperate, he walks towards the only place that is familiar to him, the spot from where he had just been unceremoniously ejected a few moments prior. With great caution he sits down on the stoop and again attempts to compose his thoughts.

His head begins to throb, the pain hammering inside. He slowly rubs a large bump on the right side of his head. Every single part of his body, from his hair follicles to the tip of his toes, aches. He looks down at his feet and realises that he is not wearing any shoes. It becomes harder to breathe with each passing second, he can feel the speed at which his heart is pounding in his chest, and he is failing miserably in his attempt to compose himself. He brings his knees to his chest, wraps his arms around them and begins rocking back and forth. The volume and intensity of questions coursing through his mind only intensifies the throbbing in his head.

"Where am I? What am I doing here?"

He flinches when he hears creaking from the opening of the steel door behind him.

"Ehhh, you are still here?"

He turns around just in time to see the woman bending down to take off a leather slipper from her right foot. His eyes widen as

9

she lifts it in the air and hits him on his head and back. "Gerrout of here you, you thief, you want to rob my shop abi?"

Up until the moment he feels the pain of the flat sole of the shoe on his back, he does not believe that she would dare hit him. He stands up quickly, turning to look at her with righteous indignation, his mouth gaping open.

He does not flinch as she rushes towards him with the slipper in the air. Instead he clenches his fists and declares, "Hooooow daarrreeee yooou!" He looks her up and down. She stops midway through her swing, her scowl disappearing as her eyes widen and she drops her hand to her side.

"Do you know who I am?" the boy continues. He clenches his jaw and puffs out his chest.

"Ehhh, and who are you?" she enquires.

The boy opens his mouth with the explicit intention of letting this obviously uneducated woman know that she had crossed the line and this would surely result in serious consequences for her, not him.

His eyes narrow as he takes a long deep breath. "I am..." he pauses for a moment, tilts his head slightly to the left, and then clamps his mouth shut.

He looks back at the woman who is staring at him with a look of nervous anticipation. His mouth feels dry and his chest tightens. He licks his dry lips and takes shallow breaths. Why is he struggling to utter the words? His name is at the tip of his tongue, but it seems to fade further away with each passing moment. The blaring horn sweeps it away everytime he thinks it is within his grasp.

He takes another deep breath and tries again "I AM..." the

silence in his head is deafening. He puts his hand back to the bump on his head and then wipes the sweat on his forehead with the back of his hand. His eyes dart from right to left rapidly in a desperate search for answers. They finally rest on his adversary almost in ironic desperation that she would have the answers.

"I bu onye iberibe," the woman jeers and kisses her teeth. "Stupid boy, talking as if you are somebody!" He is too slow to react as she continues her assault with the slipper. He raises his arms to protect his face and back of his head, while the leather sole she swings at him stings the skin on his arms, back and legs. "Oww, oww, what… are… you… doing?" he yelps as he tries to block the blows. The pain forces him to scurry away like a rodent. She continues hurling insults at him even when he is a good distance away from her establishment. He feels humiliated, something he instinctively knows he has never felt before. He walks about in a daze, eventually resting on an abandoned car tyre where he puts his head in his hands in despair. "Think, think, think," he mumbles as he fights to hold back the tears. *Don't cry. How did you get here? Why don't you remember your name?*

He takes a few short and shallow breaths, gradually increasing them in length and depth. As he focuses on each breath, his senses slowly begin to shut out the world, the noises and the smells. The thumping of his heartbeat begins to slow down. He falls into a trance-like state as the jumble of thoughts and images flooding his mind begin to dissipate and he is able to focus on just one. He opens his eyes and whispers, "Temilola, my name is Temilola."

Emboldened by this revelation he attempts to complete the exercise again. Closing his eyes, he whispers, "Focus, focus, focus."

This time he is unable to conjure any images, and is only able to focus on the pain emanating from his empty stomach. He knows any further attempts will be futile until he sedates his hunger; he has to find food quickly. He stands up and it's not until he feels the sharp pains on the soles of his feet that he remembers he is not wearing any shoes. He does not dwell for long on this and begins walking back in the direction he had just come from. With his mind a little clearer, he studies the environment in astonishment.

It looks as bad as it smells, he thinks. He deduces that he is in some sort of transportation hub based on the dozens of rows of minibuses and station wagons, parked with their boots and doors open. Several young men are shouting different destinations and trying to coax people towards their vehicles. The place is a kaleidoscope of activities, people, colours, smell and sound. As one vehicle full of passengers leaves through the gates, another enters to drop passengers. He quickly understands that pressing on the horn upon entry and exit was a requirement. There are formal men in suits with ties carrying briefcases, distinguished men wearing traditional outfits, and young men either topless or in string vests. Most of the women are in traditional outfits, though some wear chic outfits more suitable for a fancy evening dinner rather than the rough and dirty streets of Lagos. Temilola is astonished by the physical strength of a number of the women, who are carrying huge loads on their heads with ease. He stares at a thin, young woman carrying a medium sized generator on her head while talking on a mobile phone and he realises that despite his predicament, he is fascinated by this new environment.

"Ehhhh, sssss… cummut." Temilola turns around just in time

to see a young man wearing a white vest, sweating profusely and pushing a wheelbarrow full of mangos directly at him. He jumps out of the way just in time and the overloaded wheelbarrow misses him by a few inches. The perfectly ripe and sweet looking mangoes cause him to salivate as they roll past him. A thin thread of their sweet aroma cuts through the dense acrid smell in the air.

"Bloody idiot," Temilola mumbles under his breath, "why didn't he just go around me?" He throws the man a look of contempt, desperately wishing he would stumble and spill his load. He cannot believe his luck when the man does not notice a mango that falls out of the wheelbarrow. He waits for a few moments, and salivates as he imagines what it will be like to bite into the perfectly ripe mango. It feels unnatural, even undignified, the hope that one mango represents, as if it is the key to the cessation of his hunger. He licks his lips as he bends down to pick it up. A foot wearing black Nike trainers suddenly kicks the manago away when his fingers are just millimeters away. It takes a few seconds for his brain to decipher what is happening. He stands up to see a light skinned, muscular boy scoop up the mango while it is in motion. To add insult to injury, the boy is holding the mango in his hand as if it is a trophy, laughs and says, "The Vipaar has struck," before turning around and running away. Temilola does not know whether it is hunger or anger, or just a refusal to be humiliated for a third time, but he starts running after the boy who has stolen his mango.

CHAPTER 2

Beep! Beep! Vipaar turns in the direction of the car horn and sees a female hand with long blue fingernails motioning him over. He runs and reaches the blue Honda Accord within 10 seconds of hearing the horn.

"Good evening madam," he greets the young woman who he guesses is in her early twenties. She has a long straight weave, sunglasses, and is wearing a low cut white shirt, which is loose enough for him to get a bird's eye view of her cleavage—the only highlight of his day and one of the few perks of the job.

"Give me charger for Samsung," she barks without looking at him.

"For the house or for the car?" he asks as he jogs to keep up with the car, which is moving slowly in the traffic.

"For the car, my phone is dead," she answers tersely. "Make sure the one you gives me works o, the last one I bought from you people didn't even last one hour."

"I only sell quality good products madam…"

The car accelerates as the pace of the traffic suddenly increases, forcing Vippar to hasten his speed whilst simultaneously retrieving the product from his inventory. His predator-like instincts enable him to focus on the car, as he swerves to avoid several other street hawkers in his path and the vehicles speeding past him on both sides.

"Aah aaa, what took you so long? Do you think I have time to waste?"

"Sorry madam." Although it has only been a few seconds, he has to sound contrite.

She snatches the charger from his hand, plugs it into the cigarette lighter in the car and inserts it into her phone.

"You see, I tell you I only sell quality," he says cheerily when the charge sign appears on the phone.

"How much?"

"800."

"Ahh, ahh, for what," she exclaims. "Take 300 jare."

"Ah, madam, I beg, ok 700."

He is so engrossed with his desire to make a small profit that he does not notice that the pace of the traffic has increased and the car accelerates again. His bowler flies off his head when he bursts into a sprint. He is a few meters from the Honda Accord but he stops and turns around to see it land directly in the path of a speeding Grey BMW X5. His heart nearly breaks through his chest as he fears he is about to witness the destruction of his most prized possession. He is surprised when the car screeches to a halt with the right front wheel sliding but a few inches from the hat. He looks at the driver who is smiling and motioning for him to collect his property.

He picks up the hat and shouts, "Thank you Aunty." He hopes she heard him over the barrage of horns and insults directed at her from the other motorists for disrupting the flow of traffic. He wants to thank her properly but he has to find the customer who has his charger. He runs at full speed for about a minute, scanning the license plates of all the blue saloons until he sees the Honda Accord.

"Hello madam," he puffs hard, hoping to elicit some sympathy. "Ok, ok, because it is you, I will take 650 ma."

"Ehh, I thought you had dash me," she says drolly. "Anyway don't you worry, I have managed to was-sup my boyfriend and I will soon be home."

Vippaar watches in disbelief as she removes the charger from the car while texting and hands it back to him.

"Ok, madam 600, final price."

"I SAID I DON'T WANT AGAIN, AH, AH, na by force I must buy your charger, you put jazz for mouth?" She kisses her teeth and speeds off.

Angry and deflated, Vipaar watches as the car disappears into the traffic and then jogs onto the pavement. As irony would have it, he is standing in the very spot he had seen the sun rise in the morning, and is now watching it descend, over his adopted city of Lagos.

"Oh Lord have mercy!" he exclaims and shakes his head as he counts the day's takings.

"Chai, one thousand and eight," he stares at the money in his left hand in disbelief. "This won't even cover the tax for the day. From morning to night!" He puts the money in his jeans pocket and then takes it out almost immediately to count it again. He takes the hat off his head, looks at it and wonders if things would have been different if he had continued his pursuit of the car rather than going back to pick it up. He lets out a wry smile; he knows deep down he had made the right choice. The bowler hat is an integral part of his identity and the last connection he has to his home and his past.

"Well, tomorrow will be better," he says aloud to himself.

Self-consolation is the only way to stem the rising tide of bitterness of such paltry returns after risking life and limb for 14 hours in the baking sun and hard tarmac. The congested artery of Lagos's roads, which was the bane of most motorists, is the lifeblood for street hawkers like him. They are the heartbeat of the city, even though they are undervalued and often vilified. Lagos cannot function without them. They are indispensable to the fabric of Lagos as they provide essential goods and services to the residents and visitors of a city which is always on the move. There is a saying amongst the street hawkers—*'Lagos without Hawkers is like England without Iya Charlie. (The Queen of England)'.*

Hundreds of single flames, from fuel lamps lit by vendors and Hausa men selling suya on the side of the road, penetrate the darkness that has now fully descended on the city. Exhausted and extremely famished, Vipaar accepts that he is unlikely to make another sale and decides to go home. Failure to make his daily quota means he has to choose between taking transport and eating dinner. The walk home will take about three hours, so he decides to buy food en-route. During his long walk, he reflects on the three years he has spent hawking on the streets of Lagos and how things have got gradually more difficult over the past year. An already harsh existence was made considerably harsher by the state government's crackdown on street hawkers and the constant threat of being caught and thrown in jail by the Kick Against Indiscipline Brigade (KAI), a bunch of thugs in uniform as far as he is concerned.

His thoughts make him angry and he is livid by the time he reaches Oshodi Motor Park. He is approximately an hour from home when he stops to buy some fresh akara (bean cake) from the vendor situated by the entrance of the Motor Park.

"Iya Rotimi, how body?" he asks jovially as he approaches the rotund woman pouring batter into the large cauldron full of hot oil.

"It dey inside cloth o," she pauses, looking up to see who is greeting her. She breaks into a wide smile when she recognises Vipaar.

"Ah, Vipaar, my handsome bobo from the East," she exclaims as she continues with her task. "How is business? I hope the KAI don't disturb you too much."

"We thank God o, KAI never go catch me," he chuckles. "Vipaar be my name, abi no bi so?"

"Na sooo!" she responds in agreement.

"I beg give me 10 akara and one pure water." He takes N250 out of his pocket.

"It will be some minutes o," she warns as she stirs the akara with a giant spoon.

"Please hurry o, I am too hungry."

Vipaar knows the food will not be sufficient, but that is the consequence of having a bad day. As he watches Iya Rotimi, something moving in the dark catches his attention. There is a boy, walking aimlessly through the near empty motor Park. From the little he can see in the dark, and by the way he walks, it is obvious that he does not belong there. He looks like a little lamb that has wandered into a wolf's den. Vipaar looks around to see if the boy is with somebody, but does not see anybody. Curiosity forces him to abandon his place in the queue and he follows the boy as he wanders deeper into the motor park.

"You go at your own risk o, I don't sell cold food o," Iya Rotimi warns him as he walks away.

"Don't worry, I will soon return."

He doesn't know what his intentions are as he watches the lost lamb who has now settled into the doorway of a single story building for a few minutes. A single light bulb lights the front, which is enough for him to see the fear and confusion etched on the boy's face as he lays his head on the concrete floor and closes his eyes. Vipaar notices that three other boys are also approaching the lamb, and his competitive instincts come alive as they all rush towards the boy. Vipaar is the first to reach the boy, who has now fallen asleep, and he goes straight for the gold chain around his neck. He slowly begins to feel for the clasp of the chain while the other boys search his pockets with great care. Suddenly, he feels a foot brush him aside and hears someone say, "commut jo."

He stands with the full intention of thrashing the person who has dared to kick him, but takes two steps back when he realises it is RPG.

RPG stares at him. "You know you have not paid your dues this week abi," he growls.

"Yes sar, sorry sar," Vipaar replies with his hand behind his back. "I will come and give it to you tomorrow morning sar."

"Don't make me come and find you again, my friend." RPG glares at Vipaar intensely for a few moments and then turns his attention to the boy who seems dead to the world.

Vipaar watches helplessly as RPG bends down and snatches

his prized asset from the kid's neck. This causes the boy to rouse abruptly from his slumber. Vipaar feels a twinge of pity when he sees how frightened the boy is, yet he does not feel anything when RPG punches him in the face, knocking him out cold. As RPG walks away, one of the street boys continues rifling his pockets, so Vipaar goes for his trainers. He is about to take off the first one when he hears a groan, and is surprised to see the boy stirring. He is shocked at the boy's swift recovery; he had seen RPG knock grown men out cold on numerous occasions. The lamb begins to scream and thrash his legs. Vipaar sees one of the street boys pull out a knife from his waistband and without thinking slams the little lamb's head into the concrete. Silence returns to its partnership with the night.

"You dey craze," Vipaar berates the street boy who, based on his bloodshot eyes, is clearly out of his mind on drugs. He looks at Vipaar blankly, then stands up and walks away. Vipaar takes off the boy's trainers without looking at his unconscious face and returns to Iya Rotimi.

"Fine boy, your food is ready," Iya Rotimi says as she hands him a small plastic bag with the akara wrapped up in newspaper. She looks at the trainers Vipaar has tied together and flung around his neck, and then focuses her gaze directly at Vipaar.

"N200." She is astute enough not to ask any questions.

Vipaar gives her the money and continues on his journey home. He gets home just before midnight. As he lays down to sleep, he knows he will have to dip into his meagre savings to pay RPG. He also thinks about the little lamb, wondering about the circumstances that would lead him to the motor park and how long he would survive. He estimates two days, and then, upon recalling how quickly he had recovered from the blow delivered by RPG, gives him an extra day.

Vipaar wonders if the boy has even survived the night when he wakes up and begins to get ready the next morning. He puts on his Manchester United shirt, his lucky bowler hat and his newly acquired, and extremely tight, footwear. He leaves home just after 6am, which is late by his terms, and makes his way to Oshodi to see RPG. Although his plans are to go straight to RPG's, he is again at the mercy of his curious mind. He diverts to the now bustling motor park and stands a few meters away from the building where he had left the boy. He feels a fleeting sense of relief to see him alive. He is sitting on the stoop with knees to his chest and is unable to react quickly enough as a woman begins shouting and beating him with her slipper. The boy must have said something intriguing because the woman looks stunned and stops beating him. This only lasts a few seconds and then she continues her assault looking even more irate. Vipaar looks at his watch; he knows he has to leave, but something about the boy fascinates him.

"Five more minutes," he says to himself as he moves closer to where the boy is sitting on a car tyre, seemingly deep in thought. Vipaar is about to leave when he sees a man pushing a wheelbarrow full of mangoes directly in the boy's path. He loses his second battle in the space of a few minutes as he relinquishes his ground to the wheelbarrow. Something nefarious overcomes Vipaar's mind upon seeing the delight on the boy's face when a mango falls on the ground. He runs toward him, kicks it away and picks it up while it is still in motion.

"The Vipaar has struck," he shouts and laughs as he runs into the crowd. He turns around and is surprised to see the lamb is running after him. Vipaar cannot help but admire the boy's boldness for daring to give chase inside his own territory. His admiration quickly turns to anger when he hears the boy shout from behind.

"Come back here with my mango, you thief."

Vipaar would have found the boy's accent comical if he had not called him a thief. He stops and turns to face the boy with a menacing look and is surprised to see him continuing with his charge. Vipaar recognises the look in the boy's eyes; hunger is what drives him. He nearly feels sorry for this little lamb charging at a wolf but he has to teach him a lesson. His punch lands squarely on the boy's jaw, sending him sprawling to the ground. Lying on his back, the boy rubs his jaw and looks around as if hoping somebody would come to his rescue. Vipaar stands over him and drops the mango on his stomach. Something about the boy's eyes unnerves him. "Here, take your dirty mango," he says scornfully. "If you want to survive here, learn to pick your battles."

People are starting to look at them so he walks away, but not before turning to look at the boy again, who is now sitting up.

"The name is Vipaar, remember it."

He looks at his watch. "Shit, shit, I am late." His competitors will have already taken the best patch, making money from the morning traffic while he is here playing silly games with the boy. He still has to go to see RPG, whom he hopes is at his Oshodi HQ, or the whole day will be lost. He walks for 15 minutes and sees RPG sitting on a high stool reading a newspaper; he is wearing a black vest, which shows off this muscular frame. Vipaar walks past an area boy slapping a motor boy, each slap is punctuated by the question, "owo mi da? (where is my money?)". From the little Vipaar can gather from the boy's pleas for mercy, his boss, the danfo (commercial bus) driver, had fled after failing to pay the daily operating taxes for picking up passengers on RPG's patch.

"Good morning sar," he greets RPG.

"Where is my money?" RPG asks as he flips through the Punch newspaper without looking at Vipaar.

Vippar put his hand in his pocket and hands over ₦3,500.

RPG folds the newspaper in half, takes the money from Vipaar and puts it in his trouser pocket. He stands up, looks Vipaar in the eyes and says, "Don't be late with my money again. Don't think that because of anyteen or sometin, I won't deal with you." He uses his chin to indicate for Vipaar to look behind him at the motor boy who is now bleeding profusely from his mouth and a swollen eye. "Next time I will send my boys, you unstan."

"I understand sar," Vipaar replies. His voice quivers. "Goodbye sar," he says as he turns to leave.

"Vipaar, you know dee election is coming soon," RPG calls to him. "You can come back and work for me instead of running up and down the road like a goat."

Vipaar continues walking away.

"You know that old woman won't be around forever," RPG shouts contemptuously.

Vipaar wonders why the sight of the motor boy being assaulted made him uncomfortable. He had seen worse violence than that during his time in Lagos. However, that is when he realises that it was the sight of the area boy beating the life out of the motor boy which caused him so much angst. He has always prided himself on having the courage to escape that life, but based on his actions last night and that morning, he was no better than the area boys who worked for RPG, causing terror and mayhem. It was getting harder and harder to ignore the cold, savage part of him, a part that he hated and struggled to control.

"The incident with the boy is a one-off anomaly," he thinks to himself. He shakes his head hard in an attempt to remove the image of the boy's face from his mind. He flags down an okada and is about to tell the driver his destination when he sees the boy wandering around looking confused just a few meters away. He gasps in horror an his eyelids widen in alarm by what he sees. An overwhelming feeling of agnst courses through him and without being aware of his actions, he was running towards the boy.

CHAPTER 3

"Come back here with my mango you thief," Temilola screams and chases after the thief with a bowler hat without thinking. Pain shoots through the soles of his feet, but he desperately wants his mango. He wants to slow down when the thief stops and turns around grimacing, but the sight of the mango forces him to maintain his trajectory. The punch to his jaw, which sends him sprawling onto the ground, is swift, accurate and painful. Dazed, he rubs his jaw and looks around for assistance to apprehend this thug, but to his surprise, none is forthcoming. Temilola looks up as the thief stares down at him, tired, red and broken. Something about the thief's shirt is very familiar to him. Staring at the badge on the left chest, he realises that it is a Manchester United shirt. He feels the mango land on his stomach and then roll off onto the ground. In his state of confusion, he is unable to understand what the thief says to him, but he is certain it is not pleasant based on the contemptuous look on his face. Temilola sits up when the thief stops and says victoriously,

"The name is Vipaar, remember it."

As he walks away, Temilola notices the name "Henry" printed on the back of Vipaar's shirt. He knows the shirt and the name are incompatible, but he is too hungry to decipher why at that very moment. He picks up the mango from the ground and attempts to stand up. The residual effects from the swift but painful beating causes him to stumble, but he finds his footing after a few hesitant missteps. He walks in the opposite direction to Vipaar, clutching his most prized possession closely to his chest. He stops by an abandoned yellow bus without an interior, steering or tyre. He licks his lips and is about to bite into his hard-won prize, when he notices that it is muddy. He rubs it on his thigh in an attempt to clean it, but his actions only make the mango dirtier. His mouth becomes moist as he stares at the fruit in anticipation of the sweetness of the first bite. If he waits any longer, he will begin to drool. He bites the top of the mango and rips the skin off it with his teeth; the sight of the yellow inside nearly makes him delirious.

The first taste is so mesmerising, it makes the beating he received for it worthwhile. He licks the mango juice running down his forehand; nothing can go to waste. He is in his own world; it is just him and the mango. He wants to savour the sweet taste by eating the mango slowly, but the hunger makes him ravenous, and the occasional taste of mud does not even bother him. He is just finishing peeling the other half when he hears a deafening noise behind him which causes him to jump and drop his mango. He turns around to see a yellow bus entering through the gates of the compound, blaring its horn. He picks up the mango from the floor and inspects it. It is muddy and beyond salvaging. His shoulders and his head droop. He feels cheated, the sudden extraction from his fantasyland feels worse than the beating he had received a few minutes earlier. He drops to his knees on the ground and begins to sob uncontrollably. The magnitude of the situation dawns on him.

He is lost, hungry and alone, in an alien and hostile environment, and worst of all he has no memory beyond that morning.

Then he hears a soft voice, "Why are you cryin'?"

He looks up and sees a woman carrying a pail on her head. He wipes the tears from his eyes quickly and stands up. He sees that the pail she is carrying contains various brands of drinks, which are embedded in large chunks of ice. She is also holding notes of various denominations between her fingers. After a morning of beatings and humiliations, when he had desperately wanted someone to come to his rescue, those kind words soothe his pain a little. He wants to say, "I am lost and scared, can you please hold me?" Instead, he says, "I am fine, thank you for asking." He regrets it as soon as the words come out of his mouth. He cannot understand how he let his pride supersede his desire to ask for help. Luckily, for him, someone who wants to buy a drink distracts her.

She looks at Temilola. "Hep me carri dis down." He does not fully understand what she said, but he quickly deciphers that she wants help with bringing down the load on her head. He eagerly helps her lift the pail from her head and puts it on the ground. The heavy weight surprises him, and he is impressed at how she managed to balance it on her head with such ease. He looks on as the customer rummages through the beverages available.

"You no get Mountain Dew?" he asks.

"No sar," she replies, and bends her knee.

After what seems like an eternity, the man picks an apple flavoured drink, which causes the other drinks to shift positions. He hands the woman a ₦1,000 note.

"Ahh, uncle, I no get change o," she shows him the notes in

between her fingers as proof. "Please sar, do you have small change?"

"I don't have anything smaller," he replies as he opens the bottle cap with the opener attached to his key ring, puts it to his lips and begins drinking.

"Then why didn't you pay for the drink before you started to drink it?"

The woman and the customer look at Temilola who is staring at the man with disdain. The words had come out of his mouth freely, and he quickly regrets them.

"Are you stupid boy?" the man he glares at him. *"So fu omo yin ko sho are o or else ma se le she* (Tell this child be careful or I will do him harm)."

"E ma bi nu sir (don't be upset)," the woman says as she puts a protective hand across Temilola's chest. Petrified, he stands behind her. Without her protection, he is certain he will receive his third beating of the day. The woman looks in her money belt, takes out some notes, adds it to some of the ones held within her fingers and gives it to the man. He snatches the money, while looking at Temilola with utter contempt. He counts the change and puts the money in pocket.

"Learn manners, boy," the man points his index finger at Temilola and walks away.

The woman turns to Temilola. "Boy, do you want to do yourself injury? You don't speak to people like that."

"I am sorry," he replies, looking down at his feet. He feels an apology is necessary, despite not understanding much of what the woman is saying to him.

"Why you dey speak like dat?"

"Like what?"

She looks at Temilola from head to toe. "Mpph, whare you dey come from?"

"I don't know."

Temilola can tell by the look on her face she wants to ask more questions, but does not know what questions to ask.

"Help me carry this," she says as she adjusts the rag she is using to balance her load on her head. As Temilola helps her to reposition the pail, she asks again.

"Why were you crying?"

"I am hungry ma."

"What is your name?"

"Temilola."

"Whare are your shoes?"

"I don't know."

The questions become too much and Temilola begins to tear up again. The woman stares at him for a few seconds, a look full of pity; he hates it. She flips through the notes in her hand and hands him a ₦50 note.

"Go dere," she points into the main road, outside the gate. "Dere is some people selling boli on the corner. Go and buy one and eat it."

Overwhelmed with the generosity, he bows his head and says, "Thank you ma." He stops for a moment.

"Erm, excuse me, two question if you don't mind. Where are we now, and what is boli?"

"We are in Oshodi, Lagos," she replies after a few seconds of stunned silence. "Boli is roast plantain."

"Thank you."

"Cold Lacasera, cold Fanta, buy your ice cold drinks here," she shouts as she walks towards the rows of cars and mini buses. As he walks slowly out of the entrance of the bus garage, there is one gate, with twisted bars, still barely hanging to the concrete pillar. His brain struggles to process the thousands of vehicles and mass of people walking in different directions. The horns are so constant that he concludes they are connected to the accelerator.

There are so many things to look at, his eyes struggle to focus on one thing. There are yellow buses that people attempt to enter before they come to a complete stop. He cannot believe his eyes when he counts seven people disembark from the back seat of a tiny taxi, which by the laws of spatial logic should take a maximum of four. It feels like he is stepping into an even stranger and more frightening world. He considers going back to the relative safety of the tyre in the bus park, but hunger forces him forward.

Temilola sees several women selling boli, but his eyes fixate on one particular elderly woman wearing a hijab and he walks towards her. He feels sorry for her when he sees wrinkles on her face, but there is something about her eyes which suggest an inner strength. She looks like she hasn't had a day of rest in her whole life. He approachs her tepidly.

"Good morning ma," he says softly, with his head slightly bowed. "How much is boli please ma?" She looks up at him, and raises her eyebrows. She points to the different size bolis on the makeshift grill, which is a tyre rim filled with charcoal and wire mesh, pricing each one at a quick pace.

"Dis one is ₦40, dis one is fifty, dis one sisty naira, and dis one is ₦80." The smallest one is ₦40 and looks the least appealing. The one he can afford is ₦50 and it looks marginally more appealing than the smaller one. Whilst contemplating, he sees a bag full of water sachets just behind the woman which causes him to swallow dry spit.

"How much is the water please ma?"

"One sachet cost ₦5," she responds while turning the boli on the grill.

Temilola finds himself in a quandary. Does he satisfy his hunger fully, or quench his thirst?

"I will take this one," he says, pointing at the ₦40 boli. The old woman raises her head and squints as she looks at Temilola from head to toe.

"It will soon be ready," the old woman says as she reaches behind her for a sachet of water. "How many do you want?"

Looking at the ₦50 note in his hand with contempt, "I will take two please." She takes two sachets from the half-empty bag and hands it to him. He is disappointed the bags are luke-warm but he tears into the corner of one and begins to squeeze. It seems like the water bypasses his mouth completely and begins to soothe his aching throat. It hits his stomach with the force of water hitting the base of an empty calabash. He is tempted to drink the second sachet immediately, but concludes it would be foolish because he will not be able to quench his thirst after eating the boli. As he desperately squeezes the last drop of water from the empty sachet, a bald man carrying a briefcase and wearing a suit which is obviously too big for him stands beside him. He looks at the boli on the grill, twists his face like he is inspecting vomit, and asks the old woman, "How much is the boli?"

She points at the one she has already sold to Temilola and says, "This one has been sold," and went on to price the rest as she had done a few minutes earlier.

"Ahha how can you charge ₦50 for that one? It not cost more than ₦30. I will take those two for ₦60."

He points at the two bolis priced at ₦50.

"Ejo sir eba mi ra fun ₦70, ogede ti won (Please sir, help me buy it for ₦70, plantain has become expensive)."

"They are too small, I cannot pay more than ₦60," the man replies adamantly, sticking his bottom lip out as if to emphasise the point.

"Ok sar." She begins to wrap the bolis in a newspaper. Temilola feels the urge to intervene but decides against it based on his earlier experience. He suddenly realises that as bad as he thinks he has it, he is standing in front of somebody who probably has it worse. He looks at the man with disgust as he badgers the woman into giving him his boli first, "Oya oya, please horry, I have to catch bus to Ibadan." He stands next to the old woman and eats his boli under the battered beach umbrella because he has nowhere to go. He begins to survey his surroundings while eating his extremely soft boli, which has burnt patches on the outside. As he scans the hundreds of faces going about their business, he finds himself transfixed on one face in particular. It belongs to a bald and muscular man, with a scar which runs the left side of his face. Temilola does not understand why this person is of such interest to him as he continues to eat his boli slowly. The man is looking at something intently, which causes Temilola to look in the same direction in an attempt to find out why the man is so captivated. In the midst of the crowd, he focuses on a light-skinned boy who is staring at a light-skinned woman carrying what looks like an expensive leather bag. He is watching the woman's bag intently and within a few seconds, Temilola knows why. The light-skinned boy begins to unzip the bag hanging off the woman's shoulder. Temilola stops eating his boli midway, intrigued by what he is seeing. The would-be thief boy is successful in opening the bag and he begins to lift what looks like a thick rectangular shaped envelope out of the woman's bag. The woman looks down at her bag, turns around and realises what was going on. She grabs her bag and slaps the thief three times across his face, shouting at the top of her voice, "OLE, OLLLLE, THIEF, THIEF!!!!!"

Temilola is certain the thief is about to retaliate because his face swiftly went from being startled at being caught to angry at being slapped.

There is a sudden commotion as people around look at the source of melee. The thief must sense all eyes on him as he quickly jumps over the black and white block barriers he had leaned on during his failed attempt to relieve the woman of her phone. Within seconds, two men jump over the barrier and chase the thief. Temilola finds the whole incident fascinating but people immediately continue what they are doing. He finishes his boli quicker than he expected, and although he is grateful for the temporary halt of the hunger pains, he is sad he will now have to leave the safety of the umbrella.

"Thank you ma," he says as he steps out from under the umbrella holding the only treasure he has in this unknown world—his water sachet.

"You are leaving?" Her soft tone suggests she is concerned.

"Yes ma." he replies with a small smile.

She looks like she wants to say something deep, but she says, "O se oko mi, olo du mare a shu e (Thank you dear, God will protect you)."

He does not understand what she says, but based on the softness in her voice, he assumes it was some kind of prayer.

"Thank you ma."

As he leaves the safety of the umbrella, he sees a policeman approach the victim of the attempted robbery. His humongous gut precedes him as he approaches the visibly angry woman without a sense of urgency. In fact, he looks irate. Temilola is not close enough to hear everything she is saying, but based on the wild gesticulations and the pointing of her index finger inches from the policeman's face, it is obvious she is berating him for presumably not performing his duties. This abuse does not faze the policeman; his body language suggests that he is encouraging the woman to forget about the incident. Temilola's heart is beating so fast from the excitement that he nearly forgets about his thirst. He tears off the corner of the plastic sachet and begins to squeeze the bag slowly. This water seems to serve a different purpose from the first; it tastes sweet and is successful in quenching his thirst. He enters into his own little world, and for a few seconds he leaves the troubles of the world behind. As he returns his head to its primary position after tilting it back to squeeze the last drop of water from the sachet, he is abruptly heaved out of his temporary utopia by an ear-splitting noise. He looks left and sees a yellow juggernaut approaching him at full speed. Fear paralyses him and he involuntarily relinquishes his breath. His life flashes before his eyes and it does not go past the last hour since he woke up. He steels himself to be hit by a powerful force, but instead of steel, the `mass` he feels is muscle and flesh. He hits the tarmac hard and the weight on top of him doubles his pain. He looks up as he struggles to breathe and is shocked to see that his savior is the same boy who had swiftly dispatched him not less than half an hour ago—minus the bowler hat.

"Omo aje butter, this is not Janz or Yankee o, this is Lagos," he says, his eyes scornful. "Open your eyes and your ears well well."

The anger in his voice forces Temilola to wonder why he saved him. The look of disgust shortly turns to what Temilola considers one of softness before his adversary, or saviour, turns around and begins walking away. People gather round to help him get to his feet and some begin to scold him while dusting him down. "Are you blind?" "You want to die?" "Where are you from?" "Who does this pikin belong to?"

Temilola becomes light headed, his heart begins racing and he struggles to breath as he desperately attempts to gather his thoughts in the midst of the commotion around him. He longs for the safety of the umbrella and the old woman selling boli.

Someone suddenly shouts, "Hey, hey, where are you going?" at Vipaar, who has picked up his bowler hat and is walking away.

Temilola sees his assailant turned rescuer turn around and shout, "Fada, na you sabi, I no fit take this omo aje butter."

In the midst of the numerous people shouting over each other, Temilola manages to hear, "Come back hare, na bi your responsibility o, God wanted to take him, you interrupted so he is your responsibility."

Temilola looks on as people argue about him as if he is not there. He locks eyes with his rescuer again and he seems to see into his soul—they belong to someone who is in pain.

CHAPTER 4

Vipaar sees the boy standing in the middle of the road drinking a sachet of pure water, oblivious to the danfo that is coming at him at full speed. Without thinking, he runs toward him and pushes him out of the way and they both land on the ground. As he stands up to look at the boy, his first thought is, "why did I just do that?"

The boy is now looking up at him probably thinking the same thing. Vipaar looks into the boy's eyes and something about his face makes his heart begin to pulsate faster.

"Omo aje butter, this is not Janz or Yankee o, this is Lagos. Open your eyes and your ears well well," Vipaar scolded him.

People gather round and begin to volunteer their unsolicited opinions. They are asking him questions about the boy, which he cannot answer. As he attempts to walk away, a priest demands he take the boy with him.

"Fada, na you sabi, I no fit take this omo aje butter." Vippar cannot believe what these people are asking. How can they expect him to take responsibility for this boy? He is furious with himself because if he had minded his own business, the boy would be dead and he would have won the bet he had made with himself. He locks eyes with the boy; something about him reminds him of someone from his past, someone he has not thought about in a very long time. His face unlocks a door to his past, and he is petrified.

"If you care about him, you take him," he snaps as he storms off and hails an okada. He wants to put as much distance between him and the boy as soon as possible. He attempts to get the incident out of his mind and concentrate on the long day ahead of him. He still hopes he can catch the tail end of the rush hour traffic. His fellow street hawker's have packed Teju-osho near the express road to Ogun state by the time he arrives. Some are chasing after slow moving cars, while waiting to be hailed by a driver or passenger. All types of products are on sale, from quail eggs, soft drinks and live snails, to picture frames, mirrors and curtains. There are a few others selling phone chargers, so Vipaar knows he has to work hard to make today better than yesterday.

The sun is blazing and Vipaar begins walking up and down the express road with his assortment of chargers.

"Samsung charger, Motorola charger, phone cases, anything you want, I get them," he repeats every couple of minutes. His newly acquired footwear's obviously too small for his feet but he refuses to take them off. His feet have never felt this level of comfort; it feels like he is running on a cloud. It takes a few minutes for the soles of his feet to adjust to not hitting the tarmac with their usual force. The rest of the morning does not go to plan; he gets into an argument with an okada rider who nearly knocked him down, traffic moves at an even faster pace than the previous day, and there are more hawkers on his patch today than usual because of KAI raids all over Lagos.

The day wears on slowly; he is more lethargic than usual

which causes him to miss a couple of potential sales. Seeing that boy had caused deeply buried memories to resurface and he cannot concentrate. He fails in his attempts to banish them. He begins to think about his mother and feels guilty when he realises that he has forgotten what she looks like and has not thought about her in a while. During moments of rest, he thinks back to when he first started his career as a street hawker. One of the first lessons he learnt was that those who stood still didn't make money in this game. Secondly, a momentary lapse in concentration could result in serious injury or death. He had seen many of his 'colleagues' hit by cars, danfos or trailers. During one gruesome occasion in his first week, he witnessed a small girl selling peanuts pulled under the wheels of a car as she stretched to collect money from another speeding car. The driver tried to escape but got stuck in heavy traffic. The okada riders and motor boys waiting idly by the side of the road instantly mobilized and swarmed around the car like an army of ants. Ultimate chaos descended on an already chaotic environment. Vipaar could only watch on helplessly as the man was dragged out of his car by the mob. Vipaar heard the man's screams and pleas for mercy despite the noise of the vigilantes.

They threw him on the floor and began beating him. He saw a boy walking menacingly towards the baying mob carrying a jerry can. At that moment, Vipaar knew there was no possibility of the man's desperate request being granted. The size of the mob had grown considerably and the driver was lost amongst them. He was mesmerised by the surreal spectacle and he only came out of the trance when he saw a tyre around the man. He became scared and wanted to turn and run away, but his mentor forced him to watch as kerosene was poured on the man as he pleaded for his life.

They set him alight and the man's screams as the fire engulfed his body haunted Vipaar for weeks after that. This event and similar subsequent ones caused his once gentle heart to harden. What was once stuff of nightmares soon became the norm on the streets of Lagos. Within a few weeks of hawking on the streets, his spatial awareness and dexterity had increased exponentially and he was able to avoid being hit by tons of steel. The old adage 'survival of the fittest' was the most profound in the new world which had forced him to abandon his childhood and innocence prematurely. His ascent into the world where life decisions had to be made on a daily basis had been arduous and painful. Within a short space of time, he had gone from dreaming about going to London to play football in the world famous Emirates Stadium to thinking about where his next meal was going to come from. He would always wonder whether he would see the sunset when he woke up every morning, or see the next sunrise when he went to sleep at night. Those days of hope and dreams were long gone. Now, he dared not dream of a better tomorrow because it only increased the bitterness which had staked a permanent residence in his heart. He had experienced many dark moments, but the advice his mother gave him when he was about ten years old, "circumstance rule man, man doesn't rule circumstance," kept him going. She said a Greek historian named Herodotus said it. He felt he had moved to a higher intellectual plateau, although he didn't understand what it meant—he eagerly repeated it to his friends at school the day after he heard it. He had waited all day for the right moment to deliver his newfound knowledge; it was during a football match after school. He had scored his fifth goal of the afternoon and an opposition player had accused him of only being able to score because he hung around the goal. As they pointed their accusatory fingers at him, he eloquently said, "Circumstance rule man, man doesn't rule circumstance, my old chap." The blank looks on their faces merely confirmed that they were intellectually inferior to him. He was immensely proud that he was sharing knowledge all the way from Greece with the village boys. In order to survive the rigours of the streets of Lagos, he altered the adage to "man rules circumstance, circumstance does not rule man."

With this momentary trip back in time, he doesn't react quickly to the hissing of the driver of a minibus that goes past him. These are the crown jewels of the express because they usually carry multiple occupants. By the time he extracts his thoughts back into the real world, his competitors have the jump on him. Two boys selling phone chargers and recharge cards have secured the driver's side and by the time he goes behind the car to reach the passenger side, it is too late. Other hawkers are there trying to sell everything from soft drinks to standing mirrors. He tries to force his way into the scrum but it would have been easier to thread a rope through the eye of a needle. He decides to try his luck again at the driver's entrance with more aggression. He begins to shout, "commot commot, he called me, move before I deal with you." They ignore him, each concentrating on plying their goods to the driver who is moving at the speed that the traffic dictated. Vipaar's friend Sunday FM, who is selling snails, drops out of the hunt when the driver waves him away. "I don't want."

Vipaar quickly took his place. "Oga, oga, you called me first," he pleads.

"Mo pei ode duro si be bi are (I called you and you stood there like a statue)."

"Ma worry, Big Daddy has already bought what he wanted."

Vipaar looks past the driver and sees a big man sitting in the back seat counting a wad of cash and buying three phone chargers from his competitors on the other side. He knows that this is a lost cause; he is annoyed at the wasted energy but he is angrier at the cause. His reminiscing has cost him a sale and it is down to saving that stupid boy earlier in the morning. Life experiences have caused Vipaar not to believe in omens, but he cannot help but feel that his rotten luck is punishment for saving that boy this morning. By 12:30pm, he has not sold any chargers and he is extremely hungry. He is in two minds about leaving his section, but needs to recharge and refocus. The bowler hat is not having the desired effect and he takes it off.

"Vipaar, come we go chop at the buka." He turns around and sees Sunday FM walking towards him. His body twitches with envy when he sees that he has sold all his stock.

"I no fit chop jo, I no sell well today," he replies.

"No wahala broda, I go buy. I sell all my snails to one big Alhaji just returned from Yankee."

"WELL DONE Sunday FM, my oga at the top, your money don arrive o."

Vipaar hopes he has masked his envy well enough.

"Make we go chop for buka." Sunday FM looks around for a moment, thinking where to go to eat.

"Oya, let us go to Mama Afusa buka."

Vipaar decides to follow Sunday FM when he assesses the fast moving traffic express. This is the first good thing that has happened to him today and he is not about to let his pride affect his stomach. The walk to the local eatery is uneventful. Sunday FM talks about the fine babe he slept with the previous night, and the one the night before. Vipaar is used to Sunday FM's boasting, although it is white noise to him; the constant yapping confirms why Sunday got the nickname FM—he was always talking. Vipaar usually preferred to go to eat at the buka by himself because it was an opportunity for him to escape the harsh realities of the world. On a good day, he could afford to buy agufe (goat meat) and a bottle of mineral, but he usually bought rice and three or four small pieces of meat. The fundamental reason he ate at a buka, apart from the delicious and affordable food, was that it was probably the last place in this Godforsaken country where people from all walks of life could mingle. Vipaar saw and experienced the effects of the gap between the rich and poor every day, but upon entering a buka, the rich and the poor ate at the same table without judgement.

Vipaar and Sunday FM make their way to the buka, which is three shipping containers welded together. Sunday FM is a popular and lively character; as soon as they walk in there is a chorus of people calling out his name. "Sundaaaaaay FM, omo ta!" "Fine boy Sunday, how your body?"

"Omo olowo ti de ooooo!" He responds to each patron with a humorous quip.

"Who is finer than me, the don bon am yet," he replies to the praise and adulation. "My money no dey arrive yet, it will soon come, it dey for road."

At the food counter, perhaps still on the high of the exaltation when they entered, Sunday FM says to Afusa, the owner's daughter, "Give my broda here anything he wants."

Pride and hunger are jockeying for position within Vipaar; he is hungry but does not want to feel indebted to Sunday FM, so he orders three amala with ewedu and gderi soup. After the young lady scoops the amala from the cauldron, she passes the plate to an older lady sitting next to her who is responsible for pouring the soup on the plate. After she pours the soup over the three layers of amala, she asks Vipaar what meat he wants. With the intention of retaining some of his pride, he asks for two small pieces of meat. He sees her look at Sunday FM before dipping the big spoon into the pot with the egufe meat, lifting a big piece out and putting it on his plate. It is obvious this is at his friend's behest and he feels humbled. He is so accustomed to the cutthroat environment of the streets that he has not allowed himself to accept help from anyone in such a long time. The warm feeling that goes through him feels foreign.

After Sunday FM pays for the meals, and two bottles of minerals, they both walk to a table at the far corner and sit down on a plastic chair meant for the beach. They take their seats at a table already occupied by two other patrons wearing suits. Vipaar guesses they are either executives or high-level civil servants. Sunday FM stops talking and goes into a Zen-like silence as soon as he sits down to begin eating his meal. Vipaar is grateful for the quiet time. It is an opportunity to reflect on his day and change his strategy, but the first thought that pops into his head is the face of that boy. He forces himself out of his reflective mood by listening to the conversation of the two men sharing the table. From what he can gather, the man sitting next to Sunday FM is a businessperson based in Nigeria and the man sitting next to him is a potential investor from London who wants to set up a software training business in Nigeria. The Nigerian businessman is dominating the conversation, which is about a software called SAP which is the next big thing in Nigeria. The conversation becomes boring and Vipaar zones out. Eating the delicious hot food enables him to put the challenges of the past few hours behind him. He feels rejuvenated and concludes that with some hard running and a little bit of luck, he can still recover the morning's loss. His teeth bite through the egufe meat like a hot knife cuts through. He starts to pay attention to the two men's conversation again when they begin talking about how much Lagos had improved thanks to the changes made by Governor Mashola. The businessman who had obviously never lived outside Nigeria made valiant attempts to speak with an American accent. "I am telling you Mr John, this is the best time to invest in Nigeria, the economy is booming and Lagos is the epicentre of the explosion." He only stops briefly to tear into the meat and then continues, "All the major companies are using SAP software and there is a great demand for the training now."

"Oh yes, I heard. I am really looking forward to coming back to live in Nigeria," the foreigner replies. "Lagos has really improved from the last time I was here. Traffic is still bad, but it's a bit cleaner and I can really see the improvements."

"I am telling you Mr John, it is all down to the Governor Mashola. He is a great man with great vision. Have you been to Oshodi?"

"No I haven't, but I heard it has improved a lot."

"Improved is an understatement. You won't recognise it now." In his excitement, he has reverted to his Nigerian accent. "Two years ago, you couldn't drive through that place, but Mashola cleared out all those street traders who were blocking the road. I am telling you, the improvements you see in Lagos now is down to the Kick Against Indiscipline Brigade."

"Really? Wow, that is good!" Mr John chipped in as he nodded his head.

"They cleared out all those market traders, hoodlums, street hawkers and all those other delinquents. I am telling you Mr John, that place was a travesty of magnificent proportions. There was even one occasion when he lambasted an army general who was using the BRT lane, the general was prostrating. He is a great man, I am telling you, he should run for president."

Vipaar realises Sunday FM is also listening when he notices he is staring at his plate and has stopped eating. He feels his friend's anger rising and he knows the reason why. They have both experienced the brutality of the KAI Brigade first hand; they are the bane of the street hawkers and traders existence. The sight of the bright lime shirts could be compared to the wildebeest stampede on the Serengeti caused by the sight of a predator. The friends lock eyes and Vipaar knows what is about to go down. Sunday FM's temper and fight for justice was legendary.

"Sar, I am sorry to interrupt but I have to disagree with what you are saying. My friend and I have experienced the brutality of your heroes of Lagos many times," Sunday FM says calmly and eloquently in a heartbreaking tone, looking at each man in turn. "They treat us like we are dogs."

They both look at him blankly before the native businessman responds, "My friend, why you dey poke your nose in our conversation." He waves his hand at Sunday FM. "I beg, mind your own business."

"You see Mr John, these are the kind of people the KAI Brigade are fighting against, ruffians and delinquents who made Lagos a dangerous place to live."

Sunday FM stands up very quickly, knocking the plastic chair over. He turns to look down on the businessman who is still sitting down.

"Oga I take umbrage, severe umbrage. You have insulted me and my friend, and I demand an apology."

"You must be mad." The businessman shakes his head and continues.

"Sunday, don't disturb my customer o I beg," the owner, Mama Afusa, pleads from behind the counter.

"Mama Afusa, this idiotic buffoon is trying to impress his akata (Westerner) friend by insulting me," Sunday FM said, wagging his finger in the man's face.

"My friend, I should take you outside and deal with you. Do you know who I am?" the man shrills as he stands up. "The eagle does not fly at the same level as a sparrow, do you understand?"

Vipaar wonders if the man would have said what he said if he knew that Sunday FM had a degree in Political Science from Obafemi Awolowo University Ife.

Vipaar, who has been a spectator to the events, attempts to defuse the escalating situation. "Broda, I beg leave am, just finish your food and let us go."

He knows his friend is deeply enraged because nothing ever comes between Sunday FM and his food. He feels sorry for Mr John who has stopped eating, and is now sweating, breathing hard with knees shaking. Mama Afusa leaves her station behind the counter and approaches their table. Sunday FM and the businessman are now squaring up to each other and some patrons have begun to pay attention.

When she reaches the table, she immediately goes to the akata's side, kneels down and begins to apologise.

"Please sar, I am very sorry for the disturbance sar. My shop is not normally like this." She then turns to Sunday FM. "Sunday, why are disturbing my customers? If you can't behave yourself, I beg leave my shop." Vipaar cannot not help but see the irony in the situation. The equality bubble, which shielded the buka, has burst; the inequality of the outside world has penetrated his sanctuary. Vipaar looks at his friend's face and he is sure that he can hear the proverbial heartbreak. The same person who had shown him friendship and affection fifteen minutes ago has rejected him in the most hurtful way possible. Status and money have trampled over friendship and loyalty once again.

"Gentlemen I apologise, I did not intend to disturb your meal." Sunday FM's statement was full of grace and eloquence. The businessman let out a long breath and relaxed his shoulders.

Sunday FM continues, "Please continue to come to eat in this fine establishment." He turns to Mama Afusa and bows his head slightly, "I beg, no vex."

Vipaar cannot comprehend what is going on. There is a legendary story on the streets that Sunday FM once got into an argument with a rock, by the end the rock had shrunk into a pebble. The two patrons look equally bemused and the one who was ready for combat moments ago is lost for words. Sunday FM picks up the chair from the floor, sits down and continues eating his food. The mood in the buka turns sour as the other patrons eat their food in silence. Vipaar and Sunday FM do not say anything to each other during the 10-minute walk back to the Tejo Osho express. Vipaar has known Sunday FM for a few months and has never known his mouth to be stagnant for more than a few moments. He can only imagine what his friend is feeling. He had watched helplessly as pain descended on his friend's face like a flash flood when Mama Afusa rebuked him in front of outsiders. He is about to offer his friend some words of comfort when Sunday FM turns and puts his left hand on his shoulder blade and says, "Vipaar my friend, he who is courteous is not a fool."

Vipaar does not understand what the proverb means but he feels obliged to hail his friend and hopes it cheers him up a little. His arms are half way up in the air when he hears shouting and sees people running from the direction of Teju Osho express. They both walk quickly towards the commotion and Vipaar's whole body becomes limp with despair. He shakes his head in disbelief at the irony of the situation and the continuation of his rotten luck. There are over 40 KAI officers, most of them wearing the lime coloured uniforms and some in plain clothes. They are arresting and beating the street hawkers and seizing the goods of the traders who have set up on the side of the road. He looks on feebly and listens in anguish at the cries of the women who are pleading for the return of their seized goods, but their pleas fall on deaf ears.

"Ejo, mo fi ti olrun be yin, e da rin ji mi (please I beg you in the name of God please forgive me)." The KAI officers respond, "There are signs, no hawking, no trading, I beg commot before I slap you face."

They seize pails of soft drinks, phone chargers, mirrors, chickens… Anything they can get their hands on they put into their trucks. A lucky few who have managed to escape run in different directions with their goods.

Vipaar sees two uniformed officers dragging one street hawker who had attempted to escape past a plain clothes colleague who is taking a bribe from another street hawker in exchange for not seizing his goods.

"Bros, I go dash… make we go." Vipaar turns to where Sunday FM had been standing but he has disappeared. On one hand, he is thankful that they escaped the latest round up by the KAI brigade; on the other hand, he is angry because he has to find another location so late in the day. He has not made enough money to take transport; instead, he walks to Ikeja hoping to have better luck. The whole day is a disaster, as he is not the only one who has the idea of relocating to Ikeja, which overflows with hawkers for most of the afternoon. He manages to sell one phone charger by sunset. It is 7:30pm, Vipaar is physically and mentally exhausted when he starts his long walk home. He walks into the living room and lights the lantern that is by the doorway. He lifts it up and as light fills the dark room, he sees someone lying on the sofa. He turns on the torch light on his phone and walks slowly towards the figure who is snoring loudly. What he sees makes his head spin in bewilderment. He shines the torch directly on the face of the person and it feels

like his heart is going to burst out of his chest when he confirms
that it is the same little lamb from Oshodi bus garage.

CHAPTER 5

In the midst of the noise and chaos, Temilola watches as Vipaar dismisses the pastor who has been most insistent on taking responsibility for him. As he struggles to compose himself, he hears snippets of the arguments, "you sabi", "aje butter". The momentary look of vulnerability has long disappeared and the depths of his anger becomes visible as Vipaar gesticulates wildly. He slaps his palms together and raises them adjacent to his shoulders with each palm facing outwards saying, "He no be my problem." Temilola watches as Vipaar stomps away, only breaking stride to pick up his rucksack. Then someone suddenly grabs him forcefully by the arm, dragging his eyes away from a retreating Vipaar. "Where are you from? Where is your house? Where are your parents?"

Temilola looks on in silence.

"How you get here? Where are your shoes?"

Temilola desperately wants to answer the barrage of questions but each one only serves to make him feel more helpless.

"What is your name?" The questions continue.

After a couple minutes of intense questioning, the crowd thins out as people begin to leave one by one. Temilola initially thinks that they are leaving because he has frustrated them with his inability to answer their questions. He deduces that it was not the sole reason as the pace of the disappearance increases. The size of the crowd reduces from about fifteen to just three in a matter of seconds. The three people who are left have been the most vocal in their questioning. They begin to argue amongst themselves about who is going to take responsibility for him.

"We can't just leave him now abi?"

"Look at him; looking like mumu, I don't want his death on my conscience."

"Let us just take him to that policeman over there," the older man holding a leather bound bible, who Vipaar had called fada, says as he points with his index finger. Temilola looks in the direction the old man is pointing, and fearful scepticism washes over him when he sees that it is the policeman who was speaking to the attempted robbery victim earlier. He then shudders in panic when he sees that the policeman is deep in conversation with the would-be thief and the man who had jumped over the barrier to give chase.

"Sssss, Sssss! Officer, officer!" the pastor calls out to the police officer, who is still in deep conversation with the two companions. The police officer's eyes flash with aggravation when he looks in their direction and he sticks up his index finger to indicate that they should wait. Temilola's fingers begin to twitch and he mutters to himself, "Oh no, no, no, no." He wants to flee, but he has no idea where to run. He is a prisoner in a place where everyone around him is walking freely. His eyes dart around quickly in the hope of finding an escape, but all directions seem equally unappealing. He watches the policeman shake hands with the thief and then put something straight in his pocket. He is not sure why, but he is certain that money exchanged hands. Temilola cannot help but note the policeman's resemblance to a walrus as he ambles towards the pastor slowly, like he is master of time and all that he surveyed. At about 15 meters away, the policeman suddenly raised his palm to his temple and saluted, "My chairman." Temilola looks towards the recipient of the salute and then begins to run. It is the man with the scar on his face and the small capuchin monkey on his shoulder. He is not sure why the sight of this particular man causes him to take flight, but he has a gut feeling he is bad news.

"Where are you going, come back here," he hears the pastor shout behind him, but he continues running as fast as he can. He only stops when he runs out of breath, then hears a familiar voice.

"Omo mi se ko si (are you ok my child)?" Temilola has inadvertently run back to the boli stand. The old woman asks again, looking him straight in the eyes, "Are you alright?"

He is still attempting to catch his breath when he hears, "Mama, does this boy belong to you?"

He turns and finds himself facing the walrus policeman's humongous stomach. The old woman looks at Temilola and then back to the policeman. "Omo, mi ni, he belong to me," she replies.

His face shifts from sheer terror to absolute relief as he locks eyes with his saviour and she smiles.

"Mama, do you know that it is a crime for children not to be in school during these hours in Lagos state?" the policeman says, pointing at the watch on his left hand with the index finger of the right. Temilola has gone through a myriad of emotions since he woke up but the feeling he has, based on what he sees next is probably the most difficult one to deal with. A mixture of anger, helplessness, and searing gratitude roils within as he watches the old woman get on her knees and apologise to the policeman.

"Ema binu sa, iya travel lo si Ejubu ni, odo mi lo ma duro si lani ni ka. Ema binu ejo (Don't be angry, his mother travelled to Ejebu, he is just staying with me for today)."

Temilola inadvertently groans in despair, because the old woman is grovelling to this gigantic waste of space because of him.

"What is your name?" the walrus asks, sneering at Temilola, who in turn only feels the urge to pick up the nearest rock and throw it into his fat face. The thought of this big bully sprawled out in the gutter causes him to let out a cheeky smile.

"Who is this?" the walrus asks, pointing at the old woman with his black wooden rod.

"She is my grandmother sir."

They lock eyes like pugilists in the middle of the ring moments before the bell rings to indicate the commencement of the first round. Temilola is confident of what the outcome of the contest will be based on his opponents obvious disregard to the code he has sworn to uphold. "Ok, make sure I don't see him here again, you hear me?" the policeman says as he waves his batton at Temilola.

"Yes sar," the old woman says as she stands up. She turns to look at Temilola for a few seconds before sitting on her bench.

"Alhaja, kilo shele. Kini olopa yen fe (Alhaja, what happened, what did the policeman want)?" Temilola understands the question that one of the other traders asks without realising it.

"Ema da loun, olo buku. Aye lon se, eri bo se dudu be elede susun (Don't mind him, he looks like a roasted pig)." She says this loud enough for the fellow traders to hear once the walrus has disappeared into the crowd, tucking his wooden baton under his right armpit.

Laughter spontaneously rings out in the immediate vicinity. This is when Temilola realises that he is unwittingly part of a cast performing for an audience. A number of the market traders have been watching the events and, with the arrogant policeman gone, the old woman has suddenly turned from a pleading, feeble old woman to a razor sharp lioness.

"Tani omo yen, Alhaja (Who is the child)?" somebody shouts from behind.

"Omo min ni (He is my child)." The tone is curt, which results in the curtailment of further questions.

She shifts sideways on the bench she is sitting on, which Temilola takes as the invitation it was to sit, and he duly obliges. Sitting under the umbrella provides him with immediate relief from the intensity of the blazing sun. He doesn't realise how exhausted he is until he sits down. It is the first time since he woke up that morning that he is able to get off his feet, and as soon as he sits down, the soles of his feet begin to throb with pain. He looks at the old woman, "Thank you ma." She does not acknowledge his words of gratitude as she turns a boli on the grill. He puts his right leg on his left knee with the intention of rubbing the sole of his foot, but stops when he sees the grime and mud on it. He is reluctant to transfer the dirt onto his hand, and contemplates whether to provide relief to his feet at the expense of his hand.

"Oya, go over there and wash them," the old woman hands him two sachets of pure water. He takes the sachets, and washes his feet a few meters away from the boli stand. He walks back on his heels in an attempt not to dirty his recently cleansed feet. He lets out a wide grin when he finds a pair of white flip-flops in polyethylene on the bench when he returns. The act of human kindness shown by the old woman was like nothing he had ever experienced before, despite his loss of memory. He begins to sob silently as he puts on the flip-flops, which cushion the soles of his feet as if they are resting on clouds. He wants to repay her somehow, but he has no money or possessions. He touches his collarbone and squints as if intuitively knowing something is missing. For one reason or another, he expected to feel a chain or necklace of some sort. With no other recourse, he goes to prostrate, but stops midway through and hugs her instead. She has a peculiar smell, which makes him want to recoil initially, but the warmth of another human being causes him to hold her tightly for what seems like an eternity.

"Oya, joko joko," she instructs as she shifts to the side on the wooden bench. Temilola sits down again and instantly feels odd after sitting idle for about a minute. As if able to read his mind, she hands him a bottle filled with peanuts and shows him how to pour it into a small polyethylene bag.

"You pour some in the bag like this, and then tie the bag and put it here." Temilola watches, relieved that at least he will have something to do. He picks up the bottle, pours some nuts into his hand and attempts to pour it into the bag as has been demonstrated. He finds that it is a lot harder than it looks as half of the nuts in his hands miss the small bag opening. He looks at the old woman, petrified that she will scold him, or even worse send him away. She grunts in annoyance but he is relieved when she softly says, "Patience my child, you must to fill dee bag correctly, not quickly."

He nods to indicate he understands what she means. When he starts again, he pours the nuts in smaller portions and fills the bag three times. He concentrates on the task, hoping to make an impression and show his gratitude. He fills the bags carefully, and though a few nuts fall to the ground, after filling approximately 15 bags, he considers himself proficient. Within a few minutes, he becomes so totally consumed with what he is doing that all the noise and chaos around him fades away. His mind conjures hundreds of images, which he cannot put in any constructive order. There are faces and places, which he is not sure are memories or just his imagination. He is immersed in the task and his own thoughts when he hears a commotion, which causes him to exit the realms of his mind and re-enter the real world. He hears a loud pulsating horn, keenly distinguishable from the hundreds of other constant beeps and the sight of a humongous white mini-bus approaching his position. In front of it, a mini-stampede of street traders desperately attempt to clamour out of the way to avoid being hit. People begin to rain insults at the conductor hanging from the doors, who seems oblivious to the volume of abuse and the visible anger emanating from the crowd.

Temilola is sure he is about to see a lynching, but within a few seconds things are back to what could be considered normal. The conductor solicits for customers, calling out his destinations at breakneck speed. Temilola listens intensely with the hope that one of the destinations would sound familiar and spark something in his memory. Alas, it is in vain. The torrent of syllables are spouted too fast. Temilola concludes that the conductor has not been trained in customer service etiquette because of his level of aggression. When a young woman wearing a business suit attempts to confirm the destination of the bus, he looks her up and down and responds with a resounding "ENTER". Still calling the destinations at the top of his voice, he jumps aboard the bus as it begins to move. Temilola continues with his task in silence, now maneuvering the peanuts with much more dexterity into the plastic bags. Although still very worried about the predicament he has found himself in, the feeling of despair begins to subside slightly. He realises his position is better than it had been when he woke up, and he begins now to fully absorb his new surroundings. As if a spectator in a grand theatre, he sits back to enjoy the kaleidoscopic array of events he is witnessing. There are hundreds of characters performing their respective roles seamlessly. After a couple hours of intense observation, he deciphers who most of the characters are. The principle players are the traders, who consist of hawkers, food traders, and those selling all manners of goods from baby clothes and toothbrushes, to gold jewellery and leather shoes. The array of products on sale cause Temilola to quip to himself, 'Jason's quest for the Golden fleece would not have been so daunting if he had come to Oshodi.'

Then there are the bus drivers who could be described as reckless or extremely skilful, depending on your point of view; some would even consider them the opera singers of the streets. There are also upholders of the law, who ironically are not police officers and do not wear uniforms, but are young men who stand at strategic points and either hand out tickets to taxi and bus drivers or collect money from them. The men in uniform seem to be the element creating the most havoc; constantly harassing the taxi and bus drivers, causing the traffic to build up. And finally, there are the customers. The main reason why the place existed; they came in all shapes and sizes and were just transiting through a place where he found himself stuck. He watches them enviously as they arrive from and depart to various destinations. He assists the old woman over the course of the day as best he can. A new batch of plantains are delivered a few hours after he arrives and although he does not fully grasp the exchange between the old woman and the supplier, she seems to chide him for the poor quality of the previous supplies. Temilola performs menial jobs, such as tearing the newspapers in preparation to wrap the boli, and helping her to fetch charcoal. At one point, a man goes around and begins collecting money from the traders in the area where he is sitting, but when he gets to the old woman he looks at her and promptly goes to the next trader without acknowledging her. The boy thinks this is a little odd, but he just adds it to the list of many odd things he has observed.

Over the course of the day, new set actors arrive on stage. There are school kids on their way home from school and then office people on their way home from work. As it gets darker, the stage is set for the third act, the night dwellers. He naturally expects the traders to begin to pack up for the night, but the number of entrepreneurs merely increases. The night brings a new set of characters. Within a couple of hours, the landscape has changed and multiple food stalls have been set up. An array of barbecue stands selling an assortment of meats roasted over open flames sends clouds of woody, peppery smells to tickle the noses of customers. The main source of light is now from motor vehicles' headlight beams and open flames from the kerosene lamps or those being used to cook the various foods. His level of anxiety begins to rise as darkness descends around him. He begins to worry how he will deal with the new challenges that the night will surely bring. *Would his saviour's charity be limited to the daytime*, he thinks to himself. He has no idea where he is going to sleep and does not know whether she will be willing to put him up for the night. If the place was scary during the day, his imagination now conjures up images of the world ruled by Hades. He wants to ask her if he could follow her home, but again pride plays a reluctant part in stopping him asking for help. But the primary reason is that he does not want to be a burden. She has done so much for him already and he doesn't know how he is going to repay her. He concludes that not having a choice is the worst position anybody could find him or herself in.

He decides that he will have to ask for help. He takes a deep breath and steels himself. "Alhaja, thank you. I will be going now."

"Again? You stupid idiot," he mutters to himself. He cannot believe he has just uttered those words. Despite the darkness, the light from the open flame enables him to see a look of surprise appear on her face. His guts twist in apprehension as all his senses desert him.

"Where are you going to go?" Her eyebrows raise. "Are you going to be fine?"

A sufficient amount of his senses return which enable him to shrug his shoulders and murmur, "I don't know."

She tilts her head slightly left, while she looks him in the eyes. "My son, who is supposed to help me carry my load? Please help me carry dis home. I don't live far; I live in Mushin."

"Ok ma," he replies with all the humility he can muster from the lower echelons of his heart. "Thank you ma," he adds with a trembling bottom lip as he struggles to stop the tears from flowing. He assists the old woman in packing up her stand. He is surprised that most of the traders look like they are settling in for a lot longer. He rushes towards her when she begins to lift the unsold plantains onto her head. "Alhaja, I will carry it ma."

He takes it from her and puts it directly onto his head as he has seen other people do over the course of the day. "Mpph, oh my goodness." It is heavier than he expects and he swerves right and left as he attempts to maintain his balance. The old woman bids goodnight to her fellow traders and motions for Temilola to follow her. Temilola is grateful that he has taken the old woman up on her generous offer because the night is a lot scarier than the daytime.

He is exhausted by the time they reach the old woman's house. He is not able to see the front of the house before they enter a dark hallway. As dark and scary as it is, he feels safer in here than outside. There is no light and he has to rely on the old woman's small torch to illuminate his immediate surroundings. Because of a combination of exhaustion and hope that his day's experience has just been a nightmare, he falls asleep on the settee almost immediately.

After what seems like only a few seconds of sleep, he feels someone poking his ribs and he rouses from his slumber. He quickly sits up and begins looking around the dark frantically as he tries to get a sense of where he is. Panic races through his body and he begins to hyperventilate. The seconds feel like hours as his eyes struggle to adjust to the darkness. His heart nearly jumps out of his chest when they focus on the source of light. He puts his hand to his face and squints at the single bright light shining into his eyes.

He can just make out a silhouette carrying a lantern. He squeezes his eyes shut, shakes his head hard and rubs his thumb and index fingers into the ridges of his eyes. He gasps and his body shudders when he hears a familiar voice, "Eh, eh hey what are you doing here omo aje butter?" He blinks rapidly and focuses on the single yellow frame from the lantern as it rises higher until he is able to see a face. His mind reels when he realises it is the same boy who had beaten him up and then saved his life earlier that morning—Vipaar. "I SAY WHAT ARE YOU DOING HERE." Temilola's whole body begins to shake uncontrollably, his throat dries up and then, "AAAAAAAAAAHHHHHHHHHHHHHHHHHHH!"

CHAPTER 6

"Eiii eiii, eiii, don't start screaming, I beg," Vipaar says frantically as the boy rises from his slumber. It is the next morning and he has been standing over him for a good two minutes, wondering what forces in this cruel world keep putting this boy in his path. This is the first time he has studied the boy's face. He is reasonably good looking and, based on his flatness of his nose and the fullness of his lips, he is from the Egba tribe. Based on his height, weight, the way he spoke, the tint spots spread across his face (puberty spots) Vipaar guesses that he is no more than 14 years old. Of all the people in Lagos, even in Oshodi, that the omo aje butter could have gone to, what are the chances that it would be his guardian, his beloved Alhaja? When the cock crowed, he gently shook the boy's shoulder in order to wake him up. He is scared of a repetition of what had happened when he got home last night. The lamb's shrieking had shaken the proverbial wolf to the core of his spine. As the lamb rubs his eyes, Vipaar tries his best to smile in a non-threatening way, but the look of apprehension that appears on the lamb's face strongly suggests that this is counterproductive. "Erm, how did you sleep?" he asks in the softest tone he can muster.

"Fine," the lamb replies meekly as he stands up, ensuring his eyes are focused on Vipaar the whole time.

"Mmpph…" Vipaar looks around. "What is your name?"

Temilola, who is now standing up straight, gives Vipaar a blank look and remains silent. Patience is not one of Vipaar's most endearing qualities and he automatically takes the silence as an insult. He takes a deep breath, and clenches his jaw. "I say what is your…" he says as he moves slightly towards the boy who instinctively takes a step back.

Vipaar bites his bottom lip hard and his eyebrows lower in irritation. "Listen you omo aje… listen well well," he pulls his right ear lobe and takes two steps towards the boy, "if I want to do you 'arm, I will have let the danfo kill you yesterday. Your life belongs to me!" Vipaar's eyes widen and he points his index finger at Temilola. "I don' know how you get here but if you hurt her or get her into trouble, I will kill you, you understan'?"

Vipaar is shocked at the severity of his own words. This type of aggression is required to survive on the streets, but he realises that he has gone too far in this instance. The lamb continues to look on blankly. Vipaar cannot decipher whether he is scared, brave or indifferent because his face is devoid of any emotion. Vipaar only realises the impact of his words and actions when he looks at the boy's feet and sees that he is standing in a puddle of his own urine. Vipaar goes weak in the knees when he hears Alhaja's bedroom door open. The curtain shifts and she enters the sitting room.

She stands in the doorway, looks at both boys and studies the scene. Deep jealousy replaces anger as Alhaja strokes the boy on the back. "Pele oko mi," she says in her usual soothing tone. He frowns and grinds his teeth, "Why is she showing this stranger such affection?" he thinks to himself. He has come to believe those words of endearment were exclusively for him. If Vipaar disliked the boy before, he really hates him now.

"Go to the room over dare," Alhaja points towards the bedroom door and places her right hand on his back as she guides him. She closes the door behind him and turns round to face Vipaar who drops his gaze to the ground.

"Daniel, what do you say to make this boy mess himself?" She pulls out a brown chair to sit down. "Is the answer on the floor? Look at me when I am talking to you," her voice is raised and terse. Vipaar looks up at Alhaja who, although small in stature, has a presence that would intimidate the harshest tyrant and soften the most hardened heart. He cannot bear to see the disappointment on her face and his eyes return to staring at the floor.

"Remember what we talk about las' night." She begins to recap the previous night's conversation. "I tell you dat you must look afta dis boy." She pauses as she leans forward and places her elbow on her knees, clasping her hands together.

She takes in a breath and sits back up. "Daniel, remember when I bring you to come and live with me. I have always tell you dat you will have to be looking afta somebody one day."

Vipaar nods in agreement and feels a chill travel down his spine where he stands. As Alhaja speaks, his mind wonders why fate keeps pushing him and the boy together. He had been able to dismiss the pastor and all the others poking their nose in Oshodi the day before, but he knows he will not be able to dismiss his beloved Alhaja so easily.

"But Alhaja, I cannot look after him. I have to go to school then I have to go work in the evening," Vipaar pleads.

"Skool en?" Alhaja stares at Vipaar directly in the eyes. "Did you go to skool yesterday?"

"Yeyes of course," Vipaar stutters, caught off guard by the question and avoiding her penetrating eyes. She had stopped asking if he went to school a long time ago, but regularly asked, how school was. They both knew that his attendance was irregular at best. She knew he spent most of his time hawking on the streets, although he tells her he only does it after school.

The look on her face suggests there is more to the question than meets the eye.

"Do you think that it is chance dat you save dat boy yesterday?" Without looking at Vipaar's face, she says, "You are surprise abi, the boy tell me somebody had save him and I know it is you even before he describe you."

With his eyes widening and his heart pounding, "wh... wha..." Vipaar whispers and swallows his spit. "What else did he tell you?" He tries to mask the fear that is coursing through his veins.

"He say he cannot remember anytin' before yesterday morning."

Vipaar internally heaves a great sigh of relief. He has not been found out for assaulting or robbing the boy. Still, he worries.

"Alhaja I cannot look after him. We cannot take him, we cannot even feed ourselves. A bag of rice now costs 2,000 naira. We don't even know who is or where he comes from." Vipaar speaks quickly without taking a breath as he paces around the small table in the centre of the sitting room.

Alhaja looks up at him and smiles. "What is dat thing you are always saying; men rule sarcuuumstances, abi."

Vipaar's lips part to speak but words have deserted him.

"You know that I am not an alakowe (educated) like you," Alhaja says. "Did you rule the sar-cumstance when you save that boy life yesterday?" Alhaja continues, demonstrating wit and wisdom that cause Vipaar to drop his chin to his chest in shame. He had rolled his eyes as she attempted to pronounce circumstance, but he concedes that she makes a valid point with which he cannot argue.

"Yes… erm… no… I mean yes… you are right but," Vipaar licks his lips and scratches the back of his head, "dat is not how it work… you see… what dat mean is…"

"Wa, joko," Alhaja motions for him to come and sit next to her. He drops his shoulders and smiles as he walks to her. He always feels good when she speaks to him in Yoruba.

"Se eru ba nie (Are you afraid)?"

Vipaar nods slowly.

"Kilon be leru (Why you are afraid)?"

"What if I turn out like Jamiu?"

"Ahhhhhhhhh," she replies comically as she clicks her fingers three times while swinging her right hand over her head. With each motion she emphasizes her actions by saying, "Awusubila", "God forbid bad thing" and "Olrun maje".

Alhaja's reaction makes Vipaar chuckle. Such was her desire to exorcise such thoughts from the world, she said the same thing in three languages and evoked the Yoruba ritual of swinging one's hand over one's head in a circular motion while clicking the middle finger and thumb. Within that split second, Vipaar couldn't help but notice the contradiction of Alhaja's actions. She had invoked Allah in Arabic but intuitive traditions were still strong. His life experiences had caused him to have a low tolerance for religious and traditional beliefs. He believed that each element on its own is dangerous but even worse is the result of the combination of the two—he was a living witness and a victim.

"I know you will never turn into someone like Jamiu," Alhaja says softly and slowly. "Do you know why?"

"No," Vipaar replies now, looking directly at Alhaja's face.

"Esho, kole wo okon e," Alhaja says as she places her right hand on Vipaar's chest. "Do you understan'? The devil cannot enter here. Jamiu is my son, I tell you the devil has taken him a long time ago."

She shakes her head slowly and pauses. Vipaar can see the grief and sorrow in her eyes. "Ami mi ni mo bi… ami ni mo to, yes, I bon him and I raise him. I have look after you as well so I know what is in your hart. You will not be like him ever, you have a good hart." She places her palms on his chest.

"Thank you Alhaja," Vipaar responds glibly, "but I still cannot look after him. He is very soft… he is a omo-aje…" He feels the force of Alhaja's palm make contact with his left cheek. Vipaar holds his cheek and looks at Alhaja. "Wha…" She has never been so impatient with him before.

"Remember dee night I bring you into dis house?" Alhaja says, now standing over Vipaar whose left hand is still on his left cheek as if to confirm that he had actually been slapped.

"Se o ron ti, do you remember?"

"Yes ma."

"Will you be here if I did not take you from that place? Answer me now! Look at you, now you can't talk. Those boys will have kill you if I did not dare. Do you remember?"

"Yes ma," Vipaar replies, his voice wavering.

"When I bring you hare dat night, Iya Rotimi said that you are going to kill me in my sleep. Do you remember?"

"Yes ma."

Vipaar shudders as he recalls the night he and Alhaja first met; she had saved him from certain death.

"Do you know what you and that boy have and Jamiu does not; okon," she says emphatically as she pokes her chest with her finger. "How you say… erm… courage abi?"

"Yes Alhaja."

"You see, my own grammar is getting serious," she smiles widely, which breaks the tension and makes Vipaar laugh.

Vipaar instantly recalls his interaction with the little lamb over the past 24 hours and he is forced to admit he had seen that very same virtue in him as well but he didn't want to admit it to himself.

"Daniel," Alhaja calls out soothingly as she places her hand on his left shoulder, "aja to maa run oka a laya; ologbo to maa je akere a ki oju bo omi."

There is a silence, which lasts for about 30 seconds; it is a standoff. She wants him to ask for the translation to show humility but for him, showing humility on the streets was the quickest route to starvation. Asking for help or assistance in any way, shape or form was a sign of weakness. His innate quest for knowledge subjugated his arrogance and he asked, "What does that mean ma?"

She smiles and begins to explain, "A dog dat will chew dried corn must be brave; a cat that will eat a frog will dip his face in water."

Vipaar thinks for a few moments, then lifts his left eyebrow. "So am I the cat or the dog?" he asks with the innocence of a small child. This causes Alhaja to burst out laughing. Without realising it, he is glad to be reminded of his youth and innate innocent nature. She is about to explain further when she looks towards the bedroom and says, "Ba wo ni oko mi."

Vipaar looks in the same direction and sees the boy watching them both. For a few precious moments he had forgotten about the ills of the world, and it had just been him and his beloved Alhaja in their bubble. Not only had the boy invaded their precious moment, he was using his towel.

CHAPTER 7

Temilola stands up quickly as he attempts to get his bearings. It takes him a few seconds to realise where he is. The sight of Vipaar's face dashes all hope that the events of the previous few hours have been a nightmare. He is taken aback when Vipaar smiles and shows his teeth. It reminds him of one of Aesop's Fables about the lamb and the wolf. He suddenly pictures himself sitting at a large table with a stack of books staring out of a window at a large empty field with meticulously cut green grass. A white man in a black waistcoat and a bow tie is calling his name. The picture is fleeting and disappears quickly.

"What is your name?" Vipaar asks.

Temilola wants to answer but he is so petrified that no words come out. He instinctively takes a step back when Vipaar approaches him and begins to shout and berate him. He wants to answer, but instead he stands frozen to the spot as if he had looked into the eyes of Medusa. He only realises that warm liquid is descending his right leg when he follows Vipaar's gaze to see a yellow puddle forming by his left foot. Temilola notices the change in Vipaar's face when he hears the sound of the bedroom door opening. Vipaar's aggressive stance disappears and he shifts from side to side on the spot. The dynamics change when Alhaja walks into the living room.

The would-be tormenter becomes a small child in a blink of the eye. With his protector's soothing hand on his back, he gratefully accepts the invitation to enter the safety of her room.

Temilola looks around the small and sparsely furnished room. There is a single bed by the window, which is missing more than half its glass pane. There is an oak single wardrobe and what looks like an antique dressing table. He notices the dressing table because it looks out of place in its surroundings. Where everything else appears dilapidated, the dressing table looked grand with a lot of history. He then notices a very thin mattress, rolled up and placed next to the wardrobe. His eye also catches sight of something very familiar, the ridiculous bowler hat Vipaar had been wearing the day before. He sits on the edge of the bed with his elbows on his knees and puts his face in the palms of his hands. He attempts the same exercise which had helped him to remember his name earlier, but he gives up after a couple minutes of trying without success. He overhears snippets of the conversation in the living room, so he gets up and goes to stand by the door. The interaction seems emotionally charged. He hears the name Jamiu, school, and Alhaja speaking in Yoruba. Even with the limitations of being in the next room, he can hear Vipaar's emotions swing between frustration and despair like a metronome. His nose catches a whiff of a stench, which he assumes is coming from the room but quickly realises is emitting from himself. The combination of old sweat and dried urine makes him want to vomit and he has an overwhelming need to escape the confines of his clothes. He begins to undress and feels very vulnerable standing in his underwear, so he takes a yellow towel, which is hanging by the door of the wardrobe. He twitches when he hears

Alhaja raise her voice. He picks up his clothes, takes a long deep breath then parts the curtain and walks back into the living room. Although flimsy, moving the curtain to one side feels like knocking down a brick wall.

Alhaja and Vipaar turn around to look at him. The look of frustration Vipaar throws at him feels like a dagger through his chest, while Alhaja simply asks, "How are you?"

"I want to have a shower please."

Alhaja turns to Vipaar, "kilo wi?"

Vipaar giggles, "Alhaja, he says he wants to use the bateroom."

"Ehhhen, you want baffff?" she looks at Vipaar. "Oya, Daniel take him to bateroom," she taps him on his knee and motions for him to get up.

Vipaar screws his face in annoyance, and Temilola feels it is akin to smelling cow dung at a local cattle market.

"Oya, come les go," he barks as he stands up grudgingly and walks towards the front door. Temilola looks at Alhaja but she fails to provide him with the reassurance he is desperately seeking. He takes the sombre look on her face to mean he is on his own.

"Eyy, I said les go my friend, I don't have time to waste today."

He follows Vipaar as instructed, walking into the dark hallway with only a towel to cover himself, making him feel even more vulnerable than before. He walks a few steps behind Vipaar silently and notices his muscular arms and his broad shoulders. They walk past a few doors, which look the same.

"Broda Vipaar, who is your friend?" a soft voice shouts out from behind them.

The enquirer, a little boy, runs past Temilola as he turns around and is followed by three other little boys.

"Broda Vipaar, Broda Vipaar, Broda Vipaar," they chant in unison.

"Who is you friend?" the tallest of the four asks again. They all stare at Temilola as if he is an alien and he feels like a newly discovered species of mammal out on public display.

"Gerrout of here you little rats," Vipaar bellows and smiles, as he feigns lunging at them by stamping his right leg a couple of times. The words hit a nerve with Temilola because they are one of the insults that has caused him such humiliation the previous morning. The kids giggle and laugh at him like a child would laugh at a clown. "Bye bye," they scurry past, back in the direction they had appeared.

"Vipaaaar, my Chaaaairrrrrrrman," the echoes from the salutations reverberate along the narrow hallway. Temilola turns around to see a skinny man wearing a white vest and boxer shorts leaning on a doorframe a few meters in front of them.

"The one and only, any other one is a counterfeit," Vipaar replies with vigour as the two slap palms.

"Whare you slaughtering a pig last night?" the man says with a wide grin, showing off his perfectly white and straight set of teeth. "The noise from your apartment last night scared me o. I think it is arm robber."

"Mr Emeka my oga at the top. I beg no vex o, just some confusion," Vipaar replies. "Even I am surprise o, a big police sergeant like you afraid of arm robber."

"Na you sabi, who wan die." He turns to Temilola. "Who is this one?" Vipaar looks at Temilola. "Mphh, this one! It is Alhaja who bring him home yestiday."

"Another stray, just like you abi," Mr Emeka chuckles. "I remember when she bring you hare, Iya Rotimi call a tenants meeting," he begins to laugh. "He say you will rob and kill all of us." Temilola looks at Vipaar, whose face is contorted with scorn, and then back at Mr Emeka who is still laughing.

"Oya, les go, I don't have time to waste on you," Temilola turns to see Vipaar stomping away toward the door, which is the only source of light in the dark hallway. He walks quickly to catch up to him while holding the towel firmly around his waist. He steps through the doorway into the bright sunlight which exacerbates his stench. "Pheew, damn it's hot," he mutters to himself. He looks around his surroundings as he follows Vipaar, whose shoulders seem to have become wider in the daylight. He did not know what he expected the bathroom to look like, but he is shocked at the rudimentary contraption he is looking at. The so-called bathroom is constructed with the same sheets of metals he had seen at the market the day before. There is a large red and yellow metal drum with a logo of seashell, which is full of water right beside it. He is so consumed by the 'bathroom' that he only hears fragments of what Vipaar is saying. He jolts when he hears, "Hay, small boy, I am talking to you."

He looks at Vipaar, whose eyebrows are down and together.

"Pardon me, sorry I was not listening."

Vipaar rolls his eyes and sighs in annoyance. "I say, take this bucket; get the water from over there," he points at the metal drum. "The soap and konko is in the bucket." Temilola looks at the metal bucket, narrowing his eyes and pursing his lips and then looks at

Vipaar. "What?"

"Lissteeeen, omo aje, this is not dee Continental Hotel or the Sharaton, you understand." Vipaar smirks. "Dis is Mushin, di water is di same, oya go and take your baff."

Temilola does not fully understand what Vipaars says but he takes the bucket knowing he does not have much of a choice. His stench is so overwhelming he would willingly jump into a croc-odile infested river to cleanse himself. As he fills the bucket with water, he feels multiple eyes watching him from the windows of the two-story building. He takes the bucket into the relative privacy of the bathroom, removes the towel and hangs it on a nail by the door. His muscles quiver and his heart pounds as he bends down to scoop water from the bucket with a plastic pail. He closes his eyes and pours it over himself from shoulder height. The sensation of the cold water causes him to breathe rapidly. "Oh gosh, oh my gosh." His heart rate elevates, his mouth begins to quiver and his body shakes. He feels pain and relief at the same time. He pours water on his body a couple more times and just as his body and senses are adjusting to the shock of the cold water he hears, "Ok, I will meet you inside when you finish."

"What… er… please don't leave. Wait for me… please." He waits for what feels like hours for a response, and relief washes over him when he hears, "Ok, I will wait, but don't be long, I am already late."

Temilola quickly lathers himself with soap and scrubs his body. He does not want to know the limits of Vipaar's patience and generosity.

"How did you meet Alhaja?" Vipaar asks.

"Erm… I bought boli from her yesterday, and then I ran towards her when a policeman began to chase me."

"Why was the policeman chasing you?"

"I don't really know," Temilola says. "Yesterday was really blurry."

"What is blarry?"

"Blurry! I mean confusing; I am still trying to decipher all that has happened in the past 24 hours. Everything is so surreal."

"It is well?"

They both go silent, the only noise is from street hawkers advertising their wares, music from loudspeakers and the water hitting the floor after removing the soap foam from Temilola's body.

"Why did you save me from getting hit by the bus?" Temilola asks after a couple of minutes.

"My friend, will you hurry up? I don't have time for your questions, I tell you I am already late!"

"So sorry, I will be out in a couple of minutes."

"I now know your name is Temilola, what is your surname?"

"I don't know" Temilola says, his voice trembling. "All I can remember is my first name."

"Where are you from?" Vipaar asks after what feels like an eternity of silence. Temilola stops midway through pouring the water over himself. He has asked himself the same question since his nightmare began.

"I don't know, I don't remember. I woke up in that market yesterday morning not remembering anything."

Answering Vipaar's questions feels oddly cathartic. It feels liberating to share his experience with somebody else. Temilola mulls over the statement as he pours the rest of the water over his head, his body now adjusted to the temperature.

"Why do you speak like that?"

Temilola steps out of the bathroom with the towel around his waist and asks, "Like what?"

"You sound like an omo-aje bu…" Vipaar catches himself and decides to rephrase. "You sound like you are from Jans or Yankee, or those people who live on the Island."

"Pardon me, sorry I don't understand. Which Island?"

Vipaar looks at Temilola and lets out a heavy sigh. "Don't worry. Let us go, I am already late."

As they walk back towards the building, Vipaar begins to sing along to music which is playing from speakers in one of the surrounding buildings.

"Its not her fault you know
"You cannot blame me though
I wanna have them all
I know it's wrong but the … … "

Temilola begins to sing along,

"Oliver, Oliver, Oliver Twist
Rebete rebate rebate
Labat, Labata, Labata
Sebede, sebede, sebede"

Vipaar stops and looks at Temilola as they are about to enter the building. Temilola wonders as to the cause of the perplexed look that appears on Vipaar's face.

"What's wrong?"

"How can you sing to the music, but you cannot remember

your surname or where you are from?"

This realisation hits Temilola like a ton of bricks. His lips part and he tilts his head as he frowns. Firstly he had not realised he was singing, secondly Vipaar's comments make sense. Why is he able to sing along to a song without thinking, but his monumental attempts to recall his memories have been fruitless? A fleeting picture of a boxed room with a brown desk and a black stereo appears in his head, but it does not make any sense. He also realises that he had been happy for the few seconds he had been singing. The feeling of despair instantly returns to usurp the ray of hope. He drops his head and mumbles,

"Oh cruel cruel world, how quickly hope turns to despair."

"Haaay, haaay, Shakespeeer! Listen, we don't have time for a sonnet, I have places to go," Vipaar says sharply.

Another layer of confusion is added to Temilola's already complex thoughts. Vipaar is a walking paradox—first he had given him a swift beating and threatened to take his life, but then subsequently saved his life. He spoke with the same aggression as the bus conductors he had seen the day before, but he also knew about Shakespeare and sonnets. Temilola stands still, staring at Vipaar and blinking rapidly. "What are you looking at? Are you surprised dat a street boy like me know about Shakespeer?" Vipaar replies with his nose blaring and eyes bulging. He kisses his teeth and continues leading them back to the flat. "Nonsense and Ingredient."

Temilola wants to respond, but feels embarrassed because Vipaar has exposed his haughtiness. There is no defence in reply to Vipaar's accusation, the best thing he can do is be silent and follow Vipaar back to the apartment.

CHAPTER 8

"**N**onsense and Ingredient." Vipaar tries to show he is insulted, but inwardly he is pleased that he has shown the boy that he is book smart, an intellectual. They walk back to the flat and seeing what Alhaja is preparing stirs his sense of mischief like Loki. She has bought akara from a passing vendor and is getting the eko they had for dinner three days previously from the plastic basket on top of the fridge. He is curious to see how their new houseguest will react to having to eat such basic foods. It will enable Alhaja to see how soft and snobbish the boy is and finally agree to absolve him of the promise he had made.

"Go and change," Vipaar commands like an army sergeant giving orders to a subordinate. He feels he has to assert his dominance in his territory. He watches Temilola walk to the bedroom and his heart nearly jumps into his mouth when the boy looks intently at the sneakers he had placed at the entrance to the bedroom. He is petrified he will remember the event of that night and his beloved Alhaja would find out about his deplorable behaviour. He cannot bear the thought of breaking her heart, especially after she had shown so much belief in him earlier that morning. She believed that he would not be like Jamiu and he believed it. He lets out a huge sigh when the boy enters the room. He looks at Alhaja, who is now staring at the trainers also, and hopes that she has not noticed the guilt on his face. He only hopes Alhaja will not notice his ashen face. He quickly attempts to divert any questions.

"I have asked him where he comes from."

"What did he say?" Alhaja asks as she continues to remove the eko wrapped in banana leaf.

"He say he does not remember." Vipaar pauses for a second, "But he remembers that song by D Banj."

"Tan je be?" she asks.

"D Banj. You know that musician now, Alhaja. He sang that song Oliiver, Oliv…" Vipaar trails off after noticing the blank look on Alhaja's face. "Anyway, it does not matter. The point is, how can we look after him? Why don't we take him to the police station."

"Olopa ke!!! You wan us to take him olapa?" She stops putting the eko on the plate, looks up at Vipaar and smirks. "So you have already forgotten dee slap I gave you not long ago abi?"

Vipaar shifts backward slightly and raises his arm to his chest in a defensive position. "No, I am just saying. I can talk to Mr Emeka, he is a policeman."

"That mumu," Alhaja kisses her teeth. "Did you go to the police when you arrived here, eh? Answer me now."

"No ma," Vipaar concedes.

Alhaja continues her rebuke but stops when Temilola walks back into the room.

"Oko mi, sit down, we are about to eat eko and akara."

Vipaar watches Temilola watching Alhaja unwrap the last eko from the banana leaf. His face contorts as he stares at the white triangular shaped eko and Vipaar begins to giggle.

"Do you know how to eat eko?" he asks with a smirk.

"Er… I… don't think I have ever eaten it before."

"Well it is what we have, you will eat when you are hungry." Vipaar glares at Temilola.

"Don't mind him jare, sid down," Alhaja says quietly.

Temilola sits down on a chair. He senses the tension in the air and knows that he is the root cause. Vipaar picks up two pieces of eko from the basket, unwraps them from the banana leaf expertly, and then takes five pieces of akara from the oil soaked newspaper.

He watches as Temilola slowly puts a piece of eko in his mouth and chews. He laughs as Temillola screws up his face as he chews, pushing out his bottom lip and finally spitting out the eko.

"Don't you like it?" Vipaar asks Temilola, but looks at Alhaja whose eyes are flickering with pity.

"Pele oko mi," Alhaja smiles.

"I am sorry ma," Temilola mumbles. "It made me vomit."

"Sorry o, do you want bread and egg?" she says softly.

Vipaar is annoyed that Alhaja was apologising for not being able to provide an English breakfast for this brat.

"Do you want some coka-pops or Kellog Frosteee?" Vipaar asks, biting his bottom lip in an attempt to stifle his laughter.

"Yesss Pleeaaase," Temilola responds with widened eyes and a high pitched voice.

"Kilon je be?" Alhaja asks as Vipaar stands up and walks over to the side of the fridge where they kept most of the food. "It is cereal Alhaja." He keeps his back turned so that she will not see what he is carrying. He turns around and the unspoken words between Alhaja and himself shows that she knows he is up to something sinister.

He puts the bowl in front of the little lamb who blinks rapidly. His bottom jaw drops and then he squints as he looks up at Vipaar. "This is not cereal, this is Garree!" he exclaims in shock.

"My friend, this is the original cereal." Vipaars's tone is stern.

There is silence as all three look at each other, then Alhaja begins to laugh.

"Daniiieeel, you are a rascal!"

Vipaar and Temilola join her in laughter almost simultaneously, the tense atmosphere now a distant memory. Vipaar laughs the loudest but stops abruptly when he realises that he has not laughed this hard in a while. What is even more surprising, he seems to connect with the boy. A feeling akin to joy seems to race down his spine. He locks eyes with the boy and he does not know how to react when he smiles at him. He takes two steps back when he realises that the boy is reciprocating in kind. He has let his guard down. He had always been able to keep his emotions in check and it scares him that he was smiling without realising. A long time ago, he had made a personal vow that he would never get close to anybody for as long as he lived. Alhaja is an exception from his vow because he is repaying a debt. She had saved his life, and his honour superseded his vow. A few minutes previously, he had been lobbying to get rid of the boy. Now they are laughing and playing happy family. "Why am I laughing *with* the boy? The plan was to laugh *at* him," he thought to himself.

He hates to admit it, but the boy's laughter has penetrated a part of his armour. He attempts to wrestle himself out of the situation he has accidently found himself in. He looks at Alhaja who is now concentrating on her food, so he decides to do the same. He finishes his food quickly and in silence. He looks at the boy a couple of times and he seems to be lost in his own thoughts as he eats the garri and akara. Vippar stands up quickly, causing the chair to fall to the floor. "I am going to have my baff," he says as he picks up the chair. As he leaves the room, he glances back and cannot help but notice how much the lamb reminds him of his friend Ejuku.

He walks towards the backyard thinking about Ejuku, who he has not thought about in such a long time. He had forcefully blocked the image and memory of his best friend but this time around, instead of the pain and anger that usually accompany this memory, he smiles as he remembers the happier moments in his life, before the darkness descended. He is so lost in his thoughts that he doesn't realise he has reached the bathroom until he hears somebody behind him say, "Vipaar, are you going to enter?" He looks around to see one of his neighbours, Gladys, standing behind him.

"Aunty Glady Glady, how is business o?" Vipaar greets her with a jovial smile.

"Business slow jare. I only get one customer all night," she shrugs. "I even had to accept ₦3000 so that my night would not be wasted." She adjusts her towel under her armpit. "He didn't even want to use a condom. IMAGINE, chia!"

"Sorry o, don't worry my dear sister," Vipaar sighs with sympathy. "The election will soon come, it will soon come and the money will soon be flowing."

"Business betta pick up o, I need to pay school fees," she says with a hint of despair. "I pray that God bless so that I can meet one Senator like this, chai."

Vipaar laughs as he watches Gladys clasp her hands together in prayer and look up at the sky.

"Or if I can just get visa to go Italy for three or four years, make my serious money quick. I know one girl who I went to primary with, she go to Italy some years ago, come and see the house she has built now and the car she is driving. Chiiiineeeeke." She puts her hand on her hips and looks Vipaar straight in the eye. "She is now a big madamme o!"

She looks as if she is waiting for a response, but "It will be well," is all he can muster.

"Please hurry, I have to go to class and I don't want to be late," she says, as she turns around to go back into the house. It is an open secret that Gladys is a lady of the night and she's studying accountancy at the University of Lagos. She had been his staunchest advocate when he first arrived and helped to convince the other tenants to let him stay with Alhaja. Vipaar had fallen in love with her the first time he saw her, but she always treated him like a younger brother. He felt that Gladys was a perfect representation of the unfairness of the world. A woman of such natural beauty and grace who always carried herself with pride should not be working as a prostitute. She was friendly with everybody in the building and most of them came to her whenever they had problems or issues. She always went back to her village every three months and always cooked a pot of peppered snail for Alhaja without fail when she returned to Lagos. She was the one who always collected Alhaja's medicine from the Chemist before Vipaar arrived and took over.

Vipaar sometimes sensed her loneliness when she spoke of her brothers and sisters back home- she was the oldest of nine. He had heard from one of the other tenants that she was responsible for paying for all their school fees. Approximately nine months previously, as he was leaving for work at dawn, he saw Gladys coming up the stairs. He could tell something was wrong as she took one step at a time slowly and was holding onto her rib cage. She ignored him when he greeted her and attempted to hide her face but he could see her swollen lips and bruised eye. It was obvious she had been beaten up again, either by a customer or one of the other prostitutes on the street. He sorely wanted to offer her words of comfort but he was unable to muster any.

Vipaar had fantasised about making love to her many a time, in fact she had been the star of his first wet dream. He gives a last admiring look at her perfectly shaped buttocks just before he enters the bathroom. Each pail of cold water he pours over his head enables him to abandon the fantasy world and get back to reality. He thinks back to his conversation with Alhaja and he knows she is serious about him taking the boy to school; there is no point in arguing. Once her mind was made up, nothing was going to change it. After finishing his bath, Vipaar walks back into the flat to hear the tail end of the conversation between Alhaja and Temilola.

"… …don't worry, Daniel will look after you," she says, wiping his tears away with her Ankara wrap.

The die had been cast; he is now officially responsible for the boy. This is not because of the instructions she had bestowed upon him, nor because she was trying to comfort the boy; her words show that her belief in him was total and unwavering. She is startled when she sees him and smiles.

"Oya oya, get ready or you will be late for school. Go and get dressed." He hurries into the bedroom and she follows him slowly.

"Pele oko mio," Alhaja says when she enters the room.

"Ese ma," Vipaar replies as he puts on his trousers underneath his towel and then turns around to see Alhaja putting away her money tin.

"Take this." She is holding a few bank notes in her hand, inviting him to take them.

"For watin Alhaja," he gulps and frowns.

"Give two thousan, five to dee headmaster and give wan thousan to his class teacher. Tell dem that he is my grandson who is visiting from Abuja because his mother is sick, and he will be attending dee school for one week."

Vipaar begins to sweat as the gravity and reality of the situation dawns on him. This one major task placed upon him is greater than the 12 tasks of Hercules combined. Despite all the challenges he had faced and the reputation he had built as a survivor, this one gigantic task shakes him to his core. For the first time in a long time, he has doubts about his own abilities.

CHAPTER 9

Temilola slightly hears the conversation in the bedroom from the living room. He looks around the small room, which is protecting him from the unknown. He thinks back to the events over the past 24 hours and he realises that the most useless thing he has done was to cry. Fate, the kindness of strangers and God's will are the only reasons that he is still alive. He slouches back on the couch as he feels a wave of shame come over him as he realises that he had cried when Alhaja told him that he would be going to school with Vipaar. "Crying is not going to accomplish anything," he whispers. Enthusiasm surges through him in that moment and he leans forward. His heart is pumping and he decides to abandon fear, which has been his constant companion and has stalked him from the moment he opened his eyes the previous morning. He stands up and puffs out his chest. "The best way to repay my debt to Alhaja is to let hope reign," he says quietly. He believes that fear has been restricting his thought process, and has been the reason why he cannot remember anything. Belief in hope could open the floodgates. He sits back down as it occurs to him that he needs fear to survive. It had served him well yesterday when he instinctively ran to Alhaja for safety. Hope is a fickle companion as had been demonstrated earlier that morning. He scratches the top of his head and the back of his neck and paces on the spot as he struggles to retain a coherent thought process. His innate desire for survival means that in his current situation fear is probably his most suitable companion. Abandoning fear would be to his detriment. He sits back down, clasps his hands together and decides that the best course of action will be to attempt to conquer his fear and let hope be constant.

He closes his eyes, takes a deep breath and whispers, "Every new day is a second chance… an enlightened being is one who gives thanks upon seeing a blind man." He does not know what this means, but he manages to slow his heart rate down and control his breathing. He opens his eyes when he hears Vipaar call to him.

"Oya, come and get ready, I am taking you to school."

This statement signifies a new chapter in what has already been an eventful 24 hours. The sense of euphoria deserts him immediately. He desperately wants to curl himself into a ball and stay on the couch. He looks into Vipaar's eyes, which flicker in aggravation. "Okaay, I am ready to go," he says as he bounces up from the couch. His stomach feels fluttery when he notices Vipaar's left eyebrow raise slightly. Temilola can tell that he is surprised by the change in his character.

"You cannot wear those to school o," Vipaar says, looking at the flip flops on Temilola's feet. "Go and wear those sneakers over dare," he points at the pair by the bedroom door. Temilola had noticed them when he walked into Alhaja's bedroom earlier. He walks towards the door and puts first his right foot, then his left, into each shoe. He stamps his feet and his pulse rate increases as he stares down at the trainers that feel strangely comfortable and oddly familiar on his feet.

"Oya let us go." Temilola jerks and looks up at Vipaar who breaks eye contact immediately. "I no fit be late for school."

Temilola does not fully understand what Vipaar says, but assumes that it is time for school. He takes a deep breath and walks towards Vipaar who is standing by the front door.

"Have you taken okada or danfo before?" Vipaar asks with his back to Temilola.

"I took the danfo with Alhaja last night, but I don't believe I have ever ridden an okada."

Vipaar lets out a loud breath and drops his head. "Jeeeesuuuuss, dis boy gon die," he whispers under his breath, then turns around sharply with a scowl which makes Temilola take two steps back.

"Listeeeen here, and listeeeeen well well." Vipaar takes a step towards Temilola. "Whare we are going, you cannot be talking all like some omo aje butter, denfoe, okadarrr." He twist his lips and rolls his eyes to imitate Temilola by speaking in a high haughty voice, which causes Temilola to laugh.

Vipaar is taken aback by the reaction, and attempts to inject some urgency into his tone. "Hey, hey, liiseeen, I am not joking. You can not be doing smeh smeh out there o, you have to be…" He stops when Alhaja walks back into the living room.

"Are dee both of you ready?" Before they could answer, she continues, "Temilola, make sure you liseen to Daniel." She looks at Vipaar. "Daniel, don't forget what we just talk about just now."

Vipaar looks to the floor. "Yes ma."

She hands Temilola a yellow notebook. "This is for school."

"Thank you ma." He smiles at her and turns around to see

Vipaar is already out of the door. He scampers to follow. By the time he runs down the stairs, Vipaar is a silhouette at the exit of the building and he runs to catch up to him. As he enters the light, his senses feel the full force of an array of noises, sights and smells. It instantly takes his mind back to the previous morning when his nightmare began. It feels as if all the blood has drained from his head. His vision becomes blurry, his legs wobble and he puts his palm on the doorframe to stay upright. All he wants to do is run back to the safety of the apartment and Alhaja. He stands by the doorway for a few moments, as he takes short breaths and his vision slowly stabalises. All his earlier thoughts about letting hope reign are fallow in the real world. Reality hits him hard; hope without taking into account reality would be to exist in a fool's world.

"Pheeeeeeewwwww!" He instinctively knows the call is for him and he looks at the direction it is coming from. Vipaar is standing on the road, motioning for him to hurry up and come along. He resists the urge to retreat into the building and jogs towards Vipaar, reaching him as an okada stops by where they are standing.

"Oya get on," Vipaar orders Temilola and turns to the okada driver, who is wearing a red woolly hat despite the immense heat, and says to him firmly, "Aboki, surulere." A feeling of excitement runs through Temilola's whole body and he lets out a wide smile. His mouth becomes dry and his chest feels light. Despite his memory loss, he knows he has never ridden a motorcycle before. He steps up and sits behind the driver who smells like a farm animal, and Vipaar gets on immediately behind him. The driver revs the throttle and the motorcycle lurches forward. The sudden jolt forward causes Temilola to grab hold of the driver's torso tightly. He had forgotten

Vipaar was behind him for a millisecond and is relieved to feel a gentle hand on his back. He shifts his buttocks to get more himself and then he feels the adrenaline pulsating through his veins as the machine weaves in and out of the morning traffic like a mouse through a maze. The driver only stops for cars and pedestrians at the very last moment. The way he manoeuvres suggests that he is either very confident of his skills or audacious enough to believe that no vehicle would dare hit him. Temilola resigns himself to the fact that until they reach their destination, his life is in someone else's hands. He enjoys the effects of the wind as they travel at considerable speed. Temilola notices over the driver's shoulder that they are approaching a blind corner and expects the driver to slow down, but the speed does not reduce as they get closer. They reach the corner at full speed and whisk past the white Toyota with milli-meters to spare. Temilola closes his eyes and tightens his grip on the driver's torso. He is sure he is about to die. When he opens his eyes his mouth gapes open in surprise when both Vipaar and the driver begin to trade insults with the Toyota driver. "Oswo, modafucker, eron ko," are the only words Temilola hears. A few minutes after the incident, the driver begins to speed again but Vipaar reprimands him from behind, "Hey hey hey aboki, slow down, you wan kill us." Temilola is moved by the "us" in the statement, but is immediately deflated when he hears the conclusion, "if I die I go kill you."

Approximately fifteen minutes after beginning the journey, they arrive at their final destination. They both get off the motorbike and as Vipaar pays their fare, Temilola looks around and immediately feels out of place again. There are hundreds of kids converging on the dilapidated building which doesn't have a gate and which has letters missing from a signboard.

"Oya lets go." Temilola flinches and follows Vipaar, holding on to his yellow book fastidiously as he follows behind Vipaar.

"Er, how do you know that boy?"

"Which boy?"

"The boy who drove us here."

"I don't know him, why do you think I know him?"

"You called him by his name, aboki."

Vipaar stops, looks at Temilola and begins to laugh hard. "I call im aboki because he is a Hausa man." Again, Vipaar's laughter goes a little way to relieve some of his anxiety. It takes him a couple of minutes to realise that the children are stepping aside for Vipaar as they walk towards the school building. They are all looking at him with what Temilola interprets as reverence. They look at Vipaar first and then look at him as if he is a wart at the top of someone's nose. They whisper to themselves; some are laughing, and some just look at him blankly. Many of the kids wear battered sandals, a lot of them look malnourished, and all the girls have shaved heads. Vipaar greets a few of the bigger students as they walk past classrooms with little or broken furniture. They finally reach an office which Temilola knows belongs to the headmaster despite the missing 'e,m,t' on the door. Before they enter, Vipaar knocks on the door and, in that instant, Temilola sees a docile side.

"Good morning sir," Vipaar greets a bald man sitting behind a desk, which looks like it should have been used for firewood a long time ago. The man looks up, and Temilola is shocked to see the amount of scars on his face. He has four large ones on both sides of his cheeks, three on his forehead and another three on his chin.

"Daniel my boy, how are you, it has been a long time!" He greets him warmly and smiles. "You know your YEC/JAMB exams are coming soon."

"I do sir, may I please speak with you sir?" Temilola frowns as he stares in surprise. He almost sounds erudite, he thinks.

"Of course, please sit down." Vipaar sits on the wooden chair and turns to Temilola as he pulls out the other chair. "Go and wait outside."

"What?"

"I said, wait outside."

Temilola stares at Vipaar and grinds his teeth. He does not appreciate being ordered around. Still brooding, he walks outside slowly, stands outside the office and stares out into the horizon, muttering, 'What next I wonder?'

CHAPTER 10

Vipaar has not been to school for a few weeks, but he knows that there will not be any consequence. Alhaja has placed a burden on him, which he knows he cannot shirk. On the way to school, all he can think about is the look on the little lamb's face when he put on the sneakers. On the one hand, he hoped that it would jog his memory but on the other hand, he was petrified that he would also remember the events of two nights previous. As the little lamb looked at the sneaker, Vipaar tensed up and clenched his fists, shouting, "Oya let us go," out of desperation.

While on the okada, he wonders how the boy will survive the day; his accent alone is a dead giveaway just by the way he pronounces okada and danfo. When they reach the school, he leads them to the headmaster's and orders him to wait outside the office. He cares about the angry look Temilola shoots at him, but he has to deliver Alhaja's message in private.

"How is my dear Alhaja?" the headmaster asks.

"She is fine sir. The boy outside is her grandson from Abuja. His mother is sick, so we are looking after him sir."

Now sitting behind the desk, he looks at Vipaar. "Ok, ok," comes the sombre response.

"She has asked if he could attend school for some time until his mother gets better."

"Mph mph mph, is that so." The headmaster clasps his hands together and leans forwards and shakes his head slowly. "My boy, that will not be possible. The school is already full to capacity. I will not be able to accommodate that young man." Vipaar continues, unfazed; this was all part of the dance. "Alhaja told me to donate ₦1,000 to the school library sir," he said, putting the single note on the table.

The headmaster leans back in his chair, "Well that is very generous of her, but the library needs many more books." He points at the note on the table, "This will only buy about 10 or 15 books, that's all," he says as he takes the money from the table and puts it in his pocket. He looks out of the window, "and also I have to pay teachers' salaries." He turns to look at Vipaar. "This is a public school; I have not been able to pay their salaries for three months."

Vipaar places another ₦1000 note on the table before the man finishes speaking.

"Errr, this is highly irregular," he says after he places the money in bubba (wrapper). "Tell Alhaja the school appreciates her generosity. We will be able to take the boy for one to two weeks. So, how old is he?"

"I think he is 13 sir."

"Ok, he will have to go to SS1." He bends over and writes something on a piece of paper, and hands it to Vipaar without looking at him. "Take this note to Mrs Ogunleye."

Vipaar takes the note as he stands up."Thank you sir."

"Don't forget to deliver Alhaja's message to Mrs Ogunleye," were the headmaster's parting words as Vipaar exited the office.

"Yes sar."

"Oya let us go," he barks at Temilola, who flinches as usual. He walks slowly as he gives him instructions.

"Listen, if anybody asks you, tell them you are Alhaja Mariam's grandson. You will be here for some weeks and you live in Abuja. You are not here to play. You better be serious, or people will deal with you. Do you understand me?"

"Yes, yes," came the response from a visibly shaken Temilola. Vipaar sees his fingers trembling but he continues, "You cannot be doing smeh smeh here, you understand." His words are meant to prepare the boy for life in an environment that will shock his systems. Without thinking, he puts his hand on the lamb's shoulder, looks him in the eyes and says, "Listen, if anybody causes you trouble, tell them you are my bro…" Vipaar pauses and removes his hand from Temilola's shoulder. "Err… tell them you are with me."

He had nearly let his guard down again. He decides to wipe the smile off the boy's face. "Listen, why are you smiling? I am doing this because of Alhaja, don't think I like you! You have given me nothing but headache since I met you that nig…"

He pauses again, breaks eye contact and kisses his teeth. "Listen, if anybody asks you anything, just tell them watin be your concern."

"Oya, repeat it."

"Errrmm, weeten… waten… beez, your concern." Vipaar drops his head and exhales hard. "Chai, go wid god."

He continues to give the boy instructions, informing him what class he will be in. "You have to be sharp sharp, you understand."

They reach the classroom and wait by the door because the students are in the middle of reciting the national anthem. When the teacher sees them, Vipaar raises the note to beckon her over to him. She walks over to where the two boys are standing. "Good morning, how can I help you?"

"Good morning, Mrs Ogunleye." Vipaar bows his head slightly and smiles. "Err, the Headmaster asked me to give this to you," he hands her the note. She takes the note from Vipaar and when she opens it, she looks startled. She scrunches up the ₦500, reads the note quickly and motions Temilola to enter the classroom. "Come in, go and sit at the back."

"Thank you." Vipaar turns to walk out the door but stops when he hears, "Hey, Mr Man, come here," The tone was sharp and obviously irate. He stops just a few centimetres from the class entrance and watches the diminutive woman stomp toward him with a face like thunder. He feels intimidated and aroused at the same time.

"Listen here," if her look was scary, her words were even more terrifying, "do I look like mopo police to you. How dare you insult me? Do that again and I will deal with you."

She throws the ₦500 note at Vipaar and walks back into the classroom. Vipaar is stunned; he does not know how to react. He initially thought that she was insulted with the paltry sum he had provided, but then she threw the money at him. This is all new to him; he has never known anyone to reject a bribe without it being a ruse to show the current amount was not sufficient. As he bends down to pick up the money he comes up with the only plausible reason for her rejecting the money.

"She is still new, maybe she has contacts that helped her to get the job, after three months of not getting her salary, she will get with the programme," he says to himself with a chuckle. When he reaches his classroom, he notices that it is unusually full. He intends to apologise for being late as soon as he walks in but the teacher does not give him a chance.

"Mr Daniel, where have you been and what have I told you about entering my classroom late?"

The students called him Ghana teacher. Although nobody had ever confirmed he was from Ghana, it was a known fact that he was not Nigerian.

"I am sorry sar, I was with the headmaster. My small brother is registering in this school sir."

"Registering? So late in the term?" He stares at Vipaar as if waiting for a response. "Ok, go and sit down. I hope you have been studying for your exams."

"Thank you sar." Both know the true meaning of the "thank you" was for not taking out his cane to beat him. Vipaar takes the last empty seat at the back of the class. He has to utilise the skills of the streets to navigate to the back of the room because the class is full beyond its capacity. After a quick assessment of the dimensions of the room, anybody with a brain would have deduced that it was built for a capacity of not more than 25-30 students, but there were approximately 50-60 students in the classroom. He sits down on the edge of a bench already occupied by three other boys, two of whom Vipaar knows well. They shift when they see him coming towards them, and they greet each other as quietly as possible, but this still brings the ire of Ghana teacher who shouts at them from the front of the classroom. "Who is talking? I said who is talking?" he bellows from the front. The class falls silent, at which point he turns around and continues to write on the black board.

Although he had been reluctant to come to school, Vipaar feels a sense of relief at the change of pace. He has not had the opportunity to reflect since he met the boy. He is lost in his own world and he tries to process what had happened in the past 24 hours. The boy has conjured up memories he thought he had laid to rest a long time ago. He tries to come to a firm conclusion about his feelings for the boy, then he begins to think about the future, and why Alhaja's request is such a burden on him. Being responsible for somebody means that he will have to think past today; he will have to think of tomorrow and the day after. His philosophy was "survive today, and let tomorrow bring what it may." He begins to think about the future, what would happen if the boy did not regain his memory, would he live with him and Alhaja forever? He quickly dispels this thought from his mind because it leads him to a place which he does not want to acknowledge but knows is inevitable. The years were starting to take their toll on his beloved Alhaja; time is the cruel thief of youth. At the back of his mind, he knows that one day the inevitable would happen but he refuses to think about it. On the other hand, if the boy did regain his memory, he could not bear to fathom the look on Alhaja's face if she found out what he had done that night. He is caught between a rock and a hard place. He begins to think back to the last time all the responsibilities he had were house work, fetching firewood and looking after his siblings. He was forced to grow up faster than he wanted. He thinks about his brothers and sister, and is picturing his mother's face when he feels a sharp pain on his back; it is the unmistakable lash of the pankere. He looks up and sees Ghana Teacher staring down at him. He had made it all the way to Vipaar without him noticing.

"When you are in my class, you concentrate!" Ghana teacher shouted.

Vipaar stands up, "Yes sar." He is now angrier than ever. This is the second time in as many days that his daydreaming has cost him dearly. When he sits back down, he begins to think about how he is going to make money for the rest of the day. The express would be busy with people going home for the weekend, and Deeper Life were going to be meeting at the mega church this weekend so there would be a lot of traffic. He could drop the boy with Alhaja and go to the Lagos-Ibadan expressway. As much as he tries to think about making plans for the afternoon, his mind keeps going back to the boy. He wonders where he could have come from and under what circumstances he had appeared in Oshodi market that night. He also could not help but acknowledge the insurmountable probability; he realises that he is worried about how the boy is adjusting.

Chapter 11

Temilola had seen the teacher read the note Vipaar handed her and saw her face curl up in annoyance as she read it. He enters the classroom as instructed and realises he has started another journey in addition to the journey without an end. Each passing moment forces him to dig deep into his fast depleting resources of hope and courage and he is finding it increasingly difficult to adhere to his newfound philosophy. Upon seeing the classroom, he now fully understands why Vipaar was so vigorous in trying to prepare him for what lay ahead. He had tried to imagine what the classroom would look like but his imagination would not have in a thousand years been able to fathom what his eyes and brain are trying to assimilate. His journey as an existentialist is short and ends abruptly; he has to return to the path of the realist. The classroom looks like a war zone, half of the ceiling is missing and it is just a matter of time before the rest disappears based on the water patches. There are approximately 30 to 40 students in the class and all eyes are on him, some smiling, others looking stern—they were all looking at him inquisitively. If they knew what he was thinking, he was sure they would rip him apart on the spot, they all looked so poor and unkempt. There are more students than chairs and he wonders where he is going to sit. The sense of loss has returned although in a different form. Vipaar's words now feel like a spear and shield with which he takes courage to continue each tentative step into this new world.

He does not know where to walk to, he is hoping the teacher will give him more instructions but she has gone out to speak to Vipaar. He walks over to the teacher's table, which is at the front of the classroom. He does not know where to look as everyone is staring at him and giggling. The teacher stomps back into the classroom a few moments later looking visibly annoyed. He thinks he hears her mutter "insult" under her breath.

"What is your name?" The smile on the teacher's face does not correspond with the brash tone with which she asks the question. "Tell the class your name and where you are from."

"My name is Temilola and I come from Abuja." His mind flashes back to his conversation with Vipaar and the answer came out just as they had rehearsed.

"What is your surname, or you don't have a surname?" Mrs Ogunleye asks.

With all the preparation that they had gone through in the morning, Temilola realises that they had not covered the most basic part of the cover story. He thinks fast, "Samson ma, my name is Temilola Samson."

"Welcome to St Joseph Primary School Temilola Samson," the class says in unison.

Although it is a fake surname, it feels good to have an identity. He takes a seat in the middle of the classroom as Mrs Ogunleye has instructed. He desperately hopes that he has masked the obvious fact that he feels like a fish out of water. He sits next to a boy who has a mesmerising smile; he is as dark as charcoal and his teeth are as white as snow.

"You are welcome," he greets Temilola as he sits down. "My name is Joshua. Don't worry, I will look after you."

"Hello, how do you do?" The words leave his mouth before he remembers Vipaar's instructions.

The boy giggles. "Is Vipaar your broda?" he asks quietly, eyes lit up in eagerness.

"Errr, no... no... he is not my brother... but I am with him." Joshua frowns and leans back slightly. Temilola begins to sweat and looks away to avoid Joshua's penetrating eye. "E, yeah, I am Alhaja's grandson."

"Ehnn, ehnnn, ok, very good, very good. Yes tell him dat me, Joshua, am looking afta you, you hear."

"Okay." Temilola does not know what to make of the situation. It is obvious that Joshua is in awe of Vipaar and probably thinks he can use him to get access or something like that. "NO, TALKING, MR SAMSON." Temilola looks to the front of the class and sees Mrs Ogunleye looking in his direction. He looks left and right and then realises she is talking to him.

"Today you are doing a test on geography and history." She turns around to write on the blackboard and Temilola purses his lips as he notices her perfectly shaped behind. The lessons create a rollercoaster of emotions within Temilola. He is high in confidence when he hears what the morning subjects were but by the end of the morning, he feels as lost as a Bedouin in a desert sandstorm does. He was sure he was proficient in both subjects. However, his heart sinks when the first question asked is about how many states there are in Nigeria, the dates they were created, the capitals of the states etc. He does not have a clue about a majority of the questions; the only questions he answers correctly are about international countries. The history lesson is even worse. He feels dumb because he cannot answer the majority of the questions. The questions are about Nigerian leaders in the past, unfamiliar names like Nmamdi Azikiwe, Obafemi Awolowo, and Murtala Muhammed. Questions about when Nigeria was created. He sits on the bench with his butt cheeks clenched for most of the morning and looks on as most of the kids answer questions eagerly. He intuitively knows that his lack of knowledge is not the result of his memory loss. He looks around him and everybody else has his or her head down writing. He feels even more out of place than when he first entered the classroom. He believed himself to be highly intelligent, but he quickly realises that intelligence is relative. Vipaar's instructions had not prepared him for this. His discomfort must have been palpable because he feels Joshua nudge him and motion for him to copy the answers from his exercise book.

"No thank you," he says quietly. Instead of graciously accepting the kind offer, he rejects it and he can tell he has injured the boy's feeling because his smile disappears instantly. Temilola knows that the real reason he rejected the offer is that he does not want to accept help from somebody who is beneath him. His chest feels hollow as his breaths become slow and shallow. He realises that before he can let hope reign and develop the courage required to survive in this new world, he needs to develop one virtue above all others—humility. Demonstrating humility when he told the woman selling water he was hungry resulted in her giving him

₦50, which in turn led to meeting his current guardians—Alhaja and Vipaar. He decides to show some contrition, so he leans over and whispers, "Thank you, but I don't want to get you into trouble." Joshua's smile returns immediately.

At break time, Joshua makes sure that Temilola follows him outside. Many of the boys give him the thumbs up and the attention makes him feel uncomfortable but he responds in kind with a nervous smile. Joshua leads Temilola to a group of boys playing football. They stop playing when they see Joshua and they greet him while looking at Temilola. "Kilonshele, alaiaye mi." Temilola feels like a rare species that has been captured and is on public view.

"Tani ore (Who is your friend)?" a short boy holding the football asks Joshua.

Still smiling, "Is my guy, Aburo Vipaar ni (He is Vipaar's brother)."

They continue speaking in Yoruba. He cannot understand most of what they are saying, but from what he can gather, they are speculating about where he comes from and what he is doing at the school. The guesses range from VI, or Abuja, to London or New York. Temilola squints as he listens intently, hoping that a location may trigger his memory, but this only results in giving him a headache.

"Can you play baw?" The presumed leader of the group asks, looking at Temilola directly with a smirk on his ashy face.

"Pardon?"

The smirk turns to stifled laughter. "Baw baw, I say can you play?" he holds up the ball for emphasis.

"Yes of course." Temilola lifts his right eyebrow. "You kick the ball in the net, simple."

"Ha, ha, ok you will be on my own team." At this conclusion, everybody resumes their previous positions on the gravel football pitch. For the next fifteen minutes, he abandons his troubles and predicament. In fact, from the first few minutes of the game, he is in awe at the universal feeling of joy, happiness and laughter that surrounds him. Despite the obvious poverty that the vast majority of kids have come from, they exhibit a collective spirit and resilience which he instinctively knows he does not have. Although he cannot dribble, kick or run with the ball, he tackles hard, which draws applause from the boys. Playing football makes him feel alive. The ball is losing air, but the boys play with the tenacity of a world cup final game. For a while, he does not feel lost or like an outsider. He belongs—the feeling seems new.

After the game, he realises that he has laughed and experienced the freedom of a child. As he walks back to the classroom after the break, he cannot help but appreciate the innocence of being children. He has gone from being an outsider to being part of a group within the space of twenty minutes. His joy is short lived because reality hits when one of the boys asks him, "Hey bros, whare are you coming from?" He wants to solidify his newfound friendship by answering truthfully but Vipaar's instructions are thundering in his ears. He decides to be prudent and answers, "Watin be your concern?" There is a momentary pause, Temilola smiles and then the boys start laughing.

Chapter 12

Vipaar is unable to concentrate on the teacher all morning. Each minute that passes equates to money he is losing not being on the streets. It is all down to the omo aje butter. He reminisces about the days he loved going to school and learning. Those were the days when he had hopes and dreams. He wanted to become a doctor, make enough money to build a big hospital in his village and heal everyone for free. Now, he does not allow himself to think about the future. Life on the streets has taught him that life is cheap. There is a story about a street hawker who became a big afrobeat musician after appearing on a television show, but the vast majority die on the streets, in prison or just disappear. Those who made it to the top had to sell their soul to the devil. He finds himself thinking about the little lamb, and wonders what he is doing. The reasons for him wanting the time to go faster changes from wanting to return to the streets to wanting to check on the boy as soon as there is a break. He worries if the ruse has been rumbled because of the boy's accent or that he was alone.

During the break, he is happy when he sees the boy is lost in play. He is laughing and joking with his new friends and looks like he belongs. Vipaar feels a warm feeling of happiness run through him, followed immediately by trepidation. He hates to admit it but he feels some pride at how quickly the boy has adapted. It also gives him a little hope that, like Hercules, he too would be able to accomplish his gargantuan task. He wants to call him over to confirm the time and location they should meet after school, but he decides to be magnanimous and continue to let him play football. He knows how quickly joy can turn to despair; there is no way of knowing when the boy's memory will return and these may be the last moments of joy for a while.

"Sssss, you come hare!" he orders one of the younger boys who is walking past. The boy is a little startled but he gingerly changes direction and walks towards Vipaar.

"Yes sar."

"You see that new boy over there," Vipaar points to Temilola. "How is he in your class today?"

"He is alright," the boy shrugs his shoulders and sticks out his bottom lip. "He was ok."

"Ok, good, good, hare take this," Vipaar hands the boy a ₦50 note. "Tell him to meet me by the gate at 2pm. Deliver my message well well, you undastan."

"Yes sar." The boy puts the money in his pocket. "2pm sar," and he walks away.

Vipaar spends the rest of the day thinking and planning how he is going to look after the boy while hawking on the street. As time goes on, he decides to make the best out of the situation. He realises that his biggest fear is failing Alhaja, so he puts a plan in place to ensure that the task he has been set is successful. Even if Alhaja does find out about his shameful behaviour, his dedication to fulfilling the task would go some way in deflecting the disappointment if she ever found out. He decides that he will take the boy on as a protégé and his heart flutters at the prospect of passing on his knowledge to somebody else.

The boy delivered the message as instructed and Vipaar sees Temilola is waiting at the gate at the designated time. Vipaar decides to begin the boy's lesson immediately. He calls one of his friends over.

"Segun, how body?"

"Heeey, my guy, it dey inside cloth o." They shake hands and click fingers. "I hear you bring your broda today."

"Whaaat, liissseen, is not my broda, you understans." Vipaar stares at Segun, leanes back and shakes his head. "He is just one small boy Alhaja bring home yesterday. I am looking after him for some days."

"Errm… my guy, I beg no vex," Segun's eyebrows squirm, "is just that… er… that is…"

"Psst, no shaking broda, the boy got no liver so I wan test him." Vipaar turns round and points to Temilola. "He is dee one standing over dare holding dee yellow book and looking like mumu."

Segun looks at Temilola and grins.

"Watin you wan me do to am."

"Mmmph," Vipaar snorts and rubs his tongue over his top gum. "Go and mess with him small, take his book but don't hurt him o I beg."

Vipaar looks on from a safe distance as the boy looks ever more apprehensive each minute. He is holding the yellow notebook close to his chest and is moving his head in all directions. Segun swaggers towards Temilola and Vipaar watches as they exchange a few words. He can see that the boy is visibly shaken. He takes a few steps backwards and his eyes are darting around. Vipaar smiles when Segun snatches the book from Temilola, turns around and begins to walk away. He stops suddenly, walks back towards the boy and slaps him across the face. "Oh lord, oh lord, oh lord." Vipaar realises the flaw in his plan, which is swiftly getting out of control. A crowd has formed immediately around Segun and Temilola, who wobbles from the slap but is still standing, which blocks Vipaar's view of the incident. With his heart pounding in fright, he begins running towards the crowd which is blocking him from seeing what is happening with Temilola and Segun. He is already planning the excuses he is going to give to Alhaja when they return home as he pushes his way through the excited crowd. His mouth gawkes open when he sees Segun moaning on the gravel in the fetal position and Temilola standing over him, quivering.

The streets had gone a long way to dumb down his senses and nothing really shocked him anymore, but he recognised he was witnessing an anomaly.

"Eh… whaat… what happen?" Vipaar asks Temilola, who exhales in relief.

"He, he, he tried to take, to take…" Temilola begins to explain. "He, he… I was standing here…" Vipaars turns to a boy standing next to him. "Hay, what happen hare?"

There is no doubt that the tone demands an urgent and exact answer, which is reflected in the speed and excitement in which the boy gives an exact eyewitness account.

"All I see is the small boy dash sand in the face of the big one and den he use his head to hit him in the piyom."

The reason for Segun's current position becomes clear. Temilola head-butted Segun in the groin.

"Ye, ye, ye, epon mi oooo (testicales)." Temilola flinches and goes to stand behind Vipaar when Segun begins to rise to his feet. Vipaar's fears are allayed slightly. The test has yielded unexpected results, and it shows that the boy has spirit and a brain. Segun stumbles towards Vipaar crumpled over, grimacing and holding his testices. His eyes are red and teary. Temilola takes a step back behind Vipaar who feels a sense of pride that the boy has sought his protection.

"OYA, EVERYBODY CUMMUT THIS INSTANT." Vipaar looks around the crowd, anger etched on his face. The crowd disperses quickly, murmuring as they leave.

"Vipaaar, you are a liar o, you tell me that boy is an omo aje… yie, yei," Segun exclaims as he struggles to breathe and puts his right hand on Vipaar's shoulder. "Dis no be omo aje butter o, dis one get serious liver."

"Na bi your own fault," Vipaar snaps at Segun. "I say jus take his book and test him, did I tell you to slap him?"

Segun stands up straight, still holding his testicles. "Yes, yes, bet after I take his book, he insult me, he called me a ingno, ignora, ignia." He looks at Temilola. "Alaiye me, please wat word is dat you call me?"

Vipaar turns to look at Temilola who is blinking rapidly and biting his bottom lip. He opens his mouth to speak and closes it again, looking at Vipaar for guidance.

"What did you call him?"

"Erm." Temilola wipes the sweat from his forehead. "I called him an ignoramus."

Vipaar really wants to laugh, but he knows he has to chide the boy.

"Listen to me boy, you have to use your brain and think before you act." Vipaar grudgingly sneers at the boy, it is for his own good. Although he passed his first test, there are still bigger, tougher and more dangerous tests to come.

"But, he sla…"

"And so what?" Vipaar shouts, the veins in neck bulging. "Do you know who dis man is? Are you on his level? Who are you to call him an ignoramus? If he slap you, you say thank you sar."

With the events of the morning still playing on his mind, Vipaar attempts to find a balance between keeping his own emotions in check while still ensuring the boys receives the message.

"But, but…" Temilola's bottom lip is wobbling and he looks close to tears, "I didn't do anyt…"

"Don't answer me back. Listen to what I am saying to you well, well." He points to his left ear with his index finger. "Yes, he slapped you. And so what, do you think he is your mate?"

"Vipaar, take it easy now," Segun pleads. "The boy is a champiooon."

Vipaar is grateful for his friend's interjection, he had not meant to be so harsh with the boy whose posture shrinks by the second. He takes a deep breath. "You are right my chairman, you are right." He turns to Temilola.

"Listen, I am not saying you should not fight," Vipaar's tone is soft, "bet next time, if you have to fight someone bigger than you," he pauses and puts his left hand on his protégé's right shoulder, "you eider have to know where to run or you dismantle him completely. Do you understand?"

"Er, yeah… yes, I do." Vipaar looks into Temilola's eyes, whose innocence betrays his valiant attempt at showing bravado. They both know he does not fully understand. Vipaar wants to continue to ensure that the boy fully grasps his warning but he chooses to be altruistic and to let the boy preserve innocence for a while longer. As Segun and Vipaar bid each other goodbye, Temilola apologises to Segun. "I am sorry I hit you sir."

"My champion, abeg, no vex," Segun says with one hand still on his testicle and looking uncomfortable. "Make sure you listen to my chairman, you hear." With this, he limps away.

"Oya, come let us go." Vipaar's stern tone has returned. Temilola scrambles after Vipaar, holding the book tightly like a champion does his hard-earned trophy. As they walk out of the gate, they see some of the boys Temilola had been playing football with waving enthusiastically. Vipaar smiles as he watches the boy respond with the same vigour. Melancholy washes over him because he knows Temilola would have to make the leap from childhood to adulthood that afternoon. He suddenly has a deeper understanding of what Alhaja meant when she gave him the task of looking after the boy. In addition, he also realises that he had known what she meant all along but did not want to admit it. Looking after the boy meant going beyond the physical; he is also responsible for his emotional wellbeing as well. The weight of responsibility he felt earlier feels like a feather in comparison to what he is carrying now.

"Come on my friend, we have a lot of work today," he snaps. With that, he flags down an okada. "Iyana-Iba, Ojo."

As they make their way to their destination, Vipaar has no idea what the future holds for both of them, but by the end of the night, he is no longer questioning why fate has put them together. As he and Alhaja watch the little lamb sleeping on the couch that evening, he feels a sense of pride.

"How, did he do?" Alhaja asks softly.

"He did well ma," he replies with a wide smile. "He did very well. He is a survivor."

CHAPTER 13

Temilola is standing by the school gates as the boy in his class had instructed him to after the break. He chews the inside of his cheek, taps his fingers on his thigh continuously and searches the yard hoping to see Vipaar. He takes a step and gasps as a gangly boy with sagging posture approaches him with his nostrils flaring, his eyes low and head cocked to the side.

"Yooouuu, give me dat book now, now." His voice is coarse.

"Pardon?" Temilola takes another step back and clutches the book tightly to his torso.

"I saaay give me di book, or are you deaf?" His frown becomes deeper as he jerks from side to side and then snatches the book.

Temilola looks at the boy as he walks away. He clenches his fists and his biceps begin to twitch. He feels the blood flow through his veins as he steps forward.

"Give me back my book, you stupid ignormarous." He knows he is in trouble when the boy stops and turns around with a face like thunder. "Hooolly shit."

"Paawwff." He hears the slap before he feels the sting on his cheek. His throat dries up instantly as his breathing increases. He gets tunnel vision and things go dark. The next thing he knows, he looks down to see the boy lying on the gravel curled in a fetal position. "Ohhh Jesus, Jesus, Jesus." Temilola begins to sweat, his lower lip trembling as a tear slips from the corner of his left eye. Relief surges through him when he sees Vipaar emerge; the way it feels is akin to a thirsty Bedouin finding a lush oasis in the desert. His knees are shaking and he looks on as a boy explains what has happened to Vipaar who fixes his eyes on Temilola. He is shivering and can only babble when Vipaar asks what happened. Vipaar's jaws slack as the short boy explains what had transpired.

Temilola looks at Vipaar in awe for a few moments as the crowd disperses upon hearing his command. Confusion reigns in his mind as he shelters behind Vipaar, listening to the conversation between Vipaar and the boy. Although he initially struggles to understand what they are talking about, he quickly figures out that it was set up. He does not have a chance to process the realisation as Vipaar scolds him, his attacker defends him and then Vipaar tenderly puts his hands on his shoulder and speaks to him softly. He feels a little remorse at head-butting Segun who turns out to be quite amiable. He waves goodbye to his friends and sits on the okada that Vipaar has flagged down.

The okada journey is not as exciting as the one earlier, mainly due to the density in traffic which means they do not travel as fast. He also has to concentrate on ensuring that he does not drop the bag Vipaar has entrusted him with. During the journey, he realises that life is all about perception. To him all he can see around him is chaos, but to the indigenes of this environment it is normal, they are living and surviving. He cannot force this world to adapt to his needs; to survive he will have to adapt to the world around him. Approximately fifteen minutes after leaving the school, they arrive at a Total petrol station. When they get off, Temilola looks around and Vipaar hands the okada driver a ₦100 note.

"150," he shakes his head and looks at Vipaar stone-faced.

"From where to where?" Temilola looks at Vipaar who has returned to 'street mode', a term he has coined to distinguish between his different moods.

"Aboki, you dey craze, I beg take jo, you are wasting my time."

"Pssst, 150."

"Abi, you want me to do you injury?" Vipaar deepens his voice and screws up his face. "Listen, aboki, take this my friend, you are wasting my time!"

These words send a chill down Temilola's spine, he is sure Vipaar is going to smack this aboki.

"Bros, petrol has gone up," the driver is now becoming irate, "plus you carry load."

Temilola is relieved when Vipaar adds ₦20 to the two 50's in his right hand and smiles. "Aboki, you are lucky today o, I have my trainee here so that is why I am not wasting my time with you."

Temilola is confused when the driver takes the money and smiles at Vipaar. He was so sure that a fight was imminent but it was resolved without the other losing face. His heart is still fluttering from hearing Vipaar refer to him as his trainee as he follows him to the entrance of the petrol station.

"Give me dee bag," Vipaar says.

It dawns on Temilola that he is here to work.

"Do you remember anything yet?" The question catches Temilola off-guard; he had actually forgotten that he had lost his memory. His brain is already in survival mode and he was expecting a lecture from Vipaar. He pauses and thinks for a few seconds before responding, "No."

"Mpph, okay. I am sure it will come back soon, don't worry." Vipaar's voice hardens. "Now the reason I have brought you here is to train you, you unstan!" He ignores the look of trepidation that appears across Temilola's face and continues speaking, "You see dose people running afta dee cars and selling things to people in moto vehicles?" Vipaar points to numerous boys and men chasing after cars plying their goods. "People call us street hawkers, sometimes street urchins, but we call ourselves hustlaarss, you unstan?"

Temilola nods eagerly and strains to listen to what Vipaar is saying, which is difficult due to the noise coming from the cars, danfos and trailers speeding past.

Vipaar looks Temilola in the eyes. "I know you are scared, so the first lesson I am going to teach you which you must never forget is that, 'Fear of the unknown is worse than the manifestation of the fear.'"

Temilola leans back and his lips part as he looks at Vipaar in awe but no words come out. He looks down and is about to ponder this profound philosophical statement when Vipaar begins to laugh.

"Hahahaha, I beg, do I look like Wole Soyinka to you? My friend, the only rule on dees streets is Don't Die!" He widens his eyes. "You will learn everything else based on that."

Temilola is disappointed. His mind was prepared to take tutelage from a great master, but it is not to be. For the first time since they have met, he begins to look at Vipaar as a human being rather than a creature. It is obvious that he is a highly intellectual and witty individual—he knows about Shakespeare and Socrates. He realises he has not given credence to his intellectual capabilities based on his own deep-lying arrogance. He wonders what his story is, where his parents are, why is he on the streets, and how did he get on the streets? The questions flooding his mind are numerous and complex. He realises he is lost in his train of thought when he sees that Vipaar is staring at him, waiting for an answer to a question.

"Pardon me?" he asks sheepishly.

Vipaar breaths in and rolls his eyes. "Liiiiisssseeeeennnn, open your ear and pay attention, I said, 'you wan chop'?"

"Yes, yes I am quite hungry."

"Ok, now this will be your second test. You must work for your food, you unstan. Go and buy rice, beans and two meat from that fat woman over there."

Temilola looks toward where Vipaar is pointing in disbelief; it is on the other side of the busy road across four lanes of traffic. The woman has four different coloured coolers perched on a bench and is serving food to three customers. She certainly is rotund but Temilola felt calling her fat was a little uncouth. Then again, this is not his world, and who is he to judge? He turns back around to face Vipaar, desperately hoping he was speaking in jest. He sees women who are selling food on their side of the road. Vipaar is holding out ₦500, he has noticed Temilola see the food sellers standing on their side of the road. Temilola lifts his hand to point to the women but puts it back when he sees the stern look etched on Vipaar's face. He interprets it as, "say something, I dare you," and takes the money from his hand instead. Vipaar unsuccessfully tries to hide the look of surprise on his face. Temilola swallows hard and turns around quickly because he does not want Vipaar to see that he is petrified. His heart rate increases and he takes the first tentative steps towards the edge of the tarmac.

There are not many cars passing so he takes a deep breath and steps on the tarmac. He gives himself a count of ten and leans forward, but his legs do not move. He turns around and sees Vipaar looking at him with his arms crossed. Temilola takes another deep breath and begins the countdown again. As he rocks back and forth he murmurs, 'five, four, three, two… one." His leg muscles tighten up, he lets out a big puff, then begins running across the hard tarmac. He nearly defecates himself when a blue Nissan comes within inches of hitting him. Things seem to slow down as the car speeds towards him, horns blaring. The car is a couple of centimeters aways when he pictures Vipaar's face saying those immortal words: "don't die". With that, his hips swing and bend like he is a trapeze artist, in a way in which they have never done before. "Oh my goodness, sheesh." The window rolls down as the car drives past and he hears, "Olo shi, ofe ku, you wan die abi, don't worry I won't be the one to kill you." His senses are heightened by the time he reaches the barrier and he feels like he can fly. "Wow." He is laughing without knowing why. His stomach is fluttering and his heart is pounding.

He wants to look back at Vipaar but decides to focus on the second leg of the crossing as he climbs over the unpainted concrete barrier. There are more cars and danfos speeding on this side and he does not see how he is going to safely cross two lanes of fast moving traffic. He studies the pace of traffic for a couple minutes and hopes that something will happen which will force the cars to slow down, but it is just too dangerous. The feeling of elation turns to trepidation. He turns around with the intention of climbing back over the barrier to cross to the other side, however the smug look on Vipaar's face makes him more determined to complete his task. He looks around and notices other people are also experiencing the same challenges in trying to get across safely. His eyes widen when he notices that some have formed into small groups and are crossing the road together. He suddenly pictures herds of wildebeest bunched together to cross a crocodile infested river. He sees three of four small groups formulating a few meters from him and, with the notion of 'safety in numbers', he walks over to join them. His survival instincts direct him to this group purely on the fact that he would be one of the most agile. Three of the women are a little weighty, there is a man carrying a suitcase on his head, and a young woman wearing tight jeans and low heeled shoes. He calculates that if somebody was to be knocked down, it would be one of them. As soon as the man with the suitcase steps onto the road, the whole group follows and cars are forced to slow down as the group moves across the lanes as one bunch. They all disperse when they reach the other side and he lets out a sigh of relief as his heart leaps in triumph. He looks back to see if Vipaar has been watching but he has disappeared from the spot where they had been standing. The adrenaline coursing through Temilola's veins repels any worrisome thoughts as he makes his way towards the 'fat woman'. His eyebrows arch in astonishment when he sees Vipaar standing a few meters away from the food seller, but he does not acknowledge him. Temilola watches with curiosity as the woman serves two customers before him. While waiting, he uses his shirt to wipe the sweat from his forehead and reflects on his short journey across the four lanes. Instinct and calm logical thinking were required when he faced the two different types of challenges. His sense of accomplishment is nearly shattered when he makes an onerous realisation about his thought process. He had been cold and calculating when deciding which group to cross the road with; his survival instincts meant there was no room for any sort of compassion. He feels uneasy about his thought process and wonders where it had come from.

"What do you want?" she asks in a tone which Temilola would have considered rude just 24 hours previously, but now accepts as the norm.

"Yes, may I please have rice, beans and two pieces of meat?" Temilola asks with a wide smile.

The woman's eyes narrow as she stares at him for a moment before lifting the lid from the yellow cooler and scoops the rice.

"Do you want a plate or take away?"

"Erm… I will take the plate ma." He assumes Vipaar had crossed over to eat here. As she scoops the rice into the plates, she looks at Temilola inquisitively.

"Where are you from?" she asks finally.

"I am from Abuja." The question was expected and the answer was returned swiftly. "Aunty, please put some more beans." The last statement is meant to deflect further questions and to show that he has street smarts. He has picked up a few things from watching Alhaja's interaction with her customers the day before. She smiles and puts a little more beans on both plates. Vipaar walks over as she hands Temilola the first plate full of food, which he gives to him. He takes the second plate with his left hand and gives her the money with his right hand. "Oh yeah, and two pure water please."

She asks a little girl sitting next to her to take two sachets of pure water from the bag, and hands them over to Temilola. As he takes the bag, he cannot help but notice how pretty she is. Her smile makes his heart flutter. He wonders how such a rare beauty emanates in this jungle of noise, smug, and chaos. "Change," the woman says as she gives the change to Temilola who puts it in his pocket.

"Thank you," he says and walks towards Vipaar who has begun to eat his food.

"Well done," he says without looking up from his plate. "Well done my apprentice, you do ok, you do ok."

"Thank you sir." The words are like sweet music to Temilola's ears.

"Oya chop chop, quick, and by the way, always count your change," Vipaar says with his mouth full. "Everybody in Lagos is a thief, you unstan!"

CHAPTER 14

"The boy has done very well; he has a natural instinct for survival," Vipaar thinks to himself. He notices that Temilola's face beams with delight when he refers to him as his apprentice. The thing that impresses him most is how quickly he could read his environment and adjust well. "OHHH LORRD," Vipaar had cried out and put his hands on his head at the sight of the blue Nissan coming within inches of hitting the boy. Relief and admiration swarmed through him as he watched Temilola move with the dexterity of a hare in order to escape from the jaws of the wolf. Vipaar only became aware of his level of anxiety when he realised that both his hands were clasped on top of his head. He quickly put them back down. The boy kept looking right and left as he attempted to cross to the other side of the road. Vipaar began to think he had set too harsh a test for the boy and concluded that he was not ready. He would have failed the test Alhaja had set him if the boy got killed. He would not know how to face her. Failure was bad, but the possibility that she might think that he had been responsible for the boy's death was unfathomable. He picked up his bag and made his way towards Temilola with the intention of helping over the last stretch. By the time he reached the barrier, Temilola had made his way towards a group of about five or six people who were also attempting to cross. He decided to let the boy continue on his own, so he crosses the road and waited for him on the other side.

They eat their food in silence. Vipaar watches the boy observe his surroundings. The chaotic atmosphere seems to fascinate his apprentice. They finish their food and return the plates to the 'fat woman' whom Vipaar notices looks at the boy inquisitively a few times.

"My friend, are you ready to work?" Vipaar asks Temilola, who is finishing off the last drop of water from the sachet.

"Yes sir," Temilola responds with enthusiasm.

Vipaar is pleased the boy is taking his role as a trainee seriously and leads him back to the original spot by the Total petrol station.

"Ehh, ehh, so we all sell many different things on dee road, you unstan," Vipaar begins. "First things first, we must give you a name." He stares at Temilola sternly for a few seconds and then says, "From now, your name will be… the chammmpioooon."

"Oh, wow thanks," a wide grin appears on Temilola's face.

"You see on dee streets, you must earn your name. They call me Vipaar because of my speed and my fighting skills. I am too fast, nobody can catch me." He performs a few boxing moves and shadow boxes bobbing and weaving his head in order to prove his point.

"Now, as you can see, each one of dee hustlaars have different specialism, you unstan?" Temilola nods and then Vipaar turns to the street hawkers who are lined up on the road. "Dee biggest sellers are phone cards, then come soft drinks. There is nothing we don't sell on dee streets. Some people sell snail, mirror, curtain, even marble. You must have speed and stamina to make money." Vipaar's feet shift in excitement, he gesticulates with his arms, and then his voice goes deep. "You have to be strong and make sure that nobody mess wid you. You can't be doing smeh smeh here o, or else trailer will catch. Do you understan?"

"Er… yeah, I mean yes, yes." Temilola nods slowly. Vipaar is unconvinced by his apprentice's response but he continues regardless.

"You have to watch out for KAI, if dey catch you, de will seize my merchandise."

"Who are the KAI?"

"Good, you are listening," Vipaar nods his head in approval. "Hay, dey are the Kick Against Indiscipline Brigade. Anyway don't mind them jare," Vipaar waves his hands dismissively, his voice filled with contempt. "Now, you see, morning and evening is dee best times to make money, which is what we are hare to do, make money. If you don't make money you don't eat, you unstan? Do you have any questions?"

"Errr, what do you sell?"

"Well done boy," Vipaar smiles as he bends down to open his bag. "Now you see, I sell Phone Charger and Re-Charge card." He picks a few chargers out of the bag to show Temilola. "But before I used to sell pure water. I have sold gala and sometimes I sell CDs. When I have saved some money, I will open a small shop and will start making serious money." He looks at his watch, "Are you ready?"

"For what?" Temilola asks as he blinks rapidly.

Vipaar frowns and pauses. "You are going to sell these phone chargers."

"What now? But I…"

Vipaar's instinct is to respond with something sarcastic or shout in order to demonstrate the gravity of the situation. He places his hand on Temilola's shoulder, "Yes, my friend, don't be scared." He pauses, stands up and puts his hand back on his side. "Sometime you don't know what you are able to do until you have to do it. Let me tell you a story my father once told me." Vipaar leads them to a secluded spot further into the petrol station and then notices that Temilola is shaking and twitching his finger nervously. He begins to wonder if he has placed too much faith in the boy's ability. The look of innocence on Temilola's face reminds him of how scary and difficult it was when he first started. Vipaar wants to comfort Temilola but he knows it would not benefit him. Street hawking cannot be taught in the classroom, it is 100% practical and 90% instinct.

"Now as I was saying," he continues his story, and avoids looking his apprentice in the eye.

"There was once a veeeerrrrry rich Igbo Chief. He has dis beautiful daughter." He alters his tone of voice to mimic an old wise man.

"All dee men in the village want to marry dis fine babe. But Chief no gree o, he say no man, no matter how rich or strong is good enough to marry his daughter. One day sha, dee Chief send message to dee village that he will only give his daughter to the bravest man in dee whole village. He request that all dee men who believe themselves worthy to come to his palace to take just one test."

Vipaar notices the boy's apprehension visibly subsiding; he is obviously enjoying the story.

"So, all of the single men and some married men went to the Chief's house on dee selected day. A lot of them have muscles like no man's business, some ware the fastest in the village, some ware wrestlers and odas were hunters and blacksmiths and thin's like dat. When it is time for the Chief to reveal the test, all the men stand unda the balcony to listen to Chief. The Chief say that the only man wody of marrying his daughter is dee one who could swim dee length of his swimming pool, which is full of crocodile, chia! All dee men begin to grumble and complain, who wan die? Abi no bi so?" Vipaar pauses, expecting a response, but continues when Temilola looks on wide-eyed, mesmerised by the story.

"Anyway, all of the sudeen, there is a big splash. Dare is a man in the pool and he is swimming hard; dodging and punching dee the crocodiles who try and bite him. He swim the whole length of dee swimming pool without any of dee crocodile biting him. When he get out, he shout, 'Chiiineeeeeeke, who push me?'"

Vipaar smiles and watches as Temilola squints, tilts his head to the right and looks up at Vipaar.

"Erm, so who pushed him?"

Vipaar's whole body deflates. He is sorely disappointed that his apprentice did not get the morale of the story. He starts to realise the magnitude of his task. "Dis boy has no street smarts kobo," he murmurs to himself. He desperately wants to explain the significance of the story, but time is not on their side. He wants to maintain his apprentice's innocence for a little longer, but ultimately it is his responsibility to prepare him for this new world no matter how temporary it may be. He wanted the story to be the introduction to the mantra which he lives by: "Man rules circumstance,

circumstance does not rule man." However all his wants seemed futile. He considers sharing his mantra with the boy but he decides a more direct approach required.

"Listen well well, my friend, if you don't sell today, you don't eat tonight, you understan?" Vipaars hands Temilola five chargers from his bag.

That seems to jolt the boy into action. No matter how rich a man is or how many women he has, food will always be the ultimate motive.

"Oya, go over dare, don't go in dee road yet, just stay on dee side." Temilola takes a deep breath and begins to walk in the direction Vipaar is pointing.

"My friend, it's between you and God now o," Vipaar advises as they part. "I have to huzzle, don't let anybody mess with you."

As he watches his apprentice walk towards the unknown, he decides to give him one piece of advice. "Temilola," he shouts.

This is the first time he has called the boy by his real name. Temilola must have also realised this because he has a smile on his face when he turns around.

"Don't forget to count your change, you must always balance," Vipaar says. "Every..."

"-one in Lagos is a thief, yes I know, I know." Temilola rolls his eyes as he finishes the sentence. With that, they exchange smiles and walk in opposite directions.

Vipaar feels uneasy as he prepares himself for work, the burden of responsibility weighing heavily on him. He watches Temilola stand tentatively on the edge of the road. Vipaar knows he has a long way to go when he flinches at the sound of a trailer horn speeding past. He watches for a few minutes as the boy stands on the edge of the road looking around trying to make sense of what to do next. He resembles a lizard trying to fly. The boy takes the approach of copying those who stand on the edge of the road waiting for cars or buses to stop. Vipaar spots a commercial bus, which is dropping off customers, that is a prime target. Unfortunately, his new apprentice misses the opportunity and can only look on helplessly as the experienced street hawkers swarm the bus from all sides like an army of ants around sugar granules. Temilola looks totally out of place; Vipaar knows how he feels because he had been in the same position just a few years ago. He wants to go over to his apprentice to give him some further guidance, and even comfort, but he knows that he has to learn to survive the streets on his own. He also needs to recoup the money he missed during the morning rush hour, so he goes to work. "Nokia, Samsung, LG mobile phone charger, mobile phone charger for sale."

Vipaar works in an area where he can keep an eye on his apprentice. Business is okay, it is Friday and people are going home for the weekend. Competition is fierce and he sees his apprentice struggle against the more established professionals. It is obvious that he has a hustler's spirit, and he quickly realises the opportunities the commercial buses presented. Temilola runs after each new commercial bus, but he did not have the guile or street smarts to make any inroads. Within an hour, he is sweating profusely; the heat is relentless and it is obvious that he is struggling badly. He looks like he is going to collapse at any minute.

Vipaar goes to where he was standing. "My chaammmpiion." Temilola does not respond, so Vipaar taps him on the shoulder.

"Oh, hi."

"How are you doing?"

"I am fine, I have sold one charger." Temilola's eyes light up with glee and Vipaar does not want to dampen his joy.

"Well done, you are doing well. Go sit over there and rest." Vipaar points at the Total petrol station, which has become their temporary HQ. He does not want to come across as soft. "I don't want you to die on me."

The primary reason Vipaar tells Temilola to take a break is because he needs to concentrate on hustling without worrying about him. Temilola gladly accepts the offer and walks quickly to sit on a concrete slab with some shade. With his apprentice in a safe place, Vipaar is able to concentrate on making money. He works for about two hours, sticking relatively close to the petrol station so that he can keep an eye on the boy. He makes a decent sum—he definitely sold more chargers than he had yesterday and decides to take a break and check on his apprentice. His heart skips a beat when he sees that Temilola is no longer sitting on the concrete slab. His pace quickens as he begins to hyperventilate. He looks all around him but still cannot see Temilola. He goes further into the petrol station and asks the mechanics in the back if they had seen an akata looking boy but they say no. He jogs back to the spot. His mind is spinning and he becomes disoriented from scanning all directions. The thought of returning to Alhaja without the boy is incomprehensible. In his state of disarray, Vipaar does not notice a man stomping towards him. It is too late by the time he becomes aware of his presence. The man grabs him by the arm. "You are under arrest!" It was an undercover KAI officer. "Don't you know that street hawking is illegal on the streets of Lagos?"

Vipaar cannot believe the situation he now finds himself. Normally, he could sense a KAI officer from miles away, but he was so consumed with finding the boy that he had let his guard down.

"Oga I beg, I am waiting for somebody, I am not selling anything. Please oga," he begins to plead. "I no fit go prison, my mother is waiting for me… oga please."

"Shut your mouth, before I slap your face," the officer sneers. He looks at Vipaar as if he is an irritant. Vipaar continues to plead with the officer who holds him in a vice-like grip to release him but he only drags him towards a waiting pickup truck. Then he hears, "Excuse me sir, where are you taking my father's servant?"

Vipaar cannot believe his eyes. He frowns and his jaw slacks open when he sees Temilola standing in front of him. The KAI officer stops and stares at Temilola. His eyebrows squish together, his mouth opens, but nothing comes out for a few moments except a mumbled, "Pardin."

"Sir, I ask again, where are you taking my father's servant?" Temilola stares the KAI officer in the eyes without blinking, his tone oozing utter arrogance and sublime confidence.

The KAI officer looks at Vipaar and then back at Temilola. "Errr… he is a street hawker. He is selling." His feet shuffle and he wipes his forehead with his free hand. His words lack the confidence of a man in authority. "I am putting him under arrest; he is a street urchin."

"Don't you dare refer to him as that," Temilola bellows with his nostrils flaring, as he takes a step forward. "I have already told you that he is my father's servant! We are on our way back to Victoria

Island. My car stopped here so that I could use the loo."

With this, he points behind Vipaar and the KAI Officer at a black Mercedes S Class, which is parked by the exit of the petrol station. The KAI officer looks at the car and then back at Temilola. He glances all around him and scratches his chin.

"Is he your friend?" he asks Vipaar, who has become a mute.

"Sir, do I look or sound like a servant to you?" Temilola's lips curl in disgust and sound a bit more indignant. "Do you know who I am?" By this time, a crowd has started to gather around them. The two lock eyes for what seems like an eternity.

"Ok, you incompetent buffoon, take out your phone and google Son of Chief Admiral Ola Ibrahim."

These words force the agent to loosen his grip on Vipaar but not entirely let go. The KAI officer taps his pocket, "No, no credit."

Vipaar, seeing that his apprentice is at an advantage, belatedly joins in the play.

"Oga, I come look for you in toilet and this man come say I was selling."

Temilola takes a deep breath, ignores Vipaar's comments and speaks directly to the agent. "I have witnesses here. If I don't return with my servant or any harm comes to him, you will pay dearly I promise you."

Vipaar's mouth becomes dry and he gasps as Temilola walks away nonchalantly. This gives him the confidence to find his voice and forcefully release himself from the agent's now loose grip. "Oga, wait, o."

When he reaches Temilola, he is shocked at what the apprentice does next. He raises his right arm and before Vipaar could move, gives him a back handed slap.

"Idiot!" he says loudly enough for the agent to hear. Vipaar follows with his head bowed low as they both walk towards the black Mercedes Benz. He has no idea what they will do when they reach it. His plan is to engage in discussion with the driver before disappearing into the crowd. When they are a few meters away, he and his apprentice stand still, dumbstruck as the Mercedes engine starts and begins to drive away and join the slow moving traffic on the expressway.

CHAPTER 15

Temilola's heart starts to pound like a jackhammer when he returns to the concrete slab to see Vipaar being dragged by a man wearing a native outfit. He knows he only has seconds to decide what to do and without thinking he walks quickly towards Vipaar, who is resisting and pleading with the man. He has no clue what he is going to say until the words "Excuse me sir, where are you taking my father's servant?" come out his mouth. He is as stunned as Vipaar, whose mouth falls open. He does not know how or why, but he can feel each heartbeat which is slow and steady. His breathing is measured and it feels like ice is running through his veins as he locks eyes with the man. He is not conscious of the words coming out his mouth. It feels like somebody else is talking, somebody powerful, but he does not know who. His nerves begin to wane when the man asks Vipaar if he knew him. He intuitively knows that he has to dominate the conversation and show he is in control. He changes his tone and asserts his authority. He is genuinely indignant when he says "Sir, do I look or sound like a servant to you?" At this point his nerves are shredded and he knows that it is only a matter of time before everything falls apart and so he focuses his eyes on the black Mercedes Benz. He knows he has won when the man begins to mumble something about not having any credits. He takes a deep breath when Vipaar mumbles something but avoids eye contact. "I have witnesses here, if I don't return with my servant, or any harm comes to him, you will pay dearly I promise you!" That is the last ounce of gumption he has in him and he slowly walks past Vipaar and the man holding him. At this point, his chest tightens and he becomes dizzy, but he keeps his shoulders wide, knowing the man will be watching. It feels like a rock is stuck in his throat and his body feels light when he hears Vipaar say, "Oga, wait, o." Temilola desperately wants to hug him; he does not realise he has slapped him until he sees him rubbing his cheek. It feels satisfying to see the look of utter shock on his mentor's face. He stomps towards the Mercedes with his chest puffed and his chin slightly raised but he has no clue what is going to happen when they reach the car. "Oh fuck," Temilola lets out a few drops of urine and wants the ground to open up and swallow him as he watches the black Mercedes drives off.

Vipaar is equally stunned. "Oh my goodness," he murmurs. They both look back at the KAI Officer who is standing with his shoulders slumped and is blinking slowly as he watches the Mercedes drive off. The moment he realises he has been duped is comical and priceless. Temilola would have laughed if he were not so petrified. He looks back at the boys and his mouth slowly prises open. His eyes widen and he starts shouting, "Hay, hay, stop dos boys," as he scrambles for his radio. He begins running towards them. "Stop! Stop!" while trying to use his radio. Temilola stands rooted to the spot. His senses completely deserts him. He looks to Vipaar for guidance and is shocked to see that he has already taken flight. His survival instincts kick in and he follows. He catches up with Vipaar and he immediately feels a sense of déjà vu as they weave through the sea of people. Temilola looks back again and is shocked to see two uniformed officers have joined in the chase. Vipaar is moving at a remarkable speed for someone carrying a bag. Suddenly he stops, looks around him and scratches his head.

"Why did you stop running?" Temilola asks in a high pitched voice as he wipes the sweat from his eyes. He glances between Vipaar and their pursuers who are getting closer by the second.

"We must stop running or people will think we are thieves," came the calm response from Vipaar.

They continue to move through the crowds at a quick pace. Temilola looks back a few times and curses their pursuers' tenacity. He had hoped they had done enough to blend in, but in the midst of the crowd and chaos, he locks eyes with their pursuer. He looks at Vipaar as he gasps for breath, praying that he will find a way out of their predicament. He sees a grin appear across Vipaar's face as he says, "Oya we have to catch that," and he points behind Temilola.

"Nooo, bloody way," Temilola gasps, when he turns around and sees a pickup truck moving relatively slowly on the expressway. "Are you serious?" Vipaar does not hear the question because he is already making his way towards the expressway and Temilola follows him. Their pursuers are close enough for Temilola to see anger etched on the KAI Officer's face. He resembles an enraged bull. They both run towards the truck, which is now speeding through the traffic. Temilola thinks that this is both a gift and a curse. Their chances of escape increase if they manage to jump on the truck, but for each traction its speed increases, their chances of escape decrease. There are not many cars on the road but the tarmac is hard and painful on the soles of his feet and his knees despite wearing trainers. In addition to this, his strength is waning. He begins to slow down as his breathing becomes shallow. All hope is seemingly lost, but then he hears words that galvanise him.

"Temilola, don't stop." Vipaar looks back. "We are nearly there!" Just as Temilola gets his second wind and speeds up, one of the straps on the bag Vipaar is carrying snaps. This causes him to lose his rhythm as he tries to prevent it from falling onto the road. They are now running side-by-side and are just a few metres from the truck. Temilola's second wind only lasts a few seconds and the likelihood of a third wind is extremely remote. Then he experiences what he will forever refer to as the "moment." He hears the loud clunking of the gears of the truck changing and watches the sudden injection of speed as it lurches forward. In that moment he knows that his destiny is still in his hands for a few seconds and, at the very least, if he misses that window his future will be grim.

"Go, go, go," he hears Vipaar shouting from behind, "we are nearly there." Temilola feels the blood surge to his calf muscles and he wills himself forward. He stretches his hand, grabs the iron bar welded to the back of the truck, and heaves himself forward. The millisecond between being lifted off the ground and jumping onto the truck is terrifying. In addition to the odour of engine oil and diesel, there is an overwhelming smell of farm animals. If he had time, he would have observed that the pick-up's last cargo package was cattle based on droppings. A gust of wind nearly knocks him over as he attempts to steady himself and he weaves back and forth, but manages to stay upright by holding onto the bar tightly. Holding on to the right side of the vehicle, he stands up and is aghast to see the distance between the truck and Vipaar has grown. Vipaar coughs and struggles to breathe as the truck's exhaust fumes blow directly in his face as he fumbles with his bag full of merchandise. Temilola's trepidation increases when he sees their pursuer getting into a blue, official Toyota 4x4 with the letters KAI written on the side in white. He can see the energy draining from his mentor with each second that passes as he struggles to hold on to the bag, which is slowing him down.

"Come on, please, don't stop," Temilola pleads. "Please, they are coming!"

He can only watch helplessly as the distance grows even further. "Drop the bag pleeaaase!" He stretches out his hand. " PLEEEAAASEEE... I NEED YOU, GRAAAAB MY HAND!"

Although they had met in inauspicious circumstances just over 24 hours ago, he feels that their fate is intertwined, well for the near future at least. Their eyes meet; they both know that it is a life altering moment as these words give Vipaar the boost he requires just as he is on the cusp of accepting defeat. He drops the bag, lunges forward and grabs Temilola's hand. He watches as his apprentice grimaces at the force of his grip. Vipaar knows he only has one chance and one chance only to make the jump. With perfect timing, Vipaar put his right foot on the bumper, for at least two seconds his life is literally in Temilola's hands again. His trainee's strength impresses him. Temilola uses all his energy to pull him up. He knows that with one little mistake they could both fall out of the truck. The relief that he feels upon the confirmation of Vipaar's safety is short-lived. They are still being chased, so he cannot relish the rewards of his effort. Vipaar smiles and says "thank you" in between gasps of breath. They both stand up on the back of the truck, knowing that whatever happens next is totally out of their control. Fate and faith will determine where they will sleep tonight; either in jail or in what would be a grand palace in comparison—Alhaja's apartment. A sense of serenity blows along with the wind across Temilola's face. Fortune has smiled upon him so far. Fate would not be so cruel as to bestow upon him a calamity after making such a gargantuan effort to keep him alive, or so he hopes.

"Why you dey smile," Vipaar says as he paces on the spot while breathing heavily. "You go sleep in prison yard tonight!" For the first time since they met, Temilola sees fear in Vipaar's eyes. The KAI car had now turned its sirens on and was getting closer. The truck slows down slightly because traffic is building up in front.

"We must jump," Vipaar commands. Temilola ignores him. His attention is focused on the oil tanker about thirty yards in front of them. This is the reason the cars have slowed down. Temilola gently places his hand on Vipaar's shoulder who has bent his knees, ready to jump. "No, wait." His eyes are fixated on the oil tanker, which is blocking the road as it attempts to cross to the other side of the expressway.

"Hay, hay, you dey craze, pshh, abi you want me to slap you sense." Vipaar grabs Temilola by the shoulder. "Pshh, I beg jump my friend."

Temilola knows that Vipaar will not leave the truck without him. "NO!" Temilola forcefully pulls his arm from Vipaar grip. Temilola's confidence forces him to look at the oil tanker. He is not filled with the same confidence as his apprentice. "My friend if I die... chai chai," he takes a deep breath, "if I die, I go kill you, you hear me? I go kill you."

They both watch as cars in the lane closest to the barrier press their horns and increase their speed. Temilola knows that fortune has not deserted him when he feels the vibrations of the gear change under his feet, the prolonged pressing of the horn and the increase in speed. He holds his breath as their truck speeds through the ever-shrinking gap and misses being shunted in-between the barrier and cab of the truck by a few millimetres.

"Oloshi buruku," he hears the driver shout, "koni da fu en." Temilola cannot help but contrast the different reactions between missing death's whiskers. The relief that flows through his veins is in stark contrast to the anger felt by the driver.

"We made it," Temilola smiles and looks at Vipaar, whose face is sullen. "What is the matter, aren't we safe?"

Vipaar looks at him. "We must get down now." Temilola had not realised that the truck has slowed down. For him, time had stood still; he could not tell how many minutes had passed. He looks around him, looking for anything familiar as he jumps off the back of the truck.

"Where are we?" he asks Vipaar, who has begun to walk a few meters ahead.

"Where do you know?" he snaps as he walks into the parking lot of Tantalizers restaurant. He sits on the cement floor with his back resting against the yellow wall. Temilola stands looking down at him, not knowing what to do or say. He is petrified, so he says what comes naturally to him. "Are you ok?" The look that Vipaar gives makes him feel like he has asked a stupid question. "Where did you go?" Vipaar asks with the back of his head, leaning against the wall with his gaze focussed on the sky above. "I told you to stay where I put you—all this is your fault."

The fragility of Vipaar's hard exterior was becoming visible and this terrifies Temilola.

"I had to go to the toilet," he mumbles. "I had to urinate into the bush."

"I lose all my merchandise and my money when I drop dee bag on dee expressway."

The reality of their situation hits Temilola as hard as a black-smith's hammer hitting an anvil. "How are we going to get home?" he asks with an innocence that confirms his naivety.

Vipaar springs to his feet, looks at Temilola and sticks out his bottom lip as he mimics him. "How are we going to get home?" The British accent causes Temilola to burst into a fit of laughter. In between a fit, he manages to say, "I don't sound like that, do I?"

Vipaar lets out a stifled grin. "My friend, we have to walk home." The laughter seems to be short lived as a dark cloud descends upon him.

"Oya, let us go." Vipaar walks toward the gate and avoids a purple Toyota people carrier that is navigating its entry into the parking lot. Their eyes lock again for a few seconds as they both remember the events of the day. Temilola feels like they have formed an unbreakable bond. The look on his mentor's face is very different from the one which had threatened to take his life earlier that morning. Even with the thaw in his disposition, Vipaar's face suggests an inner struggle, which Temilola hopes he will share.

"Don't think I have forgotten that you slap me, my friend!" Vipaar smiles and rubs his cheek. "Tomorrow morning, I will take you home." Temilola's heart begins to race. His eyes widen. "You know where I live?" he squeals. His eyes and words are filled with a thousand hopes.

"Eh? No, but you, I thought your memo…" Vipaar tilts his head left. "You said your father is Chief Admiral Ol…" He trails off as his apprentice's smile disappears. His head droops and he stares at the ground.

"Oh, I made that up," came the quiet reply. "I saw the name in front of a newspaper when I was returning from the toilet." He looks up. "I still don't remember anything."

CHAPTER 16

Vipaar's body tenses up and he takes a deep breath as he watches hopelessness consume his apprentice like carnivorous bacteria. Temilola's bottom lip trembles and he sluggishly walks away with his head hanging low. Vipaar takes a small step forward and reaches out, but stops. He wants to comfort his apprentice but he cannot allow him to wallow in self-pity.

"Hey, my champion," he calls out as he walks past Temilola. "Whare are you walking to, do you even know dee way home?"

Vipaar feels a sense of guilt because the elation on his apprentice's face when he thought that he would be going home weighs heavily on him. He knows from experience that the only thing worse than no hope was false hope.

"Are you ready to walk?" Vipaar's voice is deep and he frowns. "It will soon be dark, oya les go." It will take about four hours to get home and he knows his apprentice will struggle to make it, but they have no choice.

"WHAT!!!" Temilola cries. "Hold on… Wait a minute … we are really walking home?"

"Yes o, I also lose all our money when I was running to catch the trailer." Vipaar's voice is monotone. "Sebi you have eaten, you will be fine."

"Yes, but… but how long is that going to take? I am so tired, and it's getting dark."

"Don't worry, we will soon be home," Vipaar says as he takes a sharp right, and begins to cross the road. He means to send a message to his apprentice to expect the unexpected. He does not look back to check he followed him, but he lets out a sigh of relief when he hears Temilola mumble something under his breath as he comes alongside him.

"Pardin?" Vipaar stops and turns to look at Temilola.

"I said thanks for *waiting*." Temilola looks into Vipaar's eyes and smirks.

Vipaar's eyebrows come together and his head flinches backwards. He stares at his apprentice for a couple of seconds, cocks his head sideways then he takes deep breath.

"Listen my friend, and liiiissseeeenn well well, chai… I should…" Vipaar bites his bottom lip. "I no get time to baby you, you hear me." His nostrils flare as he pulls the lobe of his left ear. "I have lost all my money and all my merchandise. And you want to be talking nonsense about me waiting for you to cross the road."

As he turns, Vipaar looks the boy up and down, kisses his teeth and walks away. He stops and turns around when he hears his apprentice mumble something else under his breath.

"Cooouuttttsssssiionn your sef, you unstan," Vipaar roars, wide eyed, the veins in his neck bulging. "If you say another word my friend, I go leave you here. You hear me? So you betta coutsion your sef."

Temilola stares at Vipaar, his chest puffed out and his jaws clenched.

"Oya, say somteen, I beg, say somteen, I will demolish you."

Temilola lets out a long breath and bows his head. Vipaar turns around and stomps away. *Petulance must be stamped out immediately or it will spread like wildfire*, he thinks to himself.

With the attempted subversion now quashed, Vipaar's thoughts turn to finding a solution to their dire predicament. He had spent the last of his money on buying the phone chargers and paying RPG his dues. His plan had been to raise enough funds to upgrade to selling products that would yield a higher return for low volume such as curtains or bed sheets, maybe even snails. He shudders as he considers the thought of having to go back to working at the pure water factory. It was arduous, backbreaking work for minimal reward. He has worked so hard to reach the stage of the phone charger seller, the indignity of returning to selling pure water is incomprehensible. Although they had maintained the notion that Alhaja was responsible for him, he had long become the bread-winner. His earnings supplemented what she brought home from selling plantain and peanuts in the market. Her welfare had long been the primary motivation for his survival, he wanted to be able to make enough money to enable her to stay at home and no longer go to the market. Now he finds himself thinking about how all three of them were going to survive. A million thoughts are racing through his brain as he scrambles for solutions to his problems. Each path seems to lead to a gate which he had worked so hard to avoid—RPG. He had put too much time and effort to start all over again, so he begins seriously considering taking up RPG's offer.

They have been walking in utter silence, except for the occasional berating to walk faster, for about an hour. Vipaar can see that his apprentice is exhausted, but rather than acknowledge his impotency to remedy the situation due to lack of funds, he periodically gives what he feels are words of encouragement: "we will soon be home" and "if you fall, no go carry you o."

As they are walking through Ilupeju, Vipaar has to grab hold of Temilola by the shoulders because of the huge crowds. As dusk approaches and with no viable solution in sight, Vipaar slowly begins to accept that RPG is the only option available to him. He is lost in his own world when, in the midst of the horns and other commotions, he hears "Ssss, sssss, Okada".

Vipaar's brain refuses to acknowledge what he knows he hears—the engine of an okada stopping and "Whare to?"

"Ahhaa, ahhaaa, look at dis bou, you dey craze?" Vipaar's eyes confirm what he already knows, the boy has hailed an Okada. "We no get one kobo—you go pay with your teeth." The only reason he does not slap him is that he believes that exhaustion had made his apprentice delirious.

"I was trying to tell you earlier," Temilola whispers. "I sold one phone charger and I have some money."

Vipaar stares at Temilola, motionless. He resists the urge to smile.

"Why did you not say anything before?" he shouts. "We have been walking all this time and you had money, are you stu…"

"I did!" Temilola curls his lips.

Vipaar swallows hard. "When?"

"You told me that if I said another word, you were going to leave me behind." Temilola gets onto the waiting Okada and then looks directly at Vipaar whose lips are parted, "Remember?!"

Temilola's demeanour echoes that of a chess player who had willingly sacrificed all his pawns and was basking in the victory of capturing his opponents Queen.

Vipaar is shook and looks on dumbly as his apprentice gets onto the motorcycle with a slight grin on his face. It is obvious that his silence earlier was another act of petulance rather than contrition as he had assumed. His body stiffens when he realises the apprentice—the omo-aje-butter had duped the master.

"OYA, get down, before I give you one serious back hand." Vipaar raises his right arm with the back of his hand facing Temilola, his voice dictatorial. "I look like mumu to you abi? We are walking home tonight or we are sleeping on dee street, you unstan?" Master and apprentice stare at each other in silence.

"Whare you de go?" the okada driver breaks the standoff between master and apprentice. He literally lived by the adage, "time is money," and so every second he is stationary is costing him money.

Temilola looks to the ground and murmurs, "I'm sorry."

"Pardin, I didn't hear you?" Vipaar leans forward and points his ear to Temilola. "Say dat one more time."

Temilola looks up "I said I am sorry for disrespecting you... sir."

Vipaar exhales discreetly in relief, he himself is exhausted and does not relish the long walk home. His apprentice would not make it and he would have failed his task. He also takes it as a sign that he must do what he does not want to do. "Papa Ajao," he instructs the driver as he gets on the okada behind Temilola. They get off at Papa Ajao before taking a danfo to the place where it all began:

Oshodi. Vipaar leads them through Oshodi. He has always found it intriguing how office workers who spend the day working on the Island are always stone-faced when they wait for the buses and danfos to take them into the mainland. He had theorised they were angry because, after spending the day in the plush surroundings of Victoria Island, they had to return to the realities of their one-bedroom apartments and 'I better pass my neighbour' generators.

"We have to stop somewhare quickly before we go home," he snaps at Temilola, who is walking very slowly, and whose breathing has become laboured. "I have to see somebody."

"Ok." Temilola's reply is flat, he is too tired to complain or argue.

Vipaar tells Temilola to hold on tight to his belt and they make their way through the hundreds of people who he is certain have all their own worries. He knows it is risky taking Temilola along to see RPG, but he is too exhausted to go home and come back out again. They walk through a series of alleyways, all the while his apprentice looking more petrified the further into the labyrinth they go. He greets all the people who hail him as he walks past their shops; he has purposely taken this route in order to avoid the motor park. He finally sees RPG standing casually next to a NEPA pole, overseeing his boys collecting the tax from the danfo, taxis and okada drivers in the usual undiplomatic manner. He follows the due process and speaks to one of RPG's boys.

"Bros me, how body? I beg, tell your Oga I want to see him."

"Wait hare," the boy walks off toward where RPG is standing. Vipaar sees RPG look in their direction and then walk into a building a few meters away. The boy who had delivered the message walks back towards them slowly. He turns to his apprentice whose eyes are darting around and who keeps rubbing the back of his neck.

"Don't worry," Vipaar says to him softly, "nothing will happen to you here. I know all deese boys. I use to manage them."

Temilola raises both eyebrows and then frowns. He parts his lips to say something but the boy returns to them.

"Oga says you should meet in his office."

"Thank you broda." Vipaar turns to Temilola and puts his arm across his shoulder blade. Let's go."

They enter a building through a door made of roof sheet metal and find themselves in a crowded courtyard. There are approximately fifteen people in there, and all of them are smoking marijuana and drinking alcohol. There is a policeman sitting directly by the entrance holding a machine gun in one hand and a bottle of Hennessy in the other. Vipaar feels his apprentice's shoulders tense up so he squeezes gently and says, "Don't worry; everything will be fine, trust me."

"Daniiieeeel," RPG bellows, "have you come to accept my offer?" Vipaar looks at RPG who is sitting on a leather couch grinning with two skimpily dressed women sitting either side of him stroking his chest and thighs. One of them is his ex-girl-friend, Folashade, who averts his gaze and looks away. As they walk towards him, Vipaar notices RPG's eyes firmly fixate on Temilola. His eyebrows squish together, his head flinches back slightly and then he leans forward and smirks. Vipaar's heart beats faster when he realises that RPG recognises Temilola. He quickly greets RPG, "Good evening sar," and bows his head. His stomach turns and there is a bitter taste in his mouth. He hates to kowtow to RPG in front of his apprentice, but he is not in a position to be prideful. "Can I see you privately sar?"

"You want to see me," RPG inspects his fingernails and picks his teeth with a tooth pick, "about what... my broda?"

"It is a private matta sar."

RPG smiles as he stands up. "Anything for you my broda, anything for you." He walks towards Vipaar but keeps his eyes on Temilola. "Let us step into my office, my broda." He continues staring at Temilola as he walks past them towards the entrance of the house. Vipaar turns to Temilola, "Wait for me here, I will only be a few minutes."

Temilola grabs him by his left forearm and squeezes. "No, no, don't leave me here, please."

"Hay, hay you cannot show any feere here, you understand?" Vipaar's tone becomes stern, "You are representing me, so do not fuck up."

The change in tone forces Temilola to release Vipaar's arm and he watches as he follows RPG into the darkened hallway.

"Is that the boy from dee other night?" RPG asks as soon as Vipaar walks into the room.

"Yes, Alhaja brought him home dee otha night," Vipaar replies. "He say he has lost his memory. He is now my apprentice!"

"Ha, dat woman sha," RPG shakes his head as he pours Hennessy into a glass.

"So you have come to accept my offer abi?"

Vipaar stares at RPG as he sips from a tumbler; he knows that the response will determine his destiny. He thought about

Alhaja and the boy; working for RPG would enable them all to live comfortably.

"No sar," Vipaar's feet shuffle slightly as he swallows. "Ahem, I am wondering if I can borrow some money sar?" He stands with head slightly bowed and his hands behind his back. When the decisive moment came, he could not betray his beloved Alhaja. He had promised her he would not re-enter this world and he intends to keep his promise. "I lost all my money and merchandise today so I need to restock."

"Look at you, just look at you." RPG sneers in contempt "After all dis time, you still selling on dee streets. Afta everythin I have taught you, you are still chasing cars, chia… what a waste!"

"I am sorry, I cannot," Vipaar replies after a few seconds of silence. "I have made a promise to Alhaja."

RPG puts his elbows on the table and looks at Vipaar. "You know she will not be arand for eva abi." His face is solemn.

"Yes, I know," Vipaar responds without looking up.

RPG sits back in his chair and stares at a clock on the wall. "How is she?" he asks Vipaar without looking at him.

"She is fine."

RPG lets out a wry smile, looks at Vipaar for a few seconds, and takes a deep breath. "It is well, so how much do you want to borrow, my broda?"

"Thirty thousand sar."

"Haahahaha, look where you are, begging for small change." RPG downs the rest of the drink and stares at Vipaar for a full minute. Vipaar begins to sweat and his shoulders droop further, his chest feels tight and his face begins to twitch. All he wants to do is turn around and walk away, but he knows that RPG would make sure that his boys give him and his apprentice a good thrashing.

"Chia, what a waste, you can have been sombodee." RPG smiles slowly as he unzips a Ghana-Must-Go bag next to his chair, which is full to the brim with cash. He takes three bundles from the top and throws one bundle at a time to Vipaar. "Oya pick up the small change." Vipaar takes a deep breath and drops to one knee as he picks up the money from the floor. The only thing that softens this act of humiliation is the promise he made to his beloved Alhaja.

"I want all my money back in 40 days." RPG stands up and puffs his chest out. "If I don't see you in 40 days wid all my money, I will not send my boys, *I will come myself*, you unstan?"

"I understand sar, thank you sar. I will give you your money in 25 days sar." Vipaar grins. "Remember sar, I larn from you." The last statement is a reminder that, despite where RPG is now, they both know where he started. He leaves the house to see Temilola doing his best to look fearless with his chest puffed out. The image is ruined by his yawning.

"My champion let us go." The relief on his apprentice's face is palpable.

"Did you accept the offer?" Temilola asks when they are about 500 meters away from the compound.

"What!" Vipaar's tone rasps with exasperation.

"That man, he said, have you come to accept his offer. Did you accept his offer?"

"Err, I have managed to borrow some money from RPG, so tomorrow we will restock," Vipaar spoke almost in hushed tones. "I have to huzzle hard, because we have to pay it back very soon.

By dee way, you must not tell Alhaja what happened today and the money we have borrowed."

"Ok," he replies. "Yeah, erm…"

"What is in your mouth, make it come out jare," Vipaar snaps.

"Errrr, RPG," Temilola begins. "How do you know him?

Vipaar stops and looks at Temilola. He exhales. "His name means Rocket Propelled Grenade, he was dee one who trained me and give me my name."

"Oh wow." Temilola's eyes beamed. "When he was staring at me, he looked very familiar."

Vipaar went weak in the knees, "What do you mean?"

"I don't know," Temilola scratches his head, "it's like I have seen him somewhere before, he is just so eerily familiar."

Vipaar looks into Temilola's eyes and takes a deep breath. "Okay, this is what happened, you see on that night…"

"Ohhhh, I know where I have seen him before," Temilola shrieks with excitement and snaps his finger. "I saw him yesterday morning just after I woke and was walking around in a daze. I must be exhausted, how can I forget that face?"

Vipaar exhales, "Oh."

"There is something else about him," Temilola licks his lips and scratches his chin. "I can't put my finger on it, it's his eyes, something about his eyes, they look sooo fam…"

Vipaar takes another deep breath and whispers, "His real name is Jamiu, he is Alhaja's son."

TEMILOLA'S STORY

Temilola Michael Akinola was born into a life of extreme wealth and luxury at the Portland Hospital for women and children in London. His mother Patricia is his father's 2nd wife and he is their only child together. He has six older siblings, the oldest of whom was 32 and the youngest 19. Despite being born into one of the wealthiest families in Lagos, he was lonely most of the time. The age gap with his siblings meant that they did not have much in common and were not close. He didn't like them much and they made it clear that they hated him. His oldest sister, Bidemi, told him on his 12th birthday that Temilola's mother had stolen their father from their mother when he started making money. She called his mother an ashewo (prostitute) and he retorted that her mother was a troll with no class. She slapped him hard across his face—that was the first time he had been hit in his whole life. She continued to ramble on about how he was a spoilt brat who had not experienced poverty like they had growing up. Her mother had done all the work to enable their father to make it in politics, then his mother arrived and opened her legs. Temilola calmly walked to his father's game room, picked up two balls from the snooker table and used them to smash the windscreen and back window of her brand-new Range Rover.

Throughout his childhood, his siblings had always made him feel like an interloper and he had never felt he belonged within the family. One of the main reasons they hated him was because they felt he didn't show them the respect they deserved and because he talked back too much. From this perspective, he was merely stating the facts as he saw them, and highlighting the limitations of their intelligence.

Based on the old family pictures that he had seen, the house they had all grown up in was smaller than the guest house next to the family house. The first four siblings went to School in a danfo or walked, but he had been driven to the top private international Primary Schools in Africa in one of their father's luxury cars. The news that he had passed the entrance exams and had been early accepted at one of most prestigious schools in England, Harrow School, was the catalyst for the argument with his sister Bidemi on his birthday. The ironic thing is that he was envious of his siblings in those old pictures, because they all had each other growing up, he didn't have anyone.

His mother is the most beautiful woman in the world as far as he is concerned and the only one who really showed him any sort of affection. She had been a Nollywood actress but gave up the career when she married his father, a rising star in the governing PDP party. Their union benefited them both. She used her connections in the entertainment world to elevate his social status, and this helped him make the right connections with the party, win major contracts and within a few short years become a Senator in the Nigerian Senate. She in turn became one of the most powerful socialites in Lagos. Her parties were legendary, and to be considered a somebody on Lagos Island one had to be invited to one of her parties. He lived a life of luxury in a 12-bedroom mansion with a pool on Banana Island. His parents bought him anything he wanted and he had met most of the AfroBeat musicians. He was playing on the latest X-Box and PlayStation games consoles in his bedroom three months before they were released to the public. For his 12th birthday, his mother took him on a shopping trip to New York where she had arranged for him to shop alone in a Foot Locker for one hour—he bought 12 pairs of trainers. After that he went to a bookstore and bought 27 books. He spent most summers in England or New York, either with his mother or with a chaperone when she returned to Lagos to prepare for the summer parties.

Elevating their status in the political and social entertainment worlds meant that his parents did not have as much time for him as he would have liked. He spent more time with the drivers, house maids, gardeners and other domestic workers who worked at their mansion in Lagos. Around the age of 10, he became cognisant that he experienced two different worlds on a weekly basis. He went to school with kids from countries from all over the world and all different races. Their parents were international diplomats, domestic and international businesspeople, politicians and the Lagos elites. The curriculum was English and the majority of the teachers were white. As a result, he hardly spoke Yoruba. At home, he interacted with the 'natives', the domestic workers who made sure that his family's every need was met. He was fascinated by them because they were different from him and his family. Any attempt to make conversations with them was always awkward because of the gulf in their status and class in life. Additionally, it was hard to be friends with someone whom he ordered around. He wondered where they went when they walked out of the gates at the end of the day. On the rare occasions he left Lagos Island and travelled to the mainland, he always stared out the car window in amazement. He could not understand why there were so many poor people every-where. He sometimes heard them talking about how there was no light or how armed robbers came to their neighbourhood. These were things he never worried about; his house was powered by two giant generators and there was 24-hour armed security. He didn't fully understand or appreciate the privileged life he lived until the morning he left for boarding school in England. There were two boxes full of books that had been sitting idle for a couple of years in his wardrobe. He left both boxes in the kitchen before he went to sleep with a note for the cook, "Please give these to the kids in your neighbourhood, your kids, thank you for all your hard work—I will miss your snails". Her reaction when she saw him the next morning totally baffled him.

As he watched the driver load his suitcases into the back of the Cadillac Escalade, he heard screaming coming from the kitchen quarters. He turned around and saw the cook running towards him screaming, holding a book in each hand and waving them in the air. She dropped to his feet and began rolling around on the floor saying, "Thank you Jesus, thank you Jesus, thank you sar, thank you sar." He could not understand why she was so hysterical, but it felt good that he had made her so happy. She then stood up, took him by the hand and began praying. This made him extremely uncom-fortable and he took his hand away—this was crossing the line. She noticed the distress on his face, apologised and took a few steps back and continued thanking him from an appropriate distance.

Temilola rarely saw his father; he was primarily based in Abuja and his appearances at the Lagos mansion was fleeting. When he did come home, he was mostly in meetings with politicians, business executives, pastors, and celebrities, looking to curry favours. His father was 54 when he was born; maybe this was the reason why they never bonded. They were also very different physically and intellectually. His brothers were carbon copies of their father. He knew more about him from newspapers and magazines. Every article highlighted his tough background growing up in abject poverty and how growing up in the toughest neighbourhood in Lagos made him a successful businessman and politician. Temilola loved reading books and poetry, and horse riding, a very different life to that of his father. On the rare occasions his father paid him any attention, it was mostly to chide him for always having his head in books. "You have to be tough boy, and you have to learn to fight. You are too soft. What is Socrates going to do when you enter a fight? You have to be stronger, like your brothers." Temilola had never had a reason get into a fight; nobody who knew ever dared challenge or accost him. Most people did not actually see him, they saw his parents, and they treated him with reverence. He was never just Temilola, he was "Temilola... son of..." He cried himself to sleep many times after such conversations. The one occasion he received a crumble of the affection and kindness he had been seeking from his father was when he taught him how to play chess when they were in Dubai. He took to the game like fish to water; something in him came alive. The ability to seek and destroy his enemy using pure intellect, and using their own weakness against them made him feel powerful and he loved it. He picked the most complex moves within an hour and, when he won his first game, he heard the words he had longed to hear for so long. "That's my boy, I am proud of you." They played for four straight hours, and during the game his father ignored a phone call from the state Governors. That was the happiest period of his life and he vowed to make his father proud. He joined the Harrow School Chess Club the day he returned to begin his second year. Temilola Michael Akinola, despite all the trappings of wealth and power, was an extremely lonely and unhappy young man. All he desired was to be loved and to feel like he belonged.

PART TWO

PART TWO

CHAPTER 17

It had been approximately six weeks since Temilola was rudely woken on that fateful morning in Oshodi bus garage. Every morning he arose, hoping that his memory had returned and every night went to sleep praying that he had spent his last day as a stranger to himself. He has accepted his circumstances and adapted relatively well to the environment he found himself in. He now has a routine along with Alhaja and Vipaar; despite this, he still finds it difficult to accept that no two days are the same. He has become a contributing member of the odd family. He would go out in the morning to buy bread, go to school and then return to help Alhaja at the boli stand in the evenings. The first day he went to school by himself was both scary and exciting; he lost his bearing a few times, but he felt a great sense of pride when he arrived safely. He had a strong feeling he was being followed and he thought he saw a figure, which looked suspiciously like Vipaar lurking amongst the crowd. His favourite days were those which he forgot that he had lost his memory. Sometimes he felt content just being with Alhaja and sadness would only resurface at the prospect of his memory returning and then having to leave, such was the deep affection he had for her. He felt alone a lot of times, and in his private moments he would wonder if his family were looking for him. He didn't even know if he had a family.

The first seven days with Alhaja were the most physically uncomfortable on account of the bout of diarrhoea he suffered. He hardly ate, but he continuously needed to use the toilet. Having to take a shit in the middle of the night with the single flame from a candle or the torch from Vipaar's phone as the only source of light was one of the many challenges he had to overcome. Alhaja gave him some herbal medication called agbo iba, which was extraordinarily bitter but was effective in stopping the diarrhoea. His respect and affection for Vipaar had also grown, and he suspected that the feeling was mutual, although acts of affection were few and far between. A thousand questions went through his mind daily, but one question always stood out—why me? Sometimes the question arose because of new challenges he faced, other times it was upon reflection of how lucky he was to have Alhaja and Vipaar when he saw or heard the experiences of others on the streets. He did not fully understand why, but he knew that Vipaar had purposely kept him from seeing the darker sides of his new world. What troubled him most was that he knew he had a purpose, but he did not know what it was. The second day of his memory loss was always a reference point when hope sometimes became distant, and anger drew close. Amongst the array of what had happened that day, finding out that the RPG was Alhaja's son was what nearly caused him to lose his sanity. Having to keep Vipaar's secret still weighed heavily on him. When they got home that evening, they found Alhaja on the prayer mat. He had been worried that she would be worried about them, but when she finished her prayers she said, "Eku le ein Oko mi (how was your day)?"

Her manner was suggestive of somebody with a total belief of their safe return. Exhaustion had diminished his burning desire to share some of the experiences of the day. The last remnants of his energy had been used to prostrate, and the last ounce was used to say "Thank you ma," as he lay on the settee.

As he drifted off to sleep, he heard Alhaja and Vipaar whispering.

"How did he do?" Alhaja asked.

"He did well, ma; he did well."

Temilola went to sleep that night with a smile on his face as he could hear the pride in his mentor's voice.

"Oya, Oya go and buy bread," he was unceremoniously woken up the next morning by Vipaar shaking him lightly.

"I beg don't scream ago. I don't have time for that kind wahala today."

It took a few minutes for Temilola to gather his bearings, for the first time since he could remember apprehension or fear did not accompany this task.

"Good morning," he mumbled. "Oh my God, my body aches. It feels like I have been in a ring with a boxer." He stretched and yawned. "Oh my gosh, look at my arms, those bloody mosquitoes," he exclaimed, scratching his forearms. "I am famished."

"What are you talking about"? Vipaar asked.

"What do you mean?"

"I don't understand anything you are saying; you are speaking so fast." Temilola realised that he was speaking with freedom and without apprehension.

"What time is it?"

"It is 6 am. I have to go to Alaba International Market to go and re-stock the phone chargers."

"Can I please come?" Temilola grinned widely.

"No, you cannot come. It will be very rough, I cannot look after you."

"Aw, but what will I do all day?" Temilola stuck out his bottom lip.

"I don't care if your whole mouth fall out," Vipaar snickered. "Go and help Alhaja at the market," he added as he made his way to the door. "Go and buy bread from the corner and make her Milo."

He gave instructions about how to make Alhaja's breakfast. "Buy bread from Iya Rotimi at the corner," and "make sure she eats the bread." The tenderness by which he spoke showed he loved Alhaja; it was in contrast to threats made the previous morning about killing Temilola if he hurt his beloved Alhaja. Temilola felt honoured to be trusted with such essential duties.

"Come hare," Vipaar motioned him over to the door in a soft tone. "Don't forget, don't tell Alhaja about the money or the lost merchandise."

"How are we going to pay back RPG?"

Vipaar's raised eyebrow suggested he was surprised by the "we"; Temilola only reflected on the statement later on in the day. It was not a conscious thought, it just came out naturally. He felt a sense of responsibility for the predicament Vipaar had put himself. Alhaja came into the sitting room as Vipaar was about to answer. They both greeted her and Temilola could hear the apprehension in Vipaar's voice.

"I must go to the market ma," Vipaar said as he averted eye contact. It amazed Temilola how Vipaar shrank when he was with

Alhaja.

"Don't be long Oko mi," she replied while looking at Temilola who was standing with his arms crossed and his face twitching.

"Yes ma," Vipaar replied as he walked out of the front door. He looked at Temilola, "Go and buy the bread, my friend."

Temilola followed Vipaar's instructions to the letter but making the breakfast was a task that he was not able to complete by himself. He was not able to turn on the kerosene stove and had to ask Alhaja for assistance. They ate breakfast in relative silence. She asked, "How he was, how was school, how is Daniel?", all to which he replied "fine". He nearly choked on his bread when she asked about Vipaar. He felt guilty for having to lie to her, but he had made a promise which he would not break.

"You help me at dee market today," she said to him after he had finished having his bath. "Wear those clothes over dia," she pointed at a few t-shirts and shorts she had laid on the settee.

"Thank you ma," Temilola nearly teared up. He was not looking forward to wearing the same clothes he wore the day before which stank to high heaven.

"They used to belong to my son Jamiu."

Temilola froze and stopped chewing. Luckily for him, Alhaja had turned her back and did not see his bulging eyes which would have betrayed the secret he was hiding. His ego had been severely dented en route to the market. He felt responsible for Alhaja, and he took on the role of the self-appointed guardian, but he felt more than useless. She held his hand when they crossed the roads, and despite her outward fragility she moved with zeal when necessary. By the time they reached her stall, he was sweating like a racehorse.

As the day went by, he was not as fascinated by the events going on around him as he had been the two days previously. Boredom soon set in and after a few more days of assisting Alhaja at the boli stand, it felt like he was watching the same movie with the same actors.

They gossiped all day—a soldier killed a danfo driver, who would be next governor of Lagos, the election.

His tutelage under Vipaar continued. He had given Temilola an additional nickname, "Question", because of the amount of questions he asked. Within a relatively short space of time, Temilola had picked up some critical street slang and knew who the actors on the streets were. He discovered that the street dwellers operated on a political and legal system of their own, outside the law of the state or nation. There were hierarchical systems in place; taxes were paid, and borders robustly defended, mostly through violence. Taxes were the most lucrative income stream. Temilola would listen in amazement as Vipaar explained the complex systems which governed the 2nd citizens of Lagos.

"There are area boys; they are always fighting for control of the streets." Vippar would tell the stories with vigour while they were on their break or walking home. "Commacia vehicles, taxi and Okada's pay the touts to operate in the area, you unstan."

"What if they don't pay?" Temilola asked naively.

"Don't pay ke? Dey cannot operate, simple thins. If they catsh you, they will beat you marcilessly o." Vipaar would almost salivate when he spoke with vigour as he taught his apprentice about life on the streets of Lagos. "Dee motor park is big, big money, you understand. RPG is de union leader of the six zones and the whole of Oshodi. One day I will tell you how he become dee big man."

Temilola found Vipaar's habit of finishing his stories with "One day I will tell you…" very annoying, but he soon got used to it. There were always stories to tell. Vipaar seemed to relish telling the stories of violent encounters between the touts and Temilola enjoyed listening to these the most. It was equally scary and exciting. He gained an insight into a world he knew he had never experienced despite his memory loss.

"Come and see fight just some time ago when I first arrive in Lagos and start working for RPG".

He told this particular story many times with the same vigour and excitement, and Temilola enjoyed listening.

"A man from Jans bought land and paid protection moni," he said, "but dose stupid boys from Idi iroko dont want to share di moni equal. Dey cannot gree a sharing formula. Four days, I am telling you, four days, dey ware just killing each otha, with broken bottle, knife, and shooting guunz."

Vipaar would become very animated as he described the violence and mayhem. "Po, paa, kapaassshhh."

The first time Temilola heard the story he asked, "Where were the police?"

It was also the first time he saw Vipaar burst out in a fit of laughter. "Police? Police? Did you say police?"

His laugh was warm and infectious; it warmed Temilola's heart because for a few moments he saw beneath the layers of emotional armour he wore constantly.

"Dey don't want to die. If they see arm robba, they jump in the gutter. Dey jus wan chop money. Even sometimes they support who pay the most money; they will want their own cut now, abi?"

It was also on this occasion that Temilola realised that Vipaar didn't take kindly to being laughed at.

"The whole of Mushin was like dessert," he continued.

"Dessert"? Temilola interrupted.

"Yes, dessert," Vipaar responded emphatically.

Temilola squinted and scratched the top of his head. "I don't understand, what do you mean?"

"There was nobody on de street."

"Ohhh, you mean desert," Temilola said in a fit of laughter. "Dessert is what you eat after dinner." The frown on Vipaar's face brought the laughter to an instant halt. "Did you ever get into fights?"

"Chai, I am fighting nearly every day," Vipaar's enthusiasm returned. "It is by the grace of God I am not dead. That is how I get my name; I am so quick, pap pap, two punches and those yeye boy were on de floor. That is even how I met Alhaja; I was fighting some boys and…"

He trailed off into silence and looked down at his feet. Temilola sensed the tension and chose not to follow up. After a few seconds of silence, Vipaar continued.

"I was working as a conductor for some weeks after I arrived in Lagos."

"Where are you from?" Temilola inquired. "You never talk about your past or how you met Alhaja."

Vipaar swallowed hard, and was silent for a few seconds before continuing with his story. "I am always arguing wid the drivers who don't want to pay me the correct money. Sometimes I have to fight oddars to pick up passenger. Chai it was hard, hard life," he concluded, shaking his head. "It even became harder with the LASTMA; they will sometimes just seize our bus and take it to Ikordu."

"Brother Jamiu... I mean RPG is first a danfo driver when I meet him." Temilola noticed that Vipaar always spoke about RPG with a combination of reverence and fear. Temilola didn't know whether to admire him or fear him, but he knew that Vipaar had a tremendous amount of respect and fear for the man.

"He help plenty when I first arrive. He gave me my name because of the way I was fighting; nobody could touch my face."

During this period, Temilola met a few of Vipaar's friends and was always introduced to them as "my apprentice". The most colourful of the lot was the one called Sunday FM. Temilola could not believe how much this man talked. He was most comical when he spoke in an American accent, "Yu know, whram seyiiin meeen, yin na minz."

Vipaar and his friends spoke almost exclusively in broken English and slang. These were the times Temilola would feel a little jealous and that sense of loneliness would arise. Sunday FM's use of grandiose vocabulary annoyed Temilola no end. He also revelled in the praise he received anytime he used a word which he didn't understand the meaning of. One day he used the word "perpendicular", and all his friends began to shower him with praise and adulation.

"Sunday FM", "The highest honourable", "Alailaye mi"; each one paying homage in turn. "Even the oyinbo who invent dee English no go understand your grammar", "higher and higher you will go".

"That is me o, higher and higher we are all going to go my brothers," he responded jubilantly. Temilola was lost, as usual, by the speed and the slang used in the conversation, but on this occasion he did manage to decipher the crux of the discussion. Sunday was going abroad, and his friends had come to see him off.

"I go land in Libya, and den take boat to Italy. I hare dee babes dare are bombastic. I get one cousin like this in Jans; he say he go get me a job for London."

"We go join you soon o," they chimed in support. "Don't forget us o, when you are making da pound starling."

"Habba," Sunday FM said, feigning insult. "My crew, I no go forget you o, I pray God make Nigeria better so I can come back soon." He continued cheerily. "I go call you as soon as I land, as soon as I get job, I go send you beer money."

Vipaar was the first to indicate it was time to leave. "Bros, I beg no vex, I must take my paddy home." He stood up, shook Sunday FM's hand, and said something Temilola could not hear.

"Bye, bye," Temilola said as he waved, "have a safe trip."

"Paddy mi," Sunday FM said in a serious tone, in-between pulling on a cigarette, "look after my guy o, das my guy."

"I will," Temilola suspected it was more for Vipaar's benefit than his. He had learnt that affection was demonstrated in many ways on the street, but never directly.

At home, Temilola had begun to notice subtle changes in Alhaja's health and behaviour over a few weeks. She had started to pray more and for longer, especially at night. She had also developed a habit of walking around with her prayer bead and repeating the same thing over and over again in Arabic, "Kun, fay ya kun."

She ate less and became gaunt. Also, she slept a lot more and didn't go to the market often. When Vipaar and Temilola got home after leaving Sunday FM, Alhaja was praying, which in itself was usual, but the length of time she had spent praying over the previous few weeks had increased.

The first time Temilola asked Vipaar if Alhaja was ok, he looked at her and said softly, "She is fine, she is just tired small." The third time Temilola asked, Vipaar shouted at him, "I say she is fine, what is your problem. Ah ah, I have been looking after her all dis time, I say she fine."

The anniversary of the 92nd day he met Alhaja was the happiest and most serene he had ever experienced since he was abruptly woken up on that fateful morning in Oshodi market. He woke up to use the toilet in the middle of the night around 4:30am and was grateful that there was light. He heard Alhaja reading the Quran and was surprised that she was still reading it when he woke at 9:30 am. He was also surprised to see Vipaar still sleeping and woke him up approximately 30 minutes later, worried that he may miss the church traffic. Temilola looked at him for a few seconds, sleeping peacefully. Vipaar smiled and then mumbled, "Ejuku". It was not the first time Temilola had heard him say this name in his sleep. He had not dared ask who it was.

Temilola shook Vipaar gently on the shoulder. "Vipaar, wake up, we will be late."

"We are not going out this morning, today is environmental," Vipaar said drearily as he stirred. "I am tired jare," he mumbled as he turned on his side and continued sleeping.

Temilola decided to take the initiative and peel yam and eggs for breakfast. "Well done my guy," Vipaar praised Temilola when he saw the freshly cooked yam and egg on the living room table. "You are larning, well done, well done."

Those words were music to Temilola's ears; he became giddy with joy at his mentor's praise. "Aunty Gladys's helped me with the eggs, but I prepared everything else," Temilola replied, his voice beaming with pride.

Alhaja came out of her room and Temilola sensed she had a different aura about her; "Up NEPA O," she said with a smile. "They give us light till morning."

"Alhaja, look," Vipaar's grin was wide as he pointed to the food on the table, "Temilola has made breakfast."

"E ku ishe ein Oko mi, well done." Alhaja smiled as she looked at Vipaar and Temilola, instead of the food on the table.

"Thank you ma," came the simultaneous response. They both watched her eat the yam and eggs slowly. Temilola had not felt so at peace and content in a long time. The constant fear which stalked him had been banished to the outer realms of his psyche. He listened to the conversations between Vipaar and Alhaja as they reminisced and laughed about the past. The biggest came from the story about the time Alhaja slapped the NEPA man who brought a bill when there hadn't been electricity for three months. Temilola and Vipaar also reminisced about how they had fooled the KAI man but left out the loss of their merchandise and borrowing money from RPG. Alhaja watched them both in silence and beamed with pride as they mimiced the KAI man's face and slapped palms. "No, no credit."

"Clear dees plates and go an get ready," Vipaar ordered Temilola after they had finished breakfast, "we are going to the Lagos Ibadan express." Temilola had noticed Vipaar frowning when Alhaja pushed her plate away after only eating one yam.

"Ema ja de ni ani," Alhaja said softly. "Efi ara ba le, rest, dare is no need to go out today, rest today," she continued as she walked slowly with her back hunched into the bedroom.

Temilola and Vipaar looked at each other after watching Alhaja enter the bedroom, not knowing how to react. Although gentle, her tone suggested that protest or bargaining would be futile. The rest of the day proceeded at a blissful pace. They all watched a Nollywood movie on the TV, which caused Vipaar and Alhaja to laugh and express sadness, shock or anger at specific points during the film, all of which Temilola missed. For him, the movie was unnecessarily long, with too many subplots and holes in the story, but his companions were none the less engrossed. When Alhaja returned from saying her afternoon prayers, Vipaar elaborately relayed all that she had missed. Vipaar slept most of the afternoon after watching the movie, while Temilola read a book he had found, *Things Fall Apart*. In the time they had known each other, Temilola had not heard him snore as much as he did over the course of the afternoon. The lights went out just as the sun began to set. There was a collective groan and a myriad of insults from the other tenants in the house as a result. Alhaja went to pray again after they had eaten what had become Temilola's favourite dish, plantain and beans. Temilola followed Vipaar out onto the veranda, which was lit up by the full moon.

"Where is Alhaja?" Vipaar asked, leaning over the railings.

"She went to pray," he answered and joined him as they watched the world go past. They were both in their own worlds.

"Wow, a full moon. And look at all the stars. I can't remember the last time I saw a full moon," Temilola said in awe.

Vipaar stared longingly at the full moon for about a minute, let out a loud sign and murmured, "It reminds me so much of home."

Temilola stared at his mentor. His heart was racing as he asked, "Who is Ejuku?"

Vipaar turned to look at Temilola sharply. "What?" His mouth is open wide and he is blinking rapidly.

"Ejuku," Temilola replied. He had sensed some vulnerability in Vipaar when he stared at the moon and decided to ask the question he had wanted to ask for ages. "You have said the name a few times when you are sleeping," Temilola tilts his head sideways and frowns. "Erm, actually, come to think of it, this is the first time you have ever mentioned home."

Thoughts about home were always a painful experience for Vipaar, but this time he looked at Temilola and smiled. He turned back to lean on the steel veranda railing, looked into the darkness, took in and let out three long breaths and began speaking.

"Ejuku had been my friend. We were born on the same day, within one hour of each other in a village in Delta state. My parents had five children, of which I am the oldest. My mother used to teach English at Delta State University and my father was a taxi driver. We were poor because the University always paid my mother late or sometimes not at all, and my father did not make a lot of money from driving the taxi. When I was small, she read me books all the time and when I became older, she brought me books from the University library. She always talked to me about William

Shakespeare and she had all his books. I tried to read Romeo and Juliet, but I could not understand the English and my head began to hurt. Ejuku and I sometimes went to meet her at work after school, and we would watch her argue with the other professor about writers like Plato, Socrates, and Wole Soyinka. One day I asked her why she was always reading books by oyinbo people, so she giae me a book called The Three Musketeers. She said the author, Alexandra Dumas, was a black person. She told me that with books, I could travel around the whole world without leaving my home. I read the book and I found myself in Paris. That was when my love of reading began—I read Treasure Island and the Jungle Book in four days. The best book ever written is *Things Fall Apart* by the great Chinua Achibe. My mother gave me the book *I know Why Caged Birds Sings* by Maya Angelou to read before she died. I cannot bring myself to read it.

One day I asked her why we were so poor? Instead of answering, she gave me a book written by Harodotous and asked me to read the line she had underlined. That was how I learnt the line, "Circumstances rule man, man does not rule Circumstances." But when I arrived in Lagos, I changed it to 'man rule Circumstance, Circumstance does not rule man'. She was sick for a short time, and she died one day before my 14th birthday. I cried everyday for a week after she died. My father began to drink more and more after she died and he married quickly afterwards. It was one of the women from the village who brought food to our house regularly after the funeral. One day she brought us food and didn't leave. She soon get belle, and the baby arrive six months after they married— that was when the wahala begin. My father crashed the taxi and so became a labourer which meant less money for the house. When he was drunk on palm wine or 33 Beer, he would beat me, call me a witch and blame me for killing my mother. My stepmother hated me because I would not allow her to hit my brothers and sisters. One day, I grabbed her hand and twisted hard when she wanted to hit my sister. She swore that I would pay dearly. I thought she meant she would tell my father who beat me severely that night when he returned drunk. I could not understand how my father went from being married to a beautiful angel like my mother to marrying an ugly troll.

Ejuku was like my actual brother; he was the only reason I smiled. We did everything and went everywhare together. People used to say we knew each oda before we ware born. The only difference between us was that I loved Manchester United, and he supported Arsenal. We saved money to buy a football shirt, so we decide to buy Manchester shirt and put the name Henry on the back. His father always beat him a lot also. His father used to say he is a witch and beat him with wire hanger. One Sunday morning, one week before our 15th birthday, a pastor from another town gave a sermon in our church about how to find witches through the behaviour of children. When we were returning from church, he told me that he could not handle his father beating him anymore and he wanted to run away that afternoon. Our dream had always been to travel to England to visit the Emirates stadium and Old Trafford. He said that we could start our journey that afternoon if we went to Lagos and got jobs as street hawkers. He was not scared of anything; he had a plan, we will huzzle for some months and then make enough money to go to Yankee or London. I was very scared, and I told him to give me a few days to think about it. He said he will not leave without me and I should tell him when I was ready to leave. The next morning, I waited for my friend where we usually met to go to school, but he was not there. I thought that maybe he is sick so I went to school by myself. All day I could not concentrate, I felt something has gone wrong; my mind was not at peace. On my way home, I noticed a lot of people looking at something near Ejuku's house and others looking at me as they walked past shaking their head. My heart began to beat quickly as I got close to the house and I pushed through the crowd. I cannot ever forget what I saw—it was the burnt body of my friend Ejuku. His father was standing, looking at him when he saw me. He said, "My son is a witch, I beat him and beat him, but the demon will not leave so I must burn him. My son is now free." I wanted to scream, but no words come out, I felt hollow. It was my fault my friend was dead. If I had agreed to leave the day before, he would still be alive today. My friend was the most kind, funny and strongest person I knew and he had been killed and burnt like a goat. He was very, very black, like charcoal. All I could recognise were his teeth. That is the day my fight with God began, and my heart hardened with hate. I vowed to kill Ejuku's father. After that day, nobody talked to me and people avoided me at school, and my father began to beat me more and more. One night, about two weeks after Ejuku was killed, that same pastor who gave the sermon at the church before Ejuku was killed came to our house at night, and I heard him talking to my father and stepmother. I was very scared when I heard my stepmoda say, "He and that boy are the same, they are demons. They know each other before they are born. Ejuku will take revenge through Daniel." That was the moment I knew she was getting her revenge. "He will bring harm to this house and the whole village. They are the same, they both killed their modars. They are twins born from different modars." The moment I saw my fada nodding in agreement, I knew I had to leave that very night, or I will end up like my friend. I put on our football shirt and my father's bowler hat. It was his pride and joy, so I took it to cause him pain. I woke up before the sun rose and I walked three hours to the bus station in town. I decided that I would go and stay with my uncle in Lagos. My mother had two brothers. One was a big director in Lagos, and the other one lived in Yankee. The one in Yankee visited some weeks before my mother died, the one in Lagos, who they call director, visited us every Christmas. My plan was to meet the director in Lagos, stay with him for some months, then go, and meet the uncle in Yankee. Chia, I was a serious mumu back then, I did not know that all men have is mouth. When the uncle from Yankee come and visit us, me and my brothers and sister ask him what he has brought for us. I can still remember clearly in my mind like it was yesterday. "Meeeen, I gat something for ya'll. I gat a toy gan for you, I gat you a football, I gat you a baseball, I gat you a basketball. But you know what meeen, the damn airline lost my laugauge. I will send it to ya'll as soon as I get back to New York." I waited for my basketball until the day I left home.

The uncle who lived in Lagos always told everybody he was Managing Director of one big factory like this in Lagos. I planned to go there because I had the business card he left for my mother, which I took before I left. My mother gave me 12 thousand naira two days before she died, she tell me not to tell my father. I took moto from my town, and it take me two days to find my uncle factory. Lagos was scary place and I didn't think I would survive a day. When I arrived at the factory, I approached the gate. I was shocked and wanted to cry when I saw that my uncle, the director, was the gateman. I expected to see him in a suit, carrying a briefcase, but he is wearing black security guard uniform. He is very surprised to see me and also embarrassed, but he hugged me and told me to enter the gate man house. I explained everything that had happened and he told me that I did not hear correctly, maybe I was dreaming. He said that as the oldest, it was my responsibility to look after my brothers and sisters. I began to cry when he said that, leaving them was the hardest thing I ever had to do. God took my mother, the devil took my friend, but I had to leave them. Since that night, I have prayed every day for their forgiveness. I told my uncle about my plan to go and live with my uncle in America, work and send them money to go to good schools. He looked at me and said, "You get passport and visa?" That question shattered my dream instantly. I slept in my uncle's apartment that night, but the next morning he told me I must leave. He had called my father and it had been confirmed that I was a witch. He said that I could not stay with him. He gave me one thousand naira and pushed me out of his house. I was very scared. Lagos was harsh and I quickly realised that to survive I had to be hard. For the first two weeks, I was living like an animal... I thought I was hungry before in my village... but Lagos taught me what real hunger meant. That is when I begin to use "man rule circumstance, circumstance does not rule man", you understand. I slept on the street at night and did different jobs during the day. I work for a forga, I work in pure water factory, I unloaded trailers at the market, anything to survive. It was a tough life. I got into many many fights; it is by GOD'S grace I still alive. But things have been better since I met Alhaja."

Temilola listened in absolute silence as Vipaar recounted his story. Multiple chills went down his spine and he shuddered when his mentor finished speaking. He wanted to say something comforting, but he knew no words that would soothe his friend. His love and respect for his mentor increased tenfold. The story had broken the barrier; their relationship would be changed forever. Vipaar's ability to share and show such vulnerability meant that he trusted and loved him. For the first time since he woke up, he felt that he belonged.

"So when did you meet Alhaja and RPG?" Temilola asked after a couple of minutes of silence.

Vipaar turned to look at him. His eyes were teary and he smiled, "Ahhhhh, my broda, that is a story for anoda day."

Something else puzzled Temilola about Vipaar's story—the delivery. "Ahem, " he fidgeted with his fingers, "erm… please don't take offence…but… how…"

"What do you want to ask me?" Vipaar began to laugh, his shoulders bobbing up and down.

"Erm… yeah." Temilola bit his bottom lip.

"You are surprised I can speak good English abi?"

"Well, yeah."

"Do you think I will survive three years in Lagos if I speak like you are speaking now. I have to give up many thins when I arrive here. Do you know dee most painful thing I give up? My books. I have not read one book in three years."

After a few minutes of silence, Vipaar looked at Temilola. His eyes were sombre. "I have something else to tell you. Please don't be angry, it is about the day we met."

"You mean when you stole my mango and punched me in the face?" Temilola laughed. "Don't worry, I have forgiven you."

"No there is something else," Vipaar smiled. He avoided Temilola's gaze and looked down with both his hands in his trouser pockets. "I am dee one..." He looked into his apprentice's eyes. "I am the one re..." He stopped when Alhaja came onto the balcony carrying her mat. She laid it on the floor and sat with her back against the wall. The boys turned to look at her, and she was looking up at both of them with what looked like a sense of satisfaction and pride.

"I remember when I was a small gel in Abeokuta, the moon use to shine like dis also," she began speaking softly. "On dee nights like deez, my fadas mother will tell me and my friends old stories about the tortoise with the broken shell, and dee crab." Temilola listened with eagerness though he didn't understand most of the stories because she spoke with a mixture of old Yoruba and limited English. She spoke continuously for approximately two hours, talking about what it was like the first time she saw a white man, and her journey back into her childhood caused her to laugh in a childlike manner, which in turn caused Temilola and Vipaar to laugh with her. She told two proverbs before getting up to go to sleep; she got the boys to repeat in and made them promise to memorise it.

"A ki i ri a re-ma ja; a ki I ri a-aja-ma ree."

She called Vipaar into her bedroom. He came out five minutes later and told Temilola, "She wants to see you." Alhaja was sitting on the edge of the bed when Temilola walked in. He could not help but suddenly notice how frail and withdrawn she had become. The brightness in her eyes seemed to have diminished a little. She patted the space next to her, "wa joko" and he sat next to her on the bed.

"Oko mi, I want you to look after Daniel," she spoke quietly, almost whispering. "It is not by accident you have met each oda."

Temilola gave a blank look. "I guess so," was the only reply he could muster.

"Oni la ri, ko seni to mola," Alhaja's tone demonstrated wisdom which only came with age. "Today is all we know, nobody knows tomorrow."

"Yes ma." He didn't understand what she meant but didn't want to disappoint her.

"Goodnight ma." He prostrated as he walked out of the room.

"Oda ro oko mi, remember what I have told you."

"Yes ma," Temilola said. He looked back at her just before he went through the curtain, and in those few seconds he felt a wave of affection flow through his veins. He stopped and fully appreciated all she had done to protect him, and he loved her for it. She smiled at him, and he smiled back. He went to sleep thankful for the beautiful day he had experienced. He decided to give up on his quest to regain his memory and imagine what his previous life was like. He was happy with his new life, and he was going to dedicate himself to helping Vipaar achieve his dreams. He was not to know that night would be the last tranquil night's sleep he would have for a long time. He was awoken the next morning by his mentor's painful scream.

CHAPTER 18

Vipaar wakes up sweaty. His heartbeat is sluggish and there are chills running through his fingertips. He knows something is amiss the moment he opens his eyes on Monday morning. For years, his morning began when Alhaja went out to perform her ablutions and returned for her morning prayers, but he didn't hear her shuffling through the sitting room this morning. When he opens his eyes, his first thought is of his apprentice who is sleeping soundly on the settee. It feels as if he had just closed his eyes for a few seconds. He can hear the silence around him as he stands up and walks toward Alhaja's bedroom. Before he pulls the curtains aside and opens the door, he feels his stomach churning.

"Alhaja," he whispers when he enters the room. Everything is still, even the air. "Alhaja, Alhaja," he repeats as he inches towards the bed. She looks like she always does when she sleeps—at peace. He notices her prayer beads in her hand. He touches her shoulder gently, and at that moment he knows she is gone. He grabs both shoulders firmly and shakes her again with a bit more force. "Alhaja... Alhaja, please..." Vipaar falls to his knees when she does not rouse from her slumber and a teardrop falls on her face. "Goooooooooooood, noooooooooo." The force of Vipaar's screams weaken his whole body. "WHHHHY GODDDD, Whhhhhy. Not again, God not again please."

He takes hold of her left hand, which is cold, and sits on the edge of the bed, sobbing while rocking back and forth.

"Alahja, pleeaaaase wake, pleaaaaase don't leave me." He struggles to breathe and his vision becomes blurry. "My Alhaja, not you too, please not you too." He strokes her cheek with the back of his hand and wipes the teardrops that have fallen on her cheek. He then feels a hand on his shoulder. He had not seen Temilola come into the room. Through the flood of tears, Vipaar could just about see the bewildered look on his apprentice's face.

"Alhaja is dead," he mumbles, the pain in his voice tangible. "My Alahja is gone." He buries his head in Temilola's stomach and screams, "What am I going to do now? Why has God taken her away from me now."

"I will look after you... I promise," Temilola's voice is ragged with fear and grief. "I promised her I would."

"She knew," Vipaar mumbles as he stares at his beloved Alhaja. "If it was not for her I would be dead, or will have killed someone by now."

Hearing the screams, Gladys bursts in the room.

"Lord Jesus Christ," are her only coherent words before she begins rolling on the floor, uttering what can only be described as gibberish. The next tenant to inquire is Mr Emeka, the policeman. He peeks behind the curtain. His eyes widen and his jaw drops open when he sees Alhaja's body.

"Haaa, Alhaja ti ku (Alhaja is dead)," he jumps back like a cat being attacked by a cobra. In lieu of the grave situation, his reaction would have been considered comical. Within a few minutes, the corridor is filled with sounds of shrieking screams, "Jesu Christy", "mo gbe", "olo du mare".

Vipaar wipes his tears and sees Temilola's eyebrows raise at Mr Emeka's reaction.

"What the…" He turns to Vipaar. "Why did he run?"

"Because he scared of dead body."

Vipaar looks at Alhaja's still body on the bed, and a single tear rolls down his left cheek. "She knew it was coming," Vipaar whispers. "That is why she did not allow me to go out yesterday, she knew."

"What are we going to do now?" Temilola asks after about a minute.

Vipaar looks at Temilola and his chest tightens, as if suddenly feeling the weight of the world on his shoulders and realises the magnitude of responsibility that has befallen him. The responsibility he had towards Alhaja while she was alive seems to pale in comparison to now.

"Hey, hey, hey madame, do you wan wake up the dead," Iya Rotimi enters the flat and her stern words bring Gladys to silence instantly.

Iya Rotimi does not show any emotion as she walks into the bedroom and sees Alhaja. She looks at the body for a few seconds and turns to Vipaar.

"Have you send somebody to tell the omo oloku?" Iya Rotimi's voice croaks.

Vipaar's neck jerks backwards. "What… I don't understand, what is omo oloku?" Vipaar asks.

Iya Rotimi looks at Vipaar in the eye and then looks away as she tightens her wrapper. "De owner of the body."

Vipaar feels like he has just been punched in the chest when he realises who she is talking about. He opens his mouth, but nothing comes out. His body goes numb. "No, not yet," his voice croaks. In life he was her son, and everyone treated him as such, but death brought the painful reality that she was not his mother, and he was not her son. He has no claims to Alhaja at all. He will have to relinquish her to the one who had caused her so much pain—her son RPG.

Vipaar is angry at the speed at which the day progresses, as if time itself was an illusion. The hours that passed between him discovering Alhaja's body and her burial seems like minutes. The reality of her death does not fully hit him until the body, wrapped in white cloth, is placed next to the grave. He has spent most of the day in a daze, and he feels utterly useless as the burial preparations are being made by the Imams from her mosque. The religious and tribal traditions relegate him to the role of a bystander. Looking after her when she was alive had given him purpose, and he wanted to hold on to the sense of achievement for a short while longer.

Approximately 50-60 people are gathered around the gravesite, most of whom he recognises from Oshodi market. Others claim to be family friends from various states from South-West Nigeria, but mostly from Ogun state. The burial ceremony is complete within 30 mins. The Imam reads from the Quran and speaks in old Yoruba about Alhaja Mariamu Funmilayo Azeez. When Vipaar hears the united Ameeeen, it confirms that another chapter in his life is closed.

Everybody begins to disperse as soon as the Imam finishes, but he and Temilola stand next to the gravesite and watch the body being put into the ground. He puts his hand around Temilola's shoulder blades as he weeps silently. Through the dispersing crowd, he sees RPG standing a few hundred yards away. Vipaar feels calm and grateful as he watches sand being poured over the body and smiles—"She is at peace." The grave diggers are talking about their mundane lives as they work. Vipaar wants to tell them how special she was, how much he had loved and cherished her, but to them it was another job. Tears begin to roll down his cheeks as soon as the gravediggers leave. Once again it was just his beloved Alhaja, his apprentice and him. As he stares at the freshly covered grave, he begins to reflect on the day's events.

Iya Rotimi had prevented him from entering the bedroom. "You cannot enter," she ordered sternly. "They are washing di bodi."

When he did enter the bedroom, his subconscious still expected to hear the words, "Pele oko mi." His beloved Alhaja lay on the bed with a white sheet covering all her body bar her face, and there were two cotton buds up her nostril. He had fought to compose himself upon the realisation that he would never hear her voice again. The room had been his sanctuary during his darkest moments. She had found words that curtailed many moments of anger which would have driven others in his situation into the darkest abyss, never to return.

He is so engrossed in his thoughts that he does not realise when Temilola leaves the grave site. This is the third time death has robbed him of someone he loves in his short 17 years on Earth, but this is the first time he feels sorrow instead of anger. He had dreaded this day for months as his mind had refused to acknowledge what his eyes saw and his heart knew. Alhaja had been gradually growing physically weaker over time and his greatest fear had been that he would lose his sense of purpose she had given him.

"Are you now going to send me away?"

Vipaar looks at his apprentice, who has returned to the gravesite. "What did you say?"

Looking straight at the grave, he said, "Are you going..." Temilola took a deep breath, "Are you going to send me away, now that Alhaja is gone?"

Vipaar is shocked that his apprentice has asked the question, and he is also a little hurt. He looks at him for a few moments, and his mouth suddenly tastes bitter and he feels awash with shame. He realises that he has been so immersed in his own grief he has failed to acknowledge the pain his apprentice is also going through. It dawns on him that he had been jealous of the boy and was angry with him on a subconscious level because he didn't think anybody could love Alhaja as much as he had done.

He smiles, "My apprentice, you know when I am first staying with her, people ware saying that I will kill and rob her. She tell them to mind their own business."

"Yeah, I know, you told me yesterday," Temilola rolls his eyes, and his tone is curt and uncompromising. "Are you going to take me to the police station? I heard you when you were talking to Alhaja that time."

"Do you know she gave a dirty slap that morning sha." Vipaar begins to emit laughter and tears simultaneously and puts his palm on his cheek. "You know they call me Vipaar because of my speed, but I did not see the back hand coming o, kapow."

Vipaar's description causes Temilola to burst into a fit of laughter also. "Like she did the Nepa man?"

"Yes o, chai."

Silence follows for a few minutes which is then broken by, "She told you to look after me abi? So how can I send you away?"

Temilola breaks into a wide smile of relief.

As they make the 30-minute journey home, they do not speak, each in their own private thoughts. Vipaar knows from experience that the void in their lives will not have an impact immediately and is keen to prolong the eventual consequences for as long as possible.

Vipaar quickens his pace when he hears music coming from their compound and becomes dizzy when he reaches the house. He looks around for about a minute with a slack mouth and wide eyes. The tenants of the house and some people from the neighbor-hood are eating and drinking, chairs and tables have been hastily arranged, and three drummers are playing the gan gan (talking drum). Seeing this makes him realise the love and respect Alhaja had commanded in the neighbourhood.

"Omo lo ku ti de o," somebody shouts from the crowd. "Dee owner of the body has arrived."

Vipaar stands rooted to the spot, he does not know how to process what he is seeing. He can only mutter to himself, "What… how… who… how…"

Then he sees Gladys dancing towards him and Temilola.

"How did this…" he stutters when she hugs him.

"The tenants all contributed for the rice and minerals," she replies as she hugs Temilola. "The market people hire the chairs and table, and somebody sent a cow for slaughter. She was all our mother."

"Thank you, aunty Gladys," Vipaar smiles. Although she does not say so, he knows that she had organised the event. "Les go and eat," he places his hand on Temilola's shoulder. The party is a useful distraction and delays what will be his biggest challenge so far, going back into the flat. After the party, Vipaar and Temilola stare at the front door for what seems like an eternity before Vipaar plucks up the courage to open it up and enter. It feels like walking into a paradox. Everything remained the same, but also everything had changed. The flat is eerily silent. He takes a deep breath, catching Alhaja's scent which is still lingering in the air.

"I can still smell her." Temilola's tone is mixed with sadness and gratefulness.

"Me too," Vipaar replies. "I can still feel her."

Vipaar goes to sleep not knowing what or how to feel. For the first time in a long time, he fears for what the future holds for him and his apprentice. He finally drifts off to sleep with a smile as he remembers Alhaja attempting a rendition of his motto, "men rule sar... sar... sarcuuumstances, abi." For the first time in a long while, he also manages to picture his own mother's face.

His anxiety means sleep only comes in steals, which soon becomes tortuous. Every time he wakes up, he has to painfully reconcile that the past 24 hours has not been a dream and the pain of remembering Alhaja's death diminishes him each time he wakes. He finally gets up around 6am and enters her bedroom to confirm the reality of her passing. As he stands looking at her bed, he hears a hard knock at the door which causes his apprentice to rouse from his sleep. Vipaar opens the door and freezes when he sees RPG standing in the doorway with a smirk and bulging eye. His heart begins thumping widely as blood rushes from his brain to his hands and legs.

"Where is my money?" RPG's tone is frightening. Vipaar steps backwards as RPG steps into the flat. He looks around. "You were supposed to pay me de rest of my money yesterday." He is spinning a gold chain inbetween his index and middle finger.

"What... I had to pay for Alhaja's funeral," Vipaar's voice shakes. "I pay for the ambulance and the grave..."

"Hey, hey, hey, stooooorrrry," RPG waves his right palm in front of Vipaar's face. "Watin concarn me with dat one." He walks towards Alhaja's bedroom but does not enter. He is now looking around the flat, still showing no element of emotion.

"But, but, Alhaja was your moth..." Vipaar stops when he notices Temilola frozen with fear on the settee.

"You are right, a mi ni omo oloku. I am de owner of de dead." RPG touches the door, "So this house belongs to me." He stays there for about a minute with his head down.

"RPG, I beg. I go get you your money," the stress in Vipaar's voice is palpable. "I just need small time."

RPG suddenly turns around and lunges toward Vipaar, who steps backwards until he hits a wall. RPG walks closer and closer until their faces are inches apart. "What does one have to with the otha?" RPG's bloodshot eyes and the menace in his voice cause Vipaar to cower. RPG has a hold over him which he just cannot overcome. He is the one element on earth he fears most. Vipaar continues to cower and looks down submissively. He is on the verge of giving up when he hears,

"Leave him alone you fucking ignoramus."

RPG turns around, which allows Vipaar to see Temilola standing by the settee holding a hammer. RPG laughs out loud when he sees his apprentice holding the hammer. "Do you want me to punch you again, psssh,' he says inconsequentially. Vipaar sees the miniscule twitch as Temilola eyebrows raise when he hears "again".

RPG turns back round to face Vipaar. "Now you…"

"I want you and that little rat out of my mother's house within the next 1…"

"YOUURRR MOTHEEEER? YOURRR MOTHEEER?" Vipaar screams and feels a rush of freedom as the words come out of his mouth. "I was more of a son to her than you ever ware. I loved and protected her. On her last night we made her laugh, we brought her peace in her last moments. All you ever brought her was pain." He does not realise tears are flowing down his cheeks until he tastes the saltwater on his lips. RPG's gaping mouth, darting eyes and heavy breathing confirms that the hold he has over him has finally been broken. Vipaar feels a rush of weightlessness, of power, especially when RPG takes two steps backwards and blinks rapidly. They both stare at each other, not knowing how to proceed in what is uncharted territory.

"She loved us," Vipaar's voice exudes calmness as he purses his lips. "She hated you."

RPG's eyes widen, and then he suddenly lunges forward and wraps his hands around Vipaar's neck, pushing him against the wall. "YOOOUU STEAAAL MY MOOOTHEEER."

Vipaar feels like an antelope caught in the jaws of a hyena. He does not feel any fear; instead, his anger increases. He looks into RPG's eyes and he sees weakness behind the contoured look of rage. Struggling to breathe he continues with what he believes will be his last breaths.

"It is because of you… she has to sell boli in a market till she died." He begins to feel light-headed, and his vision becomes blurred. His heart rate slows. "You sell her house, the house she built, you stole….ahh… you stole her life." He feels the vice like grip become tighter and tighter. "I loved her and she… she … hated you."

Things become darker, his whole body goes limp, and his eyes begin to close. At that moment he realises that death is the only circumstance that man could not rule. He struggles to open his eyes one last time; through his blurred vision, he sees the faint figure of Temilola approaching. RPG's grip loosens and he falls to the ground. He takes one long breath and begins to cough. As his blurry vision returns slowly, he sees RPG lying face down on the floor and Temilola standing over him. When Vipaar regains his faculties, the first thing he notices is the ashen look on his apprentice's face. He is staring at RPG and his hands are shaking. "I, I hit him on the back of the head with the hammer." He looks at the hammer in his right hand. "He was trying to kill you." Silence descends onto the room as they both look at each other. Temilola is looking at Vipaar for answers, and he doesn't have any. The tension is palatable. Vipaar tries to think, but his mind is blank.

"Did, did, I kil…" Temilola's voice is trembling as he struggles to articulate his words. "I dint mean…" He pauses and steps back when he hears RPG let out a slight groan from the floor.

This prompts Vipaar into action. "We have to go." The urgency and panic in his voice is unequivocal. "Go and take your clothes quickly—we have to leave immediately." He look at RPG, still lying on the floor. "Oyaaaa, QUCIKLY!" he shouts at his apprentice who is frozen to the spot. They both scramble into the room and begin stuffing what they can into their bags. The first thing Vipaar takes is Alhaja's Quran, prayer beads and headscarf. He begins spinning around, not knowing what else to take, "We have to go far, far from here. He will kill us, he will kill us."

In his state of panic, he can feel the blood rush to his legs similarly to when he had to flee area boys, the police and the KAI brigade. He realises that he has not stopped running since he left his father's house. The moment of nostalgia is interrupted by a twist of irony. "We have to run, come on, we have to go," Temilola is pulling him on the arm. They both dash out of the room towards the front door. RPG's groan is becoming louder, evidence of revival from the enforced period of unconsciousness. Vipaar and his apprentice are halfway down the dark staircase when Vipaar stops suddenly, as if stricken by grief, and looks back at the door.

"I have forgotten my hat. I have to get my hat!"

"You can't go back for it." Temilola attempts to impart the fallacy in Vipaar's thoughts. "He is probably awa…"

"Stay hare," Vipaar orders as he pushes his way past Temiola with one goal in mind. "I have to get my hat."

Vipaar runs straight into the bedroom, takes his favourite hat from its place on the wall and runs back into the living room. By this time, the panic has dissipated and he stops to look at RPG lying on the floor, groaning in pain. Vipaar's nostrils start flaring and his breathing becomes loud. His muscles tense up as he thinks about the pain and terror RPG had caused his beloved Alhaja. Fixated on RPG, he suddenly becomes aware of the tyrant's vulnerable state. He feels empowered and in control of the current circumstance. It is a seductive and exhilarating feeling, which propels his mind into an ecstatic state that enables him to be devoid of the world around him. He doesn't feel fear, nor does he feel anger or rage; he is in a state of total equilibrium. This state of serenity is shattered by his apprentice shrieking,

"VIPAAAAAAR, NOOOOOOOOO DON'T DO IT."

Vipaar looks toward the front door and sees a look of dread etched on his face. It is only then that Vipaar realises that he is bent directly over RPG, holding the hammer in his right hand, lifted above his head.

CHAPTER 19

"She is my sister sir, please don't call the police."

"Champion, you dey craze? I cannot look after dee both of you."

Aminat looks at the two boys who had made the statements, bewildered. She does not know what to do or say, so she just looks on dumbfounded. She had not imagined she would find herself in this position when she walked out of the Olapade's compound seven days ago. She had made her way to Ikotun Irepodun market, which was closed because it was a Sunday. She had deliberately chosen the area because she believed Mrs Olapade would not come here, she preferred to do her shopping at Shoprite. Aminat knows most of the markets in Lagos pretty well because she had been to most of them to buy food that was not sold in the supermarkets for her employer. Traditional foods such as gari, elubo, fresh meat etc.. She spent most of Monday morning wandering around Ikotun aimlessly. She was extremely bored because she was not used to having so much free time. The elation of being free began to recede by Monday afternoon when it dawned on her that she had not made any plans beyond escaping from the Olapade's house. This was the first time she had been by herself in her whole life and she did not have a clue what to do. She was so used to working all the time that her body began to feel strange not doing anything for so long. A different type of fear stalked her as she walked aimlessly through the streets of Lagos. She had heard stories of girls being kidnapped and used for ritual practices and other malicious things. She then began to think the unthinkable—returning to the Olapade's house in Ikeja. She imagined the beating and extra punishment she would receive and she knew she could not return when she pictured Mr Olapade's face. She felt a tap on her shoulder as she was standing by the entrance of the market, watching people going about their daily lives.

"Hay, I have seen you here before."

She turns around to see a diminutive boy standing next to her. She is startled and takes a couple of steps backwards.

"You have come hare before," the boy continues talking as Aminat studies him. He is as dark as charcoal and has ivory white teeth.

"I have been watching you since yestaday," he spoke as if he and Aminat are lifelong friends catching up. "You cannot go around this place by yoursef, dis place is very dangerous o. You no go survive here by yourself. If danfo no kill you, somebody go take you for ritual."

Aminat continues staring at the boy in silence and frowns in bewilderment.

"My name is Ibrahim," he pats his chest. "I have seen you carry heavy load so I know you are strong. Do you want to work?"

"Yes," Aminat's eyes light up in eagerness and her body feels the urge to go back to what she does best—working.

"My Oga is dee Union Leader for dis market; he will get you a job carrying load for people. Oya follow me."

She follows Ibrahim through a series of alleyways and open sewers before entering a doorway without a door. She walks into a room and freezes when she sees a small group of children of different ages sitting on the floor.

"Sid down, sid down." Aminat sits down close to the entrance as Ibrahim has instructed. A paunchy man with wide tribal marks festering on both his cheeks, forehead and chin, enters the room a few minutes later. He is holding a bottle of Gulder in one hand and an empty tumbler in the other.

"Listen to me," he looks each and every kid in the eyes. Aminat is instantly mesmerized when he looks at her and smiles. He is very ugly, but he has a comforting smile that makes her feel safe. She leans forward and listens to him start speaking as he pours the beer into the tumbler.

"They call me Uncle Emmanuel, I am the Union Leader for Ikotun Irepodun market," he pauses to drink his beer. "It is very very dangerous in Lagos for small children like yourself. Dare are people stealing children and using dem for ritual. As union leader, God has sent me to take care of the street children and I am di only one dat will keep you safe."

Uncle Emanuel continues his monologue for 15 minutes and by the time he finishes, Aminat feels like her prayers have been answered. Her heart flutters as he tells them that they are now under his protection if they work for him. He instructs Ibrahim to give them a meat pie and bottle of mineral drink each and continues to speak to them with affection. She could tell from his vernacular that he was from Ibadan; she had been around enough internationally educated and sophisticated Nigerians to recognise the vast difference. To her ears, his English comprehension is abysmal, but he is a skilled orator and he speaks with such confidence that Aminat allows herself to believe that she could save enough money from working with Uncle Emmanuel to return home to see her family.

She is so mesmerised by his act of kindness when he gives them a meat pie and the mineral each that she does not think it odd when he asks all the kids to give him all the money they had with them. "Dis is just a small induction fee to work in dee market," he says with sublime confidence. "Now, dee membarsip and security fee is ₦1000, dat you must pay in 7 days," he smiles at them, "bet don't worry, you will earn plenty plenty more than that when you work in my market." He spoke of camaraderie, "Work together, and you will make plenty plenty monie." He offered them safety, "Nobody will disturb you, you hear me noooo body." He stamps his right foot and looks at Ibrahim for validation.

"Confam," he obliges on cue, "confam, my oga at the top, confam," nodding his head like a house lizard.

Most of the boys are given jobs as agbros (bus conductors), the girls are given jobs as Alabaaru (load carriers) and the smallest children are "special". Uncle Emmanuel teaches the Alabaaru's how to 'toast' customers so that they can be paid well for carrying their goods for them.

"If you see dat dey be Muslim, hail them as Alhaji or Alhaja."

"If dey get Reedeem stickaa on dare, pray for Pastor Adeboye."

Although his instructions were of a serious nature, his facial convulsions were comical enough to make all the children laugh at once.

"If dey belong to Mountain of Fire, pray for dem to reesh dee top of dee mountain by the blood of Jesus Christ."

"If dey have PDP sticker, say Goodluck for president."

"If they have APC sticker, what do you say?"

"Buhari for president," they all shout in unison.

Aminat wipes a tear from her eye, a warm feeling radiating through her body. For the first time in a long time, she sleeps through the night. She sleeps on cardboard boxes near the railway tracks with some of the other children who were in Uncle Emanuel's parlour; there was a sense of safety in numbers. Uncle Emanuel has assured them that they will only have to sleep on the streets for a few days while he prepares their accommodation.

It becomes very clear that the realities of life are not as rosy as Uncle Emmanuel had portrayed within two days of working the market.

By the end of day one, she concludes that this was not a job for the weak or the lazy. She learns that there are different variations of 'hard work," as dusk descends on the market at the end of day two. Walking up to 10 miles a day to fetch firewood and water when she was in her village is hard work. Washing, cooking and cleaning from morning until night was hard work. The job as an Alabaaru is meant for animals like donkey and camels, not humans, and certainly not children. On day three, she begins to reconsider the wisdom of her decision to leave the Olapade's. A shiver travels down her spine when she pictures Mr Olapade's face. One of the only good things about the new hardships she is experiencing is that it forces her to forget the hardships she has left behind. Competition in the market is fierce; it is not a job that discriminates against age or gender. Men, boys, young women, old women, and children all qualified. Aminat saw a young woman who was pregnant when she started on Monday, and is carrying her newborn baby on her back on Thursday. The strongest of Alabaaru were the beasts of burden who unloaded heavy sacks of goods from the trailers, which entered the market every hour and distributed them to the market traders. Fights broke out often between the young men, but the shipping containers would usually be empty with an hour of arriving. Aminat's role was to take the goods that had been sold to customers to their cars, danfos, okadas etc. She had used a large chunk of the savings to pay the membership fee and to buy a large basin. She would walk through the market with the basin balanced on her head, scanning for people who needed her services. She carried all sorts of heavy goods on her head, meat, yam, gari, onions, cassava, cow foot, cartons of orange juice etc. Most of the customers were women, they would usually call for her services by shouting "alabaaru" or some of the traders would shout on their behalf. Some customers would walk straight to their car after loading their goods into the basin while others would do some more shopping or browsing. The worst customers were those who would spend 10 mins haggling over a minor difference in price while she stood there with a heavy load on her head in the blistering sun. A harsh job that paid very little. She would usually receive between ₦50 and ₦100 per job. She made approximately between ₦800 and ₦1200 per day, of which she had to give Ibrahim ₦500. She used whatever was remaining to buy food and drink, and to take a bath at the local public shower. The job was mainly for those with very little choice, so she just had to bear it. The job not only required physical strength, it took great skill to balance the heavy load on the head and nimble feet to navigate the very busy and muddy market. Aminat saw an alabaru fall over and spill her customer's goods on the ground—the customer beat the woman senseless.

It turns out that Ibrahim is not as gallant as Aminat had thought. She had seen him slap one of the bigger girls who was short with her membership fee, her blood curled when she watched as he and his boys beat up the driver of one of the trailers. She became very scared of him, for good reason. One day when she had only made N600, she asked him if he would accept half and she could pay him the rest tomorrow. He looked at the notes in her hand, then looked at her with bulging eyes, "Don't fuck with my money." Aminat began to shake as she gave him ₦500 and went to sleep that night petrified and exhausted. Things did not improve the next day. She does not get her first customer until midday and knows it will be a struggle to make ₦500. She loads the yam, gari, meat and fish into her basin, lifts it onto her head and follows the customer towards the main road. "My car is just over there," the woman said as she took her keys out of her handbag. Aminat sees a white Lexus Jeep with tinted windows parked next to the customer's car and becomes dizzy and weak in the legs and knees—it looks like the same car that Mrs Olopade drives.

Her eyes are transfixed and she is in a trance until she hears someone screaming, "What is the matter with you!" Aminat is extracted from her trance when she feels a slap on her back and, "You have drop my food!" She looks on the ground, her basin and food she had been carrying lay on the ground covered in mud.

"I sorry ma please please," Aminat began to plead as she dropped on her hands and knees and started putting the food back into the basin. She was unable to concentrate because she kept looking at the Lexus. Her chest tightened when the driver side door opened. In a split second, she relived the nightmare that had been her experience at the Olapade family. Relief flowed through her veins when a bald man in a suit stepped out of the car.

"Are you listening to me, you stupid girl?" Aminat was so focused on the jeep, she hadn't heard the woman berating her.

"I am sorry ma," Aminat said as she doubled the efforts to put everything back into the basin as quickly as possible.

"Don't think I am going to pay you for this o."

Aminat kept a watchful eye on the white Lexus jeep as she puts the goods into the boot, just to be sure it was not Mrs Olapade's car. The customer drove off and Aminat walked back to the market slowly, her head drooping and her body aching when Ibrahim stopped her. "You cannot be dropping load anyhow," he said, his voice laced with fury.

"I am sorry," Aminat whimpered, "it will not happen again."

"You cannot work as Alabaaru anymore," he clicks his fingers and motions for one of his boys to take away Aminat's basin.

"Please, please, sar," Aminat pleads, "it will not happin again."

Ibrahim looked at her like a nuisance.

"Lisseeen, I must set example." Ibrahim stared at Aminat and exhaled. "You can go and be washing cars over dare," he points to the busy junction near the entrance to the market. "You must still pay your daily rent, if you give me an wahala I will deal with you seriously."

Aminat knelt. "Thank you sar."

Within 15 minutes, she had a plastic bottle filled with soapy water and sponge. She hoped that her new job would be temporary because the location she is working is the most dangerous stretch of the road.

Cars travelled at great speed and the build up of traffic was very rare. When traffic did build up, she had the street guile to challenge her fellow windscreen washers who were faster, stronger and more aggressive. She washed the screens of five cars, two people gave her money, and the other three cars drove off.

The build up of cars only occurred a handful of times over the course of the day and Aminat had only made ₦40 by 5pm. Despair hung like a noose around her neck that tightened as the day wore on. She had tried her best but there were too many obstacles for her to overcome. She knows that there is little chance Ibrahim would accept the ₦70 she has, so she decides to use the money to eat and then deal with the consequences. She has given up, but she just needs 50 naira more to be able to afford rice and beans and a bottle of mineral. At about 6pm, the volume of cars increases; she manages to wash a few more windscreens and make an extra ₦50. She now has enough to buy rice and beans and a pure water sachet. She feels that fortune is smiling upon her. The next car washes may give her ₦50, and then she would be able to buy a bottle of mineral. She told herself she would wash just one more car and she would go and buy what could be her last evening meal. She felt her prayers had been answered when the traffic built up and she saw a blue BMW with a white woman in the passenger seat. She raced towards the car and reached it before her competitors. She approached the passenger side and returned the smile of the white woman. She was so engrossed in her thoughts of how much the white woman would give that she did not notice the Nigerian man waving his index finger at her. She heard the deafening sound of the car's horn just as she lifted the windshield wiper. The ferocity of the noise caused her to pull the wiper hard and she heard a snap. At that moment in time, her whole world went dark and gloom descended over her. She had pre-empted fate and now she would suffer the consequences. The man jumped out of the car and began shouting, "You stupid girl, you have broken my car." Aminat wanted to run away but stood frozen to the spot in fear. She does not hear anything he was saying, she just stared at him. Other cars begin pressing their horns and manoeuvring their cars around the stationary BMW.

"You miscreant," he screamed at Aminat as he pointed his index finger in her face. "Why do you think I want you street urchin to wash my car? I told you not to touch my car and you have broken my wiper."

He grabs her by the arm as people stopped to look from a distance and began to gather around to investigate the commotion.

"I am taking you to the police."

The congregation's unsolicited contribution turns the situation into a melee. Some were asking the man to show mercy while others were berating Aminat.

"Ejo sa ema pe olopa (please sir don't call the police)";

"Why did she touch his car? Did he send her?"

"What is you your name?"

"Where is you mother?"

"I am calling the police, I have just bought this car and she has torn off my wiper," the man's anger did not abate.

Aminat just looked on aimlessly as people fired questions at her. In that moment she accepts she is truly alone in the world.

"Who does she belong to?" the BMW driver demands, still holding on to Aminat's arm as he gesticulates. "Somebody better claim her and pay for the damage to my car."

Aminat was now fully resolved to her fate when she heard a distinctive voice say,

"She is my sister, sir, please don't call the police."

She looked at who made the statement and saw two boys in the crowd. One is tall and looks angry and the other one who was speaking to the man with the BMW is a little shorter. The taller one seems to be berating the shorter one but he ignores him. Aminat distinctly heard;

"Champion, you dey craze. I cannot look after the both of you."

CHAPTER 20

Aminat is dumbfounded. She doesn't know how to react when the boy tells the man that she is his sister. Her first thoughts are that he wants to use her like the others, but there is something special about this boy's voice—he sounds like he genuinely cares. `

Then she hears, "Champion, you dey craze we no get have time for this." The gruff tone belongs to a tall, muscular boy wearing a green vest and a black rounded hat.

"How much is the wiper sir," the smaller boy says to the driver, who loosens his grip on Aminat's arm. "I will pay for it."

"My friend, this a BMW," the driver sneers. "Se o mo eye ti moto yi cost me sha. To change this one alone will cost ₦25,000." His face curves as he continues shouting. "I tell her not to tosh my car, who asked her."

"Sorry saar," the smaller boy's "saar" seems forced and unnatural, Aminat thinks to herself. He looks like many other street kids, but something about the way he speaks makes him standout. There is a sense of eloquence and innocence about him. She suspects he has just realised the gravity of the situation when he says, "I will ask my brother if he can give me some money."

Aminat sees the taller boy's face go slack in shock when the smaller one turns to him and asks for money. Despite the noise from the chorus of horns, the crowd and the man shouting, "my friend stop wasting my time," she is still able to hear snippets of the boy's heated conversation.

"How much did you take from…"

"We cannot look after her."

"We cannot just leave her, he will take her to the police."

She watches as the boys gesticulate. It is clear that the older one is in charge, but the smaller one holds some sway over him. The taller boy motions for the smaller boy to move aside and approaches the man who is still rambling.

"My oga, I beg no vex, na serious machine you get here o. I no see this one for Lagos yet o." Aminat looks at the man's face and is glad he looks as confused as she feels. The boy smiles as he admires the car and bites his index finger. "Whooooo, my oga at dee top, this kind moto no fit for mainland. You should only drive am on VI or Banana Island."

"Yes, yes, I am on my way to home to Ikoyi," the man's tone softens. "I told this…"

"Ikooooyi, well done sar," the boy's voice booms as he raises both his hands, fists clenched, and shakes them vigorously in the air. "It is well sar, may God continue to bless you and you wife sar." He turns to the white woman in the passenger seat who is smiling with bemusement and waves at her. "Jeeeessuuuus is your muscle sar. By the grace of God, me too will one day drive a machiiine like dis and live on Banana Island sir. I pray that God will bless me and my sister like he has blessed you sar. In the name of Jeeesssuuusss, by the blood of Jeesssuuss."

Aminat is so mesmerised by the taller boy's performance, she does not realise that the man has released her from his grasp.

"Next time, don't touch people's car, you hear me," he snarls at Aminat before stomping back to his car. She nods her head and watches the boy continue to heap praise on him.

"God will reward your kindness my chairman." The older boy's demeanour changes as soon as the man gets in the car and drives off. He shoots a look of contempt in Aminat's direction, who is immensely relieved that it is directed at the smaller boy.

"You ozwo," he taps the side of his forehead with his index finger. "You have not larn anything since abi. Whare you go get money to give de man anyhow?"

"I just wanted to help her, I will look after her," the boy replies, seemingly unphased by the older boy's reprimand. He turns to Aminat. "What is your name?"

"She is not our responsibility," the older one shouts at him. "Are you deaf, what have I been telling you? I don't even know where we are going to sleep tonight."

"But we can't just leave her here."

"I cannot look after you both."

Aminat looks on silently as the two boys argue over her. She feels a sense of worth. Even though the older boy does not want to take responsibility for her, it is not because she is not worth anything, but because he could not guarantee her safety.

"Oya, let's go." Her heart starts racing and she cannot understand why. Although she had felt alone since she left her family and village, she feels abandoned for the first time as he walks away. She sees the small boy take a deep breath and let out a heavy sigh. He smiles at her and his face droops as he is forced to acknowledge the limits of his chivalry and follow the taller boy.

As she watches them disappear into the crowd, she hears "Iwo! You! Did I not tell you not to cause trouble around here." It is Ibrahim and he is with two of his boys! Before Aminat can respond or react, he begins pulling on her ear. "You want to mess up my business abi."

"Leave that girl alone." The order was firm and uncompromising. "If you don't want me to fuck you up, leave that girl alone before I demolish you."

It takes a few seconds for Ibrahim to process what he hears as he stares Vipaar down and snickers, "My friend, you dey ginger? Abi o fe ku? Do you know who I am; you want to die?" His eyes flare in anger.

"I wear death in my pocket," Vipaar responds coolly. His demeanour does not waver, even when three more boys join Ibrahim, each exhibiting exuberant levels of aggression. Vipaar looks at all of them and chuckles. "Are you all ready to die hare today?"

Ibrahim and his boys, who had resembled a pack of baying hyenas a few seconds previously, are stunned into silence and look at each other. Vipaar looks directly at Ibrahim with chilling confidence, and says,

"For me, death is my freedom. I invite it everyday, and every day it rejects me. When your boys kill me, it will be afta I have extinguished your life, you unstan." He puffs out his chest and takes two steps forward. "Now I said, leave that girl alone." He pauses before continuing, "Are you afraid to die? Because I am not."

Aminat truly believes in that moment, the boy means what he said; the look in his eyes is of someone who has accepted his fate.

Ibrahim and his boys must also believe him because they are all deflated and now resemble a family of meerkats.

"Come on, let's go," the tall boy calls to her when Ibrahim lets her go. Aminat walks towards Temilola, who looks equally stunned at Vipaar's comments.

"If I see you and that girl around here again, I go give you your freedom," Ibrahim shouts as the three of them walk away. Aminat notices that Vipaar walks backwards before turning around and she and the smaller boy follow.

They walk in silence for about ten minutes before the smaller boy speaks.

"So, what is your name?" His accent takes her by surprise, and she looks at him sideways. He sounds different from the people she usually met on the streets. He sounds like he had been taught how to speak English.

"Aminat," she replies.

"My name is Temilooolaaaa."

Aminat wants to laugh. The boy cannot even pronounce his own name correctly. She cannot understand why the boy speaks like he does, but looks like a street boy.

"Don't worry, we will look after you." He speaks softly then puts his left arm on Aminat's shoulder. This causes her body to become stiff and she stands frozen to the spot.

"Sorry I didn't … I did not…" Panic fills his voice. He was attempting to comfort her, but had ended up making her feel very uncomfortable. Vipaar had not uttered a single word until he heard Temilola apologising.

"What is the matter?" he asks, his irritation obvious. "What did you do to her?"

"Notting, all I did was put my hand on her shoulder."

Vipaar looks at Aminat, "Don't mind him jare, he is ozwo."

"What are we going to do?" Temilola asks, looking at Vipaar with his eyebrows pinched together.

Vipaar looks at Temilola and bites his bottom lip for a second before responding, "If you ask me that question one more time, I go give you one nice kung-fu kick in your face. Did you not say that you will look afta her? Now you asking what are we going to do, chai."

He rolls his eyes and curls his lips then looks at Aminat. "Aminat, you wan chop?"

Aminat notices that his tone is softer than when he spoke to the boy, but she is still scared of irking him by speaking so she nods. Within 15 minutes, she is enjoying her first hot meal in four days: plantain and beans. As she gorges herself, she scrutinises her rescuers. They are as compatible as Gari and Baked-beans. The taller boy looks like a product of the streets of Lagos—brash and aggressive, he is a survivor. He is very handsome but seems to have a permanent scowl. He is light-skinned, thin but muscular. The smaller boy is an enigma—he is darker than the taller boy, and it is evident from the way he speaks that he is from a different class. His speech and mannerisms remind her of the children of families whom she had served over the past two years that had been sent to boarding school in America or England, who then came to Nigeria for the summer holidays. It is apparent from the way he looks at the taller one with reverence that he is his guardian. She wants to ask a thousand questions, but she concentrates on her food. She steals glances at both of them as she eats, and her confusion only grows. Even in her tender years she has developed an acute ability to read people's inner thoughts and their actions. She distrusts people, but she feels safe with these two strange boys though she does not understand why. She studies them both intensely for a few minutes and concludes she knows one of the things that binds these opposite souls together. It is what she sees in herself every time she looks in the mirror—it is sorrow and pain. Maybe this is why she has imprinted herself onto them. She decides she will call the tall one Garri and the small one Bakedbeans.

"If you dare ask me a question…" the silence is broken by Garri's angry exasperation, which startles Aminat. She looks at Bakedbeans, whose mouth is frozen open. What amazes her most is that Garri is not even looking at Bakedbeans, he intuitively knew the boy was going to ask a question, a question for which he did not have an answer.

"Do you know this area well?" Temilola asks Aminat.

"I am washing windscreen of motor for some time," she replies quietly. "I work for Uncle Emmanuel for some time."

"Where are you from?"

"Why are you asking her questions? You are always talking and talking," Vipaar shouts at Temilola. "If you know where she is from, will you take her home?"

"It is not my fault we are where we are," Temilola shouts back. "I don't need you to look after me, I will look after myself."

They both stand up, toe to toe. Aminat is surprised at the level of Bakedbeans aggression. She watches as the two begin to shout at each other.

"My friend, I saved your life…"

"And I saved your life."

"Who asked you?"

"Without me, you will not have survive one day in this place."

"Yeah, yeah… whatever."

"I am from Bayan Gayi, it is a village in Niger." They both stop shouting, look at Aminat, and the anger disperses from their faces as they sit down.

"I have to go to Alaba International Market to go and buy phone chargers," Garri says calmly.

"What!!!!" Bakedbeans shrieks. "Are you crazy, you said RPG will be looking for you, it is too risky!"

"They will be looking for us," Garri retorts. "We can't even go back to the mainland, he will kil…" he catches Aminat looking at them with intensity.

"I think there is a pure water factory near here where we can buy water for cheap and…"

"No way, no way." Bakedbeans shakes his head with force. "We can't keep on chasing after cars, it's too much effort for little reward." Then he went into a whisper and leaned towards Garri. "How much did we take from RPG?"

"Why are you whispering," Garri says loud enough for Aminat to hear. "Do you think she will think we are thieves? I only took a few thousand."

"Maybe we can invest it in something that will make us more money than bloody pure water and phone charger. A product that will give us a higher return."

"Soooo, you want to be like Alhaji Dangote abi."

"Okkkkaaay," Bakedbeans rolls his eyes, "I don't know who that is but anyway we can't keep running away from the KAI."

"What about recharge card?" Garri drinks from a water sachet.

"What… are you even listening to me? We have to think outside the box."

"Listen to me, I am a huzler," Garri slams his hand on the table. "All I know how to do is huzzle, and what, what… is this box you are talking about?"

"No, no no, I mean," Bakedbeans pinches between his eyes. "I am trying to say there is more than one way to skin a cat."

"You want us to sell cats?"

Aminat becomes more confused the longer the boys speak to each other—they might as well be speaking two different languages. It is almost comical as they go back and forth, each one becoming more stressed. She becomes even more intrigued as to how these totally opposite individuals came together.

"Listen my friend," Garri's tone is firm. "I don't understand what you are talking about, cats and boxes, but I will give you till tomorrow morning to make sharp sense. Or else we are going to Ajegunle to buy recharge card, you unstan."

"Aminat, where do you sleep?" She gives him a blank look; she had assumed he was familiar with the area.

"I sleep on de railway near Lagos—Abeokuta expressway."

"We can't go dare," Garri replies after a few seconds of pondering, "those yeye boys will be around there. We will go and stay under the bridge near oju elegba."

"Hold on, hold on, what do you mean?" Bakedbeans back arches and his fingers begin to shake. "You mean we are going to have to sleep under the bridge… outside?"

"Noooo, whare did you want to sleep? We can go to the Oriental or the Charaton on dee Island."

Bakedbeans scowls at Garri. His reaction confirms Aminat's initial suspicions, it is obvious that he has never slept on the streets before and he is petrified. She expects Garri to offer him some words of comfort, but instead he berates him.

"Look at you, shaking like a goat that has just seen knife."

"Wooow veeeery clever, you belong to the pantheon of great orators."

"Are you laughing at me?"

Aminat looks on as they both continue to argue. She knows that this is the beginning of a fascinating journey.

CHAPTER 21

"For me, death is my freedom. I invite it everyday and every day it rejects me."

Temilola cannot relinquish these words from his mind as he, Vipaar and his new charge Aminat, spend hours walking in the baking heat in almost total silence. Although still wary of being on the streets in the dark, he is thankful when dusk descends around them. He is lost in his own world. Exhaustion restricts his ability to think beyond the moment and his mentor's words. He cannot understand why, in their current predicament, those words bother him so much; they are insignificant in the grand scheme of things.

"We are hare." Vipaar stops without Temilola realising, and he takes a couple of seconds to exit his trance.

"What!?"

"Open your ears here well, well," Vipaar replies, pulling his left ear for emphasis. "Welcome to Cheraton."

Temilola looks at where Vipaar is facing and realises that they are standing across the road from underneath a bridge. He is aware that Aminat is watching and attempts to feign familiarity with what he sees and nods his head. It is an absolute dump filled with danfos, okadas and people bedding down for the night.

"Wait hare and make sure nobody messes with the girl. You

betta look like you can fight o," Vipaar orders. "I am going to find somewhere for us to sleep."

With these parting words, he walks into the darkness. He and Aminat wait across the bridge as instructed as he disappears into the darkness. Temilola tries his best to look menacing. He puffs out his chest, lowers his eyebrows, crosses his arms and grinds his teeth. He quickly realises his attempt is counterproductive, even comical, when he sees Aminat looking at him with a deep frown. He feels a little embarrassed, he had merely been attempting to follow Vipaar's instructions to the letter. He starts talking to Aminat,

"Er, so how are you?"

"I am fine." Her answer is finite.

"Ok, good, good."

"Is he your broda?" Aminat asks after a couple minutes of silence.

"Who, Vipaar? No, well yeah, erm… he's my…er, he's my…" It puzzles Temilola why he is perplexed by such a simple question.

He is lost in his thoughts for a few seconds and then senses somebody is standing behind him. He instinctively puts his hand across Aminat and turns around. He lets out a sigh of relief when it turns out to be Vipaar.

"What are you looking at over there? Vipaar scoffs at him.

"I was waiting for you."

"My friend, you have to be aware of your sarandings. If I wanted to, I will have dealt with you."

"Oookkaaay," Temilola shrugs his shoulders, "what would you have expected me to do if it was one of those area boys. They could do anything they want…"

"Listen, what did I tell you about speaking grammar?" Vipaar shuts his eyes and rubs the top of his head. "Oya let us go."

Temilola feels the anger elevate inside him and wants to shout at Vipaar, "Stop talking to me like that." His deepest desire is to punch Vipaar in the face, but he is fully aware that he would be floored immediately in turn. He simply motions for Aminat to follow him, and they scurry after Vipaar. He hadn't known his hands were balled up in anger until he felt Aminat attempting to clasp her fingers into his. His rage dissipates quickly as he feels the harshness of her palms, which tell a thousand stories. He cannot imagine the hardships Aminat must have endured to cause her hands to coarsen so.

"Don't worry, Vipaar will look after us." Those are the only words of comfort he can muster. "And I will look after *you*."

Taking her hand firmly, they follow the torchlight from Vipaar's mobile as he leads them to their unknown destination. When they cross the boundaries of the bridge, Temilola worries it will be evident he does not belong here. But none of the indigenes acknowledge them in any way, and he realises he has become one of the many unidentifiable beings of Lagos—an unknown, he is not special. He feels conflicted. He is pleased that he has assimilated but also feels a little affronted they consider him one of them.

"This is whare we are sleeping." Vipaar is standing next to a pillar, with dismantled cardboard boxes on the ground at its base.

"Are you serious?" Temilola so desperately wants to say, but he does not want to give Vipaar the satisfaction of berating him again. More importantly, he wants to look sharp in front of Aminat.

"Ok," he replies as he sits down on the cardboard box that

would be his abode for the night. Aminat sits next to him, and Vipaar sits down in front of them. They both watch Vipaar open up the plastic bag and bring out the bowl of beans he had bought for their supper. Exhaustion has made Temilola forget about his hunger but the aroma from the beans awakens his stomach. Vipaar tears the loaf of bread into three pieces. Temilola notices that he gives the largest part to Aminat and keeps the smallest portion for himself.

"Thank you," Aminat says when she receives her portion.

Within a few minutes, the bowl of beans is empty. Before eating, Vipaar lit two of the candles he had bought earlier in the day, and they are now the only source of light around them as they eat in silence, each lost in their own thoughts. The satiation of hunger seems to awaken all of Temilola's senses simultaneously. He rests his back against the concrete pillar to survey his surroundings. Since his adventure began, he noticed his nocturnal abilities had increased expeditiously and, despite the darkness punctuated only by patches of light from the naked flames of paraffin lamps or occasional light bulb, he is able to see most of the activities. He thought he had encountered all the smells Lagos had to offer, but the smells within the bridge are unique: a combination of exhaust fumes and diesel fuel from the danfo buses parked a few meters from where they sat, the pungent smell of open sewers countered by a whiff of Indian hemp, and the undeniable aroma of freshly cooked moi moi (steamed beans). As he watches the residents of this desperate community, he can only imagine whose company he now kept. "These are not the type of people I would like to meet on a dark stormy night," he muses.

"Are we safe here?" Temilola asks quietly, unsure if he will get an answer, let alone one that satisfied. "I mean…" he pauses as if looking for the right words, "is it safe?"

"I have paid rent, we will be ok." Vipaar's tone is gruff.

"Well, that's not what I meant, I meant will *he* find…"

"I said we will be ok," Vipaar snaps. "I beg don't disturb my sleep with your nonsense questions."

Instead of pursuing his line of enquiry, Temilola chooses to continue with his surveillance of their dwelling. He focuses his attention on two men shouting and angrily gesticulating at each other. The afrobeat music blaring from multiple portable radios, albeit with weak speakers, makes it difficult for him to fully understand the cause of the argument.

"You go pay me my money," a man wearing a blue polo shirt is yelling at another one wearing a Arsenal shirt. "I look like gentle man, dat is why you think you can cheet me abi?"

"This one na mumu, now," the Arsenal shirtman retorts, pointing his index finger inches from the blue polo shirt man's face. "You dey craze, gerout of here, you dey talk rubbish." The two men shove each other and then begin trading blows while still arguing. The unmistakable roar of a generator engine starting up soon drowns out the noise from their fighting. A previously dark portion of the bridge is suddenly lit up by three light bulbs. Within 30 seconds, people surround the man operating the generator. Above him is a sign which reads:

"Charge your phone here; Nokai ₦50, Blackberry ₦70, LH & Huwie ₦100 Samsung ₦100; "Buy you phone card here."

In the midst of the chaos, Temilola cannot help but be impressed by the man's enterprise.

"Why are you not sleeping?" Vipaar says as he shuffles onto the makeshift bed. He and Aminat had been laying on the ground, but she had begun to doze and snore with intensity while Vipaar continuously tossed and turned, attempting to find the best sleeping position. "Don't tell me nonsense tomorrow about being tired o, you hear me." With an elongated groan he continues, "Chai, chai, chai, it has been so long since I have slept on di groun like dis."

An urge to laugh rises up in Temilola. He puts his fingers on his mouth in an attempt to suppress a giggle. In the midst of seemingly endless misery, this is a welcome relief. He lays down, putting his head on the bag that contains all his worldly possessions. The ground is hard and uneven, making him long for the couch he had been sleeping on for the previous few weeks.

"Vipaar," Temilola whispers in a hushed tone.

"Ohhhhhh, what is it, why are you disturbing my head, watin you want?"

"I can't sleep."

"An so what? I beg my friend put your head down and close your eyes."

Temilola inhales. "What did RPG mean when he said you stole his mother, and what did you mean when you said he stole her house? You still have not told me how you met Alhaja and R…"

"Chiiiiineke, Subuhanalah, Jesus Christ, I beg come and save me from this boy o." Vipaar sits and stares at Temilola, "Leave me alone and let me sleep."

"Ok," Temilola's voice is sombre, "I am sorry."

Temilola's question triggers an avalanche of memories and emotions in Vipaar. He closes his eyes tightly but he cannot sleep.

Maybe it is the sadness in his apprentice's voice, his own weariness, or perhaps the remembrance of the past and the brief and complete happiness they had both shared, but Vipaar's voice suddenly comes through the dark, soft and kind, completely contradicting the sharp admonishment Temilola had just been given.

"Well, you know I was telling you yesterday how I was always fighting. That is how I met Alhaja. I have been…"

Vipaar begins to sit up but pauses when he sees Temilola sitting with his legs crossed, with a big smile on his face, looking at him intently. Vipaar kisses his teeth in humour, shakes head slowly and then shuffles over to join Temilola, resting his back on the pillar. It warms his heart that his apprentice knew he was going to tell the story even before he did. He stares intently at the flames of the candlestick for a few seconds and enters a sort of trance. In the midst of the turmoil, he feels totally at peace. He takes one long breath, and then continues with his story.

"Anyway, as I was saying, I had been living on dee street for about tree to four months when I meet her. Dat time, things ware hard. I cannot find regular work, and I have not eaten for propa food for two days. The day I meet her, I am playing pool near army barak in Teju osho. People in the area don't know me then so I begin playing very rubbish, dat is how one mumu like this challenge me to a game. He say he wan bet me 2k for a game. I tell him I don't play for small money. He now increase dee bet to 5k, and I accept. Come and see me, I do not have one kobo in my pocket, and I am betting 5k. Chai, I was mad o bros." Vipaar lets out a wry laugh as he nudges Temilola playfully with his elbow.

"Anyway, we play pool. This mumu does not realise I am

studying him. I make a mistake on purpose, I miss shots… that is how I lose the game. As I put my hand in my pocket, I tell I want to play again but for bigger money. So we make bet for 15k… 15k that I do not have. At dis point, I do not care if I live or die. We play game, I am winning, and as I am about to take the last shot to win the game, one of his boys shake the table and make me miss. He now tell me I lost and I must pay him 20k. I refuse. Dat is how we begin arguing, him and his boys surrounding me. Someone break bottle… pow… and me I pick up snooker ball… I am ready to fight all of them. I believe I can fuck them all up, dat is how crazy I am. I am swinging, and they manage to force me into a corner. I am facing certain death, but I do not care. I believe there is nothing else God can take from me. Then all of the sudden all of them stop and turn around. I see dis old woman standing on the road and she is calling the leader to come and meet her. She say something to him, and den he call his boys, and they all leave. Shebi I should be grateful abi… noooo… I want to go and chase them and collect my 20k. She give me a look which make me stop like a statue and she ask me to come to her. When I am facing six boys with broken bottles, I was facing certain death and I did not care, but greater fear grip me when this small old woman begin speaking to me. She ask me my name, and I tell her Daniel. She look into my eyes and put her hand on my face. I feel she can see in my soul. She said, "It is not your fault." When I hear that, I begin crying like a little boy. She used her buba to wipe my tears. I don't know what she saw or how she saw it. Sometime later, I ask her what she see in me, she say that she can see that I am searching for death, but it is not my time."

Temilola notices that tears have started to stream down Vipaar's face, but he is smiling so he pretends not to notice.

"She ask me if I understand Yoruba, I tell her I understand small. She ask me to help her carry her load home. Dat is the moment she become my guardian. She see something in me, something I cannot see or understand. She did not ask whare I am from or what I have done. All the tenants in the house were very scared. Iya Rotimi is scared I will kill and rob her. Our Alhaja just tell them all to mind their own business. I believe if she has not allow me to stay with her, I will be dead now or will have kill someone." Vipaar is silent as he often is after he talks about Alhaja.

"Why did the boys stop when they saw her?" Temilola asks without looking at his mentor.

"I do not know my broda, I do not know." Vipaar plays with his finger nails and stares into the darkness. "She just has this power over people."

"But what about RPG? Where does he fit into this whole story?" Temilola asks after a few seconds of silence. "You told me he is Alhaja's son, but you have not told me how you two are connected."

"Mppph, R.P.G... Rocket Propelled Grenade," Vipaar says, shaking his head, "some people say he himself trained the devil. Even when you see him for first time, you know say he was a dangerous guy, but I want to be like him. Anywhare he go, he get instant respect. He is the one who teach me to huzzle on the streets and give me my name. Some days after I arrive at Alhaja's house, I am returning home from school when two boys block my way and ask me where I was going, saying that I cannot enter Alhaja's building. My reply is some quick blows, and they are soon on the floor. When I enter the parlour I see RPG sitting there.

'Daniel?'

'Yes sir, good evening sar.'

'I am Alhaja son Jamiu.' His grammar na wa o bros. 'I see what you do to my boys, I am watching you from my window. You are shap sha, your hand strike like a snake.' I didn't know what to say, I just stood there looking at this man, with his big muscles and shiny baldhead. Alhaja come out of the room after finishing praying, and we both prostrated. He ask her if she is well, has she eaten, how she was sleeping and everything. Alhaja tells me to take Jamiu as my older brother, and she tells him to look after me, to take me as his younger broda. He is a tailor, so Alhaja tell him to teach me trade. But he is already making money on the street; he has connection with the transportation union. Anyway, over some weeks sha, he trained me how to be smart and survive on the streets. How to chase cars, which danfo's to target, what the best time to huzzle. When I first meet him, he used to work as enforcer for Zone 1 chairman drivers in Oshodi. Widin some months, he was deputy lieutenant to the chairman of zone six. We begin to make some good money and have plenty of girlfriends. One day he tell me that he was going to get to the top by any means necessary and he want me to be by his side. He say he want to be in charge of the whole of Oshodi and all the six zones, that is how he will start making some serious money. Widin tree months, one of lieutenant to the chairman of zone 1 is dead, and RPG is promoted to lieutenant to the chairman. He always collect plenty of money from the danfo, taxi drivers and market traders, but when we are together he complain that he is not making money and giving most of it to the chairman. He is always talking to me about getting to the top. Some months later, the chairman of zone one also died. The chairman of the zone has four lieutenants, and that was when the war began. I want to go an join to fight for my brother, but Alhaja forbid me from going out. One day, he come and told me that he need serious money, like 15 million to become chairman of zone one. He has to pay some people some bribes to a councillor and the police inspector to be the chairman of zone 1. He asks me to bring him deed of Alhaja's house. He say he want to use it to borrow money and he will give it back when he become chairman and start making serious money. I want to please him but I cannot betray my beloved Alhaja, so I refuse. He become very angry with me, shouting and berating me. He said I was useless, and I am no longer his broda and he will never forgive me. Somehow somehow sha, he steal the deed to the house and sold his own motherhouse. He become zone 1 chairman, and Alhaja went from landlady to tenant in the house that she built. It is a difficult time for us o, but she is strong which also make me strong. She make me promise not to take any money from RPG, she say it is blood money. Within five months of becoming chairman of zone 1, RPG is soon the chairman of the whole of Oshodi and the six zone. Till today nobody know how he did it. Some people said he used juju, others said he killed all the other chairman's—they all disappear. He buy Alhaja a big house near Shomolu, but she refuse to move. She say she will die in the house she build herself and her son will look after her… she was talking about me."

"My goodness," Temilola says after Vipaar stops speaking. "Your life would make an interesting book."

"The story of people like me are not supposed to be heard my broda, we are the unseen and unheard. Nobody fight for us so we must fight for ourselves." Vipaar sighs wistfully. "Can I go an sleep now?"

"Er, yeah, thank you." Temilola replies, and he puts his head down. Vipaar's story touches him deeply. He sees that Vipaar has lost his only purpose for living, and now he needs a new purpose. Temilola decides it is time to step up. He knows he can not replace Alhaja for Vipaar, but perhaps he could try to give him meaning. After fifteen minutes, he still cannot sleep. Something is bothering him, and he just cannot put it out of his mind. Of all the events and circumstances which had led him to be sleeping in what he had initially considered the gates of hell, he could not understand why he kept on obsessing about the statement Vipaar made, "For me, death is my freedom." As petrified as he had initially been when Vipaar led him and Aminat to their abode for the night, he decides to stop worrying. Fate had led him to his current location and fate would determine whether he would see another sunrise. He used to go to sleep with the hope and prayer that his memory would return to him, but that issue pales in comparison to his current situation. Now he just prays that he and his companions will make it through the night. Without his memory, he cannot determine whether the extraordinary experiences and challenges he keeps facing are the norm or an aberration. He is still in shock and denial about Alhaja's passing. His mind seems to refuse to accept she has died.

He recalls being woken that morning by loud banging on the doors. The sleep he so desired disappeared from his eyes as soon he realised the imposing figure standing in the doorway was RPG. This sent him into a state of shock. Vipaar seemed to shrink when RPG walked through the door. His traumatic state initially deafened him to the conversation, and he could only look on impotently as his guardian retreated. He looked like prey being cornered by a predator. He watched in awe as the prey turned hunter and RPG began to inch backwards by the force of Vipaar's words, who looked empowered, fearless. The tally of varying emotions continued as awe turned to fear and anger when he realised RPG is literally squeezing the life out of Vipaar. The next few minutes were a blur. He vaguely remembered RPG looking at him smugly and laughing. He cannot recall picking up the hammer or hitting RPG over the head with it. He shudders as he recalls the panic he felt when RPG lay motionless on the floor, those few moments in which he thought he had taken another person's life were the most terrifying. The last thing he remembers clearly from that morning is pleading with Vipaar not to go back into the flat. Those few moments standing by the stairwell felt like an eternity. Temilola was sure that RPG had woken up and caught Vipaar. He decided to go back into the flat because of the promise he had made to Alhaja. Vipaar's fate was going to be his own. The look of hate in Vipaar's eyes as he stood over RPG, holding the hammer over his head is something Temilola knows he will never forget. At that moment, his mentor was devoid of all humanity. The shocked look on his face when Temilola shouted at him showed that he had not been fully conscious of his actions. Relief flowed through Temilola's veins when Vipaar dropped the hammer, and they both ran out of the flat. His last memory of the place which had become his sanctuary, were the chilling words of RPG shouting from the balcony:

"No matter where you go, I go find you, Danieeeellllll. Do you hear me? I go find yoooouuuu."

The horn blast from a trailer going past the bridge jolts him out of his reflective state back to the present. In the midst of the noise under the bridge, his mind still attempts to reconcile the multiplicity of surreal events of the day. His botched attempt to save Aminat weighs heavily in his mind. His ego was severely dented because it had exposed his limitations so transparently. He had watched and felt a combination of admiration and impotence as Vipaar inflated the man with the BMW's ego to astronomical proportions and then stood up to five area boys who looked like they would kill without a second thought. Multiple questions jostle for position in his mind, all of which he doesn't have answers to.

"Why did I try to save Aminat?"

"Why did Vipaar return for Aminat when they had walked away?"

"He had saved her just like he had saved him! Did he want to die when he challenged the boys?"

"What are you mumbling to yourself?" Vipaar asks irritably.

Temilola did not realised his thoughts were being broadcast. He sits up and rests his back against the wall, staring at Vipaar. A candle provides the light from their portion of the dark real estate. "What did you mean when…"

Vipaar, realising the gravity in Temilola's voice, sits up and looks at him.

"I mean did you…" Temilola takes a deep breath. "Earlier, with those boys, you said…"

"Do you have rocks in your throat, talk now ah ah?" Vipaar snaps, obviously agitated.

Temilola takes another deep breath. "Did you mean it when you said, 'For me, death is my freedom, I invite it everyday and every day it rejects me'?"

Despite the limited light being emitted from the flame, Temilola deciphers the ashen look that appears on Vipaar's face as one of surprise and shock. His lips and jaw move, he eyes squint, but no words come out. He merely looks away, avoiding Temilola's stare of expectation, of affirmation. The silence shocks Temilola to his core. He had expected a berating or at least hoped for a sarcastic response. It would have dispelled his thoughts and allayed his fears. He had seen the same look on Vipaar's a few weeks previously. It was during his first night when he had threatened to kill him if he hurt Alhaja—there was no doubt the threat was real. So deep in his heart, he knows Vipaar meant every word he said during the standoff with Aminat's tormentors.

Vipaar is now lying on his side, resting his head on his bag, but it is obvious he is not sleeping. Temilola's chest feels tight and his head is pounding. His mentor is lost and unsure of himself. This is more terrifying than spending the night amongst individuals from the lowest echelons of society. This is when Temilola realises why the statement bothered him so much; the promise he made to Alhaja was a lot deeper than just looking after Vipaar emotionally. He was responsible for his life.

"Vipaar," Temilola says quietly.

"Ohhhh, LORD HAVE MERCY, what do you want? Do I owe you money or somethin, or you don't want me to sleep abi?"

"Don't let anger get in the way of hope, please," Temilola says as he puts his hand on Vipaar's shoulder for a couple of seconds and then turns to lay down and go to sleep. As he closes his eyes, he hears Vipaar's phone ring.

CHAPTER 22

Vipaar leads Temilola and their new companion to their abode for the night. He knows RPG's reach does not reach as far as Ojueldgba. It is not one of the six zones he controls. For the first time in a very long time, he feels lost and unsure of himself. He thought he had long conquered or at least banished his greatest foe, but fear has returned to his heart, and he does not know how to deal with it. The feeling reminds him of his first few nights in Lagos, when he didn't think he would make it till morning. "I had cause to be scared then," he reasoned within himself, "but what am I so scared of now?" He is angry without fully understanding why. There are so many reasons to be angry that he cannot choose one, which makes him even more distressed. With anger, he feels he has a cause, but without knowing exactly what to be angry about or who to be angry at, he feels worthless and empty. It felt cathartic to tell the story of how he met Alhaja and RPG. In those few minutes, nothing else in the world existed apart from him and his apprentice. It had felt like he had entered a protective shield in which anger, hate, fear, envy, and all that was toxic about the world did not exist.

For a split second, and against his better judgement, he dares to dream of a better tomorrow when Temilola says to him,

"Don't let anger get in the way of hope, please." A warmth

radiates through his body.

At that moment, he admires his apprentice's courage. Despite all the upheaval he has been through, hope still keeps his heart soft. For the briefest of moments, Vipaar feels at peace—then his mobile phone rings. He knows who it is before answering the phone. He sits up. "Hello."

"Danieeeeel," the coarse voice bellowes in his ear, "I am goooooing to find yoooou. I go get my revenge, you hear me, I go get my revenge. You should have killed me. I will... no... ma... whare you ca... ru...hide... I go fi... and that boy..."

The crackling on the phone makes it difficult to hear everything RPG is saying, but Vipaar feels like his heart is going to penetrate the barriers of his chest cavity when he hears, "and that boy".

"Do you hare me Vipaar, I go find you and that boy, and I will kill the boy in front of you...and-" the phone cuts off.

"Who was that?" Temilola asks.

"None of your consan," Vipaar snaps. "You better sleep, I don't want to hear any noise in the morning."

Vipaar feels his brain overloading, unable to deal with the voluminous thoughts and avalanche of emotions. He had felt empowered when he stood up to RPG in Alhaja's flat, he didn't know where the words were coming from, but each word broke the proverbial yoke with which RPG used to hold power over him. It was a beautiful sight, he saw weakness in his foe's eyes and the hold was broken, he was totally free. He suddenly feels trapped again after RPG's phone call, but this time his jailer is love as opposed to fear. RPG's direct threat on Temilola's life made him realise how much he loves his apprentice. He is now chained by his affection, which in turn has put his life in danger. He feels a surge of anger towards him; he has made him soft. If he had let him deal with RPG, they would not be in the quandary they currently found themselves. No matter how much he wills it, sleep eludes Vipaar as a rabbit would a fox during the night. He is physically spent but mentally alert. His mind steadily churns over his long list of problems, without alluding to any potential solutions. The few minutes of sleep he manages before finally giving up before the dawn, is akin to self-torture. Everytime he closes his eyes he sees RPG in his dreams. Everytime he opens them, he remembers all he has lost.

He wakes up just before the sun rises. His heart aches and has a feeling of emptiness. He realises that deep down he has let hope for a better tomorrow enter his consciousness and, as always, it has now been taken away from him in the cruellest manner.

He sits up and leans against the wall. As he watches the sunrise, he cannot help but acknowledge the irony of seeing such beauty in the midst of squalor. He watches Temilola and Aminat who are both sleeping soundly, undisturbed by the ever-increasing noise of early morning traffic going across the bridge. He is able to take some solace in the fact that they are at peace, but the fact that they would soon have to wake to face challenges that the day would bring weighs heavily on his shoulders. He knows that when they wake up, they will look to him for answers, and he won't be able to give them any. For a split second, he considers leaving them under the bridge, but his hands begin to shake, his chest tightens, and he begins to gasp for air. This tremendous feeling of guilt that consumes him quickly forces him to dismiss that idea. He looks around his surroundings, and sees a few Okada riders doing their ablutions while others begin to gather on pavements for morning prayers. Although his relationship with God could be described as acrimonious at best, he still feels a sense of envy as he watches them. Most of the young men's most prized worldly possessions were their okada machines. Life had become more difficult for them since the Governor banned them from many parts of Lagos. Vipaar knew the life of an okada rider on Lagos roads was perilous, he had seen a few of them wiped out through collisions with trailers, or by angry mobs after knocking over a pedestrian. He wonders why they prayed and what they prayed for.

Did they pray for unattainable things like wealth and riches? Or for the most basic things, such as making enough money to eat, pay their rents and feed their families? Whatever they prayed for, Vipaar feels they are wasting their time, God does not have time for people like them. He continues to watch them, wondering what the future holds. Then he hears the call to prayer from a megaphone.

"Allahu Akabar, Allahu Akbar, Allahu Akbar."

"Ash adu Allah."

Vipaar jumps when the Aminat begins thrashing violently and wakes up with a look of absolute terror on her face. It is a look he is very familiar with, one he had seen too many times. He glances around rapidly to see what may have frightened her and looks on with his mouth open as Aminat quickly sits up against the wall, puts her head in between her knees and begins rocking back and forth. Vipaar had faced many dangers in his lifetime, yet he had never felt as alarmed as he was at that moment. He approaches her slowly and touches her shoulder.

"Daddy no, please daddy," she pleads. "Daddy… pleaasseee."

As someone who had experienced pain, he shared her's through those words. He feels a connection with her but also feels helpless. He knows that words cannot soothe the kind of pain she is going through.

"Aminat, what is the matter?" he calls out softly. "Aminat, Aminat." She keeps on rocking back and forth, using her knees to cover her ears. With her eyes firmly shut, she is mumbling to herself.

"Daddy, Daddy, Daddy."

Helplessness is a feeling he is not used to and doesn't know how to deal with. He wants to wake up his apprentice because it is apparent she has formed a bond with him. She stops rocking back and forth when the adhan finishes. This is when Vipaar realises it was the trigger.

"Are you alright?" he asks softly.

She stares at him with a vacant look on her face for a few seconds before returning to her sleeping position. Vipaar cannot understand what has just happened. The whole incident only adds to his feeling of uncertainty. He had put his life on the line when he challenged the boys harassing her, but he felt utterly useless when it came to soothing her pain.

As he watches her sleep, he recalls the circumstances which led to their meeting, and he begins questioning the creed he had come live by: "Man rules circumstance, circumstance does not rule man."

RPG's threat on Temilola's life, and the preceding day's events, confirms that fate is against him. Unbeknownst to his apprentice, Vipaar had decided to take him to the police station before his pitiful attempt at chivalry. Fate had thwarted his plans and brought the girl into their lives. He hated to admit it, but he is proud of his apprentice. He shivers in disgust as he recalled praising the man with the BMW. His apprentice looked out of his depth so he had decided to perform his last act of charity before they parted ways. Now, watching the okada riders rev their machines, he wishes he could steal one of the unattended ones and ride somewhere else... anywhere else. He begins to question his actions and motives which led to the standoff with the gang.

"Why did you go back to rescue the girl, when that yeye boy began pulling her ear? What did you really mean when you said death is my freedom?"

He is speaking to himself aloud, hoping to get some answers, but none are forthcoming. One thing he knows for sure is that he had felt the same uncontrollable urge to save Aminat as he did when he saved Temilola from being hit by the danfo. Something deep inside him stirred. It was a feeling he couldn't explain, understand, or control; a power surge of some sort. He thinks about the options available to all three of them. There are too many variables he cannot control. He seriously doubts that his apprentice will be able to survive on the streets. Although he has come far from the early days, he is still soft. Despite weeks of tutelage, he still did not speak or act like a survivor—they would both be a burden on him. Vipaar decides he would have to do what was best for all of them.

"Oya, wake up," he pushes Temilola on the shoulder hard. "I said wake up my friend." He is annoyed that he is not responding at an appropriate pace.

"Whaaaat," Temilola drolls. "Goodness gracious."

"Pssh, water, I beg get up my friend we have to talk. I tell you las night I don't want to hear any noise."

Temilola sits up, wipes between his eyes and looks around him. Vipaar gives him a few seconds for his memory to fall into place.

"Oh bloody hell," Temilola says. He drops his shoulders and swallows hard as his eyes dart around and he assimilates to his surroundings in the daylight. "Oh my goodness gracious… it was not a dream."

His reaction strengthens Vipaar's belief that he has made the right decision. He takes a deep breath. "Hay listen, I have to leave Lagos."

Temilola sits up and looks at Vipaar with a straight face. "Ahem, what?"

"I said I have to leave Lagos." Vipaar avoids Temilola's intense look.

"What do you mean 'I'?" Temilola shifts his bottom and straightens his back, all the while staring at Vipaar without blinking. "You mean 'WE', right?" He looks at Aminat, who is still sleeping. "All three of us."

"You don't even know dee girl, my friend I beg."

"So you want us to abandon her?"

"Liissseen to me my friend. I have to huzzle, and survive. I cannot do it with the both of you."

"What, but… but… why?" Temilola begins to hyperventilate and starts to blink rapidly. "Yesterday, you … you…"

"I beg my friend, talk sense," Vipaar says, still averting his eyes from his apprentice's intense gaze.

Temilola closes his eyes and takes three deep breaths in and then out. "Yesterday you said that I had till this morning to come up with how to make money."

"Lissseen my friend, we no go sell cats, you unstan."

"I didn't say we should sell…" Temilola takes another deep breath. "I have another idea."

Vipaar looks at his apprentice. He looks like the little lamb he had first met in Oshodi bus garage. He sighs and moves towards him. "Listen to me," Vipaar quietly says as he gently places his hand on his apprentices' shoulder. "You cannot survive on dee streets of Lagos. I cannot afford to pay ₦300 every night to sleep hare."

Temilola looks up quickly. "You paid ₦300 for us to sleep here?"

Vipaar ignores his question and continues, "I am going to take dee both of you to the police station in Surulare." His voice is low. "You will be safe there."

Vipaar looks like he is waiting for a response, but his apprentice keeps his head down, so he continues.

"Maybe dey will help you find your home and your family." He pauses briefly, waiting for a different type of response to the one he gets.

"Pardin, what did you say?" Vipaar hears Temilola mumble something under his breath. He had thought his apprentice was crying, but knows that is not the case when he looks him straight in the eyes.

"I said you are a coward." Temilola's tone is cold and unwavering.

Vipaar leans back and opens his mouth to speak, but no words come out. He stares at his apprentice in disbelief.

"Oh, how would you say it?" Temilola sneers. "U no get liver."

None of the blows Vipaar had received over the years had

caused him as much pain as the words his apprentice just used to describe him. It hit the very core of his being.

"Ehhnn." Vipaar is shaking. "I am not a coward, is just dat I have to…"

"Yeah, yeah," Temilola says, looking at Vipaar with purposeful disdain. "You wanted to abandon me the moment Alhaja died, that is why you said what you said to those boys; you wanted them to kill you."

Shock and pain do not allow any words to come out of Vipaar's mouth. His apprentice has pulled off the mask he had been wearing for so long. He flashes back to the night he left his home. One of his biggest regrets in life was that he left his brothers and sister at home without explanation. They would think that he had abandoned them. Did they also believe he was a coward? Vipaar feels the pain of Temilola's accusation from the tips of his fingers to the root of his hair follicles. It also reveals that he has lost his apprentice's respect in an instant. He hadn't realised how much value he had put on his admiration until now. Vipaar is desperate to explain why he feels he has no choice, he wants to tell him about RPG's phone call the night before.

You do not understand, death follows me everywhere. People around are always dying, I cannot have your own death on my conscience. These are the words his heart wills him to say, but instead, he says,

"If you would have let me deal with RPG, we will not be in dis wahala." Vipaar's voice is drenched in contempt. "When I say I will not send you away, dat is when I thot we ware going to stay in the flat, but now RPG is chasing me."

"Let's leave Lagos then," Temilola pleads in desperation.

"And go whare?" Vipaar snaps in a gruff tone of voice. "Whare shall we go? Tell me, now, tell me."

"I don't know," Temilola whispers as he lowers his head.

"First you want us to sell cats, now you want us to leave Lagos, but you don't know whare to go."

"At least I have ideas, all you know how to do is huzzle." The last part of the sentence mimics Vipaar.

Vipaar stands up and towers over his apprentice, his nostrils flaring and chest puffed out. "LIIISEEEEN, and liseeen well well, do you think because I did not slap your face when you say I no get liver, I go let you talk to me anyhow?" He wags his finger at his apprentice, "Me and you no dey from dey same catergory, you unstan?"

"But," Temilola looks up at Vipaar. His bottom lip is wobbling. "But all I am trying to say is that…"

"I no give you backhand because I think maybe hunger is diso-rientating you," Vipaar's tone matches the stern look on his face. He takes in a deep breath and expands his shoulders. "Don't forget who I am."

Temilola wants to continue on his path of defiance, but he stops when he notices that Aminat has woken up and is looking at them both.

"Why would the police care about us?" he whispers. "What makes us different from the other thousands of street kids of Lagos?"

Vipaar sighs. "I am only taking you to the police station." He pauses and looks at Aminat. "I will take her to the orphanage in Abu elgba."

He avoids looking his apprentice in the eyes. He cannot bear to see the brightness fade with each passing second. His silence is as loud as the crack of thunder, so to assuage his guilt Vipaar attempts to fill the void,

"I am sure dat your parents have come to the police station looking for you."

Temilola remains silent as he stands up and puts his bag on his back. He then looks at Vipaar,

"Will she be safe at the orphanage?"

Vipaars shuffles and given an uneasy smile, "Er, yes dey will look after her dare." Vipaar cannot guarantee Aminat's safety, but he reasons that she will be safer there than on the streets. Vipaar leads Aminat and Temilola to the main road after they finish packing their meagre belongings. It is now busy with heavy motor and foot traffic. He puts his hand in his trouser pocket and withdraws a ₦1,000 note. They all sit on a wooden bench and eat in silence at the mami kitchen (local eatery) just at the entrance to the bridge. Each one of them is lost in their own thoughts, and the silence is palpable between apprentice and master. Temilola casts his face downwards. Aminat senses the tension but simply eats her portion of bread and observes the surroundings in the daylight. Vipaar's eyes are fixated on the sign, which adorns the eatery. It is a white bed sheet, which has written on it in stencil:

MEAT PILES
EGG ROLL
FISH PILES
PLANTIN CHEPS
ROSETED MEATS.

He stares at the sign until he hears the unmistakable noise

which he refers to as "Sunday morning megaphone evangelists". He listens to the disjointed singing from multiple megaphones, which gets louder as they get closer to his position. Then he sees a group of about ten men and five women walking in line, most with megaphones hanging from their shoulders. They all wear yellow bibs with the name of their church printed on the back. The smiles on their faces, and the joy in their voices irritates him, because most of the congregation looked gaunt and dishevelled.

"What do they have to be so happy about?" Vipaar asks, as he looks in Temilola's direction, "the rich pastors who own megachurches send these mumu to us with their megaphones." He lets out a nervous chuckle, his feeble attempt at humour a desperate act to assuage his feeling of guilt. But the icy look Temilola shoots him confirms he has failed miserably.

"Are you going to eat that meat pie?" Vipaar continues with his attempt to break the silence in the midst of the increasing noise level above and under the bridge. "Oya, let us go," he stands up without warning. "We will go to Surulere first, and then I will take her to Abu elegba." Temilola and Aminat follow Vipaar in silence.

The journey to the police station is eerily silent. All three ride in the Keke maruwa (tuk-tuk). The only noise within their vehicle comes from the driver as he insults car drivers and pedestrians.

"If I hit you I no go say sorry o", "If you hit my jeep, na wa for you o." The man talks continuously throughout the 20-minute journey, for which Vipaar is reluctantly grateful. It makes the silence of him and his companions within the Keke maruwa more bearable. He also feels that he has been cursed with running into happy and hopeful people all morning. When they arrive at the police station,

Temilola's eyes are bulging and his lower lip is trembling. He looks like he is on the verge of tears. Vipaar wants to put his hand on his shoulder. His inner desire is to hold his apprentice, but he has to be strong. For the sake of all of them, he cannot afford to let emotion rule the day. Logic has to triumph, their very survival depends on it. They enter the police station compound and walk towards the main building in the middle of a large courtyard which looks like it has been hit by a bomb. There is a battered Toyota pick-up truck outside the gate with the writing, "Anit-Robbery Squad", and two bare feet sticking out of the passenger door window. The stench upon entering the dark building is overwhelming. It is a combination of sweat, chlorine, and a scent which Vipaar's senses has become too readily used to: the stench of blood. The first thing he notices upon entering the darkened room is a group of young men handcuffed together, sitting on a bench. After a morning full of jealousy, he is marginally glad to be back within the comfortable realms of misery.

"Go and sit over dare," Vipaar orders Temilola and Aminat. Temilola's face is devoid of any sort of emotion. He simply grabs Aminat by the hand and takes a seat on a wooden bench next to a wall. Vipaar has not fully planned what he is going to say to explain his apprentice's situation. He looks at the policeman sitting behind the desk. All his shirt buttons are undone, exposing his large overlapping gut as he sweats profusely. He approaches the officer sitting behind the desk, with his shoulders slumped.

"Good afternoon Sargent sar?" Vipaar asks as he stoops with his head slightly bowed. The officer looks up at him and makes a sour face.

"Did I give you parmission to approach my desk?" He wipes the sweat from his forehead with his handkerchief as he snorts, "Go and sid down over dare till I call you."

Vipaar's instinct is to pursue his request, but the officer has already turned his attention to another matter as he yells, "Afeeeez, Afeeez, whare is this boy?" A scruffy boy comes running towards the desk. "Go and get me mineral from Iya Riliwan," the officer orders the boy who runs out of the building.

Vipaar sits next to Temilola who is staring at the cracks on the concrete floor. "What did you say?" Temilola mutters under his breath.

Vipaar looks at him. "Are you talking to me or are you praying?" Temilola straightens his back and looks up at Vipaar. "I am sorry I called you a coward, but…"

Vipaar, sensing another plea, interrupts him. "Listen, let us just explain to them what has happen ok?" He stops and glances at two policemen who were arguing as they walked through the door. All Vipaar hears is, "Just give me my own cut, if you don't want trouble". They continue arguing as they disappear into the dark corridor.

Vipaar continues, "They will probably take you to headquarters. I am sure that your family has been looking for you."

"You are going to leave me in the responsibility of him?" Temilola said, looking in the direction of the officer at the desk who was drinking from a green bottle. "Do you think he will care what happens to me?"

"Er, don't worry. I will ask to speak to his superior, I am sure they will have your name on record." Vipaar puts his hand on

Temilola's shoulder. "Don't worry." He stands up and approaches the desk. He waits for the policeman to finish what he is doing before saying, "Excuse me, Sargent sir. Sorry to disturb sar, but I want to report this missing boy sir."

The officer stares at Vipaar. "Did I not say that you should not approach my desk until I call you?" His voice is loaded with exasperation. "Don't you have any home training?"

"Sorry officer, I am sorry to disturb you my oga... thank you for your time sar. I am just attempting to report someone missing sir."

The policeman places the empty bottle on the table, rests his hand on his gut and exhales, his eyes flashing in annoyance as he looks at Vipaar. "You want me to work today abi? Go an complete a missing report."

"You don't understand sar, it is about that boy over there." Vipaar points behind him without turning around. "I find him some time ago sir, he say he has lost his memory sir."

The policeman looks behind at the direction Vipaar pointed. "What boy?"

Vipaar turns around and stares at the empty bench in horror. Time stands still, and for a few moments he desperately hopes that he is dreaming. With his heart thumping wildly, he grabs his bag and runs out of the door, just in time to see Temilola and Aminat getting onto an okada outside the gates of the police station. His stomach twists with dread as he runs towards the gate shrieking, "Teeeemiiiilola pleeeeaaase nooo, don't go." He runs after them as fast as his legs can take him. He does not care about the dangers he is putting himself in by running in a police station. An overzealous vigilante could shout thief and he would be at the mercy of a baying mob within minutes. By the time he reaches the gate, the Okada has disappeared into the Lagos traffic.

CHAPTER 23

The relationship between "Garri and Bakedbeans", as Aminat had decided to name Temilola and Vipaar, has become increasingly tense. She pretends to be asleep as the two argue like the married couples she had worked for over the previous few years, their voices fluctuating between anger and softness. She is particularly surprised when Bakedbeans shout at Garri, who becomes frustrated and seems confused about the prospect of selling cats. Heightened tension has been the prevailing mood, but it seems to increase steadily over the course of the morning. Garri attempts to share a joke with Bakedbeans, who does not attempt to disguise his contempt. She is tempted to inquire as to what was going on as they eat at the mami kitchen, but they were engrossed in their own world. The two of them hardly speak until they reach the police station, which is when Aminat realises the cause of the tension. Bakedbeans looks ever more dejected and petrified as they sit on the bench in the police station, and he looks like he is fighting a losing battle to hold back tears. She sits looking at him curiously, unable to empathise or relate to his sadness no matter how much she wants to deep down.

When Garri goes to speak to the policeman at the desk, Bakedbeans whispers in her ears, "I will not stay here. I am going to run. Do you want to stay here with Vipaar or come with me?"

She is startled by the question, but before she can process it or think of an answer, Vipaar joins them on the bench. After a few minutes, Garri and Bakedbeans begin whispering. Aminat can only hear snippets of their conversation. Garri sounds conciliatory and Bakedbeans is defiant. She studies them both and realises that despite their outward differences, they share a deep connection, which she is not privy to. They both sound and look like two little lost boys who are petrified at the prospect of losing each other, but are unable to articulate their true thoughts. Temilola stuns Aminat when he stands up and walks towards the doorway as soon as Vipaar approaches the desk to speak to the policeman. She didn't actually believe he would go through with his intent to leave so quickly. He has taken her choice out of her hands. Logically she would be safer with Garri, but she feels more connected with Bakedbeans. So she stands up and follows him while the policeman is berating Garri. Temilola smiles when he sees her following him and grabs her by the hand. A few meters from the gate, Aminat hears Vipaar's heart-breaking cry,

"Teeeemiiiilola pleeeeaaase nooo!"

She looks back and catches a glimpse of the ashen look that is etched on Garri's face as he stands in the doorframe of the building. Temilola breaks into a run, which forces Aminat to increase her pace also. Bakedbeans looks around in desperation as soon as they go through the gates of the main compound. He runs towards an okada which has just dropped off a customer. Aminat looks back and sees Garri running towards them at full speed. She is surprised by Bakedbeans strength as he lifts her in one swift move and places her on the back of the okada. Temilola jumps onto the okada like a true Lagosian in one swift movement,

"Whare you wan go?" the okada driver asks.

"Just go straight, please," he pleads.

"I say whare you wan go?" the driver asks again and turns around to look at Temilola who is sweating profusely and looks back wide eyed in a panic when he sees Vipaar advancing towards them at full speed.

"Ladipo market, go to Ladipo. Ladipo." Bakedbeans' shriek reverberates in Aminat's eardrum. She can hear the panic in his voice, but having observed Garri and Bakedbeans over the previous 24 hours, she knows it is more out of desperation than fear.

The okada beeps its horn, revs its engine, and speeds off just as Vipaar reaches the gates. Aminat sees a look of desperation and helplessness in Vipaar's eyes and feels a twinge of pity. He has the same look her mother had the day she was driven away from her village. She feels Temilola's pulsating heartbeat on her back like a hammer as the okada weaves through traffic. It is beating fast then slows down and she hears him mumbling to himself,

"I am sorry, I am sorry."

After a twenty-minute ride, the okada driver drops them at Ladipo market.

As Temilola fumbles through his pockets, looking for money to pay the okada driver, Aminat stands by the side of the road on a quiet street and watches as the okada driver looks at him intensely.

"Why that boy is chasing you?" he asks Temilola.

"What?"

"I say why you are running from that boy?"

"Oh, him," Temilola responds calmly. "He says I stole his money and he wanted to report me and my sister to the police."

The driver looks at Aminat, then at Temilola and then back at Aminat, the scepticism on his face obvious.

"How much do I owe you my Chairman?" Temilola says in an attempt to deflect further interrogation.

"No shaking bros," he waves his hand to decline payment as he revs his motorcycle. "Don't stay here o bros, is not safe."

"Wait, wait," Temilola shouts as the man releases the foot break in preparation to drive off. "Where do you suppose we should go? We need to make some money."

"Bros, your grammar serious o." He scratches his chin. "Err, you can go to Kuramo or Barr beeessssh, you can make small money there but be careful o, na dangerous place, bet you can make some small money."

Temilola watches the okada go off into the distance, then joins Aminat on the pavement. He looks at her and smiles. "Are you ok?"

Aminat thinks that it is a strange question to ask, but she responds, "I am fine."

"Good, good, good" Temilola repeats as he scrutinises his surroundings. She watches intently as the smile gradually disappears and his face becomes slack.

"Oh shit, shit, shit, what have I done, what have I done," he repeats over and over. He begins to sweat as the gravity of the situation dawns on him.

"Holy crap, oh my goodness," his voice quakes. "I can barely look after myself, how am going to look after you?" He looks at Aminat, who stares back at him blankly as he scratches his head severely.

"What the hell were you thinking? How are you going to survive? Vipaar could have taken her to an orphanage, at least she would have been safe." He covers his face with his palms and paces in the same spot.

"Thank you," Aminat says quietly.

Temilola stops, removes his hands from his face and looks at her. "What?"

"I say 'thank you'," she repeats timidly, "for you are saving me from those boys yestarday."

Temilola looks at Aminat and his breathing slows down. He lets out a loud sigh and sits down on the pavement. He looks up at Aminat. "I guess we are going to have to go back to square one."

She sits next to him. "Is that ware you was living?"

Temilola tilts his head sideways. "Er… what do you mean, is that where I was living?"

"Square One!" Aminat confirms. "Is that the area you are coming from?"

"Ohhhh, no, no, no. I mean we have to start from the beginning, you know, start afresh… Don't worry about it, I will think of something."

Aminat now understands why Garri always seemed so exacerbated with Bakedbeans, he was always speaking in riddles. Aminat studies Bakedbeans as they sit in silence for about 15 minutes. He looks downcast and she assumes he is still attempting to come to terms with the consequences of his actions. She feels a connection to him without knowing or understanding why. There is something about him which makes her feel safe and comfortable. She can tell that he is becoming more and more despondent with each moment that goes by. He looks like he is on the verge of tears.

Without knowing why, she said, "I am from Bayan Gani Village."

"What, what?" Temilola squints his eyes, obviously confused.

"Yesterday, when you were fighting with your brada," she continues, "you asked me where I was coming from. I am from Bayan Gani Village, it is Niger."

"Oh wow, that's a long way from home," Temilola's squeals and nods his head.

"You know my village?" Aminat gasps in surprise.

"Err, well… actually, no. I just assume its far." Temilola scratches behind his head and averts Aminat's penetrating gaze. "Ohhh don't mind me, I am just blabbing nonsense. Anyway, how did you get to Lagos?"

Aminat squints as she looks at Bakedbeans. Nobody had ever asked where she was from, not even her 'friend' Kemi. This boy she has only known for 24 hours seems genuinely interested.

"My fada sold me when I was eight year old."

"Holy…" Temilola falls silent with his mouth wide open, his body shaking in horror.

She is unable to fully appreciate why her factual statement gives such a visceral reaction. Based on the look of absolute shock on his face, she knows that Bakedbeans would not be able to handle the whole story.

They sit on the pavement in silence for approximately fifteen minute and then Temilola stands up and begins walking towards the main road. Aminat wants to ask where they are going but she knows it would be pointless, so she follows in silence.

As they walk aimlessly in silence, she begins to imagine what her story would be like if one day she is able to tell it.

"I have been very sad since the day I left my village. My family is very poor. My father was a farmer. We ate what he grew and sometimes we ate chicken. My father had two wives and seven children—I am the oldest. It was my greatest wish to go to school, but it was too expensive. I helped my mother by fetching water, firewood, and working on the farm. This was in addition to looking after my brothers and sisters. Each day, I dreamt about going to school and becoming a doctor, so that I could come back to help my village. I will always remember the day I left my village. One evening, I returned home from collecting firewood and there was a man talking to my father, he told me that this stranger was my Uncle Jaro. My aunty sat me down and told me that I must help my family. She said I must go and work for some people in the city Niamey, and that my parents will get little money now and uncle Jaro will send money from my salary every three months. I will always remember my mother screaming and crying, and my father's last words in my language. "You will soon be home Insah Allah." When I saw Uncle Jaro properly, I became very scared. I wanted to scream and beg them not to send me away, but as the first born I was duty bound. Two of my friends had left the village a few months ago and the family used the money to buy goats and chickens and fertiliser—it was now my turn. The rain did not come again so I knew my father and mother would need the money. I saw my 'Uncle Jaro' give my father some money. They shook hands and then he entered his white jeep. My auntie told me softly that the people I will work for would send me to school, and teach me English and to read and write. She said I could

not become a doctor if I stayed in the village and she gave me a nylon bag with my clothes. As I hugged my mother and father, Uncle Jaro pressed the horn of the jeep and my auntie pulled me away from them and led me to the Jeep. I looked back and I saw my mother screaming and my father trying to hold her. I entered the back of the Jeep and I began to cry when I left my village for the first time in my life. I have not seen my mother and father since I was eight years old.

"I was in the back of the jeep for four days, and seven more girls entered on the way. We slept under the car at night and Uncle Jaro gave us little food. We reached Ibadan after six days. I did not speak English or Yoruba, which made things very difficult. The first woman I worked for I was asked to call "mummy" (as were my subsequent employers). She was relatively nice. She was a nurse an' only beat me slightly. She is a nice woman. She did not allow me to stay in the house when the family ware not home for the first three weeks I lived there, so I stayed on the veranda. I helped my mummy to cook, and I swept the whole house, which was huge. I washed clothes, polished shoes and learnt to make tea. It was a very hard job but ate very well; sometimes I ate meat three or four times a week. I followed them to Church sometimes but was not allowed to sit with them. Mummy's youngest daughter Kemi was my 'friend.' She began to teach me to read, to speak English and some of the things she learnt at school. The reading was very hard, but the arithmetic was very easy. I liked to read the arithmetic textbook. I began to help Kemi with her arithmetic homework. She got 100% every time I did her homework for her. Mummy did not like that Kemi and I were friends. She would sometimes call her away or send me on errands when she was teaching me English or I was helping her with her arithmetic homework. Kemi was not always nice to me. Sometimes, when her parents held a party or entertained guests, she would send me on errands, order me to get her and her friends bottles of minerals. One day she completely ignored me in front of her rich friends; I then heard her refer to me as an omo odo (house girl) and began laughing. I was very hurt but I understood that our friendship was with conditions and continued as before. Three months after I arrived, my mummy told me that she had registered me at the local government school. I would start the following Monday and she threatened to remove me if I did not do my work properly. I slept very well on the Saturday before I was due to start and dreamt about being a doctor. On the Sunday, I went to grind pepper when the family went to Church. On the way back, I saw 'Uncle Jaro' waiting near the gate to the house. I was worried because I thought something had happened to my parents, but he said to me that I should pack my bag and meet him by the gate when it is night because I must go and work somewhere else. I begged him to let me stay but he grabbed me hard by my arm and shouted at me in my language. He called me stupid and said he had paid my father money for three years and I belonged to him. He said he would send people to burn my father's house if I did not obey him. I looked in his eyes and I saw pure evil. I was petrified. That night, I left the clothes my mummy gave me when I first arrived, and the books Kemi give me, and left the house to meet 'Uncle Jaro'.

"My next mummy was an Alhaja. I helped her in her shop and to tidy her house. I open the shop at 7am and served customer till nighttime. I learnt all the price of the merchandise and within one month, I was in charge of the shop by myself. She talked a lot, she was always complaining all her children would not call or visit her. Sometime she will talk all night, which is how I begin to understand Yoruba better.

I was there for about three months before Uncle Jaro come and get me again. He told me to meet him at Challenge bus garage and he took me to another family in Lagos. I soon realised that I was a money-making machine. He would agree a contract with a family, collect money for two years, but then collect me before the end of the contract and take me to another family. I worked for many families in Lagos, and sometimes in Abuja too. Some people were very wealthy, rich with big houses and many luxury cars. Some of them were nice, but many of them were very wicked.

The people who could be considered nice did not beat me often. I would start working around seven in the morning and finish working around nine or 10 in the evening. I sometimes slept on a mattress, did not work on Sunday and even sometimes received pocket money or was allowed to keep the change from running errands. The wicked beat me all the time, I slept on the floor despite being in a six- or seven-bedroom mansion. I worked from 5am till 12am and was given food once a day.

The cruellest place I worked was with a family called Olapade. I cursed the day I was born because of that family. 'Mummy' and 'Daddy' were very wicked and the children were very lazy. It was one of the biggest houses I had ever worked in, with many empty bedrooms, but I always slept on the floor in the passage. I slept outside during the first two weeks because 'mummy' said I had a disease. On my first day, my new mummy say to me, "the last house girl was a lazy good for nothing. You better do your work properly or I am sending you back." She told me to go and wash the plates in the kitchen and the clothes in the back-yard. As I walked towards the sink, she slapped me in the back hard and told me to walk faster. She left the kitchen and returned within five minutes and asked my why I was taking so long to wash the plates.

I began to tremble as she dropped three plates on the floor and they broke. She began beating me saying, "Ohhh, my God, what kind of child have they brought me," and she reigned insults down, saying that people from the village were animals. After I washed the plates, I went to look for the clothes I had been instructed to wash. The compound was humongous and it took me a while to find the heap of clothes. As I was washing, I heard mummy shouting, "omo do, omo odo". I ran to her as fast as I could, but she beat me anyway for taking so long. She told me to go and prepare food for the family to eat. I served her husband and children their evening food at the dining table but none of them looked at me—I was invisible to them. I did not sleep until 1am that night and my mummy beat me awake at 4:30am the next morning, shouting and calling me lazy. After three days, I thought my body was going to break. Mummy did not let me bring my clothes inside and I was not allowed inside the house when they were not home. Sometimes daddy will come home very late and I have to wait to sarve his food. One morning, after I have been there for about three weeks, I woke up one morning and saw daddy standing beside where I am sleeping, looking at me. I got up very quickly and he told me to go and iron his shirt. After that, he would always smile at me or rub my back when there is nobody around. A couple of weeks later, I woke up to find him rubbing my leg. I was very scared because it was dark and I could not see his face. I attempted to stand up but he pushed me down and began to move his hand up my leg. He move higher and higher until he reach my thing and then he rubbed it. I wanted to move but my body became stiff like a piece of wood. Then he climbed on top of me. I felt pain inside of my body. I wanted to scream but I could not. That is when the Azan (muslim call to prayer) begin. I closed my eyes and thought of my family. I concentrate on the Azan to help block the pain. He was moving up and down on top of me and began to grunt like a pig; after what felt like an eternity his whole body began to shake and he let out a stifled scream. He stood up and walked away. The space between my legs was painful, I used a torch light to look and there was blood on the thin mattress I was sleeping on. I stood up but went back down, it was just too painful. I stood up after a few minutes because I had to begin tidying the house or my mummy would beat me. I was in so much pain but I could not cry. I performed my chores very slowly that morning because of the pain. Mummy beat me and called me good for nothing and lazy. Daddy did not look at me. The next morning, I woke up petrified when I heard the morning Azan. For the next seven days I prayed he would not come again, but he came to me after eight days. He put his hand on my mouth and he enter me again. Again I listen to the Azan, but I cannot block the pain. He come many time after that, every time daddy enter me… mummy will beat me harder and punish me more. I prayed for Uncle Jaro to come and collect me, but after six months, he did not come… so I knew I had to run away. One day, big mummy send me to the market and I did not go back to the house. I have been…"

"Haaaaa, NOW I GET IT!!!!!" Bakedbeans breaks the silence with a sudden cheer in his voice and excitement on his face. "Sorry, sorry, I didn't mean to scare you. I get the story, I get it!" He has a wide grin, bounces from foot to foot and squeals, "Man rules circumstance, circumstances does not rule man.' Oh my goodness, I finally get, I get it now." He continues to shriek and shake uncontrollably. Aminat begins to consider the possibility that she has attached herself to a mad person as she watches Bakedbeans pace backwards and forwards, seemingly possessed by his thoughts, which he is unable to articulate. He mutters to himself and giggles, "It *wasn't* about somebody pushing him in the pool," he clasps his hands together, "it was the fact that he swam in a pool full of crocodiles. He ruled his own circumstance and he survived. DO YOU GET IT?" Aminat stands rooted to the spot and continues to stare at the bizarre actions of Bakedbeans. He has the smile of somebody who has discovered a diamond mine. The smile disappears slowly and his whole body deflates. "I wish I could tell him..." He pauses and looks in the direction of Suru-lere. "I wish I could tell him I finally understand the moral of the story. He would be so proud of me." He looks back at Aminat, "Life and its cruel ironies, huh?" Aminat is unsure if he is asking her a question, so she shrugs her shoulders.

"What is dee story?" Aminat asks cautiously. She is curious as to what got Bakedbeans so excited, but is also afraid that whatever he has may be contagious. She listens carefully as he tells the story about a Chief and a man who swam with crocodiles with a beaming face. When he finishes, he has a look of expectation on his face. "Do you get it? Man rules circumstance, circumstance does not rule man."

He lowers his head and exhales loudly when Aminat asks, "So who push him?"

The story is confusing but the disappointed look on Bakedbeans' face even more so. "Don't worry, don't worry, one day you will get it." He gives a forced smile. "I promise."

"Ok, now let's review our circumstance." Temilola is looking in Aminat's direction but it is obvious he is talking to himself. "We have very little money, nowhere to sleep and I have no idea where we are. All we have is God, hope and each other."

She continues to analyse Bakedbeans, who is obviously terrified but is valiantly attempting to hide it through speaking in a high-pitched voice and smiling. As he continues chattering, she suddenly realises why she feels safe around him. He has nothing and has not asked her for anything. He is different from most of the people she met since she had left her village. The way he speaks reminds her of the rich people she had worked for when she first arrived in Lagos, which only increased her perplexity as to why he was living on the streets. He doesn't fit the profile of the street kids she had met. She thought about Ibrahim and Uncle Emanuel. They had promised so much, demanded more and returned so little or nothing at all: just empty hopes and unfulfilled promises. The few hours she had spent with Bakedbeans, she felt a sense of worth. She reflects on the courage it must have taken to come to her aid with the BMW man. Like her, his actions to venture into the unknown were born out of fear and desperation. But despite this, he still radiated a sense of hope and belief. She desperately hopes that after all the pain and disappointment, he would eventually turn out to be the Prince she has been searching for. His enthusiasm is in stark contrast to the realities they face, but for the first time in a long time Aminat allows herself to hope that tomorrow would and could be better. She desperately hopes that his sense of hope and innocence would withstand the inevitable challenges they would face.

CHAPTER 24

Fear and anger gnaws aways at Temilola's insides as he stands in the sand, staring at a cargo ship that is sailing further and further into the horizon. He has spent 20 minutes watching the ship as it diminishes in size. The further away it sails, the more his belief that hope would conquer ebbs away. He knows that once the ship disappears from view, he will be forced to make a choice that will determine his and Aminat's survival. He is not ready for the responsibility. He desperately wishes he could swim out to sea to join the ship on its voyage to somewhere else in the world. Since the day he ran away from Vipaar, he has been stripped of his dignity. He lives in constant fear and has been forced to do unnatural things in order to survive. During the 20 minutes he has spent watching the ship, he's been able to shut the world out for the first time in five days. His senses, which have been in a constant state of alert from the moment he arrived in Kuramo beach, now have some respite. This limited period of tranquillity is the only luxury he can afford. He has been forced to admit that reliance on 'hope' in his current environment is dangerous; to survive he has to be ruthless. Hope is not going to feed himself and Aminat, or protect them from the vultures and miscreants who had made Kuramo beach their home. He knows at that moment he has begun a path, which will only end in either of two ways—life or death. He begins to reflect on his and Aminat's experiences over the previous five days since arriving on Kuramo beach, which was a rude awakening.

By the end of their first full day, he had concluded that Kuramo beach was the epitome of paradoxes. Wealth and poverty, joy and sadness, hope and despair existed in the same sphere, but never assimilated. Each element was represented by humans who played their parts in the story of those who lived life and those who merely existed. It was a place where the rich and well fed mixed with the poor and hungry. While he had been living under Alhaja's roof and Vipaar's protection and tutelage, they may have been on the lower rungs of those who lived there, but together they had a purpose. Here, in this cesspool called Kuramo, his place is amongst those who merely existed, the outcasts of society, those without a purpose. His existence was made even more perilous because he had become an outcast among outcasts. Most of the events of the previous five days had been a blur. He was vulnerable and he didn't have time to think or reflect. All his actions were determined by his baser instincts for food, shelter and security—things he had no control over. His short residency on the beach has been the most physically and emotionally distressing period of his life—bar his memory loss. The signs of the hardships to come were ominous from their first morning in Kuramo beach when they woke up to find the bag, which contained all their meagre belongings, had been stolen. The magnitude of the challenges facing him was made abundantly paramount when Aminat asked,

"What are we going to do?"

Her question immediately reminded him of Vipaar and his

threat to give him a kung fu kick for asking the same question the previous morning.

"Don't worry," he replied cheerily. "Something will come up," he attempted to reassure her.

She looked at him intently, waiting for an answer before following up with, "What?"

He scratched his head. "Look, I don't know alright." He looked around, "I don't bloody know."

Temilola realised how annoying he must have been to Vipaar. He looked around and realised that he had no idea what to do next. They walked around the beach for about an hour in silence.

"Broda," it took a millisecond for Temilola to realise she was talking to him and looked at a weak looking Aminat who had her hand on her stomach.

"Are you ok?" he asked.

"My belly is hurting me," she mumbled as she sat down on a low wall.

Temilola had been expecting that moment since they woke up. When it finally came, he felt helpless and total failure. That one statement had exposed so vividly the limitations of relying on hope, and the errors of romanticising Vipaar's mantra. For a man to rule his circumstances, he had to have options. He had used the last of their meagre funds to get to their new residence and buy some food on the way. In order to fulfil his promise to look after Aminat, the only options available to him was to beg or steal. He felt a sense of déjà vu. He bit his bottom lip and sweat accumulated on his forehead. That was the moment he fully realised the fallacy of leaving Vipaar. Despite the challenges they had faced together, one of the things which he had never worried about was food or safety.

"Wait here, I will go and get you something to eat," he said with as much confidence he could muster, although hunger and the heat had made him lightheaded. He wandered aimlessly down the path for a couple of minutes until he saw a man exit the back of a building. He watched the man throw something into a giant silver rubbish bin and walk back into the building and Temilola managed to peek inside through the open door. The aroma wafting from the building was heavenly to his nose, but hell to his stomach. He concluded that the building must be a restaurant or hotel. The stench of the bin was equivalent to a botanical garden compared to some odours he had endured. As he rummaged through the bin, he wondered if his actions were driven by his hunger or desire to feed Aminat. He managed to get a whole banana, two pieces of half-eaten fried meat, a carton of Capri Sun, which was still half-full, four pieces of toast and a croissant. He gathered his paupers buffet and returned to Aminat who looked pensive until she saw him. Despite knowing that his actions were borne out of desperation, he still felt humiliated at having to rummage food out of the dustbin like a vagrant. He shared the food with Aminat, giving her the bigger portion and watching as she wolfed it down. He ate a piece of meat and two pieces of toast. She offered to share the croissant, but he refused. If he had known about the more serious challenges that were to come, he would have appreciated the buffet breakfast.

"IWO!!!! Ibo lo ti ri onje yen," Temilola heard someone shouting and looked up to see three young boys approaching him, each one trying to look more menacing than the other. He kept silent and avoided making eye contact in the hope that they were not approaching him. Luck was not on his side as they continued their trajectory and soon surrounded him and Aminat. The one in the middle who was the ugliest, and whom Temilola took to be the leader, asked again.

"You, are you deaf? I say whare you get the food from?" the boy shouted again, this time even louder and with more aggression in his voice.

Temilola's first instincts were to run, but instead he pointed toward the building. "I got it from the bin over there." His voice is shaking.

"Over dare is my tarotrary," the ugly leader continued, his voice raspy. "Nobody take food from thare except for me and my boys, you hear me?"

Although he was speaking English, Temilola had great difficulty understanding what the boy was saying.

"Pardon me." The words had come out before he realised, and he remembered Vipaar's warning too late.

The three boys looked at each other and began to laugh. Ugly looked at him, still laughing, and asked, "Why do you speak like Akata?'

Before he could think, Temilola heard himself, "Why do you speak and look like an ugly ignoramus?"

Next thing, he opened his eyes to see Aminat kneeling over him crying. The right side of his jaw was throbbing and he tasted blood in his mouth.

"What happened," he mumbled as he attempted to stand up.

"The big one punsh you in the face," she answered.

"I guess that was the welcoming committee," Temilola chuckled as he spat blood out of his mouth.

Over the next few days, the real humiliation came when he had to beg for money just so that he could buy food. During this period, he saw the depths of inhumanity as people shouted at him, swung at him or kicked him. Ironically, the worst kind of humiliation came from some of those who gave him money. Most just looked through him while others looked at him and Aminat with pity in their eyes. The hunger pains made the humiliation easier to bear. This was the first of many incidents marking their stay at Kurmaro beach. On their first full night, he and Aminat had to run for their lives when about forty area boys suddenly began fighting. Temilola had stood watching in a trance a few moments until he saw one short man break a bottle and shove it in another man's neck. His blood ran cold and he shouted to Aminat, "Ruuuuun!" As he turned to run away from the melee, he couldn't help but be impressed by Aminat's street smarts as she was already running and about 20 to 30 yards ahead of him.

The biggest and probably the most ironic paradox about Kuramo beach, was its location. Temilola considered it to be comparable to the devil's playground in the middle of a heavenly oasis. Parts of the beach were littered with shacks made out of cardboard and tarpaulin and human faeces, as well as that from the horses ridden by visitors to the beach. There were used condoms and syringes, cigarette butts, broken bottles, the jagged edges like teeth eagerly seeking new flesh to infect. Dusk brought with it an assortment of characters, and Temilola experienced firsthand the consequences of a lawless society—the ultimate chaos. By his third night, the sight of children selling drugs, smoking Indian hemp, fighting prostitutes who were just as violent as the area boys, and their clients no longer gave him pause.

The cargo ship blasts its horns one last time as it finally disappears over the horizon. Temilola realises that his and Aminat's survival will require some hard choices. He concludes that he has to abandon any hope that his memory will return. He must take the necessary actions to live for today; tomorrow will take care of itself. His heartbeat has become synced with the motion of the waves, and his feet sink deeper into the sand as the water hits his legs, but he stands firm. At that moment, a gentle breeze blows past him which makes him remember Alhaja. He remembers her kindness and gentle soul. He has not allowed himself to acknowledge or mourn her passing fully. He misses her terribly and realises how much he relied on her for comfort. He also feels anger and resentment towards her for dying. He knows his anger does not make any logical sense, but he cannot help his thoughts. Coupled with this, he feels a great sense of guilt for failing in his promise to her by abandoning Vipaar. He had always thought that when his memory returned, he would find a way to repay her generosity. She had been a blessing to him, and he had repaid her with an act of cowardice. His tears gradually subside, and his focus shifts from the ship. His thoughts turn to the characters on the beach. There doesn't seem to be any demarcation between the adults and young adults or children. Most of the children in groups smoked what Temilola heard referred to Indian hemp. Those who could walk did so in a zombie-like manner, and others just lounged all around the beach like grazing cattle. He had developed an odd acquaintance with a boy named Okechukwu, who one evening offered to share his Indian hemp with him. "Take some," he said, inhaling heavily, "it will make you sleep."

Temilola was sorely tempted, his desire for sleep was as strong as his need for sustenance. As a result of the challenges he had experienced during his first three days, he understood why so many of them smoked Indian hemp. It helped them to escape from darkness and misery, which represented the realities of daily life, even if only for a few hours. Of all the people who he came into contact, Okechukwu was the only one who didn't ask him why he spoke the way did. He did tell him a few home truths though. "Some of da boys don't like you."

"Why?" Temilola had asked. He was mildly inquisitive. "Dey say you are very pompous," he replied with no tact. "Dey are saying you are always looking down at dem, like you are betta dan us. You don't talk to us or smoke wid us, and you don't eat the barbeskui food that visitors on the beesh don finish eating, or the ebo sacrifices for the goddess of the sea."

Temilola did not have a credible defence to the accusation. He wonders why he does not rush to eat the leftover food, which the residents referred to as barbeskui, or the food thrown into the sea by visitors to the beach. Although intimidation played a part, deep down he knows that stalking and scavenging in public was beneath him. Despite his loss of memory, he knew that he was above these street kids in status. They were rough in appearance and mannerism. Aggression seemed to be their first nature and many of them had scars on their bodies, especially on their backs.

"Why do so many of them have scars on their backs?" he asked, hoping that his tone resonated with the concern he was attempting to project.

Okechukwu took a long drag of the Indian hemp he was smoking before answering.

"A lot of us ware badly beaten at home, which is why we are on dee streets." He paused for a few seconds as his bloodshot eyes looked past Temilola before he continued. "Some of us… the scars are from fighting wid bottles and knives." He then lifted up his T-shirt to show Temilola a scar on his right torso. "I was fighting some area boys in Oshodi. They tried to kill me, but I escape." Temilola was shocked at the sight of the scar, but he managed to keep his composure.

The conversation with Okechukwu forced Temilola to acknowledge his condition may be permanent. He was forced to acknowledge that "hope," which had been his constant companion for the previous months, was based on the belief that his memory would return. He had always looked at the street kids with pity; they had accepted their circumstances in life. Vipaar had told him that thinking about a better tomorrow was dangerous. He realised that one of the reasons he had been able to keep faith in hope was that he was within the safety of Alhaja and Vipaar. He did not believe he would be one of them. Fighting for food would have meant that he would have to accept the reality that he was one of them. The mere prospect of having to accept this circumstance filled Temilola with dread. His heart rate increased and he became dizzy. Without thinking he grabbed the joint from Okechukwu and took a long pull. He was as surprised as Okechukwu that he was able to inhale without coughing. For the first time in what seemed like an eternity, he was at peace. It felt like he was floating in the air.

For a few minutes he forgot all his misfortunes and it numbed the physical and emotional pain which were weighing him down with each minute that passed. Okechukwu stood up, and as he left he told Temilola to keep the rest of the joint.

The main catalyst for his reflective state that morning was an incident which occurred the previous evening. He and Aminat were walking back to their den after a day of begging and carrying people's loads, when he noticed a white Range Rover with black out windows following them. He turned around when it pressed its horn and the driver shouted to get his attention,

"You, small boy come here."

The man was handsome, approximately 40 to 45 years old. He was wearing a grey suit, pink shirt and a blue tie. Based on how he looked, the gold watch he was wearing, and the car he was driving, it was obvious he was wealthy. Temilola was intrigued, so he walked towards the car.

"Good evening sir," Temilola greeted the man, but he was looking behind him at Aminat who was still standing where he had left her. "Can I help you?" he said sternly, to get the man's attention.

The man turned his attention to Temilola, "Sharp guy, how the body?" he stretched out his hand. Temilola was surprised to feel a paper instead of skin as he shook the man's hand. He looked and saw that he was holding a crisp ₦1,000 naira note. He began to salivate at the thought of the food he was going to eat at the local buka. The thought of going to sleep on a full stomach nearly brought tears to his eyes. He was so lost in his own thoughts that he didn't hear the man's questions. He looked up. "Pard…" he paused. "I mean what did you say sir?"

Looking straight at Aminat. "I said, how much for the night?" the man replied as he smiled and raised his eyebrows twice.

"Huh, what do you mean?" Things only made sense to Temilola when he looked back at Aminat, whose chin and lips were trembling and whose eyes were bulging. She looked like she was going to faint.

"Oya talk now, how much for the girl?" the man said with an impatient snort.

"Stop wasting my time. I just take you both to my house and bring you back in the morning. I will give you another 1000 naira."

Temilola ground his teeth, clenched and unclenched his fist. His eyes widened and his body raged in fury. He was sorely tempted to pick up a rock and smash it in the man's face, but he knew the limits of his skills as a pugilist.

"SHE IS NOT FOR SALE." He said this with his face twisted in contempt. He screwed up the ₦1000 and threw it into the car through the window.

The man jerked his head back in shock, stared at Temilola for few moments, then said, "stupid boy" as he rolled up the windows and drove off. Temilola returned to Aminat, who had begun to cry and shake uncontrollably.

"Hey, hey, hey, what's the matter?" Temilola asked with obvious concern. He suspected there was a deeper reason for the reaction than the incident. "Don't worry, I would never have let him take you." He spoke softly and held her hand.

As she wiped her tears, through her babbling she said, "I... I... I..." She struggled to get her words out, then suddenly lunged at him, put her hands around his waist, rested her head on his chest, and squeezed. That was when Temilola deduced that they were tears of relief rather than fear. He felt emboldened. He had atoned for his less than successful attempt at chivalry when they first met.

"Lets go, don't worry. Nothing will happen to us." Aminat's tears subsided as they made their way back to their sleeping spot. The pride Temilola felt was slightly diminished when he saw the white Range Rover parked just 100 meters ahead. His heart sank when he saw a girl just a little bigger than Aminat enter the back seat, as a man in a vest spoke to the driver. She had no one to protect her. He felt empowered being Aminat's protector: it gave him a purpose, a valid reason to continue.

Temilola lets out three long exhalations when the ship finally disappears from view. He returns to the wooden hut on stilts, where he and Aminat have spent the previous five nights. He has quickly discovered that sleeping on sand is more uncomfortable than concrete. They had been chased away with threats of violence from the first few locations they had attempted to settle on the evening they arrived at Kuramo beach. The hut which they currently reside underneath is located at the very end of the beach near two giant pipes through which sewage flows into the sea. He had attempted to enter the hut above, but it was locked with a chain and padlock. The space underneath the hut is wide enough to crawl through on his hands and knees. He had bumped on the wood decking beneath the hut numerous times when he woke up in a panic and attempted to sit up.

He groans in pain as he bends down to crawl underneath the hut. He had learnt from watching Aminat that it was easier and faster to crawl through the beach sand on his knuckles rather on his palms. He lays next to Aminat and watches her sleeping for about five minutes. He feels the weight of his responsibility for her growing heavier with each passing minute. He has come to the realisation that he had been selfish when he asked her if she wanted to come with him at the police station, he has now placed her in greater danger.

"Aminat, Aminat," he shakes her gently. "Wake up, we have to go."

"Good morning," Aminat greets him as she maneuveres herself into the best position to crawl out from under the decking. She always said good morning to him, a last remnant of normalcy.

Temilola is tempted to say, "What's good about it," but withdraws the words at the last second and says instead, "How did you sleep?"

"Fine."

As they dust the beach sand off their clothes, he hears, "Akaaaatttttaaaaa!" Temilola's muscles tense up and he feels a tightness in his chest. It feels like his blood is on fire. He does not need to look around to confirm the voice belongs to the person who had become his chief nemesis within hours of arriving on the beach. It is Gadaffi, the ugly ignoramus who always wore sunglasses, regardless of the time of day. He turns around, stands with his feet apart and stares at the lanky, dark-skinned boy as he stumps towards them with two companions in tow. As the trio get closer, Temilola takes four steps forward as if coming out to confront the danger head-on, plants his feet in the sand and crosses his arms across his chest. He is unsure whether his act of bravado is to project strength and show defiance or to avoid Aminat sensing his fear.

"Don't get in my way today," Gadaffi sneers as he looks down at Temilola. "You are an Akata, you don't belong hare."

Temilola blinks rapidly and curls his top lip to cover his nose as Gadaffi's bad breath, combined with the smell of Indian hemp, nearly engulfs him, but he stands his ground. He leans forward and looks into Gadaffi's glasses.

"Stay out of my way or I will destroy you." Temilola's tone is laced with contempt.

This statement is met with stunned silence. The boys turn to look at each other and then erupt into raucous laughter as they clutch each other for support. Temilola smirks as they laugh. He does not avert his gaze from Gaddaffi's face. Their laughter strengthens Temilola's resolve and he feels a great surge of power flow through him—it feels good.

"You wan destroy me, I run this beesh," Gadaffi retorts glibly as he takes off his sunglasses. "What are you small akata going to do?"

"Okaaaay," Temilola shrugs his shoulders, smacks his lips and stares at Gadaffi's bloodshot eyes. He steps forward again and notices a slight twitch in Gaddaffi's cheek. " I have warned you, come after me at your own peril!" With this Temilola turns to Aminat, "Let's go."

"If I see you hare tomorrow, I will throw you and that little girl into the sea," Gadaffi shouts after Temilola as he walks away.

Aminat scrambles after him, "What did he want again?"

Temilola smiles at her and winks. "Don't worry duchess, I will sort it out. Let's go get something to eat."

As they walk towards the main road, Temilola sees a woman selling bread walking in the opposite direction and he instinctively calls out to her by pursing his lips and whistling, "pwwwweeeeffff" "pwwwweeeffff" "pwwwweeeefff" in quick succession. The woman turns around and walks towards him. He feels proud of himself. He had tried to do the call numerous times previously, but it had always ended in failure. He bought small loaves and butter with the last ₦100, which he had kept in his underwear for safekeeping. As they eat, Temilola thinks about how he is going to deal with the predicament which is Gadaffi. He feels the venom of hate coursing through his veins. He had threatened Aminat's life, and that was the last straw. He knows he has the option of relocating somewhere else, but he is tired of running. He had run from RPG, and run away from Vipaar. It is now time to take a stand. He knows he has 24 hours or his and Aminat's life would be forfeit. In that instant, he makes a decision that will change his life forever. For them to live, Gadaffi has to go.

CHAPTER 25

Vipaar's whole body is numb. His head is spinning and he is unable to comprehend what is happening around him. He runs after the okada as fast as he can, but his physical abilities cannot match his desire. He stops, disorientated, and watches helplessly as the okada disappears. His brain is unable to process the multitude of thoughts racing through his mind. He spins around a few times, looking for another available okada, which increases his state of confusion. The blaring horns and people shouting makes it difficult to get his thoughts under control.

"Cummut off dee road. You dey craze, Mentalo, you wan die."

It is only then that he realises he is standing in the middle of the road. Drivers are hurling insults at him, and pedestrians are pleading with him to get out of the road. He stands frozen to the spot. A blue 4x4 comes hurtling towards him with its horns blaring. His survival instincts have become divested from his thought process and he is unable to take evasive action. Between the times he sees the car and it stopping inches from his legs, his brain processes numerous thoughts in a concise and logical manner. Within those few seconds, he accepts that he was destined to lose everyone he had ever loved. Death had taken three from him: first his mother, then his best friend Ejuku and then his beloved Alhaja; and now his actions had sent a fourth to certain death. He has failed to keep his promise to his beloved Alhaja. He accepts that his time has come.

"Mudafucka, get off the road," the woman behind the wheel sticks her head out of the window and continues shouting and gesticulating at him. "You want to die?"

Vipaar walks back towards the gate of the police station in the midst of horns, screeching brakes and a multitude of insults in various languages. As he stands by the gates, he notices people are actively avoiding him and some are looking at him with fear in their eyes. He only realises the potential danger he had put himself in when he hears a couple of people walking past.

"Alayi ti ya ware."

"This won de serious craze."

"Mentalo don catcsh this one o."

He is acting like a mad person in front of a police station. He has seen the effects of mob mentality, and it would only take one to suggest that he should be taken into the police station before the mob joined in. He walks away from the gate and composes himself as much as he can. He stops at a shop for a cold bottle of coke, and, in an attempt to jump-start his brain, downs it in one go. It does not have much of an effect so he sits down on the wooden bench and stares at the black steel gates of the police station. He begins to think of all the places Temilola could have gone to. The options were limited—the only places he knew were Alhaja's flat, her stall in the market and school. The school would be the most likely place he would return to. In two minds about leaving the area in case Temilola changed his mind and came back, Vipaar stands up and then sits back down. He orders another bottle of coke. He would be able to sit there outside the shop as long as he held the bottle in his hand.

"Are you waiting for somebody?" the woman who sold him the coke asks.

"Yes, I am waiting for my brother," he replied.

"When ware you expecting him, you have been waiting for some hours now," she said sympathetically as she put a crate of empty bottles on the ground.

Vipaar looks at the clock on his phone. He has been sitting in the same spot for two and a half hours. Time had stopped for him.

He hangs around the area for two days, hoping that they would return. He goes to the school and sees one of RPG's boys waiting by the gates. He knows Temilola is smart enough not to go back to Oshodi. Vipaar becomes more and more depressed with each hour that goes by. He does not eat anything substantial and only drinks water. Despair consumes him as he imagines all the dangers that Temilola and Aminat would face out there on their own without him there to protect them.

A trailer could have hit them, someone could have kidnapped them for rituals. He refuses to allow himself to believe the worst.

The evening of the second day, two young boys approach him from either side. He is so lost in his own thoughts that he does notice until they have surrounded him.

"Who goes dare?" The short one on the left of him hollers.

Vipaar's eyes dart around the area and he realises he does not know where he is.

"I say, who goes dare?" the boy, who was no more than 12 years, asks again, with renewed aggression and confidence.

Vipaar knows the boy must have serious backup to be so belligerent. "Scorpion is my name." His response is weak and lacks the usual vigour.

Five other boys join the first two and survey Vipaar with malevolence asking, "Is he bam? Is he bam?" From the insignia on their shirts, Vipaar knows that they are members of the Ayelowo gang members, but he does not understand why they have taken an interest in him. They are one of the most organised and violent gangs in Lagos; even RPG did not mess with them.

It soon becomes clear when the short boy asks Vipaar, "Hey, who you dey pledge?"

"I no dey pledge, my chairman," Vipaar replies, giving the boy the respect he was due despite his tender age, "I just look for my broda."

"Why you dey wear two colours?" one of the boys asks.

Vipaar looks at his torso and realises that he is wearing a red shirt and black jeans. They are the colours of two rival gangs in the area and boys want to know which gang he is affiliated with. He knows he is in trouble. In his normal state of mind, he would think of something to say to get out of the situation, but the events of the past two days have taken their toll on him. He is physically and mentally exhausted.

"Bros, I beg no vex, I just make wrong turn," is all he can muster. He turns around to leave, and he feels a fist land on his right jaw. He is stunned but stays on his feet.

"Oya, take off the clothes this instant," the short boy orders.

Vipaar looks at the boy defiantly. He wants to lunge at him, but he knows that would mean instant death. His promise to Alhaja and his love for Temilola enables him to control his anger, but his pride does not allow him to break eye contact with the boy who had punched him.

"Oya deal with him," the short boy commands. Vipaar feels the blows and kicks all over his body. As they punch and kick him, he begins to acquiesce. He wants to feel physical pain, he wants to be punished. He feels he deserves the beating and wills them to hit him harder, but alas the beating is insufficient. In the end, he merely curls up on the floor, protecting his head and face with his forearms until they finish. The short one rummages through his pockets and takes the money he had taken from RPG.

He hadn't fought back as the boys' reigned blows on him, blows which were not painful enough to replace the feeling of guilt and failure which completely envelope him. He walks aimlessly for hours. His left eye is nearly swollen shut and his jaw is throbbing when he finds himself standing in front of the house he had shared with Alhaja. He walks into the dark hall, up the stairs and knocks on a door. As it opens, everything goes completely dark. The next thing he hears is someone calling his name softly, "Daniel, Daniel." He stirs as his nose picks up a sweet aromatic scent.

He opens his eyes, sees Gladys's light skinned face looking down at him, and feels the soft warmth of the palm of her hand as she strokes his face.

"Daniel, Daniel wake up now," she begins pushing his right shoulder. "Please don't die on me, please I beg wake up now."

"My dear sister Gladys," he smiles wearily. He feels a sharp pain in his left ribs as he sits up. He looks around and he realises he is in her bedroom. "Don't worry, it seems that death does not want me now."

"What happened to you? Where is Temilola? What happened with Jamiu? People are saying you try to kill him?" The speed at which she speaks, combined with the panic, compounds Vipaar's already thumping headache.

She stands up, walks out of the room, and returns with a sachet of water, which she hands to Vipaar along with two tablets. "Here, take this paracetamol." As he puts the tablets in his mouth, she asks the same questions again.

"You know he is now staying in Alhaja's apartment and he has come here two time looking for you." Vipaar nearly chokes on the water when he hears this. "Why would you come back here? I thought you will have left Lagos by now."

"What time is it?" he asks.

"It is 11," she answers, trying to subdue her irritation at the lack of answers to her questions. "You arrive here about two hours ago, blood over your face, then you just collapse. It took me twenty minutes to drag you into the bedroom."

"Thank you," Vipaar whispers.

"Where is Temilola? Is he alright, have his parents come to pick him?" Gladys shrieks. "Oh, chineke, what kind wahala you don bring onto us o?"

As Vipaar begins to put his head on the pillow he says, "I don't know where he is. They ran away from me, they both left me." A tear rolls down his left cheek. As he drifts off, he faintly hears,

"Who is they? Who is Aminat? Why did he run away, Daniel? Daniel?"

His lapses into unconsciousness which results in a deep journey into his subconscious. The dreams are tortuous. He is conscious within an unconscious state, which keeps him trapped. No matter how much he wills himself to wake up and escape his nightmares, he cannot. For the first in a long while, he dreams of his mother. Instead of sitting on her lap and her smiling as he had always remembered her, she was shouting at him. He sees Alhaja's face, she keeps on repeating the words she had told him the night before she died. In his dream, he is walking across the 3rd mainland bridge and he looks into the river and sees two bodies being pulled out of the water—Temilola and Aminat. They both suddenly open their eyes and whisper: "You wanted to abandon us, you wanted to abandon us."

Vipaar is sweating profusely, but still unable to wake up. He keeps on falling with no ground in sight. He is always spinning as he sees the faces of those he had lost over and over again. With all the strength he can muster, he finally escapes his nightmare and wakes up. He sits up and the first thing he notices is the wetness of the bed and then himself. He looks around to confirm he is finally free from the dream. Gladys enters the room carrying a tray, which she places on the bed. It is a bowl of Indomini noodles. "Eat something, please. You have been sleeping for some hours now."

Vipaar does not feel he deserves such kindness and wants to reject the food, but his hunger triumphs over his guilt. The food is delicious, which only increases his sense of guilt.

"Are you going to tell me what happened?" Gladys asks after he has taken a few mouthfuls.

Vipaar wants to tell her everything that has happened, but he is unable to take another person being disappointed in him.

"He ran away from me." His words are heavy. "They both left me."

Gladys senses that there is more to the story, but does not push him for answers. She stands up and walks out towards the door frame. As she pulls the curtain aside, she turns to Vipaar.

"Jesus will watch over him." Glays clasps her hands together in prayer.

These words infuriate Vipaar, he wants to shout at her, tell her to shut her mouth, but he just continues eating his food.

"Sometimes, people need to chase their own paths. The boy is strong, I pray that Jesus will watch over him." With this, she walks out of the room.

Vipaar ponders on her words for a few minutes and then acknowledges his limits and powerlessness. He feels useless and minuscule in the grand scheme of things. This was another circumstance that he could not control. He had exhausted all his abilities in his attempt to find them. He could not think of any other way. He takes a deep breath and stands up, his heartbeat picks up speed and he goes down on his knees. He puts his elbows on the bed, clasps his hands together and closes his eyes.

"My beloved Alhaja prayed to Allah, my mother prayed to Jesus, and my father prayed to Chineke. Whichever one is listening, please please look after them. Do not punish them for my mistakes, please keep them safe. If anything God, punish me. If you keep safe God, I promise to…"

At that moment, he hears banging on the door, followed by an unmistakable voice.

"GLADYSSSS, IS HE IN DAARRE, OPEEEN DEE DOOR,

IS HE IN THERE?"

It is RPG. Vipaar takes it as a sign that God really hates him. Gladys rushes into the room, her eyes frantic with fear. "It is Jamiu. Quick quick, enter the wardrobe," she gesticulates widely.

"WHO IS THAT BANGING ON MY DOOR, I SAID I AM COMING, ABI. WHAT IS YOUR PROBLEM?" she shouts as she attempts to pull Vipaar off the bed. Vipaar's reaction is the complete opposite to Gladys's; he is eerily calm, ready to meet his destiny. He enters the built-in wardrobe, which is dominated by Gladys sensual smell. "I said I am coming," she shouts again. "Don't worry, I will send him away, don't make any noise." The fear in her eyes makes Vipaar feel pity for her. There is a slight gap between the two closed wardrobe doors from which he sees Gladys wrap a towel around her and then takes off her leggings and t-shirt. She puts on a shower cap and disappears from view. He hears shouting from the other room.

"Ohhhhhhh, what do you want again, I told you he is not here. Why are you always disturbing my life?"

Then there is silence. Vipaar hopes RPG has left. He feels his heart will combust when he hears the rings of the curtain slide across the pole. He sees RPG enter the room through the narrow gap between the wardrobe doors. He considers rushing him, but decides against it. He is in no shape to take on RPG. Then he sees RPG look directly at the wardrobe. They stare at each other but Vipaar is not 100% sure he has been detected. He can hear his own heartbeat, which is beating so loud that he thinks that RPG can hear it. He makes peace with his maker when RPG begins walking towards his hiding place.

"Why are you lying to yourself?" Gladys sneers, which makes

RPG stop and turn to face her. This is when Vipaar sees the white dressing on the back of RPG's head where Temilola had hit him.

"Eh?" RPG replies.

"I said, why are you lying to yourself?" Gladys' tone softens.

"You come for two days now saying you are looking for him, for two days he is not here." She moves closer to him and looks him in the eyes. "What is it that you really want?" Her tone is now soft and tender.

They both stare at each other for about thirty seconds before RPG pulls the towel to reveal Gladys' naked body. Vipaar had fantasised about seeing her naked for a long time. Even in his predicament, he can't help but admire her perfect breasts and curvy contours. He becomes filled with jealous rage when RPG begins to stroke and squeeze her left breast, then the right one. With the volume of testosterone he feels, he reckons he could beat RPG. The only thing that stops him is the thought of Temilola and seeing Gladys placing her hand on RPG's shoulder, gesturing to him with her index finger. RPG suddenly turns Gladys around and bends her over the bed forcefully. Vipaar closes his eyes tightly for about a minute. He opens them to see RPG's hairy butt cheeks. RPG bends his knees and stands on his toes simultaneously, then he begins to gyrate and groan. Fury rages through Vipaar. RPG has taken everything good he had, and now he is taking what he desires most. Closing his eyes could not prevent him hearing the claps and RPG's grunts. He opens his eyes after a couple of torturous minutes and sees the muscles of RPG's cheeks clench up as he lets out a loud groan,

"Awwwwwwwwww, ohhh myyyy Goood."

RPG is out of breath and sounds as though he has used up the last of his energy. He takes a step back and then pulls up his trousers all the while still mumbling,

"Oh Lord, my God, my God, my God," over and over. Vipaar has to dig deep to resist the temptation of jumping out of the closet and knocking the stupid smile off RPG's face. He is sweating profusely as he walks toward the doors like a drunkard, still repeating, "my God, my God." Gladys has put on a robe and follows RPG out of the bedroom door. Vipaar hears bolts on the front door, but does not come out of his hiding place until Gladys returns.

"He has gone," she says as she returns to the bedroom. As Vipaar steps out of the closet, a whole range of emotion consumes him: relief, jealousy, anger, and bitterness being the most prominent. He looks at Gladys, and there is an awkward silence which lasts about a minute. He realises that he is angry at her and grateful to her at the same time. Even as she had likely saved his life, he seems to resent her for what she had done and how she had done it. He sits on the bed and looks at her. She suddenly looked vulnerable.

"Are you alright?" he asks.

"I am fine." Her voice is now devoid of its customary sharpness. "Men, it is all they want. Did you see how I scatter his head, walking out of here like a mumu?" She continues chattering at speed, all the while avoiding Vipaar's eye. She looks everywhere else but at him.

"Thank you."

"For what?" she snaps. "My friend, this is life jare."

The silence returns, and he watches as Gladys picks up a pink bathroom bag and walks towards the door.

"I go baff," she says as she puts on her shower cap. "When I come back, we go talk."

Vippar stands up and puts on his shoes as soon as he hears the front door close. He walks into the living room and towards the front door. He feels like a coward, but he would not be able to handle seeing the disappointment on her face if he told her that Temilola had run away because he wanted to hand him over to the police.

The dark hallway, which would typically be loud with some kind of noise, is eerily quiet. A sense of fear seems to have descended on what he remembered to be a normally lively corridor. His heart begins to pulsate, he feels like a thief in the night as he sneaks through the place which had been his home just over 48 hours ago. His heart does not rest until he is sure he is far enough away from the house. He still feels a little guilty about leaving Gladys' without an explanation, but he is sure that she would understand. He walks through the back streets and flags down an okada.

"YABA," he orders. His mind cannot stop picturing RPG's gyrating buttocks, no matter how much he tried. He feels emasculated, then guilty for being selfish, thinking about himself and not about finding Temilola. He does not realise that the okada has arrived at their destination until the driver turns around to look at him and says, "We don arrive."

Vipaar gets off and pays the driver ₦100. Walking away he hears the call for prayer, which instantly makes him think of Alhaja. He smiles for the first time since she died as he remembers how, despite not wearing a watch or having a clock in the house, she would always know when the time to pray had arrived, almost to the second. Just as the call to prayer ends, he becomes aware of his surroundings and realises that he is standing near the spot he had given his apprentice his first test. He smiles as he remembers how awkward his apprentice had been as he attempted to cross the road. As Vipaar continues to walk around aimlessly, he begins to think about the impact Temilola had on him, and realises the proverbial noose around his neck had loosened since he met him. He begins to wonder why he had saved Temilola. It was a question that had been gnawing at his subconscious, which he had ignored, but now had no choice but to confront it.

"I was seeking redemption." He said the words out loud in an attempt to conquer what had been keeping him prisoner for so long. He realises that what haunted him the most about losing Temilola was that he had lost his last chance for redemption. Despite the less than successful results of the request for help from God earlier, he decides that a 2nd attempt is required.

He looks up at the sky,

"Please God, lead me to them. I am begging you, lead me to them or lead them to me... I know I don't..."

At that very moment, he feels a firm hand grab him by his right arm. His heart begins to pound because he thinks it is RPG. He turns around to see who has seized him. The face looks familiar, but he cannot remember where he has seen it before.

"Do you remember me?" the man asks with gleeful malice. "Where is your Mercedes Benz?"

It is the KAI man that he and Temilola had escaped from a few weeks previously. Vipaar lets out a loud sigh. He does not offer any resistance or denials. He is now entirely broken. He does not have the energy to continue fighting for a life of misery and heartache. His heart stops pounding. He cannot run anymore. He finally gives up and decides to succumb to whatever circumstances fate is going to bestow on him.

CHAPTER 26

A shiver shoots down Aminat's spine when the man in the Range Rover looks at her and asks Temilola "how much" as he licks his lip. She has seen this look before. To him, she is something to play with and then discard. She exhales in relief when Temilola throws the money back in his face. She wants to say "thank you" but she is unable to speak, so she hugs him tightly and only let's go when he begins to wince. She can feel his ribs and realises how much weight he has lost since they met.

As they go to sleep under the hut that night, she realises that the events of the past five days have not only changed Temilola's physical appearance, but his personality too. She can tell by his reactions to some of the events on the beach that he is out of his depth. Although he had tried to make one of his jokes when he regained consciousness after Gadaffi punched him in the face, she could tell he was visibly shaken. He was also very slow to react when the area boys started fighting when they first arrived. She had turned on her heels as soon as she heard the bottle break. She watched him become dejected with each hour that went by, especially when he begged for money or scavenged for food. He smiled less, and though he still spoke in riddles and chuckled, she could see the brightness in his eyes fade with each sunset. She could see him looking downcast when he didn't know she was looking. Upon realising she was watching him, he would smile and attempt to speak in a cheery voice, but she knew that he was terrified. He had also begun to call her Duchess, which she loved.

"Thank you for not sending me to dat man," Aminat whispers just before she falls asleep.

"Not a problem duchess," Temilola's response is monotone. "No problem at all."

Aminat wakes up the next morning when she feels Temilola shaking her gently. He gives a forced smile when she greets him good morning. Her stomach churns and she feels her knees are going to buckle when she hears, "Akaaaaaattttttttaaaaaa" and sees Gadaffi and two other boys stomping towards them.

She is as stunned as Gaddaffi and his two companions when she hears Temilola say "Stay out of my way or I will destroy." The statement is cold and unwavering. He does not flinch as he stares Gadaffi in the eyes. She does not hear most of what Gadaffi says after he stops laughing and she scurries after Temilola as he walks away slowly. She wants to ask him to leave the beach as they eat their agege bread for breakfast, but the scowl etched on his face suggests that it would be a bad idea. He is no longer the soft Bakedbeans who had tried to rescue her just under a week ago.

"Fine boy", Okechukwu calls to Temilola as he shakes his hand a couple of hours after the incident with Gadaffi. "Dee boys say Gadaffi tell you to leave dee beeeesh. Whare you dey go?"

"What makes you think I am going anywhere?" Aminat's shoulders slump in despair. Temilola looks at Okechukwu, smiles and winks. "Trust me, I will see you tomorrow."

"Ehhh…watin you dey talk," Okechukwu shrieks. "My sista, I beg warn you broda o."

Aminat's heart begins to palpitate as Okechukwu continues to plead with Temilola who remains steadfast and continues staring into the ocean. Okechukwu finally gives up after about 10 mins and walks away, shaking his head.

By mid-afternoon, the silence and not knowing what is happening, has become unbearable for Aminat.

"Maybe we can come and leave this place."

"And go where?" Temilola snaps without looking at Aminat, who shudders in shock.

"Errr… I don know… bet what are we going to do when Gadaffi…" She stops talking and her chest tightens when Temilola looks at her with his jaws clenched and frowns deeply.

"Listen. I said. I am," his eyes widen with each word, "not. Going any…"

"TEMILOLA… TEMILOOOOLLLLLAAAA!"

They both look left and Aminat sees a tall, light skinned woman wearing a red dress and black leggings walking towards them. Temilola is also looking at the woman with his mouth gaping wide, and then he lets out a heavy sigh. Aminat feels a hint of jealousy as the woman hugs him.

"Where have you been, eh? What are you doing here? Look at you, you are so thin." Her face and voice are full of dismay. "What happened? When last did you eat?" She asks one question after another, without giving him a chance to respond to any of them. "Is this where you have been sleeping?"

"Gladyyyyy, Gladyyyyy!" A fat man wearing a blue Agbada

sitting at one of the barbeque stands calls and motions for her to come over.

"Darling, one minute I will be there," she turns back to face Temilola and notices Aminat.

"Who is this?"

"Errr…" Temilola lets out a tight smile. "She is my ward."

"Ohhh, there you go again with grammar." Gladys blinks quickly. "Who is she, is my question."

"She's my friend, Aminat," Temilola says softly. "Duchess, this is Aunty Gladys."

"Good afternoon." Aminat bends her knees slightly.

Gladys stares at Aminat, then her eyes widen and her mouth slacks open. "Ohh, Aminat."

Gladys turns to Temilola. "When last did you eat?"

"GLAAAADDDDYYYY!" the fat man shouts again.

"I am coming General," she waves at him. "Oya come eat with me and my friend."

"No thank you, we will be fine."

Aminat looks at Temilola and squints, she feels like throwing a brick in his face.

"You stay hungry with your shakara," Gladys grabs Aminat. "Let us go dear, leave him." Aminat does not resist as she follows Gladys towards the table. She looks back and sees Temilola following them.

"Darling, sorry, this is children that used to live with me." Gladys kisses the man on the lips. "Oya say hello to the General."

"Good afternoon sir," Temilola prostrates and Aminat kneels.

"Hello," the General snorts.

"Sit, sit sit," Gladys instructs them.

Aminat sits down and stares at the General. She wonders how somebody so ugly can be with a woman as pretty as Aunty Gladys. He has humongous lips, a flat nose and bulging eyes. There are two men dressed in full military fatigue, with guns around their waist, sitting at the table a few meters from them.

"Order anything, anything," Gladys instructs them when a waiter comes to take their food order.

"Can I have a bottle of water please." Temilola shifts his bum on the plastic chair.

Gladys exhales in annoyance. "Please bring four plates of jollof rice, two tilapia and four bottles of minerals."

Conversation between the General and Gladyys is limited to, "How are you my sugar" and "I am fine darling".

Aminat can tell that the General is annoyed by their presence as he clenches his jaw and lets out a loud sigh intermittently.

They all sit in silence under the umbrella for about 10 minutes when the General's phone rings. The first three phones he takes out of his pockets are not the ones ringing and he slams them on the table in frustration. He struggles to answer the fourth phone he takes out of his pocket. He pushes his thumb on the glass screen, puts the phone to his ear, says "hello" and groans in frustration when it continues to ring. "Ohhhh…stupeeed phone…aahhh."

Gladys gently takes the phone from him, slides her thumb across and hands it back to him. Aminat scratches her head in disbelief. Not only is he ugly, he is an imbecile.

"Hello, hello," the General shouts into the phone. "Haaay, my friend Boris, how are you… no dee tanker will leave… no no.. don't worry… my boys have sort it… Bori." His face becomes flared in aggravation and he begins to sweat profusely. "Don't... worry... my... eh... eh... your cargo will leave don't worry... don't mess wid my money... you hare me... transfer 10 million into my account or else."

"Is everything alright darling?" Gladys asks. The General ignores her, stands up sharply and stomps toward the sea, followed by the soldiers.

She then turns to face Temilola.

"Why did you run away from Vipaar?" she asks, teary eyed.

"What... where... how..." Temilola's back stiffens as he avoids Gladys's penetrating gaze.

"Errrr... I... I don't know." He slumps and stares at the sand.

"How are you living like this?"

"How is he?" Temilola looks up. "Where did you see him?"

"Don't worry about him." Gladys rubs his shoulders. "Pele... how are you eating? Can you remember anything yet? People are saying you try to..." She pauses when the waiter brings their food over.

"No, I can't remember anything yet," Temilola replies as the waiter opens the soft drinks.

"I saw him some days ago." Gladys exhales and shakes her head.

"He... he is doing ok?"

"Eat, eat," she instructs Aminat, who waits for Temilola's nod of approval before picking up the spoon.

"Is he..." Temilola stops as the waiter puts two whole barbecued fish on the table.

"Is he angry with me?" he continues when the waiter leaves.

"RPG is looking for him." Gladys curls her lips in disgust. "He has come to my apartment three times looking for him. He has even moved into Alhaja's flat."

"Is he angry with me?" Temilola asks again, this time looking directly at Gladys.

"All he said was you have run away... he is..." She takes her handbag from the table and opens it. "Errr... I have his mobile, I will tell him you are here?"

"Noooo!" Temilola shrieks. His eye widen as he lunges to stop Gladys taking the phone out of her handbag. "Don't tell him where I am, please don't tell him."

Aminat cannot understand Temilola's reasoning. By her logic, this is a perfect opportunity to escape the showdown with Gadaffi.

Gladys's mouth is gaping. "But why... What happen between the both you? I am sure you can..." She stops when the General suddenly reappears. His nostrils are flaring and his breathing is noisy. He begins rambling:

"These yeye Russians are messing with my money," he snaps at Gladys. "Oya oya, let us go. I must go Port Harcourt tonight." He picks two phones from the table and puts them in his pocket.

"What happened darling?" Gladys rubs his shoulder.

"Don't worry, my sugar. I just have to sort out some business."

Aminat stops eating and watches the General take out a wad of cash from his pocket as he calls the waiter over.

"Ogebni, how much do I owe?"

"Eight thousand sir."

The General counts out the money and give it to the waiter. Aminat notices Gladys subtlety nodding and rolling her eyes in the direction of Temilola. The General sighs and rolls his eyes then takes a smaller wad of cash out of another pocket, counts out a few notes and gives it to Temilola, who stands up and looks at Gladys before taking it. He prostrates, and says "thank you sir". Aminat kneels in front of the General and also says "thank you sar" as he hands her ₦1,000.

"Oya, oya let's go," the General orders the soldiers as another one of his phones rings. He answers it and begins shouting as he stomps towards the car park, followed by the soldiers.

Gladys takes out a pen and paper from her handbag, scribbles on it and forces it into Temilola's palms. "Call him, I am begging you." Her eyes are welling up with tears. She looks in her handbag, gives ₦2,000 to Temilola, and ₦500 to Aminat.

"Thank you very much," Temilola whispers. "Please don't tell him where I am…" Gladys begins to cry as she strokes his face, then rubs Aminat's chin. "Please look after him, my dear."

"Yes ma." Aminat's heartbeat quickens. "I will try." Gladys wipes the tears from her eyes, then turns and walks at a brisk pace to the waiting jeep.

Aminat looks at the uneaten food on the table. "What are we going to do with the food?" Temilola smiles. "Don't worry Duchess, I have a plan." He turns and calls the waiter over.

"Can I have 10 plastic spoons please?"

"Pardin?" The waiter frowns and flinches.

"I said, can I have 10 plastic spoons please?"

"Are you going to eat all of this?"

"They have been paid for by my friends." Temilola crosses his arms. "As far as I am concerned, what I do with them is none of your concern."

Aminat watches the waiter meekly walk away and returns with 10 spoons a few seconds later. Temilola puts three into each plate. He looks around and invites the boys who have gathered around to rush for the left-over food. "Hey, come on, please join us." Temilola points to the two empty chairs.

Three approach tentatively and sit, but don't begin to eat until Temilola starts. They are joined a couple of minutes later by three other kids. Within a few minutes, the plates were empty and the fish has been expertly cleaned.

"Toosshh knuckle," the first boy to take up the offer to join the feast offers his clenched fist to Temilola, who smiles and bumps his knuckles with the boy. The others follow suit, showing their gratitude either by slapping palms or bumping fists.

"I will see you tomorrow," Temilola says with aplomb and confidence.

Aminat is now looking at a totally different boy from the person she met six days ago.

The same boys who had shunned him since they arrived are now in awe of him.

"With a little bit of luck, a man can rule his circumstance." Temilola looks at Aminat and winks.

"Now that we have some money, we can leave."

"We cannot leave." Temilola chuckles as he leans back and rubs his palms together. "How do you know the next place we go won't be worse than this place? Anyway, the seeds have been planted, the end is near."

"I don't know," she replies, "but if we find your brother…"

"I promised I would look after you, didn't I?" He leans forward and looks her in the eyes. "Providence gave the opportunity to lay the foundations, which will change our circumstances."

Aminat rolls her eyes and lets out a low sigh. She had long given up trying to decipher his cryptic messages.

As dusk falls, Aminat sees Gadaffi walking near the fence she and Temilola are sitting on and her heart begins racing again.

"Wait here," Temilola orders and walks towards Gadaffi.

"Where are you going?" Aminat asks.

"I am just going to talk to him." Temilola gives her a cryptic smile. "Trust me, Duchess."

Aminat watches from a distance as Temilola speaks to Gadaffi with his shoulders drooped and his head bowed. She hopes Temilola has taken heed of her pleas and is apologising to Gadaffi. She then sees Temilola take something out of his pocket and hand it over to Gadaffi. As Gadaffi inspects the object, Aminat's stomach clenches when she realises that it is one of the General's phones. She blinks quickly and her throat becomes dry as she flashes back to the time spent with the General. She recalls that there were three mobile phones on the table when the General walked towards the sea, but he had only picked up two when he returned.

She begins to shake as she watches Gadaffi pat Temilola on the head and laugh as he walks away. She becomes filled with hope when Temilola walks back towards her with a wide grin.

"Will he let us stay?" Aminat's voice is shaking.

"The trap has been set," Temilola responds coolly. "We just need one more move for checkmate."

"You took the General's phone, he will come back…"

"Don't worry about it, Duchess." Temilola sits down and leans against a brick wall, staring into the ocean. "What do we always say?" he says.

"Man rules circumstance..." Aminat begins.

"Circumstances do not rule man." Temilola finishes the sentence as he takes a deep breath.

They sit by the wall and Aminat notices that Temilola keeps on looking towards the car park. Her hands begin to tremble, and she becomes dizzy when she sees the General's jeep enter the car park and one of the soldiers from earlier in the day jump out.

"Wh... what... are we going to do?" she asks Temilola, who stands up slowly and dusts the sand from his clothes. He takes a deep breath. "It's showtime," he says and walks towards the barbeque stand they had eaten at earlier with his head bowed.

"Heeeeeyyyyy... Yoouu... come hare," the Soldier shouts and points at Temilola, who looks up.

"Yes sir?" Temilola responds calmly.

"The General lose his phone, did you see it whare we ware sitting?"

Aminat's legs nearly buckle when she hears Temilola say,

"Yes I had it."

"Oya give it to me," the soldier says with his palm open.

"Well, I had with me, but a boy named Gadaffi took it from me. I told him it belonged to the General, but he said he didn't care." Temilola speaks softly and rubs his chin. "He punched me in my face and took the phone."

Aminat watches dumbfounded. Temilola is changing before her very eyes and she does not know what to make of it.

"Ehhh, what yeye boy go take my Oga's property?" the soldier bellows as the veins on his neck protrude. "Dey don't bon the person yet. Who is this person?"

Temilola looks around and points straight at Gadaffi, who is standing next to a wall holding the phone in his hand. "That's him there, the one wearing the sunglasses."

Aminat feels sorry for Gadaffi, who yelps and begs for mercy as the soldier reigns blows on him and kicks him with precision.

"Ogggga, I beg pleeeease pleeeease," Gadaffi pleads and rubs his palms together as he cowers on the ground. "Kini mo se…what did I do?"

"You wan take my oga property abi?" The soldier intercedes each blow or kick with commentary. "Who born you?"

"Oga… I didn't know… he gave… oga please… I beg…" Gadaffi's pleas for mercy fall on deaf ears as the soldier continues to pummel him.

A crowd has formed to watch the melee, and his friends look on with their mouths gaping. None are brave enough to intervene on his behalf. Within a few minutes, Gadaffi's left eye is swollen and closed and blood is drooling from his mouth profusely.

The soldier picks the phone off the floor and begins dragging Gadaffi by the buckle of his belt toward the car park.

"Shut up, shut up, thief, thief, " the soldier shouts at Gadaffi in between giving him slaps across his face. "Na prison you sleep tonight." He opens the boot of the jeep and throws Gadaffi in like a sack of potatoes.

Aminat is breathing quickly and her head begins to hurt as she tries to understand what has just happened. She looks at Temilola. His face is blank and his chest is puffed out. He has a different aura about him which makes her feel uncomfortable.

He lets out a heavy breath when the Soldier slams the boot shut, and Aminat hears him say, "Checkmate."

Beep beep beep. They both look towards the soldier's jeep, as the blacked-out windows roll down and the soldier motions for Temilola to come.

"Haaay Chaairman, come hare."

"Wait for me, I will be back in a few minutes." Temilola looks at Aminat. "Trust me." She looks on as he walks around the front of the jeep and enters from the passenger side. Minutes feel like hours as Aminat attempts to piece together all the events of the day and how they all interlinked. Her back stiffens when she realises that Temilola had planned it all. She begins to wonder if he is who she thinks he is as he walks back towards her after a few minutes. There is an aura of self-assurance about him. Gone is the scared boy who was petrified at the prospect of sleeping under a bridge a few days ago. This is a different person, steelier and oozing confidence. There is also something else about him, something she cannot explain.

Temilola is walking slowly as he flips a white card in his right hand. He smiles at Aminat when he reaches her, but not in the way he used to, and she squints. He continues walking past the crowd of onlookers who are keeping their distance and speaking in hushed tones. A cold chill runs through Aminat's veins as Temilola stops at the blood-spattered spot where Gadaffi has just been brutally beaten. Silence descends amongst the crowd as he slowly picks up the sunglasses, stares at Gadaffi's friends for a couple of seconds, and then smiles as he puts the glasses on his face. He then turns to Okechukwu who is blinking rapidly with his mouth slacking.

"I told you one of us wouldn't be here tomorrow. I will see you tomorrow."

He looks at Aminat. "Duchess, let's go," he says and begins walking away. Aminat stands rooted to the spot, frozen with fear as she realises what she now sees in him. Temilola is devoid of empathy. He reminds her of Uncle Jaro, Ibrahim, and Mr & Mrs Olapade.

CHAPTER 27

Temilola watches with gleeful satisfaction as the once mighty Gadaffi cries, yelps and pleads for mercy as the soldier pummels him mercilessly. Something dormant in him has come alive. It feels wonderful and intoxicating. Gadaffi was the embodiment of everything that had caused him so much pain since his ordeal began in Oshodi bus garage: his loss of memory, Alhaja's death, RPG chasing them out their home, Vipaar wanting to abandon him after he promised not to, and Gadaffi making his life hell. Each blow and kick that the soldier lands on Gadaffi feels like a major triumph. He revels in watching his nemesis's fall from grace in such a remarkable fashion. What makes the spectacle more scintillating was that he had orchestrated it with military precision. Although he was not the one raining the blows on Gadaffi, he was the orchestrator of his downfall, which made the whole situation even more satisfying. The watching audience looked on in shock, but for Temilola things are going according to plan.

"Oga I beg, please oga…" Gadaffi continues to plead as the soldier drags him towards the jeep. Each plea is met with a punch to the face or a kick to the torso, followed by, "Who born you… I say who born you." Despite the joy of watching Gadaffi's pummeling, the sweetest moment is when their eyes meet, and

Gadaffi's widen—Temilola is certain that is the moment Gadaffi realises he has been outwitted by a superior mind. Temilola cannot help but smirk at the look of bewilderment on the imbecile's face as he attempts to decipher how he had been outwitted by an "akata".

Temilola reflects on the combination of providence, courage, and ingenuity that had led to the execution of the perfect coup d'etat. Gadaffi had been the architect of his own downfall the moment he threatened to throw Aminat into the sea. He should have heeded the warning, but he responded in the only way he knew how, with threats and aggression. Temilola was surprised by his own steely words, "Stay out of my way, or I will destroy you." He was unaware of the methodology he would use, but he was certain of the outcome. Aminat's pleas to leave the beach and Okechukwu's assumption that he would retreat only strengthened his resolve. After all he had been through and survived, there was no way he was going to be defeated by a numskull like Gadaffi. It was his pride which enabled him to inform Okechukwu that he would "see him tomorrow."

He was initially mortified when he saw Aunty Gladys, but he quickly decided it was a sign that God was on his side. It was too much of a coincidence that of all the beaches in Lagos, she came to the one where he was located. He hated the look of pity she wore as she looked at him and wanted to smack the look of disdain, with which the so-called General looked at him, off his face. A fat oaf so ugly had no right to look at anybody with such disgust. Gladys hadn't given him a straight answer when he asked about Vipaar. A combination of pride, guilt and shame prompted his desperate pleas to keep his location secret. He wanted to prove to himself that he was a survivor. He had watched in utter disbelief and wondered how a man who struggled with the simple task of answering a mobile phone made it to the rank of General. Temilola would have seriously doubted his credentials if it had not been for the two trained killers in uniform who had accompanied him. His mind began to race and ponder how to turn the General's presence to his advantage. Within a split second, he had considered all his options, and played out a number of scenarios like a game of chess. He weighed the risks involved and the opportunities that could be gained—then he calmly took one of the phones off the table and placed it in his pocket.

He was the personification of serenity when the General returned to the table in a state of flux. He was in such a state, rambling incoherently about Port Harcourt and Russians messing with his money, he didn't notice the missing phone just as Temilola had expected. The money he gave them was an unexpected bonus, and he was loath to prostrate when he accepted the money from the General, but he knew he would be foolish to act otherwise. Aminat was a little slow, but she took the hint and she quickly kneeled and accepted the money he handed to her. The good General was soon on his way, shouting for Gladys to follow him quickly as she forced a piece of paper in his left hand and pleaded for him to call Vipaar. He nearly wavered as she stroked his face with tears in her eyes; it was a reminder of how good things were before Alhaja's death. He knew he sounded ungrateful when his response to her emotional and monitory generosity was "Don't tell him where I am... please." But for his plan to be a success he had to be staunch with his emotions. He was saddened as Gladys walked away, a feeling he had to dismiss quickly. He had successfully laid claim to the uneaten food without raising his voice, which was a perfect segway in implementing stage 2—winning hearts and minds. The beach boys were a little trepid when he invited them to sit down, but within a few minutes the only thing left on the plate were fish bones. He responded to their look of confusion when he said, "I will see you tomorrow," with a sly smile. He knew that if everything went according to plan, this would be a defining moment.

"Good afternoon sir," Temilola greeted Gadaffi in the most conciliatory manner he could muster.

"You are still here eh?" Gadaffi said with his usual abrasive tone. "You are brave o." Temilola looked down at the floor and said, "I am sorry for disrespecting you sir." He took the General's phone out of his pocket and offered it to him. "Please don't send us away," he said in a monotone voice without looking up. The big lummox took the phone without hesitation, and patted him on the head. "Go and get me a bottle of mineral," he commanded.

As he walked away, Temilola almost felt sorry for his nemesis. His total lack of intellectual prowess was not his fault, but he had sealed his own fate with the condescending pat on the head. Temilola could not help but marvel at his own ingenuity when he saw the soldier approaching him and then asking for the phone. His conscience was clear when he told him that Gadaffi had taken the phone. Temilola watched with bated breath as the soldier charged towards Gadaffi, who was blissfully ignorant that he was in imminent danger. The punch that landed squarely on Gadaffi's jaw was poetic justice, and the swift but surgically efficient dismantling of his nemesis in front of his peers was ecstatically satisfying. In order to remove any doubt about who was responsible for his downfall, Temilola smiled widely enough for Gadaffi to see through his one partially swollen eye. The 'mighty' Gaddaffi continued screaming like a scared little child as he was picked up and thrown into the back of the black jeep like a child would a doll. Temilola felt a minutia of pity for him, not because of the battering he had received or even his pleas for mercy, but for the fact that his circumstance had put him in the crosshairs of a far superior intellectual mind and now he was now paying the price. He had been given fair warning, but his hubris has led him to his particular circumstance for which Temilola had no pity.

He suddenly realises what has come alive in him: he has unshackled himself from the chains of a "hope of a better tomorrow", which unleashed something more powerful than anger—hate. He has finally given in to the dark side, and it feels glorious. He feels the power course through him like a lightning bolt from his hair follicles to the tip of his toenails. As the soldier enters the car, Temilola looks at Aminat. He has been so invested in the outcome of a master plan that he has totally forgotten about her.

"I told you I would look after you, didn't I Duchess?" Temilola had seen the look she had on her face before, but he cannot remember where. He squints and his head shakes slightly as he wonders why she looks that way.

"What is the matter?" She continues to stare at him blankly. "Duchess, are you…"

"Beeeeeeeeeeeeepp." He turns around and sees the soldier pressing the car horn and gesturing for him to come over to the jeep. "Hey Chaairman, come hare."

Temilola is caught off-guard by the unexpected invitation, but he walks towards the jeep and enters through the passenger side. The air conditioning and soft leather feels like heaven compared to his current accommodation on the beach. He smiles at the soldier and hears Gadaffi's whimpering from the boot.

"Chairman," the soldier begins, "you save my Oga o. If the EFFC seeze this phone, na serious problems for me and my oga o. He order me not to return widout dee phone, he even point gun at me."

Temilola squints as he struggles to understand most of what he is saying, but he nods and smiles.

"I am thinking I must bring my boys from dee baraks to come and destroy dis whole place."

He reaches under the seat and pulls out a thick rectangular brown envelope, which looks like it contains books. Temilola eyes widens when the soldier pulls out two wads of green cash and hands it to him. "Take, go and enjoy yourself."

Temilola's muscles become stiff and he gulps hard, as he struggles to control his giddiness when he realises he is holding dollars in his hands.

"Thannn… thaaaannk… thannnk… you," he stammers as his hands begin to shake.

"Shaaaraap your mouth, if you make me come back dare," the soldier shouts at Gadaffi who is still pleading from the boot. "You thief, I will soon deal with you."

"Where are you taking him?" Temilola asks, his voice breaking.

"This mumu mess up my day. I must now drive to Portachourt instead of plane.'

The soldier ignores Temilola's question and starts the car engine by pushing a button by the gearbox. Temilola takes this as his cue to leave, "Thank you sir, very much appreciated." He opens the door and steps back out into the baking heat. He begins to walk back towards where Aminat is standing when the jeep drives away. He knows all eyes are on him, the only way he can look or feel any more invincible would be if he were to survive a direct lightning strike. Getting rid of his nemesis is insufficient, he needs a final act to show that he is a formidable force and to plant the seed of "fear" into anyone foolish enough to consider taking revenge. His decision to take the General's phone had been spontaneous but picking up Gadaffi's sunglasses from the bloodsoaked ground is a calculated move.

"To the victor belongs the spoils of war," he smiles with satisfaction as he puts on the sunglasses. Temilola looks directly at Okechukwu. "I told you one of us wouldn't be here tomorrow." He gives a cocky smile and winks, "I will see you tomorrow." He then looks at Aminat, "Duchess, let's go."

It immediately becomes clear where he has seen the look on her face before. It was during the incident with the man with the white Range Rover. The possibility of her being scared of him halts his ascension dead in its tracks, he has to motion for her to follow him when he walks away, which she does reluctantly. They walk in silence until they reach their accommodation. He tries to engage her in conversation as night falls but she is frosty towards him. They eat their dinner in silence, and Temilola does all he can to avoid her eyes. It isn't until they are preparing to go to sleep that she asks, "What is going to happin to him?"

"Who?" Temilola responds, knowing full well whom she means.

"That boy, Gadaffi."

"I don't know, and I don't care." Temilola shrugs his shoulders. "I warned him he should have listened to me and left us alone."

Even from the single flame from the candle, he can see the look of disappointment that is etched on her face. That look and silence pricks his conscience, and he is forced to give her question some consideration. With each minute that passes, the sense of euphoria from his victory recedes, and doubts begin to creep into his mind.

"I had no choice, you know that Aminat. I had no choice, it was either him or us." His tone betrays his need for absolution from her. He continues after a minute or so which feels like an hour, "He threatened to throw you into the sea." Aminat's continued silence is deafening, which forces him to take a firmer tone. "Listen, I promised to protect you, and I was not about to break my promise like Vipaar. I had to do what I had to do." With $2000 in his pocket, Temilola had expected to sleep that night with his mind at rest, but instead anger boils inside him. "It was his bloody fault, why didn't he just didn't leave us alone? First RPG chased us out of our home, now this bully wanted to chase us away again." He is exhausted and angry. "If Vipaar had not wanted to abandon us, we wouldn't be here. Why did she have to die?" He begins to cry softly. "Why did she have to die?" he repeats quietly as he drifts off to sleep, listening to the waves hitting the shore. The question that weighs most on his mind is whether his actions were a true reflection of who he really is or who he has become.

He wakes up the next morning without the usual feelings of fear and apprehension that had accompanied his mornings, which would be followed by hunger pains. The first thing he does, like he did every morning, is confirm Aminat is still next to him. He then reaches into his trousers pocket to confirm the wads of cash are still there and the events of the previous day were not a dream. Although he has woken up without his usual ailments, his heart feels heavy and not at peace. As he crawls out from under the hut, he sees the bag, which had been stolen on their first night, on the beach resting against the hut. He smiles; it is the first of what he expects to be a result of his meticulously executed actions. He thinks about the next steps all morning. He knows that his newfound reverence will wither away without further action. He treats himself and Aminat to a proper public shower, and they eat a proper breakfast of three loaves of bread and a freshly cooked egg each. He feels all eyes are on him, and some of the beach kids are whispering amongst themselves. A couple even change direction when they see him coming. He flushes with pride. He is confident he will now be able to keep Aminat safe. She is still tense as they eat their breakfast, and he says to her, "Don't worry, you are safe now."

"Thank you," she responds with an awkward smile.

"After we have set up our business, I will call Vipaar," Temilola says as he takes the piece of paper Sister Gladys had given him out of his pocket. "I will tell him where we are, and we will be together again, I promise."

He is hoping for a smile from Aminat, but she merely stares at him without blinking as she drinks her hot Milo (hot chocolate). His heart feels heavy with sorrow when he realises that she has lost the brightness in her eyes. He meets up with Okechukwu a couple of hours later with an objective of putting the next stage of his plan into action but the first question he asks is, "What will happen to Gaddaffi?"

"Em, I think he will spend some time in military prison."

Temilola can tell that he is holding something back but he shrugs his shoulders. "Oh well, I gave him fair warning." He takes out a notebook he had bought earlier that morning and asks: "What are they saying about me?"

"Ermm… well…" Okechukwu begins.

"Be truthful," Temilola's voice is firm.

Okechukwu straightens his back and swallows—his usual swagger is absent.

"People… erm… dey is very scare."

"Why?" Temilola begins writing in the notepad without looking at Okechukwu.

"Because you use dee military to come and take Gadaffi," Okechukwu continues as he fiddles with his fingers, "some is saying you have powerful military connection, some is saying you is using juju, some is saying that you are de… de…" He pauses and looks up at Temilola, who looks up from his notepad and smiles. "Carry on."

Okechukwu scratches his head. "Some is saying you is the devil."

"Oh wow." Temilola raises his eyebrow.

"Some are happy Gadaffi is gone, but dey are more scare of you dan him."

"Interesting, interesting." Temilola turns down his lips and nods as he writes in the notebook. "What do you think?"

The question seems to catch Okechukwu off guard as his head

jerks backwards. He pauses for a few seconds then slaps his palms together. "Well you are now my chairman, and my Oga at dee top. I will assist you in any way I can."

"Good, I am glad to hear it. Now let's get down to business." Temilola puts the notebook down. "As a long-term resident of this heavenly resort, I need your insight into how things work here. I have a few ideas based on what I have observed since I arrived here, but I need an advisor or a conduit if you please to help me navigate the proverbial…" he stops talking when he notices Okechukwu is blinking rapidly and keeps on scratching his ears. "You don't understand what I am saying do you?"

"Not everythin," Okechukwu responds almost apologetically.

"Ok, let me start again." Temilola takes a deep breath. "The General has lent me some money to invest in a barbeque stand here on the beach. I want you to be my right-hand man."

"En hen," a wide grin appears across Okechukwu's face.

"I need you to tell me what I need to do if I want to set up our own barbeque stand. Who are the main players, what do we need to buy…"

"Ohh, I see, bros it's not ez o. I use to work on barbeque stand at Elegushi beesh, it iz serious work o." Okechukwu shakes his head. "Dare is a system o: first you must have parmision from dee area chairman, pay some small monies for a parmit and rent every day, den you must drop somethin for dee area boys or they bun down your shop…"

"Ok wow, you are a ray of sunshine aren't you," Temilola quipps as he writes frantically in his notebook.

"Thank you very much," Okechukwu smiles in delight and

continues, "as I was saying, dare is serious competition o. I don know if you will be able to handle it o bros."

"I live by one moto," Temilola starts slowly and pauses for emphasis. "Man rules circumstances, circumstances does not rule man."

Okechukwu frowns and licks his lips, "It is well, anyway I have dis one aunty in Asegere Fish market in Makoko who will give us good price for dee fish. You must hire some of dee boys to work for you, you must buy a small generator, you have to rent a chair and table for the area chairman... Me, I cook o. My speciality is abacha ..."

Temilola continues to write quickly in his notebook, and has to stop Okechukwu multiple times to ask for explanations about things he was describing such as abacha, which is also called African salad. They speak for approximately two hours, with Temillola spending the last hour or so focusing on the approximate cost of setting up his new venture. He hands Okechukwu $600 to change to local currency, then he looks him in the eyes. "I like you, but know this, mistakes I forgive, but disloyalty I am ruthless."

The Kuramo Beach Boyz BBQ stand was up and running within two days. Temilola's innovations, and the menu developed by his lieutenant Okechukwu, soon makes it one of the more popular joints on the beach. Okechukwu is aghast when Temilola first reveals his business model and warns him against it, but he is soon in awe. On their opening night, The Kuramo VIPs consisting of the area Chairman, the leaders of the area boys, and a few pimps who are invited to eat and drink for free.

They buy a small generator nicknamed, "I better pass my

neighbor", multiple phone chargers and two crude but colorful signs that say, "Charge your phone for FREE while you eat." Temilola instructs Okechukwu to meet discreetly with a few of the key prostitutes who are called runs girls, to offer them a business opportunity. Those who bring their clients to "their joint" would receive a 10% commission of what their client spent. The offer came with one strict condition—no fighting.

Temilola and Okechukwu had to rent additional chairs and tables within two days of opening, to accommodate the increase in their clientele. Despite the success of the business, Temilola felt that his greatest accomplishment was with the beach boys. In a short period of time, he had won their loyalty and dedication. He hires eight of them, and after some initial challenges with communication, they become fully invested in the business. Most of them had names such as Banker, Engineer, Doctor, and after getting to know them better, he understands these are reflections of their aspirations. His spine shivers every time they share stories about how they were beaten by their parents and thrown out of the house. Engineer lost his mum's ₦500 change, and he couldn't face going back home. Their experiences put his issues into perspective. He ended each interview by saying, "Make a mistake I will forgive you, steal from me I will be ruthless." Two interviewees subsequently didn't take up the job offer. "Man rules circumstance, circumstances does not rule man," became their mantra, which they chanted each morning before work. Although none of them understood the moral of the story about the Chief and the swimming pool full of crocodiles, they took the mantra on board with vigour. Temilola made them feel valued and appreciated, and they loved him for it.

Temilola and Aminat's standard of living improved significantly, and her smile returned. He bought her a colouring book and a number of children's books. Her eyes nearly welled up with tears when she received Cinderella, which she did not let out of her sight when she was not working at the barbeque stand. For someone so small, with such a short frame, she was strong, hardworking and tenacious. She was responsible for collecting payment, and Temilola quickly discovered that she had a prodigious mathematical brain and photographic memory. She was able to calculate change in mere seconds, and kept an accurate record of income and expenditures. Her intervention and detailed record keeping saved them from being bamboozled by a couple of unscrupulous runs girls named Patricia and Sunshine. They had tried to claim their 10% for bringing two clients to the barbeque stand. Temilola was about to pay them when Aminat opened her notebook and calmly pointed out the two men had arrived and ordered their food and drinks twenty minutes before they arrived. Patricia and Sunshine had merely joined the men at the table, and so were not eligible for the commissions. They left sheepishly and did not return.

Temilola thought deeply about Vipaar during the few moments of solitude he can afford. He would stare at the piece of paper with his telephone number on it for minutes at a time, contemplating whether to call him. He told himself each morning, "today will be the day I will call him," but he would go to sleep every night clenching the piece of paper in his hand. Anger turned to guilt, which began to weigh more heavily on him with each day that passes. He also had nightmares about what he had done to RPG and the possibility of him finding out where he was, or worse if he had found Vipaar. The only thing that brought him solace from his guilt and nightmares is that he had begun to teach Aminat, who was a quick and tenacious learner, how to read. One Sunday evening, during one of their reading sessions, he notices that she is not listening to him. She is staring at something or someone behind him with her mouth gaping, which has caused her to go ashen face. Before he turns around, he knows that whatever or whoever she is looking at is going to have a major impact on their lives moving forward.

CHAPTER 28

As soon as the KAI agent, whom his subordinates called "Oga Festus", grabs him, Vipaar's normal instincts to flight or fight remain docile. He does not say a word or put up any resistance as they lead him into the back of a black pick-up truck which is already full of more young men and an okada motorcycle. As he steps into the back of the truck, he hears Oga Festus say with some glee,

"God has delivered you into my hands." He keeps on looking around the surrounding area, "I have been praying to find you ever since that day. God will soon deliver that small devil into my hands. You and that boy use juju on me."

Vipaar finally accepts that his destiny is not in his hands when he hears the click of the padlock as the agent locks the steel doors of the truck. The "click" represents the final nail in the coffin of his brief flirtation with the concepts of faith and hope. Both have been heavy burdens to carry, and he feels some relief at being able to let them go. Sitting in the back of the truck, he lets out a loud sigh as he finally accepts that people like him are destined to live a life of constant sorrow. He had foreseen this outcome when Alhaja asked him to look after Temilola. His greatest fear is now manifesting—he has failed and lost another person in his life.

Upon arrival at the police station, Vipaar and his fellow captives are stripped to their underwear. The police officers and KAI agents call those without underwear animals.

"Oga I beg, I don do anyteen, I jus cross dee road."

"Who say you can talk?" A policeman hits the prisoner who attempted to plead his case with the butt of his gun. "Stupeed boy," he sneers and then begins shooting in the air. The boy defecates on himself and all the other prisoners cower in fear, but Vipaar does not flinch. He merely stares blankly ahead. The policeman who had fired the gun in the air notices Vipaar's stoic stance and stumbles towards him.

"U no dey fear?" he asks, with his face inches from Vipaar's face. The powerful smell of alcohol is not enough to mask the bad breath, which causes Vipaar to blink rapidly and recoil.

"Be careful with dat one o, my broda," Oga Festus shouts from across the compound. "Him and one devil boy used juju on me some time ago. I had catch dis one, when his friend come an jazz me. Dat is how dey escape."

The policeman begins to laugh and stares directly into Vipaar's eyes. He inches forwards until his forehead touches Vipaar's. They stare at each for about thirty seconds before the policeman blinks, drops his shoulders, smiles and steps back. "Dis one is serious." This is when Vipaar sees a man being dragged out of the back of the truck, bloodied and unconscious.

"Turn this way, put one hand on the back of your head, hold the pant of the one in front of you and march forward." The prisoners do as instructed and begin to march forward. They sit on the floor in a grungy room which one of the policemen refers to as the custody suite. Some of the prisoners begin to pray under their breath, but most look sullen, as if they have accepted their fate. Vipaar pities those who are praying and wants to tell them that they are wasting their time, God does not care about people like them. Each one of the prisoners is called to the desk and asked questions.

"Do you have money for bail?" the policeman behind the desk asks each prisoner. Most of them say "no". Hard slaps and kicks are meted out to those who dare to plead for mercy or protest their innocence.

"What is your name?" They write the name in a notebook and then the prisoners are told to sit back down. Vipaar sees one prisoner put his hand into the back of his shorts and pull out what looks like a clear plastic bag. He knows instantly that the plastic bag contains money. That was one of the first lessons RPG taught him when he began his street hawking, hide money in between the butt cheeks—he called it insurance. The man takes money out of the bag and places it on the table.

"Is dat all you have?" the policeman behind the desk snorts with contempt as he takes the money from the table. "Five thousan?"

"Yes sar," the man clasps his hand together and lowers his head. "Sorry sar, business is no good today sar, that is all I have sar."

The policeman looks at the man with his nose flaring. "Psht, you can go." He waves him away and then puts the money in the pocket of his shirt. "If I see you hare again, I will deal with you."

"Yes sir," he says and with that the man is out of the door.

"You, come hare." Vipaar knows that he is next but he does not jump up as the others had done. "Hey, are you deaf? I said come hare."

Vipaar stands up slowly and strolls to the desk.

"What is your name?"

"Daniel Samson."

"Do you have money for bail?"

"Haaay, haaay, no bail for dis one." Oga Festus steps forward, wagging his index finger at Vipaar. "He is very dangerous. He and his friend jazz me some time ago."

The policeman looks at Oga Festus and then back at Vipaar.

"Do you have somebody who can bring you food?"

"Nobody."

"Do you have money to buy food?"

"No."

"Ok, go and sit down."

"Where is my bag?"

"Are you stupid?"

Vipaar stumbles backwards and stares at Oga Festus who has slapped him and is now looking at him, his face venomous with hatred. Vipaar narrows his eyes. His nostrils are flaring, and his right fist is clenched. He can feel his muscles and veins straining against his skin. He knows that this would be an opportune moment to end his nightmare. He is about to lunge forward when Temilola's words begin ringing in his head. "You are a coward." He knows that if he lunged at Oga Festus, Temilola would have been right about him. Acting on his desire would have been an act of cowardice. He imagines the feeling of euphoria that would course through his veins from knocking Oga Festus out cold before his body is riddled with bullets. Vipaar looks straight into Oga Festus's eyes and he can see in them the burning desire for revenge. He smirks slightly, unclenches his fist and returns to his spot on the floor. His pride will not allow him to give this fat oaf the satisfaction of taking his life. He has survived too many events; too many people had made too many sacrifices only for him to be killed and disposed of like a cockroach.

"Stupid bastard," Oga Festus exclaims. The bitterness in his voice is sweet music to Vipaar's ears.

The prisoners are ordered to stand up and walk through a rusty metal gate. Vipaar is the last in the line and as he hears the gate slam shut behind him, he suddenly feels light headed. He has finally unshackled himself from the burden that came from having faith and hope—they have no place in hell. The first cell the prisoners walk past only has two people in it, one man was standing with his hands through the bars, assessing the new arrivals while the other lay on a mattress on the floor. The further they walked, the darker it became and the more pungent the smell. The line stopped. He heard clink of keys turning in a lock, the creaking of a rusty door opening and the prison guard shouting,

"Oya make space, make space."

There are load groans coming from the cell which is promptly quelled by, "If I come in there, all of you go suffer tonight."

The line shuffles forward at a snail's pace. When Vipaar reaches the cell, it is full to capacity with semi naked bodies. It is obvious that the cell was built for two, four people at the max; it had a capacity to squeeze in about six or seven bodies uncomfortably, but there are currently approximately 14 to 16 bodies in the cell. He is about to defy the laws of physics by entering the cell when the policeman stops him.

"You are not staying here, you are going somewhare else."

Vipaar looks on as the policeman pushes and struggles to close the cell door. "Squeeze in more, squeeze in more," he shouts until he manages to lock the door. Based on his recent experiences, Vipaar knows that a worse fate awaits him. He follows the policeman into a courtyard. They stop by a wooden box, which is approximately two feet high and narrow.

"Oya enter," the skinny policeman wearing an oversized uniformed orders. "Oga Festus has said you are a dangerous parsin."

Vipaar begins to shiver and he feels a tingling in his chest. He takes a deep breath, gets on his hands and knees, and crawls in the wooden box. It has a stench that has become all too familiar: death, sweat, urine and human excrement. He feels a sharp pain on the top of his head. In the dark, he feels the roof and sides of the box with his palm and realises that multiple nails have been inserted into the box. It is impossible for him to stand or sit upright without being pricked by the nails. His only option is to sit with his back arched, with his knees pulled to chest and his arms wrapped around them. His back begins to ache within two hours and he feels the muscles in his thighs tightening by the minute. The box was designed to make sleep impossible because the slightest movement results in his being punctured by the sharp nails that protruded inside the box. This is extremely painful and at one point he wishes he had swallowed his pride and punched Oga Festus in the face while in the custody suite. He survives the first night in the box the same way he survived the first few nights when he first arrived Lagos, he closes his eyes but keeps all his other senses on full alert. By day three, his body has become accustomed to the confined space and he is able to stay still for hours on end.

Through the gaps of the wooden box, Vipaar sees prisoners being put into similar wooden boxes in the compound. Some begin screaming and desperately pleading to be let out of the box within a couple of hours, while others last a couple of days. He also sees two lifeless bodies being pulled out of the box by some other prisoners and carried away. Vipaar lapses into a state of stoicism. For six days, he does not say a word or show any sort of emotions. Minutes begin to feel like seconds, and hours like minutes. He does not feel anger, hurt, guilt, sadness, or pain of any sort. His mind is blank. He does not experience any thoughts or have any inner monologues.

"Oya Cummut." Vipaar does not realise the door of the box has been opened until the policeman pokes him with a baton. "I say cummut, before I slap your face."

Vipaar crawls out slowly. His body is riddled with mosquito bites and puncture wounds. He winces as pain shoots through his back and legs as he stands up straight.

"Oya go." The police uses his baton to point in the direction he wants him to walk. Vipaar's leg muscles, which had been his greatest asset as a street hawker, are now weak and unable to sustain his weight as he falls to the ground four times before reaching the building the two policemen escorting him call, "the tiethaare".

Vipaar takes a deep breath before entering the room. He does not know or care what is behind the blue door with eroding paint. There are two uniformed policemen and another man wearing a white shirt and black trousers in the room, talking amongst themselves. Small patches of the wall suggest that the initial colour of the room was yellow, but is now mostly covered by dark mould and blood splatters. Vipaar knows he is in the "integration room" when he sees the bucket, metal rods, pliers, sticks, wires, a car battery, a machete, and whips displayed all over the table and hanging on the wall. Every street hawker knew about the "theatre". It was the one thing they all feared the most. Vipaar knows what is about to happen to him, but he does feel or show any sort of emotion.

Vipaar and policemen stare at the three men who have not acknowledged their entrance. The man in the white shirt sitting on the chair stops talking mid sentence and looks in Vipaar's direction. His eyes narrow and then he screams,

"WHY ARE YOU STANDING? DO I HAVE TO DO YOUR JOB FOR YOU, OLODO, STUPID!" Vipaar knows that this is the OCT (Officer in Charge of Torture). The two policemen who brought Vipaar flinch.

"Sorry sar." One of them picks up a rope from the floor and ties Vipaar's hands together tightly, telling him to stand on a stool which is then used to hang him to the ceiling using a ceiling fan hook. His shoulder joints begin to hurt and the rope burns his wrists as he dangles from the ceiling.

"Is dis dee one dat use juju on Oga Festus?" the OCT asks.

"Yes sar, he is dee one."

"Oya, Officer Adebisi, get to work," the OCT orders one of the shorter men he is talking to. "Do dis one slowly."

Officer Adebisi yawns and stretches before strolling towards the table in the middle of the room. He spends about a minute inspecting the instruments on the table, and then selects a pankere (bamboo cane).

Officer Adebisi dips the pankere in a basin of water for about thirty seconds and then walks towards Vipaar. His body instinctively becomes still and he feels a sudden giddiness flow through him as his heart begins racing. He lets out a wry smile of relief. It feels good to know that he still has the ability to feel something.

"Whare is dee boy Oga Festus is looking for?" the OCT asks from behind the desk.

Whaaaaapppp, Whaaaaap. Vipaar hears the sound of the cane hitting the back of his legs before his brain registers the pain. His legs feel like a thousand bees have stung them at the same time. He tightens his eyes and remains silent.

"Whare does he live?" *Whaaaaap, whaaaaaaapppp, whaaaaaaap.*

Vipaar's whole body begins to shake as he dangles a few meters from the ground. He clenches his jaw and closes his eyes even tighter. He pictures his beloved Alhaja, and his brothers and sisters and a single tear rolls down his cheek.

He arches his back in pain and clenches his jaw when he feels the sting of the cane on his back. The moment he is about to scream out in pain, he pictures his mother's smiling face and takes a deep breath instead. He can smell his own blood, and as he becomes light headed he takes shallow breaths. He opens his eyes slightly and sees the OCT staring at him.

"Just tell us where dee boy is, and you can go. No wahala." Vipaar fully opens his eyes, stares at the OCT and whispers, "Man... rule circumstance...cir... circumstance... does not ...rule...man."

The OCT frowns in annoyance and steps back. "You—bring that battery here."

"Muuummmmmmmy! Aggghhhhhhh, Muuuuuummmmmmy!" Vipaar screams and sobs uncontrollably as the volts of electricity pass through his body. His whole body is on fire and he longs for death as an act of mercy.

"Pleeeeaaasssssse, pleeeeeeaaasssse, stop… pleeeease." He urinates and defecates simultaneously. Breathing becomes excruciatingly painful as his lungs feel like they are being cooked from the inside.

Vipaar hears laughter and then, "Oya shock him again."

His eyes widen and his lips begins to tremble. "Pppp…pleaase no no, no, pl… …Agggggghhhhhhhhhh!" The voltage starts at the bottom of his feet and reach the tips of his fingers within milliseconds as his body jolts violently.

"What did you say?" The officer Adebisi puts his ear to Vipaar's lips, and begins laughing. "Ejuku won't save you now."

With the last remnants of his energy, Vipaar looks up at the blackened ceiling and mumbles.

"Alhaja, please forgive me. God, please watch over him, please." His head drops and he loses consciousness.

He wakes up with a sudden jolt when he feels cold water on his face. His heart sinks when he realises that he is not dead but lying on the concrete floor of the 'theatre'.

"You are not dead yet," the OCT scoffs. "Oya, put him back up."

He hears a commotion outside as he is being pulled up. The door of the theatre opens and two policemen enter, dragging a body.

"Oga we have a special one for you."

"What is this one?" the OCT asks.

"One soldier bring dis one in just now, he say dis steal dee phone of one Military General."

"Ehhhhhh, a whole military General ole."

"No, no no no I didn't steal the phone." The boy is on his knees shaking and bloody. "One boy gave it to me...pleeaa..."

"Shut up." This order is followed up by a punch to the face. "Leave that one and put this one there."

The policemen holding Vipaar drops him like he is a carcass. Vipaar lays still on the floor, his mind and body are finally broken— he prays that they will end his life quickly. In his semi-conscious state, and in between the screams, he hears fragments of the boy's interrogation.

"Confess, ... you are a thief... ole."

"No, no... a small...gave... it..."

"You stole the phone of a General."

"What is your name gan sef?"

The boy is blubbering and crying. "My name is Samson Ibrahim, and people sometime call me Gadaffi."

"Gadaffi, sebi you know a General is higher than a Conel?" The room filled with laughter. "So Conel Gadaffi, who give you dee phone?"

"It is one Akata boy, he say his name is Temilola, he arrive in Kuramo beesh about one week ago, with his sister... He give me dee phone sar..."

Vipaar's eyes flicker open and his heart begins to palpitate. He takes a deep breath and lifts his head to look at the boy properly.

"One akaata boy gave you a phone?" The OCT kisses his teeth. "Do you think I am an ozwar, boy? Oya take him outside."

The boy pleads and claws on the concrete floor with his finger-nails as they drag him by his feet out of the room. The OCT lights a cigarette and begins talking about the girls he had sex with that morning. The screaming gets further and further away, and then Vipaar hears,

Pop pop pop. The screaming stops, then a few seconds later he hears, "REST IN PIECES."

"What shall we do with this one?" one of the policemen asks, as he stands over Vipaar.

The OCT looks at Vipaar like an afterthought. "I am tired, go and put him in dee cell, he will soon waste."

"Temilola," Vipaar whispers when he regains consciousness in total darkness. His breathing is slow and shallow. He is sweaty and every single part of his body is in searing pain. He takes three long breaths as he tries to slow down his heart rate and gather his thoughts. He knows he is in a prison cell based on the snoring around him and the warm bodies tightly pressed in front and behind him which make it impossible to rotate. His heart begins to beat heavily when he recalls what the boy had said in the theatre about an akata boy and Kuramo beach. He desperately wants to believe that it is his mind playing tricks on him. He lets out a loud sigh when he realises that hope has returned because he is unable to get those two words out of his mind. He is hungry, thirsty, and each breath is laboured. He prays that God will end his miserable existence once and for all. His desire for death after Alhaja passed was borne out of fear; he now wishes for death as an act of mercy. Death is the master of time. It strikes whom it wishes in its own time. It taunts him with each passing minute, so close yet so far. His body is ready to go, but his mind continues to cling on to life for some inexplicable reason. The same words and image keep looping through his mind, "Akata, Temilola, Kuramo beach."

Vipaar stirs and wakes up when he feels someone kick the soles of his feet.

"Eh, this one no waste yet. This one is strong o." He opens his eyes slightly and sees a silhouette standing over him.

"Oya get up, get up," the gruff, angry voice orders and kicks the soles of Vipaar feet again. "Di de, abi you wan me to put you in the waste?"

Vipaar has given up the will to live, but against his conscious will, he stands up and limps out of the cell. He stands against the wall with other prisoners as instructed and looks on jealously as three dead bodies are pulled out of the cell—they are free.

Despite Vipaar's attempts to purge the words, "Akata, Kuramo and Temilola" from his mind, they persist. He shares a cell with six others. Most were motor boys, street hawkers or had been arrested for petty theft. In his vulnerable state, Vipaar does all he can to avoid bringing attention to himself. He does not talk to any of the other prisoners and they eventually believe that he is a mute. He spends most of his time during the day in his cell and only ventures out to empty the bucket they all use to shit in their cell. Time becomes irrelevant in prison and he loses count of how long he has been in there. Every few days, he would hear screams coming from the courtyard followed by shrieks and pleas for mercy and then the inevitable *poh, poh, poh,* "Rest in pieces."

He wakes up one morning and sees one of his new cellmates who had arrived two days earlier hanging from the bars of the cell doors. He considers taking a similar action every day but he would always see his Alhaja's face, and hear the words she said to him on their last night together. A couple of hours later, he and one of his cellmate prisoners carry the body to a waiting minibus in the middle of the compound. On the way back, he thinks he sees the back of a man who looks remarkably like RPG enter one of the buildings that surround the compound. The sight is fleeting and all he sees is a baldhead. He does not give it any further thought, and he hurries back into his cell to escape the heat.

Three days later, a police officer stands in front of Vipaar's cell door and looks at all the prisoners before pointing to him.

"You, come hare," he barks as he opens the door. "You are wanted."

Vipaar takes a deep breath, stands up, and steps over sleeping bodies laying on the floor as he exits the cell. His blood runs cold and he begins to tremble. He believes he is being taken either back to the theatre, or the compound. Either way, he knows that he is not coming back. In his final moments, he thinks about his mother, Ejuku, and his beloved Alhaja. He is about to join them. He hopes that what he thinks the Gadaffi boy said in the theatre was not his mind playing tricks on him, and that Temilola is alive on Kuramo beach. He turns left towards the courtyard but the guard stops him.

"No no, go this way. You are going to dee custody suite."

Vipaar walks into the custody suite and goes to the desk when the officer calls him over.

"So you did not die." He stares at Vipaar and scowls. "You can go, someone has paid your bail."

Vipaar goes weak in the knees and becomes light headed. He squints and shakes his head. "Pardin... what?"

"Are you deaf? I say someone has paid your bail," the policeman bellows in irritation. "Oya sign hare, take your bag and go." Vipaar's hands shake as he signs beside his name in the notebook.

He thinks it's a trick. He had prepared himself for death and now he was told he was free to go—it does not make any sense. He looks in his bag and finds Alhaja's Quran, his bowler hat, and some of his clothes which serves to increase his state of confusion. He puts on his trousers and T-shirt and begins to walk towards the main gate. He steps out of the gate and looks back at the police station, and then the area around him, and begins walking. He resists the urge to get his hopes up. He waits for the hand to grab him by the arms and drag him back to his cell. Despite his apprehension, he continues walking, unsure where he is going to end up.

CHAPTER 29

Although she has heard the story of Cinderella many times before, Aminat particularly enjoys it when Temilola reads it to her. He makes it fun by reading the story in a funny voice, and puts on different accents for all the different characters. Her favourite voice is the one of the grand duke. She always waits with bated breath for when the Prince would put the slippers on Cinderella's feet. Temilola would always skilfully increase the suspense by waiting to confirm that the slipper fitted Cinderella. He has reached her favourite part of the story when she notices a figure with a heavy limp walking towards them. She is unsure if the person is real or an illusion. Temilola notices the look on her face as he turns around. He drops the book on the sand as he stands up slowly. His jaws drop open and he does a double take when the face of the person coming towards them becomes clear.

"Vipaar," Temilola whispers.

Temilola and Aminat both stand frozen to the spot, staring in disbelief as Vipaar gets closer. Aminat's shock turns to horror when she sees how dishevelled and haggard he looks. She looks to Temilola for guidance, but he is swaying like a palm tree on a windy day and continues to stare wide eyed and mouth gaping. Aminat's breathing becomes slow and shallow, and it feels like her heart is in her throat when Vipaar is a few meters away. He does not look like the same person she had last seen just a few weeks ago. The muscles are gone, he is gaunt, and he looks like he is on the cusp of collapsing.

"How are you Aminat?" he asks her with a smile.

"I am fine," she responds. She looks into his eyes and she can see that something has changed. His eyes are full of anguish and rage.

"What happen…" Temilola manages to utter. His bottom lip is trembling. "Are you alright?"

"I am fine." Vipaar takes a deep breath as he tries to keep his emotions in control. His eyes are watery and his voice is cracking. Temilola and Vipaar stare at each other for a few moments. Aminat jumps back when Vipaar lunges at Temilola, and starts shaking him by the neck.

"WHHHYYY DID YOU RUN, WHY DID YOU RUN?" Vipaar shrieks and begins sobbing uncontrollably. "WHY… DID YOU… LEAVE ME… WHY?"

"I am sorry, I am sorry." Temilola has also begun to cry.

Aminat is too overwhelmed to move. Through her tears, she sees Okechukwu and another of the boys who works for Temilola, named Jaconde, running towards them shouting, "Ehhhh, ehh, what are you doing, leave him alone?"

Vipaar drops Temilola into the sand and turns to face Okechukwu, who is holding a bottle and Jaconde who has grabbed a stick. Before they could put their weapons to use, Vipaar has thrown two quick jabs, and they are both sprawled out on the sand. Aminat walks over to where Vipaar is standing over the two boys, with his fists clenched. She stands beside him and looks up at him. As he turns to look down at her, she recognises the look of pain and suffering in his eyes. She had seen that very same look before many times when she looked in the mirror. She places her hands over his clenched fists, and he immediately clasps his hand into hers. The two boys stand up. She can tell by the look on their faces that they want to continue the attack, but stop when they see them holding hands. Okechukwu and Jaconde look at each other, and further bewilderment descends on their faces when Temilola stands next to Vipaar clasping his hand into his left hand. The boys sense that there is more to the situation than meets the eye and walk away. The three of them stand in silence, staring into the sea for approximately 15 minutes. Vipaar squeezes Aminat hand periodically and would say something, which she could only hear parts of due to the strong wind. All she heard was,

"Free, free, free."

She looks up at the tears rolling down his eyes, which quickly turns to uncontrolled sobbing as he drops to his knees and whimpers,

"Please God, don't let this be a dream. Pleeeeaaasssee." Without thinking, Aminat hugs him as tightly as she can. She desperately wants to absorb the pain and sorrow she can sense in his voice. Temilola, who is now also sobbing, hugs Vipaar tightly too. "I am sorry, I am so sorry," he repeats over and over again.

Vipaar hugs Aminat and Temilola in a vice like grip. He only lets go when Temilola says, "Errrr, Vipaar, I... I can't breathe."

"I am tired." Vipaar's breathing is laboured. "I want to sleep, I have been walking for three days."

Jaconde walks over with two sachets of water as all three of them stand up. "Sorry sar, we did not know you were dee professor broda sar." He bows slightly.

Vipaar takes the sachets, "Thank you bros." He tears into the corner with his teeth. "I beg no vex, na my reflexes just dey… you unstan." He downs the two sachets of water in quick succession, as Aminat looks at Temilola looking at him. She has spent enough time with him to know what he is thinking. She deduces that he is trying to understand what has happened to Vipaar and whether it was his fault. Although she had only spent a brief time with both of them together, she knew that he had always looked at Vippar with respect and adulation. Now, he looks shocked and confused, and he is doing a very poor job of hiding it.

"Let's go," Vipaar commands when he has finished the second sachet of water. His voice lacks the usual command of authority. He winces as he picks up his bag from the sand and turns to face Temilola. "What are you waiting for? Let us go."

"The Charaton Hotel is this way," Temilola says with an awkward smile, to which Vipaar reacts with a cold look.

The extent of Vipaar's physical detriment becomes clearer as they walk towards Temilola and Aminat's wooden shack. It is obvious he is in pain because he winces as he walks slowly with a heavy limp.

"Lean on me," Temilola attempts to offer him support by putting his arm around his back.

"I am FINE," Vipaar pushes him away. "I have been walking for three days widout anybody helping me." Although Aminat feels sorry for Temilola, whose shoulders drop and head bows in response to Vipaar's reaction, there is some relief that he still has some fire in him.

"Sorry, I was only trying to help," Temilola replies gently. He feels hurt and dejected when Vipaar pushes him away. It is heartbreaking to see his mentor in such a fragile state and he only wants to feel useful. He does not know how to process the sight of the person who had been the personification of strength and power, now looking so gaunt and dishevelled. His first sight of Vipaar nearly brought his whole world crashing down. He had idealised their reunion, but the reality is devastating. He realises at that moment how much he had idolised Vipaar. The revelation that he was a mere human being is heartbreaking. The aura of invincibility has been cruelly shattered, and he fears that the dynamics of their relationship have now been changed forever. He had rehearsed the answer he was going to give when Vipaar asked the inevitable question a million times in his head, but at the moment of truth, he does not have one. Even as Vipaar grabs him by the neck, Temilola could immediately tell that the spark in his eyes had disappeared. They had lost their intrinsic ability to command fear and instant respect; but even in his obviously weakened state, he had managed to dispatch his rescuers with ease.

As all three stood on the beach looking into the vast emptiness of the Atlantic Ocean, Temilola desperately wanted to ask Vipaar what had happened to him and how he found them. He was on the verge of asking when Vipaar began squeezing his hand and crying. This was the second time he had seen him cry, but this time it was different. The tears after Alhaja's passing were in mourning, but these are the result of a deep sense of pain. All the anger Temilola had in him disappeared the moment Vipaar grabbed and hugged him. From the moment they had split, the anger had been building and that had been his source of power to survive. He had to consider his need to breathe with his desire for Vipaar to continue holding him; he decided that the former was essential and told him so. Temilola wished he hadn't made reference to the Charaton Hotel, it was obviously a sore point for Vipaar.

A five-minute walk to their shack took over 10 minutes as a result of Vipaar's difficulty in walking. All three walk in silence, with Temilola and Aminat giving each other worried looks. Temilola desperately wants to help but resists the urge. Firstly, he does not want to upset Vipaar again, and secondly, and more importantly, it is important for him to let Vipaar keep his pride.

"Do you want anything?" Temilola asks hesitantly as he watches Vipaar lay down on the cardboard boxes and rests his head on his bag.

"I am fine," Vipaar's voice is raspy. "I just want to sleep."

"Ok."

As Temilola leaves the shack, he hears Vipaar mumbling, "Alhaja, Alhaja, Alahja."

"What is happen to your broda?" Aminat asks Temilola when he comes out of their shack.

"I don't know," Temilola replies after a few seconds, seemingly deep in thought, looking for an answer. "He looks… I mean… I don't even want to think about it." He shakes his head and attempts to alleviate Aminat's concern.

"Hey, on the bright side, the three musketeers are back together again, one for all and…" He stops when Aminat shoots a look of unbridled anger at him.

"You think this is my fault, don't you?"

Aminat's silence merely adds to the heavy burden of guilt which is hanging around his neck like an anvil. Aminat and Temilola do not exchange words all night until they are lying down next to Vipaar, whose snoring is interrupted when Aminat says,

"You should have call him."

The heavy burden of guilt ensures that a good night's sleep is not permissible for Temilola. He is awoken suddenly just before dawn by Vipaar's screams.

"NOOO, NOOO, NOOO, PLEEAASSEE STOP!" Chills run down Temilola's spine as he hears the agony in his mentor's voice. Vipaar is sweating, shaking and thrashing on the ground. "Temilola, Alhaja, Aminat, Ejuku." Aminat has also been woken up by the commotion.

"Vipaar, Vipaar," Temilola shakes him gently. He is close to tears, so vivid is the manifestation of Vipaar's terror. Vipaar opens his eyes. He is trembling, his breathing is quick and shallow, and his bulging eyes dart around aimlessly, trying to get a sense of where he is.

"Hey, hey, Vipaar. It's us, it's us," Temilola says. "It's Temilola and Aminat, don't worry you are safe." Vipaar has taken the form of a scared little boy—he stares at Temilola and Aminat for a few seconds before reaching out to touch their faces.

"Ejuku," he says when he touches Temilola's face. He then turns to Aminat and smiles. "Alhaja." A tear rolls down his left eye when he touches her face. He lays back down and regains lucidity after a few minutes of silence, but still looks at them and rubs his eyes.

"Temilola? Aminat?" he asks, as if looking for affirmation.

Temilola again feels the urge to help Vipaar as he attempts to sit up, but decides against it. Temilola sees the extent of Vipaar's open and raw wounds when he sits up and leans against the wood.

"Holllly shiiiiit. What happened!" he exclaims as he stares at Vipaar's torso.

Vipaar experienced an avalanche of contradictory emotions when he saw Temilola and Aminat standing on the beach. His heart began to pulsate when he first saw Aminat, and it increased the closer he got to them. He considered the possibility of hunger and exhaustion playing tricks on his mind, so he forced himself to repress the feeling of relief, which was eager to surface. The closer he got to the two figures, the faster the last remnants of his energy reserves were depleted. He knew that if this was a false sighting or an illusion, he wouldn't even have the energy to haul himself into the sea to end it all. When he was a few meters away, he finally allowed himself to confirm that it was Temilola and Aminat, standing looking at him with slack jaws. He wanted to run over to hug them both, but each step he took was painful, plus he did not have the energy. When he finally reached them, the look of pity on their faces triggered something in him—anger. Everything seemed to be a blur. The next thing he knew, there were two boys laying in the sand, and Aminat was holding his right hand. For the first time in his life, he truly understood what it meant to be free as he stared into the Atlantic sea. He could no longer hold back the tears, as he hugged Temilola and Aminat. He realised that the love he has for them is greater than his desire for death. The freedom death gave was final, the freedom from love was always renewable.

He could not escape the screams and the pain in his sleep. He wakes to see two faces looking at him, mumbling something. His whole body feels like it is on fire, every single bone and muscle aches.

"I need some water." Vipaar ignores Temilola's frantic questions when he sees the scars on his torso and legs.

"Duchess, go and get him water from…"

Aminat is so transfixed on Vipaar's injuries that Temilola has to repeat himself.

"I am fine," Vipaar says to Aminat as she leaves the shack. From the worried look on her face, he can tell his attempts to banish her worries are a failure.

"Why do you call her Duchess?"

"It makes her smile," Temilola responds irritably. "What happened to you?"

"When did you arrive here?"

"Not long after I left you."

Vipaar's eyes widen. "You have been here all this time and you have survived? I trained you well."

"I learnt to huzzle," Temilola says with a smile, which Vipaar knows requires reciprocation. He duly obliges with a half-hearted smile.

"Did Aunty Gladys tell you I was here?" Temilola blurts out after a few seconds of tense silence. "Did RPG do this to you?"

"Gladys… what… how did you see her?" Vipaar frowns and cocks his head to the left. "Why will she know whare you are?"

"Wait, she didn't tell you?" Temilola flinches backwards slightly.

"Then how did you know I was here?" He shakes his head and takes a deep breath. "I am so confused."

At this point, Aminat comes back into the shack. She gives Vipaar a sachet of water and hands him two tablets with her left hand.

"Thank you, Duchess," Vipaar smiles. "How have you been? I hope you have been looking after him."

"He has been missing you," she replies as she sits down.

Vipaar downs the two tablets and consumes the sachet of water in one go then turns to Temilola. "So, you ware saying Gladys was here?"

"Yes, a while back ago, with a man, a General of some sort."

"A General, she was with a General?" Vipaar asks, wide-eyed.

"Yes yes, a General. Why do you look so shocked?" Temilola now sounds more irritated. "Stop avoiding my questions. Did RPG do this to you?"

Vipaar looks down and rubs his chin for a few seconds, as he is forced to acknowledge the possibility that what he heard in his state of confusion while in prison was real.

"Hello," Temilola waves his hand in front of his face, bringing him out of his reflective state. "Did RPG do this to you?"

"Do you think if RPG had catch me, I will be hare talking to you? No no, this happened in hell."

"What are you talking about?"

"Do you remember dee KAI agent at the petrol station?" Vipaar begins.

"Nooooo," Temilola put his hands over his gaping mouth. "He beat you up. How did he catch you, where did this happen?"

"Do you want me to tell you what happen or not?" Vipaar rolls his eyes.

"My apologies, please continue." Temilola licks his lips.

"Anyway, he catch me one evening when I am looking for dee both of you and take me to police station. You are lucky they didn't catch us that day. You will not survive that place. Come and see the animals in there, some of dem make RPG look like a small boy. Come and see dead bodies... I am telling you, that is the place where they went and collected ebola. The police beat me and beat me, they wanted me to confess to being an armed robber... but I was strong. I refused to confess... so they beat me with a cane, wire and even elec..."

Vipaar stops when he sees Aminat and Temilola giving him a pained stare. Temilola is sweating and his right hand is shaking.

"Don't worry, they couldn't break me." Vipaar smiles with pride, "so dey release me. I don't know how long I am in dare for. When they release me, I begin walking hare."

"Err," Temilola curls his lip and pinches between his eyes. "But... I still don't understand. If sister Gladys didn't tell you where we were, how did you know we here?" He squints.

Vipaar looks down and takes a deep breath as he looks up slowly. He looks at Temilola and exhales. "Do you know somebody called Gadaffi?"

Temilola and Aminat look at each other and then back at Vipaar. This is the confirmation he requires.

All three sit in silence, looking at each other, wondering the same thing. What made the three of them so unique for the universe to bring them together? The only noise which penetrates the dome of silence within the shack, is the ocean waves and winds, which are louder and stronger than usual.

"What are the chances of that happening?" Temilola breaks the silence. "I mean seriously, what are the bloody chances."

"Of what?" Vipaar asks, although he is thinking the same thing.

"What are the chances of you being in the same place as the one person on this earth who could connect us."

"It is God," Aminat chimes in quietly.

Vipaar looks at Aminat and cannot help but admire her courage. He wants to say the same thing, but he does not have her courage. He is still trying to grapple with the possibility that he is even considering the notion.

"God? God, yeah right." Temilola's voice is heavy with bitterness. "Look at us, living like animals. If he really did exist, why would he do this to us? The only thing we all have in common is pain and misery."

Vipaar is stunned by Temilola's outburst. His words are imbued with anger and acrimony.

"What did Gadaffi say?" Temilola asks.

"Is he alive?" Aminat asks.

Vipaar stares at Temilola as Aminat's question hangs in the air.

"I had to do it. He threatened Aminat, he threatened to throw her in the sea. I warned him." Temilola's tone became defensive. "It's not my fault. He wouldn't leave me alone, I was tired of running..." He averts his eyes from Vipaar's intense gaze.

"What is he talking about?" Vipaar asks Aminat, who has her back hunched over like she has the weight of the world on her shoulders. She hadn't known the extent of how much the incident had affected Temilola until that moment. This is the first time since the incident with Gaddaffi and the soldier that he has let his armour down.

"He told the soldier that Gadaffi had stolen his phone," Aminat gasps softly. "The soldier beat him up and take him away."

Vipaar begins to piece together all that he heard and saw as he lay on the prison floor. He shudders as he pictures the terror on the boy's face as he hung from the ceiling. He pieces his words together in his head; he has to relive the desperate cries for mercy and profession of innocence. His body begins to shake when he finally puts everything together, based on what he recollects and Temilola's uncontrolled babble. Vipaar has to deal with the truth. He does not want to believe that Temilola is responsible for causing someone else's pain and suffering. Even worse, he is directly responsible for the death of another human being.

Temilola sees Vipaar staring at him with a dumbfounded expression on his face as he puts all the pieces together.

"DON'T LOOK AT ME LIKE THAT." Temilola jumps up with the veins in his neck protruding. "You were going to kill RPG, I stopped you. If you had not tried to send us away, I would not have done what I did. I had no choice." Temilola is pacing on the spot with clenched fists.

Aminat suddenly realises the weight of the burden Temilola has been carrying since they arrived at the beach. It had been eating away at him, and she hadn't understood it until now. She was so desperate to see the Prince, she hadn't been able to sense how much pain he had been in. Vipaar's chest tightens as feelings of guilt, failure and helplessness descend over him like a dark cloud. His worst fears have come to pass. The world has robbed the little lamb of his innocence, and he is now on the edge of darkness.

"I am sorry for trying to send you away." Vipaar's tone is full of remorse and his eyes are watering. "I was trying to protect you. If RPG had caught you with me, he would have killed you, instantly."

"Is he alive?" Temilola asks desperately, his eyes full of the hope which Vipaar had tried for so long to keep alive. "Is Gaddaffi alive?'

"Pop, pop, pop, rest in pieces." Vipaar shivers. His blood runs cold as he recalls Gaddaffi's desperate screams and clawing on the concrete floor as he was dragged out to his execution. He is unable to get the screams out of his head as he looks at Temilola and Aminat.

"He is dead."

Temilola steps backwards as he puts his hand on the side of his head. His mind begins to spin. He feels like his chest has caved in and his body feels like it is falling into a deep, dark crevasse with no end. Those three words finally shatter Temilola's already crumbling notion that hope would eventually conquer all. He covers his face with his palms.

"Ooooh God, what did I do, what did I do," he cries out in anguish.

Aminat gasps in shock at Vipaar's words—she had hoped he would at least lie to spare Temilola the pain and anguish he was now going through, but part of her is relieved that his heart hasn't completely become hardened. As the first born to her parents, she had been looking after her brothers and sisters since she was seven years old, and the one thing she had become adept at was soothing their pain. She had always been resentful of having to grow up fast, but something maternal comes alive as she watches Temilola crumble, consumed by despair right in front of her. Vipaar hadn't known what he was going to say until the words came out of his mouth. He crawls over to the corner where Temilola has retreated to and attempts to pull his hands away from his face.

"No, no, leave me alone, don't look at me," he shrieks and turns to face the wall.

Aminat is now rubbing his back. "Sorry, sorry," while Vipaar continues with his attempts to move Temilola's hands from his face.

"Look at me, Temilola, please look at me."

Temilola finally obliges. His eyes are red and he is hyperventilating. They both look into each other's eyes.

"Do you know you save my life?" Vipaar says solemnly as he puts his hand on his apprentice's cheek. "Do you know that?"

"How?" Temilola asks, still sniffling. "It was because of me you went into prison, and I killed Gadaffi."

"If it was not for you, I will have died in that place, shebi you know." Vipaar smiles a little as he recalls the conversation he had with Alhaja when Temilola first arrived. At that moment he sees the same innocence he saw in him back then.

"The devil cannot enter here." He places his palm on Temilola's chest. "Your heart is soft. I used to think that would make me weak, but it is what makes you strong. You are stronger than me. It is not your fault. You have a good heart, and you are not capable of evil intentions. Only God knows why what happened, happen."

Temilola is still shaking and wiping the tears from his eyes.

"You also saved my life," Aminat interjects.

"You see, you saved her life too." Vipaar grins widely. "Remember that stupid man with the BMW?"

"No, this was anoda man, with a white Jeep."

"You broke anoda wiper?" Vipaar eyes grow as he looks at

Aminat, shaking his head.

Temilola giggles. "No no, it was not a wiper. Don't worry, it's a long story." He has missed Vipaar's brashness.

"So you have saved the lives of two people. Whateva happen wid Gadaffi, it is because you were scared. Do you understand?"

"But it is my fault he is dead." Temilola's voice is full of sadness. "If I had just left, he…"

"Remember what you say to me under the bridge that night?"

Temilola frowns. "Erm… no… I can't remember."

"You say don't let the anger get in the way of hope. That is how I survived the prison."

Vipaar and Aminat's words went a long way in soothing Temilola's pain and alleviating some of the guilt. His actions had weighed heavily on his conscience, but he hadn't known how to deal with them.

"Ahhhh," Vipaar screams and bends over in agony.

"What what, what is the matter?" Temilola panics.

"It is nothing, it is just my stomach that is hurting me." Vipaar winces then begin to cough. He puts his hand over his mouth and Temilola sees splatters of blood when he removes it.

"Oh no, we have to take you to a hospital."

"Do you have money to pay for treatment?"

"Actually, yes I do."

Aminat watches Temilola and Vipaar go back and forth. She realises how they both balance each other out.

"Listen bros, I tire. If I am alive tomorrow, you will take me to the hospital."

"Deal," Temilola puffs his chest out in triumph. "I am absolutely famished, let's go and eat breakfast."

All three exit the shack. Temilola and Aminat lead the way to their local eatery.

They both stop when they realise that Vipaar is not following them and is heading into the sea.

"There is a storm coming," Vipaar says with a calm authority when they join him.

Temilola and Aminat look at the calm sea and clear sky, both wondering what he sees.

"How do you know?' Temilola asks.

Vipaar takes a breath and closes his eyes. "I can smell it. That was one of the first things I learnt from Alhaja." He opens his eyes. "Oh God, how I miss her so."

CHAPTER 30

While eating his breakfast of bread and egg on the beach the morning after he arrived, Vipaar cannot help but be impressed by how much his apprentice Temilola has matured. He is no longer the scared little lamb he had met just over months ago; his apprentice had become a respected businessperson. Vipaar wants to believe it was all the result of his expert tutelage, but he knows what he has known since they first met: Temilola was a born survivor. He watches in silence as Temilola and Aminat look intently at figures in a notebook and discuss the money that had been made, who owed what, and who was needed to buy stock. Aminat stays by his side all morning with Temilola and his employees, giving him water to drink, frequently ask about his wellbeing.

Vipaar had informed Temilola that a powerful storm was coming and advised against opening the barbecue stand today. Temilola was sceptical, but he chose to heed Vipaar's advice and he informed his employees that they will be closed for the day. They all look at him in disbelief, but it is Jaconde who has the courage to voice their concern.

"Bet why? We will loose a lot of money."

"Because Vipaar said there's a powerful storm coming today and we should leave the beach."

"But today is Satiday," Okechukwu says, "the sun is shining, it will be very busy…"

"I *said*, my mentor has advised that we should leave the beach." Temilola's cold tone sends a shiver down Vipaar's spine. The boys' silence shows that they fear Temilola as much as they respect him.

The sun *is* shining brightly at midday and the beach has started to liven up with activity. The visitors and traders begin to arrive and the other food stalls have started cooking the food that would serve the afternoon visitors. Temilola can tell by the frowns on Okechukwu and Jaconde's faces, and envious glances towards the other food shacks serving customers, that they are angry. He himself doubts Vipaar's prediction of rain and he knows that his authority will be severely damaged if the storm does not happen. On Vipaar's advice to seek shelter from the coming storm, the group leaves the beach around 3pm when it is packed with customers and the sun is still burning fiercely. They walk approximately three miles to an empty building site with six unfinished bungalows and duplexes, and settle in one of the bungalows that has a roof. The clouds have begun to gather, the winds have strengthened, and the sky has become dark by the time they reach their destination. By 8pm, torrential rain thumps the roof above and the usual sounds of horns and people have been replaced by the howling wind in the darkness and the sound of steel debris being blown on the roads.

"This storm na serious thing," Okechukwu says with astonishment as he looks into the darkness through the window frame of the unfinished bungalow. He turns to Vipaar who is leaning against one of the unplastered walls, seemingly lost in his thoughts.

"Mr Vipaar sar, how do you know this is going to be serious

sar?" Vipaar looks at him and wonders what Temilola must have said about him for them to show him so much respect.

"I smelt and saw it coming from this morning. My guardian taught me how to sense it some time ago."

"But sar, how do you know it will be this powerful sar?" Jaconde continues.

"Experience, my broda," Vipaar replies with a wistful smile. "Experience."

As the group sits in absolute silence, with light provided by two portable radios which also double as torches, Okechukwu breaks the silence. "Do you think, people like us will live in a place like dis?" Despite the thunderstorm, the graveness in his voice is palpable.

"What?" Temilola asks.

"I am saying, in some months, a rich politician who has been stealing Nigeria's oil money will buy dis house, and we will still be sleeping and huzzling on the beesh that is just down there." Temilola is still able to see the bitterness that clouds his friend's face.

"Yes o broda, I tire of dis life. I tire of this country," Jaconde chimes in in support. "How long must we live like dis."

"What can we do?" Vipaar's tone is monotone. "We can only make the best of the circumstances we find ourself."

"Yes sar, I understan dat sar, bet how long must we continue with this for." Jaconde sighs as he stares into the darkness. "You know I want to go to school. I have ambitionz now, but what is the possibility with dee corrupt leaders running this country?"

Aminat and Temilola listen quietly as Vipaar, Jaconde and Okechukwu go back and forth about corruption in the government, how the biggest thieves in the country are politicians, boko haram, the pastors with seven private jets… but Governor Mashola receives the brunt of their ire.

"But bros, let us talk truth," Jaconde says. "If I ever get to the top… I go chop my own, abi no bi so."

"Confarm, my broda, my broda," Okechukwu nods in agreement. "I go chop well well."

"You see, that's the issue with this country," Vipaar's tone is similar to that of a wise sage, "my mother told me that Confucius said the grass will sway, the wind blows… the leaders at…"

"HOOOOLLLLLLY SHIIIIIIIIIIIIITTTTTTTTT!" Temilola screams, jumping to his feet and pacing with both his hands on his head. "Holy shit, holy shit, holy shit. What the hell, oh my goodness."

His companions all stare at him, unsure what to do or say.

"Are you alright?" Aminat asks calmly. She was used to his outbursts.

"Yeah, yeah, Duchess." Temilola is now shaking. "I am fine, I am fine. I am having a déjà vu moment."

Ever since Gadaffi had punched Temilola and knocked him out on their first day on Kuramo beach, he had been having some flashbacks, and patchy dreams. Yet he had not been able to put them together until that very moment. The boy's conversation triggered something in his mind. He looks at Vipaar. "I remember who I am."

TEMILOLA'S STORY

Temilola had landed at Muritalia Muhammed Airport on a British Airways flight from London, First Class. There was a short, light skinned woman wearing an official's uniform holding up a piece of paper with his name when he disembarked from the plane.

"You are very welcome," she said cheerily. "My name is Bisola. Your moda said I should come and meet you.'

Temilola smiled but remained silent. "Let me take your bag," she said as she moved forward to take his rucksack from his shoulder.

"No thank you," Temilola said sharply. "I am fine."

She attempted to make further conversation as they walked through the airport, following the yellow signs directing passengers towards customs and baggage claims.

"Do you have luggage? Tell me how it look like and I get somebody to bring it for you."

"This is all I have. I am only staying for a week, for half term."

Temilola hated this particular airport. It was always hot and stuffy. The giant fans placed along the walkways were not sufficient to quell the heat and humidity. On a positive note, this was the only airport of the many he had been to all over the world that he did not have to wait in line at passport control, customs and baggage claim. He followed the woman as they went through cordoned off areas and passed the long snaking queues. It also held the title for being the most disorganised and disorderly. Passengers were always either fighting each other or with the airport officials, and this time was no different. As he walked past hundreds of passengers waiting to have their passport stamped, he heard and saw a woman holding a toddler on her hip shouting and pointing at an official, "Oga, you betta give me back my passport if you don't want wahala for your head."

He followed his escort to the VIP car park. He recognised his father's black SUV Escalade and they walked toward it. A man about 40 years of age got out of the driver's seat. Temilola recognised him as one of his father's drivers.

He smiled and said, "Welcome back to Nigeria sar," as he took his bag from his shoulder. Temilola was not phased; he was used to people older than him calling him sir, mostly those who worked for his father.

He turned to Bisola. "Thank you for your assistance," he said. As he put his hand on the passenger side door, he heard, "You didn't bring anything back for me from London sar." She placed the back of her right arm into her left hand. She looked directly into his eyes, fluttering her eyelids, and giving him a seductive smile.

Temilola wanted to say, "Did my mother not pay you?" but he knew that may only prolong the uncomfortable moment. He took the Louis Vitton wallet his mother had given him for his 12th birthday from his back pocket, opened it, took out a crisp £20 note and handed it to her.

The smile turned into a frown as she snatched the money from his hand. "Thanks," she said and walked away.

"Don't mind her jare my oga," the driver said as he walked to the rear right passenger side and began to open the door. "Dis costom people are very greedy, don't wory she will collect plenty of bribe."

As Temilola opened the door he said, "Ahh oga, I beg please enter di owners corner," the driver exclaimed with laughter.

"It's okay, I prefer to sit in the front," Temilola said as he stepped on the rail and hoisted himself into the soft brown leather seat.

As they drove out of the airport, Temilola turned on the radio and his favourite song, Oliver Twist by D'Banj, was playing. Approximately 20 minutes into the journey on the expressway, the car suddenly came to a screeching halt. A danfo had cut them off and blocked the path of the SUV. Two other cars had screeched to a halt on either side. About a dozen young men poured out of the vehicles shouting. Some were holding guns, some waving machetes.

Temilola's whole body began to tremble. A shiver went down his spine and he began to sweat profusely even with the car's air conditioning on full blast. His heart began to beat at what felt like the speed of light; his stomach turned and he had a sudden urge to defecate. He looked to the driver in desperation, but he had both his hands on his head and was babbling, "Ye, ye ye, ye… e jo em pa mi on (please don't kill me)."

Temilola looked on helplessly as the driver was dragged out of the car, put on his knees, and shot in the head as he pleaded for mercy.

The passenger door opened and Temilola stared wide eyed at a man in a yellow string vest and a red woolly hat whose muscles glistened in the sun. He had a gun in one hand and a picture of Temilola in the other. He looked between Temilola and the picture a couple of times before commanding him to get out of the car.

"Cummut."

Temilola began screaming, which was put to an immediate halt with a slap across the face. "I told you shut up your mouth." The man pointed the gun at Temilola and motioned for him to step out of the car, which he did submissively with his hand resting on his stinging cheek.

Temilola looked around, hoping somebody would come to his aid but he knew he was alone when he saw a police officer in black uniform running away.

"Oya, put am in the moto." Temilola attempted to struggle when another of the men grabbed and began dragging him towards the danfo.

"No no no …please… please…I am begging you," he began crying and pleading. One of the men lifted Temilola off the ground like a feather and shoved him into the danfo. Ironically, he had looked forward to entering a danfo all his life, albeit not so unceremoniously. Four men got into the danfo, and the one who had dragged him from the comfort of the escalade shouted at the driver, "Alaiye, move on."

Temilola put his index fingers into his ears, covering them as his kidnappers began shooting their guns in the air. He suddenly felt a cloth doused in chloroform put over his mouth, and the last thing he heard before losing consciousness was the screeching of tires on tarmac.

He woke up a few hours later with a tremendous headache to

discover that he had wet himself. It took a few moments to recall what had happened as he looked around his surroundings with his eyes wide and his heart pulsating quickly. He was lying on a dirty mattress placed on a concrete floor in a room without a door and unplastered walls.

"Eey, you are awake," the kidnapper referred to as Samuel snarled at Temilola. "Don't cause me any trouble or else I will slap your face."

"Please, please let me go," Temilola pleaded, his voice and body trembling with fear.

His pleas were ignored as Samuel continued to read his newspaper. The other members of the gang joined him shortly afterwards and began talking amongst themselves, seemingly oblivious to Temilola's presence.

"Where am I? Why have you brought me here?" Temilola stood up and asked again, this time with more assertion. "Why have you taken me? When can I go home? Do you know who my father is…"

The leader of the gang looked at him, pulled out a pistol from his waist and put it on the table. Temilola got the message. He kept quiet, pulled his knees towards his chest, cowered into the corner, and began sobbing quietly. He did not speak again until the next morning when Samuel gave him a half loaf of bread.

"When am I going to go home?"

"You will go home when your daddy pay us our money."

As he ate the bread, which had fried egg in the middle, he saw his face on the TV. He was on the NTA news with the caption, "Senator Akinola's son kidnapped." The kidnappers all gathered around the TV. They began laughing hysterically when they heard the Lagos Chief of Police say, "We have mounted checkpoints around Lagos. We have set a special task force dedicated to rescuing the boy. These criminals and miscreants will be brought to justice."

Temilola saw his father sitting next to the police officer and noticed that he looked angrier than usual as he said, "These criminals have kidnapped my son. I assure you they will be caught and dealt with mercilessly. No ransom will be paid. We cannot succumb to criminals."

Temilola's heart sank and he felt his future was bleak when he heard one of the kidnappers say, "No ransom eh. Listen to this mumu, I want my 10 million dollar." He then turned to him and said, "You better hope your daddy pay me my money or else I will start sending your fingers."

The next few nights for Temilola were surreal. There was no electricity most nights, he struggled to sleep, he had to defecate in the bushes, and his body ached from sleeping on the mattress on the floor. Despite this, the most challenging ordeal was the boredom. By the third day, he felt like he was going out of his mind.

On the sixth day, while they were watching the news, the kidnappers suddenly became angry the newscaster was telling a story about a Government minister whom the Economic and Financial Crimes Commission were investigating for spending 250million naira on two official cars.

"Ole, Ole, Ole, thief thief," they shouted at the TV. Temilola was a little bemused. "That's the pot calling the kettle black," he thought to himself. How these hypocrites could be calling someone a thief when they kidnapped him.

"Deese are the people spoiling Nigeria. How can one parson

spend 250 million naira on a motor. If dey are spending dis much money on moto, how much will they spend on their helicopta and aeroplanes? Billions upon billions? We just want our own." They spoke as if they were honourable thieves.

Samuel, the quietest one amongst them said the thing that made Temilola feel sorry for him, and guilty at the same time.

"Imagine, I have Engineering degree from the University of Ife, 1st in my class, and for two years after I graduated, no job," he said sadly. "My mother work and borrow money to send me to University, but when I graduate and look for job, everywhere I go they say they want someone with a degree from UK or America." He became more agitated the longer he spoke.

"After three years, I took a job as a gateman just so that I can get out of the house. I take a job working as a gateman for one stupid minster like this, imagine a 1st class degree and I was working as gateman. If you see his house, la ku li ja la la la li," he exclaimed and put his hand on his head. "Every month he buy new car, Mercedes, Range Rover, Lexus… His wife, one fat ugly woman like dis, is always doing party. She even force me to shuku shuku with her… chai… come and see orobo."

Temilola did not understand the lingo, but based on how hard they were laughing, she assumed she was fat. "Dare are even some cars that he don't drive before he buy anoda one. Some of dee cars are not even release in Europe yet, but this minister have it in his compound. One day I carry a raffia bag into the house. It is fill with money, come and see dollar and pounds starlin, chai chai chai. Sometime he will not pay me my salary on time, and when I ask for salary he sack me, saying I am going to get armed robber to come to his house. Imagine that, dey call us criminal."

One of the others then joined in the conversation. "Dey steal all Nigeria money, send their own children abroad to Univasity. The children now come back to the country and take all dee best jobs, and they call us criminal."

Samuel turned to Temilola and looked him directly in the eye with his jaws clenched and his voice breaking as he said, "You know my mother died because I can not afford to buy her medicine, and people like your father call me a criminal." Turning back to face his comrades, he continued, "When these politicians get sick, they fly to America or London for treatment. All their daughters get married in Dubai and Paris, and dey call us criminals." They continued talking, and one of them spoke painfully about one of their friends who had been lynched by a mob a few weeks earlier after being caught doing a robbery. "My father is not a thief," Temilola said meekly. "He is a businessman." The kidnappers merely ignored him. The next morning he was awoken by angry shouting. The leader of the kidnappers was sitting at the table shouting into his mobile phone. "SENATOR, YOU BETTER JUST PAY DEE MONEY… AFTER ALL THE MILLION AND MILLIONS YOU HAVE STOLEN, YOU BETTER JUS PAY DI MONEY OR ELSE…" He stopped when he saw that Temilola was awake. "Come hare and talk to your fada… you betta tell him to pay us our money or else." Temilola stood up quickly and ran to take the mobile phone from the kidnapper's outstretched hand, who had put it on loudspeaker.

"Hello, Daddy? Daddy?" He began crying as soon as he heard his father's voice.

"Don't cry boy, don't cry. Be strong, remember what I taught you. Men don't cry." Temilola's body went limp. The words of comfort he was seeking were not forthcoming. "Daddy, I am scared. Please, I want to come home."

"Boy, don't show them weakness," his father snapped. "You must be strong, you hear me boy? You are my son." Temilola's stomach churned, his shoulders dropped and his toes tingled. He could not understand his father's inability to show him affection even in his current predicament. He wiped the tears from his cheeks and said, "Yes daddy." Then he heard his mum screaming in the background, "Just pay them and bring me my son…" He held back his tears and said, "I will be strong Daddy."

"Good boy, that's my boy. Don't worry, Daddy will deal with this." Temilola handed the phone back to the leader.

"Now Senator, pay dee money quick quick, or I will throw this boy in the river."

"I do not have 10 million dollars."

"I beg don't tell me nonsense."

"I can give you $100k immediately."

Temilola stared at the phone in disbelief.

"100K. 100K from 10million dollar. Senator, if you want your son back, you betta pay."

"Listen, you stupid ignoramus," Senator Akinole shouted angrily. "I don't have time for this nonsense. You take me for mumu abi? I have five sons, he is last born. My lineage will continue if you k…" The kidnapper saw the stunned look on Temilola's face, turned the speaker off and walked into another room. Temilola slowly walked back to the room and slumped on the mattress—fear had been replaced by a feeling of despondency. He looked up to see the leader standing by the doorframe a few minutes later. "My guy, don't worry. It is only negotiations… you will go home soon," he said softly.

Temilola would wake up every morning and hope it was a dream. He thought about his private boarding school in Surrey, wondered if his friends missed him, and whether Sir Tablot would penalise him for handing his Latin assignment in late. He had been looking forward to coming to Nigeria to tell his father he had won the prestigious Harrow School's Chess Championship. He was the youngest winner in the school's history, and also the first Black winner. Despite the many thoughts going through his head, his father's statement kept ringing in his head: "My lineage will continue."

While eating breakfast on the 24th day of his kidnapping, Temilola noticed that his kidnappers seemed to be in a jubilant mood. Samuel came to him. "Chairman, your daddy has paid di money, we will release you today." He had been looking forward to that moment since he woke in the house, but when it finally arrived the expected feeling of jubilation did not materialise. He merely replied, "Ok."

By 4pm, most of the gang had left the house and only Samuel remained.

"We will be leaving as soon as it is night," Samuel said to him.

"Ok," Temilola replied flatly.

Around 7pm, Samuel put a blindfold on Temilola, guided him towards the backseat of a car, and told him to lay down.

After driving for approximately two hours, Temilola knew they were back in Lagos based on the gradual increase in volume of noise from vehicles and people.

"Get up," Samuel ordered after the car had been at a standstill for approximately five minutes. Temilola sat up and Samuel removed the blindfold. Temilola blinked quickly and looked at the darkness around him. "Where are we?" he asked.

"Oshodi bus garage," Samuel replied as he handed him a sachet of pure water.

"Just wait here then go and find a policeman. They will take you back to you fada."

"Thank you," Temilola said as he tore open the door. He paused and looked back at Samuel. "How much did my dad finally pay?" After a slight pause, Samuel replied, "He pay 125k dollars."

Temilola let out a short breath. He remembered following his dad to a Rolls Royce dealership in London a few months before to buy a Rolls Royce Phantom worth 400k without negotiating on the price. He stepped out of the car, which sped off immediately. He was able to survey the area thanks to the few working street lights. There were a few people hanging around, some buying food from vendors and others waiting for buses. He had no clue which direction he should go in, but after a few moments he walked towards a single storey building which had its security lights on. He was too exhausted to be scared. Based on the trauma he had just come through, he did not care what came next. He lay down by the doorway of the building and fell asleep. The last thing he remembered was waking up to find people rifling through his pockets.

CHAPTER 31

"Next thing I remember is this guy trying to steal my mango," Temilola says as he concludes his story. Jaconda and Okechukwu begin to laugh, but Temilola sees Vipaar looking morose. The group had all listened, enthralled and in silence as Temilola told his story. There were still some gaps in his memory, but he was able to recall and share the majority of the events which led to his first encounter with Vipaar.

"So you are Senator Akinola's son, Jeesus," Jaconde says almost in a whisper.

Temiola does not respond. He is looking directly at Vipaar. "What's the matter?" he asks worriedly. "Is it your stomach? I thought you would be happy to see the back of me," he ended with a nervous chuckle.

Vipaar had listened to Temilola's story with trepidation. His level of anxiety reached climatic levels when he mentioned being dropped off at Oshodi. He had steeled himself for the fallout when Temilola said, "The next thing I remember is this one stealing my mango." Instead of relief, he was filled with despair. He looks at Temilola laughing and at that moment he knows he has to stop running. He has been carrying the guilt of Ejuku's death, abandoning his brothers and sisters, and causing Temilola's loss of memory for so long. He knows that if he does not admit what he had done, he would never stop running from himself. He takes a deep breath and then exhales. "It was me." Those three words release him from the shackles he had imposed on himself. He feels tears well up behind his eyelids.

"What was you?" Temiola asks. "What are you talking about?"

"The reason you lost your memory, it is my fault." Vipaar's voice quivers as his throat becomes dry. "That night you enter Oshodi market, I saw you enter and… I don't know why…"

Temilola bites his bottom lip and his eyes narrow. He touches the back of his head and then his neck. He begins whispering to himself and then looks at Vipaar.

"Holy shit… the trainers, what RPG said in the flat that night, that evening on the balcony… IT WAS YOU, IT WAS YOU," he begins screaming with his eyes bulging. "YOU DID THIS TO ME!"

Within a split second, he has jumped on Vipaar and begins reigning blows on him while shouting, "YOU DID THIIIISS TO ME… THIS WAS YOUUR FAULT." He sobs uncontrollably, "I THOUGHT YOU WERE MY FRIEND… I HATE YOOUUU…" Vipaar does not offer any resistance as the blows land on his arms which are protecting his face. The other three are caught off guard by the sudden change in atmosphere. Aminat looks on speechless as Okechukwu and Jaconde pull Temilola off Vipaar.

"What happen, professor I beg take it ez, kilo shele," the boys reel off questions while trying hard to hold back Temilola, who is thrashing in his attempt to get free. As Vipaar stands up, Temilola breaks free and comes rushing at him. He throws a punch which lands squarely on Vipaar's left jaw, coinciding with a booming thunder strike. The room falls silent as Vipaar absorbs the punch, as a sponge would water. Temilola, who has now stopped crying, knows he is in trouble. He plants his feet on the ground and straightens,

"Er...sorry," he says, contrite, but his apology is too late. Instincts replace contrition in an instant and Vipaar's punch sends Temilola sprawling to the ground.

"You better stay down o, oga I beg," Okechukwu warned. "Oya tell us what happen, why are fighting your broda?"

"He is no brother of mine." Temilola's face is twisted with revulsion as he sits up. He rubs his jaw. "I am really getting tired of people doing that to me."

Vipaar regrets hitting Temilola, but certain instincts are hard to control. He is deeply hurt when Temilola says, "He is no brother of mine," but he remains silent.

"What happen?" Aminat, who had been silent up until this point, asks, her tone soft with apprehension.

"It's all his fault." The contempt in Temilola's voice is almost vivid. "When the kidnappers let me go, I fell asleep in the doorway and then felt somebody trying to steal my trainers. It was him..." he sneers, as he points at Vipaar with his index finger. "I remember his face clearly now... that was when everything went dark. I woke up the next morning with an almighty headache."

Vipaar feels hollow and worthless. He stares at the ground as Temilola exposes him. He interprets the blank look on Aminat's face as one of disappointment. The pain that had been inflicted upon him while in prison is nothing compared to the pain he feels at this very moment. His only solace is that Alhaja is not alive to see his ultimate moment of shame.

"I am sorry," Vipaar says. "I don't know why I did it. Something just come ova me that night."

"Yeah, yeah, you are sorry." Temilola swallows hard and shakes his head. "It's too bloody late for sorry. I have been living like an animal these past few months... I mean..."

Temilola knows he has gone too far when he hears gasps and turns to see Jaconde and Okechukwu looking at him with their mouths slightly open. Jaconde bites his lip and shakes his head slowly.

"Errr, sorry... no... I didn't mean that. I am just so angry... plea..."

"Yes you did," Vipaar retorts. "You mean everything you said. You have been living like us, like an animal for months abi. How long have we been living like this? When you go back to your daddy's big mansion and your school in Surrey, all of us hare will still be living like animals on the street."

"And that's my fault?" Temilola places his palms on his chest and tilts his head. "How is it my fault?"

"It is the fault of people like your fada. When you are in Surrey playing chess, we will be hare trying to survive everyday."

Temilola looks on slack jawed for a few seconds. "What? You are actually blaming your situation on me?" Temilola looks at Jaconde and Okechukwu. "You too, you actually think this is my fault." He then turns to Aminat. He drops his shoulders and leans in towards her. His lips are trembling. "Duchess?"

She looks at him but does not say anything.

Temilola gasps and takes a step back. He feels light headed and does not know how to process the myriad of emotions coursing through his veins. He feels like he did the morning he woke up in Oshodi bus garage. He looks to the ground.

"Even if my father is one of the so-called corrupt politicians, is the son supposed to pay for the sins of the father?" he asks quietly.

"Anyway, life is life," Vipaar says as he shrugs his shoulders. "I am happy for you, you can go back to whare you belong. You have been giving me headache since I met you gan sef."

"Listen, I didn't choose who I was born to, it's not my fault the country is the way it is." Temilola's eyes dart around his companions, who are all averting their gaze. "You are blaming me for the action of a man I hardly know…" He lowers his chin to his chest and sits on the floor. "A man who hardly spoke to me, a man who haggled for my life… a man…" He is now crying. "A man who… who… thought I was worth less than one of his cars." Temilola puts his head in between his knees, overwhelmed by the deep-seated anger he held for his father and the people he considered his friends, looking at him with disdain. Then he feels someone sit next to him. He exhales in relief when he sees Aminat. "It's not your fault," she says gently and puts her hand on his arm.

Vipaar looks on. He feels sorry for his apprentice but is too angry to offer any words of comfort. He does not actually feel any anger towards Temilola, he is merely angry because it is clear that he is going to lose another person that he loves. They sit in silence for what seems like hours, each one deep in their own thoughts.

"I put the both of you in charge of the barbeque stand," Temilola says without looking at either Jaconde or Okechukwu. "Oh… what am I saying… it's yours. Thank you for all you did for us." The boys look at each other, stunned, and both say, "Thank you. Professor, please come and visit us once in a while." Okechukwu smiles.

"I promise."

"We all better sleep," Vipaar's tone is gruff. "We mus leave dis place very early in dee morning."

The rain is still falling heavily but the winds have subsided. Everyone goes to sleep, all knowing that his or her lives have changed forever. Temilola wonders what life will be like when he returns home. He looks forward to seeing his mother, but nothing else. As he falls asleep on the concrete floor, he pictures all the designer clothes, all the mountains of gadgets, and his collection of 124 trainers; they all mean nothing to him. He realises that he had never felt complete, despite all the trapping of luxury. Nobody, apart from his mother, had shown him the type of love and affection that Alhaja, Vipaar and Aminat had shown him.

Vipaar decides to return home to face his father and seek forgiveness from his brothers and sisters. Since he met Temilola, he's let himself dream again about being a doctor. It may be too late for him, but he vows to do all that is in his power to ensure that all his brothers and sisters go to University. Aminat feels alone. Now she knows who Temilola is, she is certain he will treat her just like her friend Kemi had done previously—he would leave her.

Temilola wakes up in a panic just as the sun is rising the next morning. He searches for his phone in the darkness and turns on the torch. He shines it on Aminat and then Vipaar, both of whom are fast asleep. He is gasping for air for a reason he cannot decipher, as he crawls toward Vipaar.

"Vipaar, Vipaar," he whispers and shakes his shoulders. "Ohhhhh, what do you want?" Vipaar flicks his shoulder. "I can't wait for you to go home so that I can finally get some sleep." He sits up and looks at Temilola, frowning. "What is it dat you want now?"

"Listen, something has been bothering me." Temilola swallows to relieve his dry throat. "Yesterday you said Gladys didn't tell you we were here right?"

Vipaar takes a long breath and rolls his eyes. "Yes and so what?"

"So if she didn't see you to tell you we were here, that means she didn't know you were in prison, right?"

Vipaar sits up fully, and exhales. "My friend, if you don't start making some serious sense, I will knock sense into you shap shap."

Temilola scratches his head. "So if Sister Gladys didn't know you were in prison, she didn't bail you out right?"

"Yes, and so?" Vipaar's eyebrows raise as he ponders what Temilola is saying.

"So if she didn't bail you out, who did?"

"VIPAAAAAARRRRR, did I not promise you I will find you and that boy?" the voice comes from the corner of the room. In his state of shock, Temilola manages to point the light from his phone in the direction the voice came from. However, it is not necessary; they both know it is RPG.

CHAPTER 32

"HOOLLLLLYYY SHIIIIT..." Temilola screams. He begins blinking uncontrollably and his whole body trembles when he sees RPG in the corner, grinning. He looks even bigger and more imposing than he remembered.

"Vipaar my broda, I have been looking at you sleep," RPG says with a snigger. "I have been waiting for dee right time."

Jaconde, Okechukwu and Aminat have been awoken by Temilola's scream and they are all in that disoriented state between sleep and sudden arousal. Aminat runs behind Temilola the moment her eyes rest on RPG. The two boys immediately get to their feet and stand beside Temilola, their chests puffed out and their hands balled into fists. Vipaar on the other hand is remarkably calm based on events over the past few months. RPG finding them is nothing to be surprised about. He is more intrigued to know how he had found them. Temilola gently holds each of the boys hands and says quietly, "No, we cannot take him." They both get the message and unclench their fists.

"WHO ARE YOU?" RPG growls at the boys.

"All three of them are nobody," Temilola says, his voice shaking. "They are nobody. They all work on the beach for the chairman."

RPG looks at them for approximately 30 seconds, narrowing

his eyes and pursing his lips before commanding, "Oya cummut." Okechukwu and Jaconde look at Temilola, confusion and fear etched on both their faces. "Don't worry, we will be fine. You are now both in charge of the restaurant. Take this useless girl with you."

The boys look at each other, unsure what to do, then shake Temilola's hand and begin walking slowly towards the exit. "Go with them," Temilola says, his voice cracking as he attempts to coax Aminat out from behind him, but she staunchly refuses, peering over his shoulder to look at RPG.

"No, no, ko lo so ibi kon kon, she not going anywhare," RPG waves his index finger. "You think I am mumu abi, she is staying right hare."

Okechukwu and Jaconde stop at the door and look at Temilola for final confirmation. He smiles at them. "Fellas, it has been an absolute pleasure." With both their faces contorted in pain, they disappear into the darkness.

"Why don't you leave us alone?" Vipaar asks calmly from where he is sitting. "I mean, don't you want peace in your life?"

"Leave you alone, leave you alone?" RPG laughs as he moves closer to Vipaar. He puts his hand in his waistband and pulls out a gun. Temilola inhales loudly and shudders, he steps backwards until he hits the wall, all while shielding Aminat with his right hand.

"What did I tell you that night when I called you eh?" RPG's eyes are bulging but he has a relaxed smile across his face. "What did I say to you?"

Vipaar remains silent, his face motionless. "Please, let her go. She has nothing to do with this," Temilola pleads. "It's me you want, I was the one who hit you."

"If you don't sharaap your mouth, I will shoot that gel." Temilola's muscles tighten. RPG's voice is filled with hate. "All my wahala is your fault." He returns his focus to Vipaar. "Daniel, answer my question. What did I say to you on dee phone dat night after, you leave me to die in my own moda house? You better answer me now, now, or I will shoot this boy." RPG points the gun directly at Temilola

Vipaar looks up at RPG. "You said, no matter where we hide you will find us and take revenge."

"Haaaa, haaaaa, yes, I say I am going to find you and this boy and take my revenge," RPG crowed. "And now hare we are."

Temilola squints and looks down at Vipaar. He tilts his head to the right and casts his mind to the night under Ojuelegba bridge. The phone call and the sudden urgency to take him to the police station now made sense—he was trying to protect him.

"Sir, I have five thousand naira," Temilola says, still shaking. "Please let her go at least, she has nothing to do with this."

"Five thousan?" RPG twists his face and snorts in disgust. "You want to pay me five thousan, I will slap your face." He feigns a lunge and Temilola jumps back in fright. "I pay forty thousan to release dis one from dee prison, and I have to pay that KAI officer 25 thousand… he want you, specifically." RPG uses the gun to point at Temilola. "He say you use juju on him… and you want to give me 5k, you ozwo, I beg go sid down my friend."

Vipaar thinks back to that split second when he was in prison and he thought he had seen a familiar face. So there it was, he had in fact seen a familiar face. It was RPG. He had thought, or rather hoped, it was his imagination. "I go in dare to do some business and I see dis one," RPG continues. "If I want you to die I will have get you kill in the prison—but it is this boy I want. Because of you, my boys are now challenging me, people are not paying… they are saying I have been beaten by my apprentice and an akata. You have mess up my business and you are going to pay. I follow you for three days…"

Temilola stares at RPG intently. He is able to see his form more clearly with the daylight penetrating the house. He takes a step forward, puffs his chest out a little and curls his lips, "How the hell did an imbecilic ingrate like you come from an angel like Alhaja?"

RPG stops, looks at Temilola with his lips parted and the gun lowered. "Eh, what did you say to me?"

"He said how our beloved Alhaja make a mumu like you," Vipaar grunts as he stands up. He senses by the shocked look on RPG's face that something about Temilola unnerves him, so he presses on.

"R… P… G… Chairman of Oshodi and the six zones," he continues, smiling. "How can you bring a gun to deal with a small boy. Are you fearful of this small akata?"

"Sharaap your mouth, I say sharaap your mouth," RPG almost squeaks as he moves closer to Vipaar, his jaw clenched and his eyes bulging.

"Imagine, the great RPG… Rocket… Propelled… Grenade." Vipaar looks him in the eyes as his grin becomes wider with each word he utters. "You know something… you owe dis small boy your life. I was going to smash your head like coconut that night, but he stop me."

RPG takes two steps backwards and then smiles. "Well that is your own mistake." He inhales and tuts as he assesses Vipaar from head to toe. "Chai, you and me, imagine… if you had been by my side you would be making serious money now. I teach you everything and you betray me, now look at you."

"You want me to betray Alhaja." Vipaar's eyes flicker in anger. "Afta everything she did for you, you stole from and betray your own mother!"

"You think you are betta than me? Are you forgetting that night you robbed that boy?"

As the two argue, Temilola and Aminat begin to shuffle slowly toward the door.

"Talk all you want, I will kill you first so that the boy can watch," RPG bellows with malevolent glee. "Yes, I know who he is, I meet with his fada to discuss some election business some time ago and I see his picture in dee office. Yes, I know he is dee son of Senator Akinola. As for dee girl, I will give her to my boys, dey will use her well well."

Temilola and Aminat are a few meters from the doorframe when he sees a knife they had brought with them to prepare the fish the previous night. He motions for Aminat to run away. She is shaking and sobbing quietly as she walks away. RPG has his back to Temilola as he bends down slowly and picks up the knife. He tip-toes behind RPG, who is still busy lauding his victory over Vipaar, as stealthily as he can. RPG suddenly stops talking and looks at the spot where Temilola and Aminat had been standing a few seconds previously. Temilola's heart begins racing fast. He knows he has milliseconds to do what he needs to do. He lunges at RPG, who turns around at the very same moment and raises his hand. Temilola plunges the knife into his arm and he drops the gun.

"Ahhhhhhh, you devil!" RPG screams as he looks at Temilola like an irritant. "You try to kill me again… I should have kill you that night in Oshodi." He punches Temilola in the face, sending him crashing to the concrete floor. At the same time, Vipaar punches RPG in the ribs and then punches him twice in the face. They do not have the desired effect, as RPG only takes a couple of steps backwards and then begins to laugh. Vipaar knows he is in serious trouble.

"Vipaaaar, you have lost your power," RPG roars spitefully as he punches him in the face. Vipaar is dazed as he hits the wall, but he still sees RPG pull the knife out of his arm and come towards him. He looks RPG in the eyes, smiles and takes a deep breath. He then feels like his body is floating in the emptiness of the clouds. He feels a sharp pain in his torso as RPG plunges the knife in with as much force as he can muster. In that moment, he sees RPG for who he really is, "a little boy who was scared of the world."

"I am free," Vipaar whispers, taking great satisfaction as RPG's eyes narrow in confusion.

"Noooooooooooooo!" Temilola shrieks as Vipaar's body drops to the floor, clutching his stomach, blood spurting violently from his mouth. RPG turns around and stomps toward Temilola like a raging bull. "You tried to kill me again abi?" He picks Temilola up from the ground like a rag doll, puts both hands around his neck and begins to squeeze. Temilola attempts to fight back by hitting RPG on the wound on his forearm but it has no effect, it is just pure muscle. He begins to feel light headed and it becomes harder and harder to breath as RPG squeezes and squeezes. Then he hears, *bang, bang*.

RPG's eyes widen and he coughs. He releases his grip from Temilola's neck and falls to the floor. Temilola begins to cough hard as he attempts to regain control of his breathing. As his vision starts becoming clearer, he sees Aminat standing motionless in the middle of the room, holding the gun with both hands. Temilola stands up slowly, steps over RPG's lifeless body, and carefully prises the gun from her hands, hugging her tightly. Her heart is beating quickly but it slows to a more comfortable rhythm as he holds her.

RPG's sudden appearance had shaken Aminat to her core. She desperately wanted Temilola to come with her, but he insisted she leave. She was crying as she walked away from Temilola, and then something suddenly made her stop after taking a few steps. She stopped crying and her body stiffened. She closed her eyes and all she could see were the faces of the people who had mistreated and abused her. In a flash, she saw Uncle Jaro, Uncle Emanuel, Ibrahim, Mr and Mrs Olapade, Kemi… the list was long. These faces unleashed a fury in her. She ground her teeth, and clenched her fist tighter and tighter. She had been scared and angry since the day she left her village, but she had not had the courage to display anger until now. RPG was another in a long line of people who saw her as a thing to use and abuse. What made her most angry was that he was going to kill the only two people who saw and treated her as a human being. She opened her eyes when she heard Temilola's scream and walked back to the room. She saw Vipaar bleeding on the floor and Temilola's legs desperately flaying as RPG held him in the air. She calmly picked up the gun from the ground. She felt a surge of power flow through her. She pointed it at RPG's broad back and squeezed twice. The next thing she knew, Temilola was removing the gun from her hand and kissing her on the forehead.

"I am so sorry," Temilola whispers as he kisses her forehead. "I told you to leave, why did you come back?"

"You are my brodas," she replies purposefully. "He is trying to kill you, so I kill him." Temilola is taken aback by the calmness in her voice, and the lack of emotion on her face. Something about her demeanour has changed instantly, but he does not have time to decipher what.

"Is that... modafucker... dead?" Vipaar's voice is raspy as he struggles to breathe.

Temilola and Aminat rush to his side. "Oh my God, oh my God," Temilola shrieks upon seeing the amount of blood on Vipaar.

"I say, is that modafucker dead?" Vipaar coughs and a little blood spatters from his mouth.

"Yes he is," Temilola mumbles as he kneels beside Vipaar. "Aminat saved my life." Vipaar still has his hands pressed to his stomach and blood is now slipping through his fingers. Temilola repositions himself and begins cradling Vipaar, whose breathing is becoming slower and more shallow. "Just wait for a little bit, I will take you home with me," Temilola blubbers as he strokes Vipaar's face. "We will all go home, I will look after all of us."

"Please forgive me," Vipaar struggles to speak. "I didn't mean to..."

"Shhhh, don't say anything. You didn't do anything wrong, shhhh."

Vipaar looks at Aminat, his eyelids struggling to stay open.

"Duchess, don't cry." He wipes the tears from her left eye and smiles. "Thank you for looking after him... promise me you will..." He coughs and winces in pain. "Promise me you will look after him."

"I promise." Tears flow from both her eyes.

"Please don't go, I still need you. I have never had a friend before. You said you will not leave me." Temilola is now wailing.

"Alhaja said to... me." Vipaar coughed up more blood; each breath was now very painful as he wheezed. "She said to me the night before she die..." He pauses to take a deep breath. "She said, 'oni la ri... ko seni to mola'...meaning..."

"'Today is all we know, nobody know tomorrow'." Temilola completes the sentence. Vipaar smiles, his teeth now stained with blood. "She tell you the same thing abi... my beloved Alhaja." He closes his eyes.

"Vipaaaar, Vipaaar, no, no no don't close your eyes!" Temilola shakes him vigorously as Aminat clutches his shoulder in desperation.

Vipaar opens his eyes slowly. "She say it is not by accident we meet each other... I am now understanding what she means... Thank you for allowing me to redeem myself."

"You saved my life, I know who I am now," Temilola says as he squeezes Vipaar even more tightly. Vipaar's body is now limp and his face is cold. "You are my brother, I love you so much. Please don't go."

"Remember what I teach you." Vipaar takes one long breath. "Man ... rules circumstance... circu..." His breathing becomes more laboured and he removes his left hand from his wound and holds Aminat's hand.

"Man rules circumstance… circumstance does not rule man," both of them repeat in unison, slowly. All three of them continue repeating their motto together until Temilola realises that he is now speaking alone. He looks down and sees Vipaar's eyes are closed. He had stopped breathing. Temilola squeezes Vipaar's lifeless body, buries his head in his neck and then kisses him on the head. He is sobbing uncontrollably. "You are the best human being I have ever met… I will make you proud, I promise. The world will know you and your story, I promise… the world will hear about Vipaar." Aminat has stopped crying, and has positioned herself next to Temilola, resting her head on his shoulder.

"I used to call you Garri and Bakedbeans," she says.

Temilola begins laughing with tears still falling from his eyes. "Yeah, I guess we were like chalk and cheese."

They stay in their positions, watching the sunrise for thirty minutes.

"We have to leave," Temilola says as he gently places Vipaar's head on the floor and stands up.

"Are we going to leave him hare?" Aminat asks as she looks adoringly at Vipaar's body.

"Yes, for now." Temilola begins to take off his blood stained t-shirt. "We will come back for him. I will arrange it when I get home." He scrunches up the t-shirt and places it under Vipaar's head. They both straighten out his body and fold his hands across his chest. He then takes Vipaar's bowler hat from the bag he had brought with him and places it gently on his chest. "He looks like he's sleeping… he is finally at peace," Temilola says softly as he touches Vipaar's cold face. "He was a fighter till the end."

393

They wash the blood from their hands using a bottle of water he had brought the night before.

"Are you going to go to you house now?" Aminat asks.

Temlilola looks at her. "*We*, Duchess…" He pauses as he walks towards her and puts his hand on her shoulder. "*We* are going to our home." Aminat's shoulders ease as relief flows through her. She begins to pack some of the things they had brought with them the night before, but Temilola stops her. "No no Duchess, we won't need those where we are going."

He walks back to Vipaar's body and kisses him on the forehead. "Rest in peace my brother." They then walk towards the exit, stepping over RPG's body, which is laying face down on the floor. Temilola stops when they reach the doorway, turns around, and runs toward RPG's body, kicking the head as hard as he can, shouting "MODAFUCKER." He turns around and sees Aminat looking at him. "Just wanted to make sure, Duchess. Thank you again for saving my life. I will be forever grateful." He looks her in the eyes. "You know you did the right thing, don't you?"

Aminat nods. "Yes, I know."

They walk out of the building and walk along the main road. "You know you are my responsibility," Temilola says to Aminat. "You are going to live with us, you are going to be safe with us, I promise you."

"Ok," she replies with a hint of scepticism. She wants to believe, but she has experienced too many false dawns. They continue walking for about 10 mins before she asks, "Whare are we going?"

"I have my memories back now. I remember where I live." Temilola's words are bitter sweet in his mouth. For him the joy of returning home would forever be tainted by Vipaar's death. As they walk, they see some of the effects of the storm. Many of the shacks on the side of the road have been flattened and parts of the road are flooded. "We have to walk to the bridge to go and get a taxi," Temilola says.

The first few taxis they see have passengers in them and they have to wait for another ten minutes before they see an empty one, a green Nissan Micra that Temilola flags down.

"Good morning sir," Temilola greets the old man who is driving.

"Good morning," he replies in a croaky voice.

"We are going to Banana Island."

"I am not going that way." The driver puts his hand on the gearbox in preparation to drive away.

"How much will you charge to take us there?" Temilola asks quickly. The driver looks at Temilola, then Aminat and frowns. "12 thousand." Temilola puts his hand in his pocket and takes out the money stuffed in his pocket. He hands it to the taxi driver. "This is five, my father will give you the rest when we reach our destination." He opens the back door and motions for Aminat to enter while he sits in the front seat.

"What are you children doing on dee road at dis time of dee morning?" The driver asks as they go over the bridge.

"It's a long story sir," Temilola says wistfully. "A very long story. Maybe you will read about it one day sir."

"Do you know where you are going?" the taxi driver asks as they drive along the Lekki-Epe Express way.

"I don't actually remember the exact address sir," Temilola bites his lower lip. "Do you know how to get to the Ikoyi club?"

"Yes," the driver replies, "I have been dare plenty."

"Okay good. I know my way home from there." Temilola's heart rate increases when the taxi turns on Falomo Bridge, because things are becoming more familiar. When they reach the end of the bridge, it feels like they have entered a new world. Left behind are the dilapidated, crumbling buildings with rusty roofs and roads with potholes. They have now made way for their replacements: smooth roads, high rise glass skyscrapers and a number of luxury yachts marooned in luxury lagoons. Temilola looks back to see Aminat staring out of the window in amazement. After they reach Ikoyi Club, Temilola begins giving directions to the driver. Some parts have changed from what he remembered, with new mansions and buildings, but enough has remained the same for him to recall his way home. They drive past pristine streets lined with humongous mansions that have high walls and steel gates. When they turn into his street, he thinks his heart is going to break through his chest plate. He has been waiting for this moment from the minute he woke up in Oshodi bus garage that fateful morning. He begins to shake when he sees his house. "That's my house over there," he points and shrieks excitedly when he sees a cream coloured house in the distance. He struggles to contain his excitement and his right leg begins shaking uncontrollably as they get closer. The driver pulls up to the gate and presses the horn. A man who looks irate steps out of the gatehouse. "Watin you want?" he asks the driver, his face twisted in anger.

"This boy says he live here," the taxi driver says.

"Which boy say he live hare?" The gateman looks past the driver into the passenger seat.

"Good morning, Christopher," Temilola says with a smile. "How have you been?"

"Ye, ye, ye, Jesus is Lord," Christopher yelps. "Mr Temilola…" He stares at Temilola with his mouth gaping like he has seen a ghost.

"Would you mind opening the gate please? I am quite eager to see my mother."

"Yes sar, sorry sar!" Christopher jumps back from the taxi and runs back into the gatehouse. A few seconds later the automatic gates slide open sideways.

"Welcome back sar," Christopher puts his two fists in the air excitedly as the taxi drives through the gates. "Thank you Jeeessuuuss."

As the taxi drives along the long driveway, Aminat is stunned by the size of the house; it is like nothing she has ever seen. The lawns are lush green surrounded by pristine rose gardens. They drive past a fleet of luxury cars, some of which she has never seen before. Christopher runs after the taxi shouting, "MADAAAMMMMME, MADAAAME!!!"

"Are you ok?" Temilola asks Aminat, who looks around her, unable to process what she is witnessing. All she can do is nod her head.

"You are now my sister," Temilola says as he holds her right hand. "Mi casa es su casa."

"Pardin? What do you mean?"

"It means my house is your house."

They both get out of the taxi and stand under the balcony next to Christopher, who is still shouting, "Madamme!"

Temilola hears his mother's voice from the balcony before

he sees her face. She is shouting, "CHRISTOPHER, YOU DEY CRAZE! WHAT KIND MADNESS DON CATCH YOU DIS MORNING, YOU STUP…" She stops when she looks down from the balcony, her face frozen.

Temilola looks up. "Hello mummy," he smiles as he puts his hand around Aminat's shoulders, drawing her close. "This is my frie… no… this is my sister Aminat, I call her Duchess… We are home."

THE END.

Acknowledgements

Praise be to Allah the most Gracious the most Merciful.

My parents Alhaji Olanrewaju and Alhaja Tasikirat Kareem. Thank you for giving me such a wonderful life. The never give up attitude you instilled in me gave me the courage to start and finish this book.

My wife Milensu, I am eternally grateful for you unwavering support and belief in me over the past five years. I could not have finished this book without you by my side. You were there to push away the clouds of self-doubt and the belief you showed in my abilities, as a writer was priceless. I love you now always and forever… My FZB

My babies—Funmilayo Likumbi and Ntanda Oluwakemi—my heroes and the reason I wake up every morning. Thank you for your patience and understanding for the many hours' daddy was writing on the computer. Thank you for the privilege of being your father, I promise to love and guide you now, always and forever.

My sisters and brother - Morufat, Moruf, Karimot- thank you all for your love and unwavering support all of my life. You have all been there for me when I needed you and I thank God for having you in life.

The Kareem-Bello and Adewunmi Family—May our families continue to grow and prosper—Insha Allah

My mother-in-law Angela Shanyinde and my sisters-in-law, Sandra Chama, and Chola. Thank you for your support while writing the book.

My nephews and niece—Ehizogie and Oluwaseun Omorogbe—thank you for helping me overcome my writers block, Finley Nasir Kareem and Eric Asuelimen I love all very much.

Patrick Omorogbe, Segun Onabajo, Fayekemi Adeyemi, Amy Branigan, Kabir Adiro, Habeeb Kareem—my brothers and sisters from another mother—it's all Love.

My best friends Tega (My Chairman—thank you for the feedback in the first draft) and Phillip Nyarko—my eternal gratitude for your friendship over the 20 and 25 years respectively. May our bonds of friendship never be broken.

To those who contributed and supported me while I was writing the book, Samantha Watson, my Tuesday night writing buddy thank your keeping focused and disciplined and for your friendship; the Brixton Fix Writing Collective—Emma Allotey and Siobhan David O' Dean—your regular feedback made me grow and develop as a writer and helped shape the book; Brixton Library—thank you for creating a safe space to nurture and develop my writing; Hursh (Papa H) Shah—your feedback on my first draft on Westminster Bridge was invaluable, Titilope Emmanuel, you copious notes on the early draft was invaluable, Alhaji Teju Kareem, thank you for your mentorship and showing me around Lagos; and a very special thank you Abigail (my dear sister) Nwaokolo—you took the time out of your busy life to help me edit and shape my manuscript to be ready for submission to a publisher. To you all, I thank you for your time, words of encouragement, I hope I have done you proud.

Valerie Brandes, firstly thank you selecting my manuscript to be part of the Jacaranda Twenty in 2020 collection and secondly for all work you did editing my manuscript during what was undeniably a very difficult period. Kamillah Brandes, thank you for the support in the design of the book cover, Jazzmine Breary, Cherise Lopes-Baker and the rest of the Jacaranda Team—thank you for helping get to the finish line. Rodney Dive, thank you for a phenomenal cover, it perfectly captures the very essence of the story. Joy Francis, I started my creative writing journey at a Words of Colour course eight years ago. Thank you for setting me on the path and for guiding me along the way. And to my fellow Jacaranda Twenty in 2020 Authors, I feel privileged to be in such esteemed company.

To my all my family and friends, there too many to mention here— just know I have you all in my heart and am grateful for the love and friendship that we share.

And finally—the street hawkers and street kids of Lagos—you were my inspiration for this book, and I hope I have told your story well. And to the danfo drivers, bus conductors, street kids, ladies of night, Mushin area boys, Agbros, and traders of Lagos. Thank you for sharing your stories and experience with me so freely—your insight was invaluable—KKB Salutes you. I hope I have done you all proud.

R.I.P Dr Partson Shanyinde.

About the Author

Kabir Kareem-Bello was born in Ibadan, Nigeria, and moved to the UK with his family in 1992. His self-published book, *Memoirs of Young African* is based on his experiences as a young African migrant in the UK. He has spoken about identity and migration at a number of public events, most notably at the University of Edinburgh and Portsmouth University . He has also written about the quest for identity on his blog www.kilonshele-kkb.com. *The Street Hawker's Apprentice* is his first fiction novel. He is currently writing his second fiction novel and developing a documentary looking at the migration of Africans to the United Kingdom in between 1980's and 2000. He plans to launch his podcast in 2021. He graduated from Middlesex University with Business and Marketing Degree. He currently lives in Buckinghamshire with his wife and two daughters.